IMBER

IMBER

DEBORAH MISTINA

Copyright © 2024 Deborah Mistina

First edition

ISBN 979-8-9903531-0-7 (ebook)
ISBN 979-8-9903531-1-4 (paperback)
ISBN 979-8-9903531-2-1 (hardcover)

Library of Congress Control Number: 2024905725

Design and illustration by Jason Arias

Printed in the USA

Published by Moon Bear Books
Lebanon, OH
www.deborahmistina.com

MOON BEAR BOOKS

For my bear

CONTENTS

CHAPTER 1

BARNSTORMING

Violet Murphy lounged on the weathered stone bench where she was eating her lunch. A tepid breeze ruffled her hair as she absently munched on an apple and contemplated the dismal historical poem she had just read.

"LAMENT OF THE EARTH"

Cool fools press power
Filthy air clings with no rain
While angry storms rage

Crops wither and fail
Seasons lost in gasping breaths
Friends long forgotten

Life battered and cracked
Fading under rising tides
Aching and lonely

Violet did not notice that Firestorm was angling for an apple of his own until his nostrils were a couple of feet from her cheek. A gentle whinny roused her from reflection. At once, she turned to look at him. "I'm sorry, buddy. Of course I have one for you!"

A plump red apple lay beside her on the bench. She snapped the fruit in half and stood to face the large chestnut horse. He had a ruddy brown coat and striking white markings that ran from forehead to nose. Violet had received him as a gift from her parents when she turned twelve. He was a wobbly foal then, but in her imagination, he swept across the pasture like a flame, and she promptly named him Firestorm.

"Sounds perfect," her father had chuckled. "Now remember, Violet, horses are extremely rare. You must care for this foal diligently and treat him like the treasure that he is." He kissed the top of her head and proceeded to explain her new daily chores. She hung on his words and watched his movements intently, striving to absorb every detail.

Firestorm ate the juicy apple pieces from Violet's hand as she stroked his neck. "Can you believe there was a time when wild horses roamed the countryside? I can picture it clearly: silver stallions crashing through the surf or spotted mares meandering in fields of flowers. The world is so small now…"

Finished with the apple, Firestorm nuzzled Violet's pocket for sugar cubes. He always knew where she'd hidden them. Violet chortled at his antics, pushing away the funk that had enveloped her. "Not yet, smarty," she teased. "Let's go for a ride first!"

Violet relished how riding could make her feel serene and energized at the same time. Wisely, they had waited until Firestorm was four to ensure that he was physically and mentally prepared to bear a rider. From the moment Violet mounted him, it was an ideal pairing. They grew together over the years, branches of the same tree, anchored by deep roots. They were parted while Violet studied at the university, but even then, she had returned to the farm regularly.

As Violet crisscrossed the paddock, she rued having chosen the gloomy poem. In her mind, much-loved voices encouraged her to *celebrate* life. "I know that's what you would want," she thought, "but it's so hard." Her parents had died exactly one year ago. After graduation, Violet had eagerly returned home to assist with the farm. Her mother was a botanist, and her father was an engineer. Living on a bucolic estate bordered by dense woodland, the unassuming couple designed and tested vertical farming techniques and sold fresh produce to the city. They instilled in Violet a thirst for knowledge and a profound appreciation for all living things.

Quieted by the meditative clomp of horse hooves on grass, Violet revisited a seminal incident from her childhood. A hawk had been killed by a hailstorm. Violet had found the beaten, mud-covered carcass near the front door of their old stone house. True acrobats of the sky, hawks had frequently swooped overhead while she played in the yard. Violet was intensely moved by the loss of the regal bird. She knelt on the sodden lawn and wept. Her mother joined her, and after a few wordless moments, she tenderly brushed Violet's hair from her tearful eyes. "We must allow ourselves to be sad, sweetheart, but only for a time," she counseled. "Then we must take comfort that the one we have lost has gone to a better place and we will be reunited someday. In the meantime, we should cherish their memory and be grateful for the time we shared."

Those words had helped to ward off the bitter grief that had threatened to consume Violet this past year. She had been home for five short months when her parents ventured to the rugged western coastline. Violet's mother was investigating a possible new flower species. She was passionate about flowers, and their scarcity seemed to fuel her fascination. A squall erupted. It dissipated quickly, but not before Violet's parents were wrenched from a sheer cliff. They broke like porcelain on the jagged rocks below, where the sea writhed with furious waves and the tempestuous foam was tinged with red swirls that mocked the tiny wildflowers peppering the adjacent slopes.

With a hearty neigh, Firestorm came to a halt near the entrance to the greenhouse. Vivid colors shone through the clear windows—lush greens, pristine whites, jubilant yellows. The greenhouse was a modest one-story extension of the farm tower, but the radiance of its residents made the building seem impossibly grand and dazzling for its diminutive size. This had been a sanctuary for Violet's mother. It was also a fertile laboratory where she labored to preserve plants that were on the brink of extinction and develop new hybrids that might have a better chance of survival.

Violet dismounted and retrieved a sugar cube from her pocket. "Here you go," she crooned, stroking Firestorm's fine, silky coat with her free hand. "You're so spoiled," she appended affectionately.

The horse nickered his appreciation for the treat, and Violet grinned toothily. For months, Firestorm had smooshed his nose against the greenhouse glass every afternoon, searching for Violet's mother. He dutifully reported to the barn to be groomed by Violet's father. Violet suspected that he knew they were gone but was unwilling to surrender these routines. A boisterous horse, Firestorm had grown eerily quiet after the accident. It was the sort of silence that accompanies the eye of a hurricane, suffocating and out of place. She was relieved to hear his lively vocalizations again.

Inhaling deeply to catalyze a change in focus, Violet announced, "It's time for me to get back to work, but I'll visit you later. Stay out of trouble, okay?" Firestorm snorted and trotted away.

Violet traversed the greenhouse, evaluating various plants along the way. Though the artificial lighting was effective, she tended to loiter where sunbeams danced on the windows. At the entry to the farm, Violet stopped next to a young plum tree with fragrant silver blossoms and dug her digital companion, or DC, from an interior pocket of her jacket. A DC was issued to every citizen at birth. The device was wholly integrated into daily life and regarded as an extension of its owner. The sleek screen illumined at her touch. "Show my tasks for this afternoon," Violet bade, brushing sugar granules from her fingers and heading into the tower. With her eyes on the list, she accidentally bumped the delicate tree. "Sorry," she whispered, steadying the trunk. As the tinted glass door closed behind her, she glimpsed a few petals falling reluctantly to the ground like a snow flurry at dusk.

Abounding with life, the farm was an airy circular structure that housed a dizzying array of crops and equipment. It was a more controlled and mechanical environment than the greenhouse, but the technology harmonized with nature as much as possible. Solar panels, wind turbines, and an innovative water capture system all supported a bountiful indoor harvest. Yet inasmuch as the farm depended on Mother Earth, it also required protection from her. At the Murphy estate, a biblical tempest was as likely as a mizzly rain shower. The farm thrived in a protective cocoon of reinforced walls that withstood the capricious weather as resolutely as a dragon guarding its gold.

Violet's parents had devoted their life's work to the farm, even though most people viewed farming as a frivolous pursuit since food generators were plentiful. Nevertheless, the operation was consistently profitable. Venerable restaurants in the city purchased their produce and cooked "natural" dishes for enthusiastic customers who regarded it as a novelty.

The majority of the population lived underground, burrowing deep into the mountains to evade the planet's heaving seas and broken sky. Fear and frustration festered until many came to despise the earth and yearned to leave it. For years, the government had been seeking a new Eden. Relatively few people lived aboveground on inherited plots passed down for generations. New habitation was prohibited. Most land was left untamed, visited only by dazed students on steel-clad field trips and adventurers inspired by folktales.

Though their ranks had dwindled, the Murphy clan still occupied the mature stone house where Violet was raised. The house was settled on a sprawling, meadowed lot skirted by acres of thick forest. Violet was now its sole caretaker and the family's only living descendent. Fortunately, the farm was just three stories high. Violet's parents did not want it to overshadow the nearby trees. With advanced robotics and automation, Violet was able to manage the estate on her own.

After three grueling hours and a particularly difficult repair of storm-damaged machinery, Violet paused. "Play classical music," she prompted, and Vivaldi sprang elegantly from the walls. "Very nice," she murmured and moved on to her next task. Engrossed in the work and music, she did not hear the visitors' approach. The abrupt intrusion of the bell startled her.

Lingeringly annoyed from the jump scare, Violet headed without haste to the arched front gate of the estate. She was surprised to find three people in formfitting white jumpers and helmets, bobbing like buoys next to a matching white microcar. They appeared to be inspecting the carpet of lime moss on the rocky arch and the petite golden flowers at its base.

"May I help you?" Violet called as she approached.

"Are you Violet Murphy?" a woman's voice shot like a pistol.

"Yes, that's me," Violet replied. "I wasn't expecting visitors today. Please state your business."

The woman mulishly waited until Violet arrived at the gate. "Per recent news alerts," she recited briskly, "the government is performing the annual census. We are completing our work in your area today. My name is Dr. Akira Tanaka. I belong to the Science Bureau, and I am leading the census." She extended her DC to Violet. "Here are my credentials."

Violet opened the sturdy gate and glanced at Akira's device. She knew about the census and had no reason to doubt the woman's legitimacy, but she could not recall having home visits in the past. "I thought I'd get a form to complete," she said. Irritation and confusion colored her tone.

"The process is more comprehensive this year," Akira explained. "May we look around your property?" With the flick of a hand, Akira signaled her companions to proceed. They did not wait for consent.

Violet exhaled loudly. She followed the trio up the path, watching uncomfortably as they recorded extensive threads of data and images. As sunset started to paint the horizon, the group dithered outside the farm, debating in low voices. Akira turned to Violet. Adopting a more conciliatory manner, she inquired, "Would you mind giving us a tour of this structure? I am acquainted with your parents' methods. Organic production is my personal area of focus."

Violet was hesitant but could not deny a request to showcase her parents' work, especially on this day. She led the scientists around the facility and answered their ready questions. As they filed out of the building, Akira noted that they had skipped the greenhouse.

"The greenhouse is…private," Violet asserted. Akira's dark, flinty eyes dissected her, but she did not back down.

"Fine," Akira said with a nod. "Remove your jacket, please. We require a blood sample."

Momentary relief dissolved to alarm. "What?! Why do you need my blood?" Violet yelped as she backed up a step. "I'm certain you have access to my medical records. Look, I've been patient, but this is asking too much!"

Firestorm was grazing in the paddock. When Violet's distress reached his pert ears, he snorted forcefully and dashed over. His sudden appearance caused a commotion. The scientists jockeyed clumsily for new positions a safe distance from the fence.

Violet scratched under Firestorm's mane and clucked warmly, "I can always count on you for some comic relief."

Akira jerked her head to signify that she was composed. She glared at her associates then addressed Violet. "The census process requires a blood sample from each citizen. Would you like to review the edict?"

"No," Violet snapped. She was tired and just wanted the intruders to leave. She removed her jacket and bunched up a sleeve of her threadbare Henley shirt. Rising moonlight and waning sunshine mingled on her creamy, freckled skin. One of Akira's minions wielded a small gadget. He held it firmly against Violet's arm until the sample was drawn. It did not hurt, but Violet still grimaced in protest.

"You'll be on your way now?" Violet asked, though it was more statement than question.

"We need a sample from the horse, too," Akira responded calmly. Violet instantly shifted to block her path. Unaware, Firestorm watched a pair of bushy gray squirrels that were bolting like puffs of smoke between the fence posts.

"Why do you need my horse's blood? What kind of bizarre census is this?" Violet challenged.

"We must account for all household members. This horse is clearly a member of your household and not a feral animal." Akira dropped her icy tone and added vaguely, "He is quite beautiful."

Before Violet could react, the phlebotomist mashed his gadget into Firestorm's neck. Shocked, the horse lurched away, reared, and fled with a shrill cry to hide in the gathering dusk. "What are you doing?! You can't just jam that thing into him!" Violet yelled.

"It's just an animal," the man responded dismissively, his tone as dry as sawdust. Pivoting to Akira, he inspected his equipment and confirmed, "We have what we need."

"We apologize for the disruption to your afternoon, Ms. Murphy. Thank you for your cooperation. The official confirmation of our visit will be sent to your DC," Akira announced without a wisp of remorse. "We will be leaving now. We can see ourselves to the gate."

Violet was anxious to find Firestorm. She mastered her tongue so that the encounter would end. Akira nodded and started down the gravelly path, but she turned back after a few steps, seeming conflicted and speaking more slowly. "Ms. Murphy, I know you haven't…*enjoyed*…our visit today. I wish the circumstances had been different because I am truly interested in your agronomy techniques and would like to learn more."

Violet did not reply. Her stiff movements as she slipped back into her jacket broadcasted her displeasure.

After a thoughtful pause, Akira continued, "Perhaps you would be willing to present at the Science Bureau." She did not await an answer. "Yes," she declared crisply. "I will make the arrangements. Please watch for an invitation. Good evening." The matter was apparently resolved.

Pale moonshine was overtaking the final blush of day, which made it difficult for Violet to spot Firestorm in the wide pasture. "Firestorm?" she called. "They're gone now, buddy. Where are you?" The horse whickered and emerged from the shadow of the barn. Violet hopped the paddock fence and rummaged in her pocket for a treat to distract him. Firestorm clopped over to meet her, soft light swaying on his silken coat. Violet assessed his neck. "You don't seem to be injured," she said, "but I'm really sorry that I didn't prevent that vampire from touching you." Leading the horse inside, she added wearily, "The whole thing seemed so surreal."

The barn was constructed from the same core materials as the house. Ancient beige and gray stones of different sizes and shades created a foggy, ashen tapestry like rolling mist on a basalt beach. The barn boasted a gabled slate roof with skylights and a compact storage silo. The spacious interior mainly consisted of a wide corridor flanked by timber benches and cabinets, two large stalls, and a tack room. It was diffusely lit, and the heady scents of fresh straw and ripened wood perfumed the air. Integrated custom technology supported its upkeep, and the structure was solidly reinforced for severe weather and earthquakes.

The familiar surroundings helped Violet to unwind. She closed the sliding doors manually and watched Firestorm amble to his water trough. He was an amiable horse who raced the produce trucks and merrily snacked on hand-fed carrots from the drivers. Once, a driver brought his daughter to see Firestorm. He rarely encountered children and seemed to recognize that this was a special occasion. He sprinted across his enclosure with such majesty that the girl was awestruck, and then he waited with uncharacteristic patience while she mustered up the courage to pet him. Violet wondered sadly if today's events would make him less trusting or sociable.

Intending to read the news but unable to keep her eyes open, Violet fell asleep on a cot that she used whenever Firestorm was ill. She was roused by damp breath and prickly whiskers several hours later. Violet chuckled as Firestorm persistently nudged her with his nose until she sat up. "It's good to see you're no worse for wear," she uttered through a yawn. "As for me, I need a shower and a warm breakfast."

As she led Firestorm into the dewy golden dawn, Violet glanced at her DC. Akira had wasted no time in contacting her about visiting the Science Bureau. In three days, Violet was scheduled to present on a concisely bulleted list of topics. Her train fare was prepaid. There was no request for confirmation. Violet sighed. "Well, it looks like I'll be taking a little trip, Firestorm."

CHAPTER 2

INFLECTION

Violet rechecked the itinerary, hoisted her rucksack, and straddled the stocky, steel-framed scooter. She adjusted the windscreen to fend off the misty dawn air, then she called to Firestorm, "Be good. I'll be back tomorrow."

Firestorm neighed. He trotted alongside Violet as she motored down the path and secured the gate, until the paddock fence blocked him and he could accompany her no farther. Once the scooter was obscured by the low-lying fog, he moseyed away, pressing his nose into the wet grass to graze.

The train station was the glossy, industrial nexus of three unpaved woodland paths. To Violet's chagrin, the winding trail from the Murphy estate was muddy, so the journey took almost an hour. She drove slowly to avoid spattering her clothes. When she finally emerged from the trees into the swath of tallgrass that encircled the station, she felt a surge of anticipation. Akira seemed genuinely interested in farming and had been meticulous in organizing this trip. For the talk, however, Violet was instructed to focus on environmental vegetation, not crop production (probably because they had skipped the greenhouse on their tour). Regardless, Akira's detailed message made it easy for Violet to prepare. She found that the woman was more likeable in writing.

Violet parked the scooter and relaxed her tense muscles. The train would arrive in a few minutes. She glanced around the small outpost. It consisted of an open-air platform, two utilitarian benches, and a freestanding wall to which a glassy half-dome was anchored, providing marginal shelter from the elements. Video display units on the wall hummed with news and advertising, but apart from the VDUs, the station was empty. This was a remote stop; Violet had usually been the only passenger here when she traveled to and from the university. Sunshine was starting to penetrate the fog, so she closed her eyes and tilted her head, inviting the rays to warm her chilled face.

A low-pitched horn heralded the train's approach. Violet's sharp blue eyes opened just in time to spot an inquisitive ginger rabbit hopping into the safety of the dense, wheat-like grass nearby. Smiling, she watched the cottontail's retreat. She pulled her DC from the rucksack to use at the ticket scanner, inhaled deeply, and headed to the platform.

Streamlined and silver-gray, the train was commonly known as the "electric eel," but actual eels were extinct, and most people were oblivious to the glib analogy. It was comprised of multiple self-contained units with assorted seating configurations. Using a subaquatic tube, it connected the planet's last two inhabited regions, though the bulk of the system operated within the city of Apricus. The train was spotless inside. Teal upholstery padded the seats, and a video strip ran the perimeter of each unit. Violet chose a window seat and settled in. She deposited her rucksack on the opposite seat and propped her feet on it to avoid dirtying the unnaturally clean furniture. Pulling up her hood and folding her arms across her chest, Violet shut her eyes and allowed the mild swaying of the train to lull her to sleep.

The alto bell was brief but emphatic. Muzzily, Violet wondered how the engineers chose that particular sound. The bell was not alarming, yet it insisted on being heard. It meant that the train was about to enter its translucent tube and cross the murky waters that were too treacherous for boats. Following centuries of abuse, the earth had seemingly revolted with ferocious tectonic shifts. By that point, the oceans were already bloated, decaying corpses smothering a half-drowned planet in barren waves. Then after the tectonic plates moved, almost all remaining land was either actively volcanic or shards of bladelike rock where no plants would grow. Humanity survived on two islands called Fulminara and Potesta. Fulminara was wild and hardy, a miracle of rolling grasslands and mixed forests teeming with deciduous trees and vibrant evergreens. Potesta was mountainous, defined by the steep inclines and whetted crests of the Olympus Range. Its terrain was largely stony and inhospitable, but there were also defiantly picturesque thickets of sturdy trees and plants. Apricus prospered within a chain of massive caverns inside the mountains. Few people lived beyond its protective walls.

Violet drew her feet off the rucksack and shifted to face the window. As the high-speed train raced by, ghostly structures materialized like giant tombs in a flooded mausoleum. Violet watched with morbid interest, knowing that she could see only the peaks of these man-made alps and that most of the lost city was hidden in the black fathoms below.

The bell tolled again when the train resurfaced. The abrupt brightness of the sunny azure sky caused Violet to squint, but she did not look away. She savored the sunshine, knowing that the train would soon plunge into the mountainside, dousing the light. Catching her reflection in the window, Violet removed her hood and tied her wavy brown hair into a ponytail with a plain elastic band. Then she scooted closer to the glass and studied the boulder-strewn landscape outside. She played a game of find-the-juniper and fiddled with her bangs until the train sped past the chiseled colonnade of the Apricus portico.

Violet retrieved her DC and scanned her presentation. Three stops preceded the Science Bureau, and before long, the train was bustling with neatly pressed commuters and uniformed schoolchildren. The cacophony of conversations and automated train announcements made it difficult for Violet to concentrate, so she gave up and simply waited for her stop.

"Government Square," a cool, feminine voice pronounced as the doors glided open. Violet exited with a horde of commuters but quickly sidestepped the hurtling crowd to get her bearings. She had visited the square when she was a student, but unlike the commuters, this was not her daily routine. Ahead, five imposing buildings formed the perimeter of a vast flagstone square made of evenly cut pavers in muted tones of blue, tan, and gray. A polished black sculpture sat in the middle of the square, circled by gray sandstone benches. It depicted a simple, rocket-like spaceship and a featureless planet, artfully positioned to show that the ship was leaving. At the base, a silver placard read: *Onward.*

There were numerous light shafts in Apricus where the original builders had tunneled through solid rock to naturally illuminate the city. Over time, many of these shafts had fallen into disrepair, but the one at Government Square was maintained, and the statue was situated where the admitted light could bathe it for much of the day. There were no fountains or gardens, though. No greenery, birdsong, or insect buzz. The square was exactly that: sharp edges and emptiness.

"What a waste of sunshine," Violet grumbled.

The buildings at Government Square were unvaryingly gray. Like most structures in Apricus, they had been erected using an aggregate of salvaged metals and other refuse. While the city's recycling process was revolutionary, its end product was as melancholy as an overcast sky. Violet used her DC to locate the Science Bureau. She checked the time and crossed the square with a self-assured stride. Inside the building, there was a circular reception desk in a well-lit, high-ceilinged entry hall. The gleaming floor in front of the desk was etched with a clean-lined white rendering of the sculpture from the square, and its *Onward* mantra was carved into a decorative cornice at the top of the walls. Otherwise, the hall was an unadorned wash of gray.

Four corridors forked off the entry hall like spokes on a wheel. Violet was unsurprised to see her host waiting at one of them. Akira wore a perfectly tailored white lab coat and held a sizable digital tablet. Her black hair was arranged in a short bob reminiscent of the helmet she had worn on her visit to the farm.

"Welcome," Akira said with a brisk nod. She wasted no time on pleasantries and swiftly ushered Violet into a small auditorium where more white coats were already assembled.

Unruffled, Violet glanced at her itinerary and said, "I'm not scheduled to present for another ten minutes, and I need to set up. First, I'd appreciate directions to the restroom." With a hint of annoyance about the lack of hospitality, she added, "I've had a long trip."

"Certainly," Akira replied.

The next couple of hours passed quickly. Having earned two advanced degrees, Violet was accustomed to public speaking. She was eloquent and poised. She skillfully balanced theory and practical application. The farm was in her blood. Every day, she was immersed in its intricate technological and biological systems. Although she rarely had opportunities to share her expertise, it came to her as naturally as riding her bicycle after a thaw.

The white coats applauded courteously when Violet concluded her lecture. Most thanked her as they filed out of the auditorium. Akira remained behind to escort Violet to the next activity, which was a Q&A session with a small subgroup of scientists.

"Well-done," she praised. "I enjoyed your talk."

While it was hard for Violet to imagine Akira *enjoying* anything, she appreciated the compliment.

Akira led Violet down a long, sterile corridor with regularly spaced doors. The gray walls were bare, and the doors were closed. White coats occasionally flitted between rooms. Violet sensed that the rooms were bubbling with activity, but the doors closed too fast to see, and the only sound was the staccato clip of Akira's heels. They turned a corner into a dimly lit passageway. To the left of each door, a video display and alphanumeric keypad were set into the wall and emitted a faint bluish-green glow like bio-luminescent algae. Violet saw the word *detention*, and her pace slowed.

Without looking back, Akira explained, "We are required to share space with the Security Bureau and military." Under her breath, she added, "It is unfortunate."

Violet was unsure if Akira had meant for her to hear the comment, so she did not reply. She waited at a distance while Akira poked a code into the keypad for Interrogation Room 5.

"We will hold your Q&A session here," she said. "I have several follow-up questions. We will be joined by a few of my colleagues." Akira perceived Violet's discomfort and tried to pacify her. "I am sorry that a different setting is not available. Meeting space is very limited these days. I recognize that the arrangements are not optimal."

The door slid open. Akira stood in the corridor, clutching her tablet and extending her other arm into the room, gesturing for Violet to enter. Violet hesitated. Interrogation Room 5 made her uneasy.

Dropping her thin arm, Akira tapped an unmarked button on the key-pad and said, "We need coffee, please." She looked to Violet who was firmly planted a dozen feet from the door. "A hot cup of coffee will make us more comfortable. Don't you agree?" she cajoled. "We grew the beans ourselves. I would value your opinion."

Violet bit the corner of her lower lip. Coffee plants were extinct, and all extracted DNA was believed to have been lost. Food generators could approx-imate the flavor and aroma of coffee, but it was probably a weak imitation of what the true bean could yield. Violet's curiosity was piqued. She had to know how the bureau's coffee tasted. She had to know how they were growing the plants. She dropped Akira's gaze and walked through the open doorway.

The room was stark. A matte metal table and six matching chairs sat glumly under a bright but cheerless overhead light. The walls were empty. Everything was gray, as if the government had an acute mistrust of paint.

Violet selected a chair facing the door, placed her rucksack on the floor, and folded her hands politely on the tabletop.

"We will get started in a moment," Akira stated as she took the opposite seat.

Three more white coats marched into the room, followed by an olive-skinned man in a black uniform carrying a serving tray with six identical ceramic mugs. The man distributed the mugs, placed the tray in the center of the table, and took the remaining seat. Violet slid her hands around her mug, welcoming its warmth.

Akira's colleagues fiddled with their tablets and muttered to one another. Violet could not pick up what they were saying, and they seemed disinclined to make introductions. The man who brought the mugs sipped his coffee and stared at Violet.

"Have you tried the coffee, Ms. Murphy?" Akira inquired expectantly. "Don't let it get cold."

Violet lifted her mug and sniffed the brown liquid. "How did you grow the beans?"

"I will be happy to discuss that at the end of the Q&A," Akira dodged, peering into her mug. "Let's finish your piece first. Then it can be our turn to share." Akira took a swallow of coffee. Her raised eyebrows pointedly encouraged Violet to follow suit.

Eager to proceed so that she could ask her own questions, Violet tasted the coffee. It was excessively bitter and altogether unsavory. Violet barely suppressed the impulse to spit it out. Her lips were tightly pursed in a grimace. She willed herself to swallow the vile swill and gradually morphed her expression into a closed-mouth smile, nodding slowly as if she were carefully considering the coffee's many merits. Everyone was looking at her. "It's good," she breathed. "Really interesting flavor."

"Excellent," replied Akira with a curt nod. "Let's start the Q&A."

Akira's colleagues pelted Violet with technical questions for the next half hour. Violet had expected a more casual discourse. She had stowed her

DC but hastily recovered it to access her data and records. Akira was conspicuously quiet, observant but detached. The man in black continued to stare. At first, Violet was invigorated by the variety of horticultural topics, from hydroponics to hay fever. Then she started to feel dazed and distracted.

The onslaught persisted, taking on a distinctly agricultural bent, with topics such as farm economics and energy conservation. Violet became dizzy and queasy. As soon as words left her mouth, she could not recall what she had said. However, the group looked pleased, so whenever it seemed she would pass out, she forced herself to refocus. It felt like a matter of professional pride.

By the ninety-minute mark, Violet was very ill. She was woozy, floating like dandelion fluff, and everything was distant. Even so, she continued to impart her knowledge. It did not occur to her to stop. Certain questions were less technical now, which felt like a pleasant reprieve. The scientists asked about the local wildlife at the estate and why she did not live in Apricus. Akira was fidgety. This struck Violet as odd, though she could not say why.

Eventually, Violet could not lift her head. She did not remember laying it down. "I don't feel well," she garbled into the tabletop.

"We're almost finished," came the icy retort. It was the first time the glowering man in black had spoken. With a vague sense of déjà vu, Violet repeated her complaint minutes later and received the same reply. The probing scientists asked about her mother's unpublished research and her father's custom circuitry.

Violet was frightened now. The inquisition would not stop, but she was barely conscious and could neither understand nor respond. She braced her chin on her folded forearms and looked pleadingly across the table at Akira. Someone was talking, but Violet was no longer listening. Unwanted tears welled in her eyes.

"We're finished here," Akira announced, interrupting her colleague.

"I was in the middle—" he protested.

But Akira shouted, "Enough!" and he fell silent. Violet rested her pounding head on the table and closed her eyes as the room emptied around her.

In the hallway, Akira grabbed the coffee-bearer's arm while her associates fled the scene. "How much did you give her?" she demanded, bunching his shirt in her hand.

The man jerked out of her grasp, but before he could either speak or strike, Akira's DC chimed in a pocket of her lab coat, loudly announcing an incoming call. "You should take that," he sneered. He tugged at the sleeve of his molested uniform and stalked away.

Akira pulled out her DC, saw *President* on the display, and steeled herself with a deep breath. "Good day, sir."

"Good day, Dr. Tanaka," the president replied genially. "I trust that your work is progressing well?"

"Yes, sir. The Murphy debrief just ended." Akira's eyes combed the vacant corridor. She elaborated, sotto voce, "However, sir, I remain concerned about the involvement of the Security Bureau. Ms. Murphy seemed willing enough to share with us. These draconian measures do not align with our values." She plowed ahead quickly. "The values on which you were elected to lead us."

The president was quiet for a moment. Akira had taken a risk with her bold footnote, but he purposely surrounded himself with candid advisors and could not hold it against her. He had no patience for sycophants. "I agree, Dr. Tanaka, that we must hold true to our values. I agree that it is my duty to protect the rights and welfare of all citizens. However, it is also my duty to justly weigh the treatment of one citizen against the greater good." The president spoke reflectively but with conviction. "I regret that unconventional methods were required today. You studied Ms. Murphy's profile. You agreed that she would not support Project Noah. We cannot afford any disruptions.

We are too close to success." He waited a beat to see if she would resist further, then he concluded firmly with, "Remember the greater good, doctor."

"Yes, sir, I will," Akira conceded. "Thank you for your time."

The president set down his DC and lolled in his chair. His eyes felt tired and gritty, so he shut them while his fingertips brushed across the uneven surface of his desk. His movements were careful and slow over the tiny, braille-like bumps and grooves of the varnished wood. To a chance observer, the president would have looked worshipful. In truth, he *hated* this desk. It lampooned the calculated exactness of every other object in the room. Nevertheless, he did not order its removal. He told his staff that using the desk was a time-honored tradition, but he really kept it because its flaws were a catalyst. Stroking the desktop helped him to think. He knew that Akira was right to question him. He knew that he was pacing the ragged edge of vice.

Violet received no medical assistance. Disoriented and lead-limbed, she lost her battle for consciousness. Darkness engulfed her for nearly two hours.

"Help us," a voice beseeched.

Awakened by the sound, Violet pried her eyes open. The room was still empty.

"Please help us," the voice rustled, then other voices repeated the plea like a sibilant echo.

Violet forced her body upright and slumped back in the comfortless chair, head lilting behind her. She stared at the harshly lit ceiling with droopy, bloodshot eyes. A waning undertow pulled at her, but she had faith that she could overcome it, if only she could focus her mind. She cast about for a theme, and her first clear thought was of Firestorm. "Yes, that'll work," she mumbled. She coerced her fuddled brain to recall his age, his appearance, his personality, and what they would do when she returned home. "I will brush him. I will clean his hooves. We will ride to the river—"

The voices interrupted, shattering Violet's fragile concentration. "Please help." Violet straightened her neck and rubbed her temples. "Focus, Violet," she reprimanded herself. But the intrusive voices came again, begging for aid, for rescue.

Violet's health steadily improved. She was rapidly returning to normal—normal, that is, except for the disembodied voices. Someone nearby must be imprisoned and afraid. "You can't possibly know that," she scoffed internally. "It's obvious that the voices are *in your head*. You're hallucinating, Violet." She needed to get her blood flowing and send more oxygen to her brain. She stood up slowly and ambled around Room 5, using the walls for support. She had to rest after a few laps, but the voices had stopped, and she was satisfied that she had regained control of her mental faculties. She dropped inelegantly into a chair, wincing at the shrill sound it made as it scraped the floor.

Akira entered the room. She took the seat next to Violet, watching her closely. "Are you feeling better, Ms. Murphy?"

"Yes," Violet answered. "You were ill, too?"

Akira furrowed her brow. The question was unexpected. It was not in the script that her distasteful, black-clad coworker had compelled her to memorize to explain the afternoon's events.

Violet interpreted Akira's hesitancy as confirmation of the theory she had been mulling over between hallucinations. "It's okay," she consoled. "Biogenesis is exceptionally complicated." With a weary, conspirative smile, she added, "I don't think your coffee was quite ready for consumption."

Akira had not anticipated this. She was prepared for a confrontation. Instead, Violet approached her as a sympathetic colleague—and that was much, much worse. Akira's guilt swelled. She rose abruptly and nearly toppled the chair. "Yes, well, I'm sure that you are eager to leave us now," she evaded. "We have kept you longer than planned. I will show you out." Her sight was fixed on the door, and her stance was rigid. Violet attributed Akira's conduct to embarrassment and did not press her.

With her rucksack slung negligently over her shoulder, Violet followed Akira back to the hallway where white coats scurried from room to room. But as she passed the closed doors this time, she felt crushing waves of desperation, sadness, and fear. Unnoticed, she stumbled and was grateful when Akira paused to speak with a minion. The ghostly voices were gone, but this was considerably worse. This was a full-on, visceral experience. The sensations hit Violet like a gut punch, leaving her braced against the wall, breathless and sweaty.

Violet could not make sense of the situation and wanted to leave, urgently. She joined Akira and cleared her throat. Akira apologized, dismissed her subordinate, and gestured for Violet to continue down the hall. Violet walked by just as the scientist opened a door to resume his clandestine work. She glimpsed a pair of mournful eyes inside the room. In that instant, she knew without a doubt that those eyes belonged to one of the voices she had heard.

She also knew that they were not human voices.

CHAPTER 3

HIGH AND LOW

Violet had planned to stay overnight in Apricus at a friend's house, but it no longer seemed like a good idea. Her primitive instincts were screaming for distance from the nebulous dangers of the Science Bureau. Even her rational brain was lobbying for a strategic retreat, to go home pronto and process what had happened. But in the end, her heart won. When Violet exited the building to be greeted by her friend's megawatt smile, she stopped questioning her plans. They shared a delicious meal and reminisced about their university years over a bottle of full-bodied cabernet. Cheerful company, happy memories, and restful sleep soothed Violet's anxiety.

The next morning, Violet waved goodbye and boarded the train, pleasingly refreshed. But as the train slithered on its way, her mood deteriorated. She was haunted by doleful eyes and a plethora of questions. She wriggled restlessly in her seat. Finally, she sat up straight, smacked her thighs determinedly, and gave herself a pep talk. "You are a scientist, Violet. You know what to do. Analyze the situation objectively and methodically." With renewed confidence, she pulled out her DC and began to record detailed notes about yesterday's experience.

In a neighboring unit, Jack Collins was also busy working on his DC. It was his day off, but he had to reply to one or two messages from his staff before he could relax. Jack was a director of retail operations. All shopping was done digitally, and Jack's team focused on order fulfillment for personal and household goods such as cleanser, linens, and perfume. He was a tall, lean, raven-haired man with clear green eyes—handsome but not flashy. Everyone said that Jack *looked* like he worked in business. He was never quite sure if it was a compliment.

When the alto bell sounded, Jack stashed his DC in a zippered pocket of his weatherproof jacket. He noticed that he was alone; everyone else had disembarked in Apricus. He relocated to a window seat so that he could track the train's progress through its underwater tube. Only instead of seeing the deluged cadavers of an abandoned city, Jack imagined a vivacious metropolis with chockablock storefronts, tree-lined sidewalks, and jolly shoppers laden with colorful bags. Having seen old photographs of Fifth Avenue and the Champs-Élysées, Jack often wondered what it would be like to manage a physical store and interact with the customers. He leaned his forehead against the cool glass, lost in fantasy.

Jack was lonely. But his aloneness was unrelated to the existential isolationism of the modern retail industry. The cause was not so grandiose. It was ordinary and apprehensible yet no less painful for its simplicity. Jack's father had died about two years earlier. Jack had returned to his childhood home to live with his mother and younger sister. Despite having a loving family and a clutch of work buddies, he struggled to repair the void of his father's passing. He was most content on days like today, when he rode the train topside to hunt in the woods of Fulminara.

Jack was mild-mannered and unimposing, notwithstanding his height. He was no adventurer, but unlike most of his contemporaries, he did enjoy spending time outdoors. His father had taught him how to hunt small animals as soon as Jack was mature enough to carry a rifle. As Jack aged, he graduated to larger game like deer and wolves. Though he felt powerful when he wielded his rifle, there was never any rush from killing. That was not what made the excursions meaningful. Jack would have been equally pleased to hike, fish, or watch the clouds. All that mattered was spending time with his dad.

To his mother's chagrin, Jack was advised by his grief counselor to continue these trips. It stung to know that he was disappointing her. She had always opposed hunting, judging it to be cruel and negligent. But her steadfast protests were quashed by the leaden weight of history. Hunting had been a Collins institution for generations. Even as the wilderness vanished and mass extinctions unraveled the tapestry of life, the Collins family clung to tradition. Jack was now its sole custodian, and the responsibility was precious to him.

The bell interrupted Jack's reverie. He welcomed the intrusion, perturbed that his shopping daydream had been sacrificed to darker subjects. He had not realized that his mind had wandered. As the train climbed to his station, Jack could almost hear his father's proud baritone. "Never forget, my boy," he would boom, slapping his son amiably on the back. "Hunting is all about camaraderie, strength, and achievement." Jack's aggravated mother would roll her eyes and exit the room in a huff, pausing only to bid them to be careful.

Alighting the train, Jack inhaled a lungful of salty sea air and looked around. He had not been here for four months, but nothing had changed. The small, sheltered station had an uninviting backless bench and a video panel with a pixelated display. It was near the coast and rarely used, at least by people. Feathered visitors, on the other hand, were frequent. The platform was chaotically spattered white in an avian version of abstract expressionism. Jack crossed it guardedly. For a while, he meandered along the granite path outside, lured by the steady beat of the surf. Although he was tempted to spend the day relaxing on the clifftops that overlooked the water, he resisted their siren call and headed inland instead. He hefted his pack to a more comfortable position and hiked through the hardy dune grass toward the forest. The narrow trail was made of crushed seashells that crunched under his boots. Gradually, the grass yielded to leafy shrubs and clusters of pink-and-white flowers, scattered like peppermints.

Jack followed the trail into the forest. The shells underfoot gave way to hard-packed dirt and fine gravel. Leaves swished gently in the onshore breeze that fanned the treetops. After an hour of uninterrupted hiking, Jack felt unaccountably edgy. The rifle was heavy in his hands, and he was bothered that his arms could not swing freely. He decided that he was overdue for a snack. Ditching the trail, he bushwhacked to a meadow where a ring of salt-pruned trees guarded a swath of bristled ferns and showy yellow primrose. Lingering traces of fire damage chronicled the lightning strike that must have birthed the clearing.

"It's amazing," Jack reflected, "how brutality can beget such beauty."

A mild frown creased Jack's brow. Hiking usually made him feel invigorated, not moody and quixotic. Shaking his head in bemusement, he set down the toilsome rifle, removed his pack, and fished out an energy bar. He sank into a pillow of bluish-green pine needles and nibbled his treat, enjoying the mellow rustle of the boughs overhead and the intermittent flute of birdsong.

The whipcrack of a broken branch startled Jack out of a light doze. He suspected that white-tailed deer were browsing nearby. He knew from experience that they favored the oaks in this area. Though the animals preferred to feed at twilight, they could be tempted from their beds in balmy weather. Rolling onto his stomach, Jack grabbed his rifle and shimmied to deeper cover. His six-foot-two-inch frame folded like origami into a tight space between exposed tree roots.

Jack scanned the meadow for his quarry. Slowly, a brown smudge detached from the trees and moved into the clearing opposite him. Sunlight unveiled a tawny deer with a sleek, compact body and slender, almost dainty legs. Patches of fur around her eyes and muzzle and under her tail and belly were as bright as bleached cotton. The doe's big ears were held at slightly different angles, muting her regalness and making her look sweetly goofy. Around her, myriad tiny seeds danced in the air like fairy dust. Jack was enthralled, mundane in the presence of magic.

Increasingly frustrated by his romanticism, Jack shifted his body brusquely and lost his grip on the rifle. Sensing trouble, the deer raised her tail in warning and froze. Jack muttered some imaginative curses but was abruptly silenced when a shock wave of fear smashed into him. His heart pounded violently, and his stomach spasmed. Jack slammed his eyes closed and fought for calm. His mind tossed about wildly for an explanation. He worried that he was having a panic attack.

After a few tense minutes, the oppressive fear subsided, and Jack tentatively opened his eyes. The deer remained motionless across the meadow, but he heard her unladylike snort as she sniffed the air. Then her ears twitched and she refocused on her meal, reaching for the new shoots of an unlucky fir seedling. Jack adjusted the rifle. The wary doe froze, comically mid-chew. Doused in sunshine, she was a perfect target. Yet Jack could not fire. Again, he was paralyzed with dread. His hands trembled. Brackish sweat dampened his hair and stung his eyes. "This is so strange," he thought. "It's like I'm feeling what she feels…but that's ridiculous."

Jack held the rifle so tightly that his hands ached. He was thoroughly fed up with himself and keen to act. The doe shuddered nervously and turned her head to stare unblinkingly in his direction. Her brown eyes were soft and pacific. Somehow, Jack *knew* she had a fawn nearby. "I can't do this," he groaned, rising noisily from his sylvan hidey-hole.

The deer bounded toward the trees. She paused in a belt of dappled shade as a little brown bundle with a riot of white spots made its way to her on wobbly legs. Jack watched them disappear into the forest. He stretched his sore muscles. Feeling overheated, he removed his jacket and piled it on his rifle and pack. For a long while, Jack strayed around the meadow, weaving in and out of the clearing and cataloging the sights and sounds. Bark flaked under his fingers. Briars scraped his pant legs. Verdant green leaves kissed his cheek. He breathed in the heady fragrance of flowers and sap. And as the afternoon crested, Jack's brittle exasperation melted like chocolate in the sun.

The rumbling of Jack's stomach warned him that it was time to hike back to the station. He fetched his DC and captured several photographs of the meadow, meticulously composing each shot. It was a sentimental gesture, but he was too blissed-out for embarrassment or self-reproach. Then, with a fortifying breath, he grabbed an energy bar, donned his gear, and headed out. The conditions were still agreeably warm and breezy, but the temperature was falling. Pop-up thunderstorms were common on Fulminara. Through gaps in the trees, Jack saw tenebrous clouds looming in the distance. He slipped a pair of water-resistant shell pants over his denim jeans and increased his pace, more excited than worried. The prospect of being topside during a storm made him feel tingly and alive. With a jolt, Jack realized that he had not been *feeling* much of anything for a long time. Until today.

He considered the incident with the deer. "It was not my imagination. I felt her panic. I knew she had a fawn. It was real…but that's nuts. I am not a telepath. I cannot talk to animals. I was *not* communing with a deer."

His thoughts spun round and round like a puppy chasing its tail to the point of exhaustion.

Unfortunately, this lengthy internal debate corroded the peace that Jack had discovered in the meadow, and his musings turned grim. He doubted that he would ever hunt again and began to resent whatever had happened, upset that it had stolen a link to his father. Unsuppressed tears mingled with the first drops of cold rain on Jack's face as he walked.

By the time Jack reached the scratchy dune grass that bordered the railway station, the caustic flare of pain had abated, and he felt unexpectedly refreshed and unburdened. He double-checked the video display and spent the last half hour of his trip sprawled on his back on the granite path. He was bundled up in his hooded jacket, head resting on his pack, being pelted with raindrops and mesmerized by the lightning flashes in the clouds over-head. When the train arrived, he collapsed into a seat, soggy and tired and wrung-out but relaxed.

There was no one else on board, so Jack removed his outerwear and laid it out to dry on the adjacent seats. He ran his hand through his short hair, leaving it roguishly disheveled. He gave his frayed jeans and cornflower-blue pullover a once-over. The clothing felt soft and warm on his skin. Empirically, advanced synthetics were indistinguishable from natural fabrics, but Jack swore he could tell the difference whenever he wore his favorite cotton clothes or wool socks or touched the silk tie he'd inherited from his grandfather.

Cozily settled, Jack pulled out his DC to scan the news and check his email. The work clutter in his inbox could wait, but a counseling reminder sent his wabbly thoughts tumbling back to his last appointment, slumping on the quilted sofa in Mohammed Devi's office. The doctor was a short, wiry man with sepia skin, graying temples, and buddha-calm eyes. He was compassionate but unrelenting, belying his diminutive appearance. He ped-dled lofty concepts such as "purpose" and "meaning." He was trying to help Jack divorce his self-image from his paralyzing grief, but Jack was morbidly uncooperative. Why couldn't the doctor see that Jack's life had no purpose? That Jack was just drifting aimlessly, more a ghost than his dead father? At the end of the session, with his patient in silent tears, Dr. Devi had gently asked, "Jack, what *else* defines you?" To which Jack had finally admitted, "I don't know yet."

Released from the memory, Jack closed his inbox. He did know one thing: at this moment, he felt less lonely than he had at any time since his father died. He scrolled through his photos of the meadow, and a shy smile quirked the corner of his mouth. When the train chimed, Jack turned to catch a last glimpse of the storm.

CHAPTER 4

OUTSIDE THE BOX

Violet was met by the rackety crackle of leaf litter under her boots. The station was blanketed in branches, stems, and muddy chunks of turf. Outside the shelter, her scooter was upended. "Windstorm," she concluded. "Not too bad, though."

The weather was pleasantly cool and calm. Violet wore russet corduroys over her sturdy lace-up boots and a fitted bomber jacket. She zipped up the jacket but removed the hood and slotted it neatly into a side pocket. As she set out through the lazily undulating prairie grass, the latent blond strands in her hair caught the light. But as Violet crossed into the woods, her tresses started to catch less desirable things like thorny twigs and low-hanging ivy. She paused the scooter. With swift, long-practiced motions, she secured her hair in a loose bun on the crown of her head.

Aside from rousting a cloud of blackbirds from a berry-laden bush, the journey was uneventful—and Violet was certain that when the little bandits took flight, it had startled her more than her scooter had startled them. She found that the wind damage was concentrated. Barring puddles, there were no signs of the storm as she neared the farm. "It was probably a microburst," she thought. "Thank goodness it wasn't a derecho or tornado. Firestorm would have been so frightened."

As if on cue, Violet heard a merry neigh in the distance. When the estate's elegant stone arch came into view, Firestorm was already waiting at the edge of the paddock. Laughing, Violet called out a greeting. Firestorm pawed at the ground impatiently while she maneuvered the gate. As she steered down the path toward the baronial stone house, the horse trotted along the fence line beside her.

Mirth and joy and relief and safety and love, love, love, love, love. And oh, it was all amplified, magnified, until Violet was breathless with it.

She was awash in Firestorm's emotions.

Happiness and security and love, love, love. It was wondrous and beautiful, and very nearly overwhelming.

Violet parked the scooter and shuffled unsteadily to where Firestorm waited. His rich brown coat and white blaze dazzled in the sun. Taking stock, Violet noted clinically that she was overwrought, clammy, and wheezy, but not ill per se. It was how one felt after crying tears of joy—drained, though not from sadness. Firestorm rested his nose on Violet's shoulder. She stroked his mane and shifted her focus to him.

Concern and hesitation and love, love, love. He was worried about her! She could hear him in her mind but without a voice or words. She just *knew*. Firestorm whinnied softly and raised his head. "I'm sorry, buddy," Violet soothed. "I'm acting strange, aren't I? Everything's fine. I'm so happy to be home. I missed you, ya big softy."

Apparently satisfied, Firestorm sauntered to the middle of the paddock. He grazed on the lush carpet of emerald-bright bluegrass and idly swished his tail at pesky insects. Occasional birdsong punctuated the quiet. Reclining on the limestone steps in front of the house, Violet watched him and pondered her strange new "ability."

"Strong emotions appear to trigger it. But unlike with Firestorm, I heard voices in Apricus. Maybe being sickened by that dreadful coffee altered the experience. My overtaxed brain may have been helping me translate the sensations. And there were *a lot* of sensations, which probably means that I connected with several—"

Violet's highly rational brain hit a trip wire.

She mercilessly ignored it.

"—animals."

There, that wasn't so bad.

"The evidence suggests that I have somehow, someway tapped into the thoughts and feelings of animals. At a minimum, a raccoon and my horse. Wow."

Violet had only glimpsed the raccoon at the bureau, but its distinctive markings were easy to recognize. "Those banded rascals are usually so dynamic. This one was still and scared," she recalled sadly. Her ruminations drifted until she realized that she had been thinking about sandwiches for at least five minutes. She gusted out a breath and went inside to make lunch.

Refueled, Violet spent the balance of the afternoon tending to Firestorm and the farm. She enjoyed the liberating routine of physical labor while her recent metaphysical experiences percolated in the back of her mind like a pot on slow boil. The sun's inexorable descent bathed the sky in ochre and mauve, and Violet paused repeatedly to admire it. When her final chore was complete, she pulled off her work gloves and sat on the cedar fence in the secondary paddock to give the light show her undivided attention. In time, the wind kicked up, and ominous clouds smothered the last blush of daylight. Regretfully, Violet abandoned her perch and headed for shelter.

Outpacing the storm, Violet ducked into the house as the first fat raindrops fell. She removed her jacket and boots in the foyer, serenaded by the staccato tap of drizzle on the thick, insulated windows. Deft hands built a fire in the great stone hearth that divided the kitchen and salon. When she was satisfied with the burgeoning flames, she walked through the amply stocked kitchen pantry to a storage room that contained a micro weather station. The equipment showed that a thunderstorm had formed off the east coast and was barreling inland but losing power. Convinced that the storm posed no serious threat, Violet proceeded to the bathroom to wash up.

After dinner, Violet curled up on a homey overstuffed couch near the hearth. The vaulted ceiling in the salon was adorned with beams of polished, densely grained wood that matched the floor. The rough-hewn stone walls were mellowed with vivid, handwoven tapestries of wool, hemp, and silk and an assortment of paintings and photographs in rustic frames. Violet rocked gently to the rain's lullaby, absently rubbing her cheek against the velvety pillow on which it rested. Minutes or hours later, a devious thunderclap jolted her out of repose.

Violet unfurled like an indolent mainsail. She sat upright and grabbed her DC off the squat, mosaic-tiled coffee table. She added her unusual reunion with Firestorm to the notes that she had logged on the train, then she reviewed it all again. And again. And again. Until her mind was a sizzling fuse box about to blow. She was almost certain that she had experienced some type of empathic telepathy. However, persistent doubts niggled at her, dulling her excitement and making her tetchy. She was troubled, too, that the animals at the Science Bureau had been pleading for help. If she did indeed have this ability, then she also had a responsibility to act.

"I need to substantiate my hypothesis," Violet mulled. "But I cannot simply ramble into the woods in search of random wildlife to talk to, especially not in the middle of the night, during a storm." She buried her face in a pillow and groaned loudly in frustration. "Maybe I should start by ruling out temporary insanity," she joked to herself.

Violet relocated to the study. While the computer verified her identity, she tapped her stockinged feet like an amped-up athlete taking their mark. A chime tinkled, then the expansive semicircular monitor awoke, and Violet got busy. She doggedly searched the city's databases for information about telepathy. Though her conceptual knowledge improved, everything she found was speculative, and the ties to her own experiences were flimsy. Disappointed,

Violet tried another tactic. She scoured the city's online "communities," which were social groups for people with shared interests. However, she found no posts that were even tangentially related to paranormal phenomena.

Unwilling to concede defeat, Violet fetched a glass of water from the kitchen to clear her head. She propped her hip against the pale alder cabinets and listened to the meditative beat of rain on the house. Suddenly, Violet's eyes snapped open, which felt all the more dramatic because she had not realized they had closed. With epiphanous excitement, she sprinted back to the study.

"Nature, wilderness, wildlife," Violet listed, narrating her keystrokes. "Surely, there must be at least one forum for people who love the natural world." In college, she had seen the animosity that most citizens had for Mother Earth. She'd learned to hold her values close—not because she was intimidated, but to avoid the wearisome scorn or pity that her ethics inevitably spawned. She had never sought to join a like-minded group, but tonight, the idea thrilled her.

"Ah-ha! Found you!" Violet exclaimed. Her monitor brimmed with the words and images of a small but enthusiastic community of nature-lovers. She browsed the content eagerly. Pleased with what she saw, she uploaded her profile and drafted a short introductory post. She wanted to end the message with a question that would suss out if anyone else in the little fringe group was telepathic—without saying it outright, of course. "Even I'm not that brash," she thought with a smirk.

> I have a special connection with animals that seems to be on a different level. Does anyone know what I mean?

Satisfied that her bait was tantalizing but safely vague, Violet shut down the computer and lumbered upstairs to bed.

CHAPTER 5

LIKE A DUCK TO WATER

Miles away, while Violet Murphy admired the sunset and Jack Collins sped home, Emily Steuben *should* have been on her way to the train station. But as was often the case in Emily's life, things did not play out as expected.

Seated cross-legged on a hard-wearing oak bench, Emily dictated to her DC, finalizing her notes for the public lecture she would deliver tomorrow at the archives. Her melodic contralto voice drifted across the courtyard like a sacred song. Her fleece dress was draped modestly over her lap, held taut by her knees to keep it from fluttering up in the breeze and giving the birds a show. Her cerulean eyes were slightly unfocused. Lost in her work, Emily appeared to be meditating.

Three stout brick houses formed a semicircle around the cobblestone courtyard. Each house had Tudor-style timber accents, a prominent chimney, and tall rectangular windows. Some of the windows held vibrant splinters of yellow-and-green stained glass assembled into imaginative grids with durable copper foil. Large weighted pots held brightly colored flowers and pungent herbs. At the far end of the courtyard, a sizable pond was dotted with orange water lilies. Bunches of cattails with brown cigar spikes flourished along the shoreline. The landscape beyond was dominated by the gilded grasses of Honey Hill. In the distance, a low stone wall marked the borders of the Steuben estate where rolling hills melted into a cool green forest.

Sundown cast the courtyard in shadow, and a chill wind blustered. Stirred by the sudden cold and the insistent thwapping of her dress, Emily realized that she was running late. She stood up gracefully, stretched her legs, and ran her hands along her flanks to smooth out the paisley fleece that hugged her curvy figure. She preferred this type of downy, feminine dress, but it was always paired with leggings and tough knee-high boots as a concession to the capricious weather on Fulminara.

A petite woman poked her head out the doorway of the left-hand house. Her hair was arranged in a natty chignon that shone brilliantly silver in the twilight. She wore a stained apron over her clothes and a smear of red sauce on her cheek. Her twinkling sapphire eyes invited mischief. Calling to Emily, she said, "You really need to leave for the station, dear. A storm is brewing."

"I'll leave soon, Grandma. Time slipped away from me."

"It tends to do that if you don't keep a close eye on it."

"Yes, Grandma," Emily replied with an affable eye roll. She hurried into the adjacent house to use the bathroom and grab her overnight satchel. She combed the wind-whipped tangles out of her straight golden-blond hair and pulled the cascade into a tidy ponytail that accentuated her facial features. Emily had fair skin with subtle pink undertones, which she liked, and a large aquiline nose, which she detested. Dithering in front of the mirror, she fretted that the ponytail drew too much attention to her maligned nose, then she chastised herself for vanity and headed out.

Menacing shelf clouds were now visible from Emily's hilltop vantage. She dashed back into the house to don a long, rainproof trench coat made of beige twill. When the cuckoo clock in the hallway rang, Emily cursed. She would need to drive fast to catch the last departure of the day. If she missed the train and could not spend the night in Apricus, she would be late for tomorrow's lecture.

Emily was a preservationist at the Potesta archives and museum. A curator and scholar, she was avidly devoted to understanding and safeguarding the world's history and cultural heritage. Her primary responsibility was to examine the debris that was harvested from the ocean in order to identify and claim significant artifacts before they were destroyed for raw materials. Intelligent and analytical, Emily had been expected to apply her skills to a practical career in science or technology, but she fell in love with history during her sophomore year at the university and could not be dissuaded.

Hurrying, Emily rounded the corner of her house to access the gravel road where a battered white sport utility vehicle was parked. The gravel cut a slim path through the fecund grasslands of Honey Hill then merged with a cracked concrete municipal road that led to the railway station. The SUV was freshly washed, heavy droplets dripping from the bumpers. "Grandpa has been busy," Emily thought fondly. She tossed her satchel on the passenger seat and was ready to climb in when a small but raucous flock of mallard ducks passed overhead, making a steep descent.

Her boot was on the running board.
Quack! Quack! Quack!

Her hand was on the grab handle.
Splash!

She checked the dashboard clock.
Quack! Splash! Quack!

Abandoning the vehicle, Emily raced back to the courtyard and uncovered a large plastic bucket that was half-filled with rolled oats and cracked corn. Her friends had just landed in the pond, and she was unable to resist their cheery ruckus. "Ugh, you guys have the *worst* timing!" she hollered.

As Emily approached, the armada of ducks flapped and quacked boisterously. Their blue wing patches and orange-yellow bills were resplendent in the half-light. Some of the birds were briefly submerging to splash water on their backs and bursting back up like heated popcorn kernels. Several drakes hopped out of the pond and waddled across the cobblestones to meet her. "Hold on, I'm coming!" she called with delight. Others jockeyed for prime positions near the shore, bobbing their iridescent green heads excitedly.

Out of nowhere, Emily felt strangely overwhelmed. Her heart thundered behind her ribs, and her hands shook so violently that she almost dropped the bucket. She stumbled to an ungainly halt as a tidal wave of adrenaline rushed her body. In its wake, Emily was breathless, and her mind was jumbled and fuzzy. Distantly, she heard clamorous, throaty quacking and the impatient smacking of little webbed feet on wet stone.

After a few taffy-pulled moments, the persistent rumpus broke Emily's freeze response, and she began to dole out handfuls of grain. Fitful wind gusts frizzled her cheeks, but she welcomed the burn, hoping that it would clear her head. She held the bucket low to prevent the feed from blowing back in her face when she threw it. Her eyes scanned the flock ceaselessly to ensure that every mallard received nourishment. An eager male tugged gently on the hem of her coat. Laughing, Emily rewarded his cleverness with a palmful of corn, then she tended to a clique of fulvous females that were farther offshore, dabbling among the water lilies so that only their tails were visible above the choppy water. The spray of grain on the pond's surface caught their attention, and they sucked up the tidbits like buoyed vacuums.

As the sated flock grew less frenzied, Emily noticed that one duck was swimming apart from the others, weaving nervously among the yellow-striped grasses that sprouted in the shallows. The clatter in Emily's mind receded, and she understood that this hen was a mother waiting patiently for food, unwilling to bring her hidden ducklings into the fray. "Why am I so sure?" Emily wondered. "We haven't seen ducklings on Honey Hill for at least three years. It's probably wishful thinking."

A quiet, rasping call from another solitary duck captured Emily's attention. A glossy male was bobbing in the waves created by his rambunctious cohorts. He floated in the same spot and ate only the grain that came within easy reach. Although he looked healthy, Emily was certain that his wing was injured, making him unable to compete with the stronger, faster birds for food.

"This is ludicrous," she said to the duck. "Where are these insights coming from? Are they even true?"

The duck merely joggled his tail feathers.

"That's not helpful," Emily reproved with gentle amusement.

Tossing a generous shower of grain to keep the others occupied, she coaxed the duck into the shallows with a separate handful. Standing in the fine silt, he flapped his wings a few times, revealing his injury. Emily gasped, in both surprise and sadness. The drake's left wing was droopy and unnaturally bent. It was obvious that he could not fly. "I'll have to keep an eye on you," Emily whispered. She gave him an extra helping of grain then watched as he swam out to dabble in deeper water. The swelling sunset ignited sparklers on the waves and draped the pond in pale purple ribbons.

Emily toured the water's edge in search of ducklings. Bellies full, the flock was dispersing. Most of the ducks sought refuge in the dense cattails on the opposite shore. Others were preening in the shoals. But the mottled brown female was still swimming among the waving grasses. Emily sprinkled grain in the water to entice her out of hiding. She quacked with gusto and sped forward, trailed by a chorus line of six tiny balls of flaxen fluff.

"Whoa, this is amazing!" Emily thought. She plonked down on the cobblestones and dispensed more feed abstractedly. "I have some sort of psychic link with the ducks. I felt generalized excitement from the flock that sharpened into specific thoughts when I focused on individual birds." Lulled by the soft whistles of the ducklings, Emily pondered this intriguing notion, and for the second time that day, she lost track of time…

Emily dimly registered the cold, damp fall of night and nestled deeper into her coat. It was dark, and the ducklings had long since retreated to safety. A blinding burst of sheet lightning torched the sky, finally yanking Emily from her reverie. The advancing storm belched a foreboding rumble—one that sounded very much like a train. "Oh no!" Emily cried, standing abruptly and slowly blinking her wide, startled eyes. The only reply was a blast of stinging rain to her face.

Like the ducklings, Emily knew that it was time to seek shelter. She would need her strength to face a different kind of storm tomorrow.

CHAPTER 6

OF FIRES AND FLOODS

Seated at his desk, the president surveyed the room. A cadre of senior deputies from assorted bureaus was delivering his interminable daily briefing. Dark uniforms and stark white lab coats flecked the office like mismatched socks. The menthol bite of breath mints lingered in the air. The briefing did not require the president's full attention, so while his perspicacious brain processed the tedious details, he entertained himself by sizing up the motley assemblage in front of him:

He is focused and pragmatic. He should be assigned more responsibility.

Her boots need inserts to increase her height.

He is an arrogant, bombastic ass who has outlasted his usefulness. He needs to go.

And so on. The president cataloged his staff with relaxed detachment. He was as cold and ruthless as a winter-hewn blade. But he hid it well, even from himself.

After decades of defeatism, the president had been elected eight years prior on a wellspring of optimism, unity, and bold ideas. Youthful and charismatic, he was wildly inspirational. He pitched a structured, sensible plan for colonizing a new planet and leaving their own empty husk behind. To blunt the jagged edge of finality, he also proposed an exploratory mission to unequivocally confirm that no other habitable regions remained on Earth. Over and over, he milked the public's deep-seated fear that they were trapped in an unsalvageable wasteland, subtly amplifying it to make them restless and angry and then saying, "Do not be angry; there is hope!" It was a masterful manipulation.

His predecessors had been fixated on bolstering the safety and comfort of life in Apricus. They sought alternatives halfheartedly, and the public became apathetic. Conversely, the president made the vestiges of humanity edgy for *more*. He stoked a fire of want. It flared into an inferno that swept him into office and delivered almost unlimited power to him. He promptly announced a comprehensive overhaul of the governmental structure and budget, and with great fanfare, he poured resources into the Science Bureau and military to mobilize ambitious space technology projects.

Years later, the euphoric rush of the president's vision continued to fuel a massive engine of progress. His daily briefings were wearisome but essential. The work was at a crucial stage. His piercing eyes made another lazy circuit of the office as the final report ended. Pleased, he nodded his thanks and smiled while the deputies filed out of the room. By necessity, the president relied on the expertise of his staff and the countless nameless workers under them. Each cog in the engine had its own tasks and goals. The work was so demanding and the energy was so high that no one questioned or even seemed to notice that only the president knew how all the cogs fit together.

Over at the Infrastructure Bureau, Mason Agu was one of the anonymous cogs that kept the president's engine thrumming. He was a gifted computer programmer and systems analyst who helped to manage the city's complex data grid. Being versatile and well-respected, he was also a go-to resource for odd jobs and troubleshooting.

Mason's early life was less auspicious. When he was eight, his mother died in a laboratory accident at the Health Bureau. He grieved intensely and struggled with debilitating bouts of depression and anxiety for more than a year, but with therapy, he eventually adjusted to the loss. Mason's father, however, never found a way to cope. He tried with all his heart to give his son the parenting he deserved, but sorrow consumed him. On Mason's eleventh birthday, they spent a wonderful day together, filled with rare smiles and laughter. He kissed Mason good-night and said he was proud of him, then he died in his sleep.

Devastated, Mason was placed in an orphanage where he barely functioned in catatonic impassivity for months. Caregivers, teachers, and counselors tried desperately to reach him. One day, Mason was staring at family photos on his DC, compulsively rocking his underfed body in a chair at the back of the classroom. His teacher had been watching helplessly when blessed inspiration hit. After class, the teacher offered to show Mason how to make the DC automatically display his favorite photos on command. It was the simplest of programs, but it awakened Mason's interest in computers. He spent endless hours emptying his misery and rage into the dispassionate and controllable realm of ones and zeros. At fourteen, he discovered an aptitude for hacking. Before his mischief could turn criminal, the orphanage secured an internship for him as a penetration tester at the Infrastructure Bureau. Mason excelled as an intern. He rotated through several roles to build his skills, and he was readily hired full-time after he graduated from secondary school.

Rising from his terminal in the dim room, Mason rubbed his eyes and stretched, crowding the tight quarters with his muscular frame. The monitors lit his espresso skin and highlighted the prematurely gray accents in his close-cropped curly black hair and beard. Today's assignment was a mind-numbing slog of programming upgrades to the train system. "I haven't had a day off in forever," Mason complained under his breath. "I never even get to travel where the trains go."

Trevor Zhou squinted up at Mason. His fingers rapped on an ergonomic keyboard nonstop. "Did you say something, Mace?" he asked. Trevor was a brilliant software developer and network architect. Multitalented, he served the bureau with distinction in numerous areas. Trevor and Mason were longtime friends, and they finagled to get projects together as often as possible.

"Mmm no," Mason replied absently. Then he took a breath and pushed aside his grumpiness. "Just need a break. Wanna try another one? I'm leading by three points."

"Sure," Trevor agreed with a puckish grin. "Hit me." He leaned back in his chair and clasped his hands behind his head.

"I am not afraid of storms, for I am learning how to sail my ship."

"Oh, oh, oh! I know this one," Trevor crowed. "*Little Women* is one of my sister's favorite novels. She needlepointed that quotation on a damn pillow. Louisa May Alcott." Trevor pumped his fist in the air triumphantly and bounced happily in his chair.

Mason chuckled at his friend's dramatics. He fell back into his chair and swiveled it from side to side, contemplating. "Technically, you should get a half point for that. It sounds like you haven't actually read the book."

"No, but I still nailed the quote." Trevor side-eyed Mason hopefully.

Mason raised a skeptical eyebrow. "Hmm…" He drew out the syllable outrageously, until a laughing Trevor threw up his hands in defeat. "Fine, fine. Give me another."

Swiveling again, Mason bit his lip and sifted through his prodigious memory. He stopped moving, closed his eyes, and offered his next words slowly, with reverence. "The world breaks everyone and afterward many are strong at the broken places."

Trevor concentrated hard, searching his own extraordinary memory bank but coming up blank. "Uh, that's an interesting sentiment. Kind of somber, though. I give up."

"Yeah, the rest of the passage is pretty dark. It's Ernest Hemingway. *A Farewell to Arms.*"

"Ah. I've read *The Old Man and the Sea,* but not that one."

They returned to working in companionable silence interrupted by short flickers of hushed conversation about the system upgrades. By and by, the afternoon passed and they tiredly boarded a homebound train. Trevor claimed a window seat and pounded an impotent fist against the glass in punishment for their grueling day, muttering "goddamn trains" in an undertone. He noticed Mason's smirking reflection and froze. Suddenly, they erupted into a fit of uproarious, unprofessional giggles. Scandalized stares from the prim commuters across the aisle elicited even *more* giggles, the men deciding that laughter was far better than fists at relieving the day's tension.

At his stop, Trevor clapped Mason's shoulder affectionately and hobbled off the train. Mason's stop was next. Walking to his apartment block, he paused at an eye-catching advertisement for the public lecture series at the archives and felt the residual fizz of laughter drain away. "I hardly ever travel beyond this stop," he mourned. "And the sensory chambers haven't been satisfying lately. Sure, the tech is incredible. The sims are so immersive they can fool me into believing that I'm really exploring a vast and diverse world. But it's just a sham," he thought sadly.

Feeling vaguely claustrophobic, Mason resumed walking and regarded his surroundings. The ambient lighting in the enormous cavern imitated a blushing dusk. Evenly spaced lampposts illuminated a wide stone path. Ahead, a sprawling residential complex loomed. Its ubiquitous gray construction was accented with rebellious smudges of color in windows and on small balconies: lavish draperies, polychrome flags and pottery, and the occasional green plant thriving in the artificial light.

Mason increased his pace in an effort to shake off his simmering discontent. He was relieved to reach his ground-level apartment. He pulled his DC from the back pocket of his pants and used it to unlock the door. The foyer lights blinked on, and Mason's peripheral vision caught an argentine blur. Grinning, he turned to watch a large tabby cat jump onto the narrow entryway table. "Hello, Pounce," Mason cooed. "How's my pretty kitty?" He scratched at the base of her dainty ears, enchanted by her soft, sweet meows.

Pounce had a snowy undercoat that accentuated her shimmery silver fur and bold black markings. She had been Mason's companion for almost seven years. She was smart and good-natured, and although she loved attention, she was independent enough that Mason's long absences did not trouble her. Domesticated animals were rare in Apricus. Most residents feared having their sedulously maintained cityscape overrun by strays. When a litter of shorthairs was born, Mason had lobbied hard for an ownership license and gladly paid the exorbitant fee for a kitten.

Mason treaded to the bathroom to wash up. The apartment was small, but the open design made it feel more spacious. Only the bathroom had interior walls. The standard-issue furnishings were well-made and the appliances were sophisticated, but they lacked warmth. It was Mason's carefully curated personal belongings that transformed the place into a home. A thickly padded patchwork quilt adorned the bed, and lovingly worn, buckram-bound copies of his favorite books were haphazardly stacked on an end table by the sofa. The walls were decorated with striking framed photographs of tigers, cheetahs, lions, and other extinct animals, predominantly big cats.

Dressed in the casual sweatpants and T-shirt that he preferred to wear after work, Mason stopped on his way to the kitchen to admire a photo of two snow leopard cubs, entranced by their spotted fur and pale green eyes. Wanderlust rolled over him like a sour billow. "The world is so achingly empty," his soul grieved. "No polar bears making dens in the ice. No elephant herds roaming the savanna. No parrots or orangutans playing in the trees of a tropical rain forest. No sea turtles or rhinos or giraffes. Even if I *could* travel, is there anything left worth seeing?"

Mason selected a container of leftover pasta from the refrigerator. He dished out a heaping portion, preferring to eat it cold. He told his DC to play classic swing music then tucked into his meal as Duke Ellington drifted from the in-wall speakers. After a few bites, Pounce entered the apartment through her kitty door. She sprang onto the kitchen counter, pawing Mason's arm and yowling loudly. All of a sudden, Mason could not pull enough air into his lungs. His fork fell from numb fingers, leaving a pinwheel splash of pesto on the laminate countertop and his shirt. Startled by the clatter, Pounce retreated to the sofa.

Mason's breathing quickly normalized, so he disregarded the incident and wiped up the mess with a dishcloth, wondering how best to remove the stains from his shirt. He carried his plate to the sofa and melted gratefully into the cushions. Pounce let loose another insistent yowl and perched on the low table in front of him. Expressive brown eyes met an intense hazel gaze. Mason froze with a forkful of pasta midway to his mouth. He had the strangest suspicion that his cat was trying to tell him something.

Unsettled, Mason concluded that he needed to socialize more. "I need a date," he mumbled with a strained, self-effacing chuckle. But before he could resume eating, a suffocating pressure returned to his chest. He put down his meal and cocked his head, eyeballing his cat as if he had never seen her before. She was motionless except for the twitchy tip of her tail. Mason felt a mounting sense of unease culminating in the inexplicable realization that there was an emergency in the adjacent apartment. He rocketed off the sofa and sprinted next door.

For the most part, Mason had a polite but aloof relationship with his neighbors. Consuelo Garcia was different; she was family. At 135 years old, Consuelo's petite frame was bowed, and her brown-sugar skin was mottled with age spots. Time had blanched her sable hair, and delicate silver eyelashes graced her wide-set almond eyes like snowflakes. She had a fundamentally kind disposition tempered with a wry wit and occasional mulishness, and she would curse a blue streak if she got riled up. She doted on Mason and regaled him with tales of *before*—before the apocalyptic earthquakes and floods, before the raging pestilence, before the dregs of humanity fled underground, cowed by a damaged world that would no longer bend to their will. Mason cherished her wisdom and affection. He always carved out time to spend with her, despite his demanding workload. He even installed a kitty door to her apartment so that she could enjoy Pounce's company when he was away.

Mason rapped on Consuelo's door as Pounce preceded him inside. Receiving no response, he unlocked it with his DC and poked his head into the foyer. "Consuelo, is everything okay?" he called, trying to modulate his volume so as not to alarm her. Mason thought he could hear the misty patter of the shower, but the apartment was unusually dark. Fearing for the older woman's safety, he stepped inside and triggered the lights. The bright colors of Consuelo's home surged out of the blackness. Mason inched forward. "Consuelo, can you hear me?"

The bathroom door was open. Mason walked toward it at an angle, not wanting to embarrass either of them if Consuelo was bathing. Soon his feet sank into sopping carpet. He slopped awkwardly into the bathroom and turned off the shower faucet. The room was flooded, and there was no sign of his neighbor. Pounce was staunchly avoiding the water, but her long, drawn-out *mrowls* floated into the bathroom and drew Mason to the raised platform of the bedroom like a fish on a hook. Consuelo was on the bed, curled on her side atop the comforter, calmly watching the water encroach on her sofa. For an instant, Mason was struck by her loveliness, certain that she must have been an uncommonly beautiful woman in her youth. He approached her warily, worried that she had not responded to his calls.

When Mason reached the platform, Consuelo unfurled slowly into a sitting position. She wore an ankle-length saffron dress cinched at the waist with a colorfully patterned belt. Mason was comforted to see that her clothes were dry. He sat beside her on the edge of the bed and gently took her small hand in both of his, noting that it was cold. "Do you feel ill, Consuelo?" he asked.

A whispery, faraway voice answered, blurred as though she were addressing him from inside a dream. "It will happen soon, *mi nieto*. The floods are coming again. I can see the waters rising."

"When did you last eat and take your medicine, Consuelo?"

The mundanity of the question seemed to break the spell. Consuelo shifted toward Mason and lovingly patted his cheek with her free hand. "I don't know," she confessed. "I honestly don't remember."

Mason nodded. He guided Consuelo off the platform and around the saturated carpet to the kitchen. He ordered her favorite soup from the food generator and deposited the bowl on the undersized dining table where Consuelo was seated. While she ate, Mason summoned a maintenance team, contacted her elder care worker, and waded into the bathroom to fetch her medicine.

Two hours later, Mason left Consuelo and her soggy apartment in capable hands and returned home. He peeled off his damp, soiled clothing and collapsed onto the sofa in his boxers. He devoured his abandoned pasta, cradling the plate as if to fend off poachers. Pounce lazed on the floor beside him, rolling around and showing her fluffy tummy. When he finished eating, she leaped up on the sofa and purred while he stroked under her chin. "You're such a good kitty. Thank you for telling me about Consuelo, sweetheart." Mason murmured his gratitude for several minutes before retiring to bed, never registering the strangeness of his words.

CHAPTER 7

HOMESTEAD

The footpath was broad and flanked by dozens of three-story row houses. The air was markedly humid in this section of Apricus, but the temperature was cool. Thin sheets of celadon moss carpeted portions of the path and cavern walls. Although the overhead lighting was off for the night, Jack had no trouble finding his way home. He walked this path every day, and the warm glow of the lamps that hung outside the portico of each home was more than sufficient.

The houses were identically constructed in an Italianate style. A steep flight of stairs led to a recessed front door that sported a large, frosted pane of glass. To the right of the door, angled bay windows bubbled out. All other windows were tall and slender with arched tops. The roof was low-pitched, with a wide projecting cornice and chunky brackets. Each structure was built using the city's customary gray building material, but the window frames were white and the doors were gaily painted in red, yellow, blue, or green to alleviate the aesthetic monotony. Slight architectural differences also emerged over time as residents sought to express their individuality. In some cases, a modest cupola adorned the roof, or the window above the portico featured a tiny Juliet balcony with a metal balustrade.

Inside, the standard furnishings were utilitarian, and the floor plan was narrow and cramped. Even so, these homes were significantly bigger than most apartments, and a partial basement provided storage. General living areas occupied the main floor. Half walls were used to make the tight quarters feel less oppressive. Bedrooms were on the upper levels. Smaller families often eliminated walls to enlarge the bedrooms or repurposed extra bedrooms as offices or playrooms. Common walls were thick to afford a degree of privacy from neighbors.

Jack sighed in relief when he spotted his own unassuming house sandwiched amid its brethren, just beyond the playground up ahead. His muscles were protesting the incline on this part of the path. A metallic jangle drew his attention to the swing set on the margin of the park. Two gangly teenage boys were huddled conspiratorially, talking quietly and twisting in the canvas seats. The heavy clomp of Jack's hiking boots caused the boys to look up in alarm, afraid to be caught breaking their curfews. In the low light, Jack watched their eyes grow even wider when they saw the long-barreled rifle that was draped across his back. He smirked at them good-naturedly, never slowing his pace.

"It's okay," one boy said. "He's cool." And with that decree, the teens resumed their private conversation.

The footpath forked to follow the row houses on the left or right, but Jack cut through the playground to shorten his trek. His aching feet savored the cushy synthetic tiles. Recycled from automotive tires, the tiles had been installed to protect rambunctious children from the rough cavern floor. No children were playing now, though. Diffuse lamplight from the houses cast eerie shadows on the vacant equipment. The slide and seesaw looked pallid and forlorn. At the epicenter of the park where no light reached, a lifeless row of spring riders seemed downright menacing. Each rider was a radiantly painted mythical creature: mermaid, dragon, and phoenix. But wreathed in darkness, they were more monster than make-believe. "I'm glad that Olivia isn't here to see this," Jack thought. "It would probably give her nightmares. Damn, it might give *me* nightmares!"

Olivia did not often visit the playground anymore. At fifteen, Jack's high-spirited sister was busy with more mature pursuits—school, sports, and boys—though she would occasionally loiter with friends on top of the climbing frame. "Ugh, the *climbing frame*," Jack groaned. He was blindsided by the crystal-clear memory of a teary, red-faced kindergartener running to her big brother for comfort after overhearing some older children clamoring to play on the "monkey bars." Olivia had stood before him in her Curious George jumper and ribboned pigtails, chubby fingers tugging on his pant leg as she moaned about all the monkeys being gone. Barely looking up from his book, he did not take the time to understand why his sister was upset and insensitively offered "jungle gym" as an alternative, which led to a total meltdown. "It's so mean!" she wailed over and over. He rocked her on his lap, kissing her forehead and apologizing, until she wore herself out and fell asleep. Jack swore he could still hear those heart-wrenching sobs. Olivia had boycotted the playground for weeks, and to this day, she insisted that everyone around her refer to the equipment as a climbing frame.

When Jack rejoined the footpath, he was only two doors away from his house. Olivia's chalk drawing was a colorful beacon that bedecked the level stones at the base of the stairs. Today, it was unicorns playing baseball. Jack grinned as he ascended the steps, running his hand along the polished metal railing. Muted light escaped the fringed edges of the antique velvet curtains on the bay windows and tinted the tartan etching on the frosted glass of the front door. As Jack reached the portico, the door opened on his mother's smiling face. "I've been tracking you, darling. Welcome home."

Abigail Collins was a full-figured woman with shoulder-length wavy brunette hair and light-brown eyes. Her lashes were ridiculously long and lush, the envy of anyone who'd ever had to brandish a mascara brush. Jack's father would get tipsy on holidays and recite clumsy, earnest poems about his lovely wife's eyes. Inevitably, he would catch her as she passed the sofa, ferrying dirty dishes to the kitchen or performing some such chore. He would pull her down on his lap and tickle her mercilessly while she threw her head back and laughed. Bemoaning this brazen display of parental foolishness, Jack and Olivia would flee to the kitchen and raid the pantry for treats until their flush-faced mother returned to tsk-tsk them. When the siblings were older, they would clean the kitchen instead, eliciting a flurry of adoring kisses from their grateful mum.

Currently, those beautiful eyes were fixed on Jack. Abigail waved him inside. The scent of freshly baked bread wafted over from the kitchen. Jack wiped his boots on the coarse faux coir doormat and sniffed the air appreciatively.

"Stow your gear," Abigail said, clucking with fondness. "I've been keeping your dinner warm. You must be famished."

"Thanks, Mum." Jack stooped to kiss her dimpled cheek then side-stepped her to descend the staircase to the left of the door. He shrugged off his pack and rifle and carried them down by hand to avoid scraping the wall. The basement lights winked on to reveal tidy shelves, stackable storage bins, and a crowded workbench. Jack dumped the gear on the floor. He added his damp outerwear and boots to the heap, vowing to clean up later.

Jack was following his nose to the kitchen when his sister came bounding down the stairs on the opposite side of the salon. "Mum! Do you know where my black leggings are?" Olivia shouted. Spotting Jack, she halted abruptly on the bottom step and scowled at him.

"Hey, Livi," Jack offered softly, familiar with this routine. He gave the dining table a longing glance but waited.

Abigail rounded the kitchen half wall, wiping her hands on a dish towel. "Olivia, don't shout. Your leggings are in the laun—"

"What did you shoot today, brother?" Olivia seethed. Her eyes were bronze fire, and her hair was a wild mass of curls. She was an avenging spirit, a Fury, in the trappings of a disillusioned teenage girl. Abigail tolerated her daughter's rudeness and silently observed the standoff.

"I didn't shoot anything, Livi." Jack's declaration was confident, but his lips were curved in an uncertain, wistful smile that did not seem entirely sure it should be there.

Olivia was guarded, unwilling to relent. Jack had presumably been thwarted by inclement weather. Yet there was something peculiar about his smile. She cocked her head and squinted. "Why not?"

Remembering the meadow, Jack spoke with dreamy, soft-edged abstraction. "I just…I had a feeling that it wasn't…what I should do. And I…I don't think I'll be doing it ever again."

Olivia's intake of breath was audible. She bounded from the stairs, gamely dodged the sofa, and tackled Jack in a fierce hug. Jack returned the embrace then leaned back to see his sister's freckled face. The unabashed adulation in her expression was the sort earned by valorous white knights and comic book superheroes. Jack ruffled Olivia's unruly hair and guffawed when she swatted his hand coltishly.

"Olivia," Abigail bade, "go back upstairs and finish your homework. Your brother needs to eat."

Olivia complied, and Abigail hustled Jack into the kitchen. He washed up at the sink while she cut the middle out of a round loaf of crusty sourdough bread and ladled a thick savory stew into the edible bowl. "I'm no psychologist," she mused, "but my intuition tells me that, somehow, this outing was a turning point in Jack's recovery." She transferred the bread bowl to a ceramic plate and carried it to the dining table. Jack was drying his hands with her abandoned dish towel and inspecting his fingernails for cleanliness, humming under his breath. Abigail knew not to jump to conclusions. She knew to tread lightly. But her son's tuneless humming and rusty smile were so welcome, so precious, that all she wanted to do was laugh and dance and hold him close.

Jack turned from the sink and lobbed the dirty dish towel into the laundry nook, missing the hamper spectacularly. "You okay, Mum? You've got a weird look on your face."

"Oh? Er, I'm good, darling," Abigail replied. She patted the back of his chair. "Come sit."

Jack stooped to relocate the uncooperative towel then ambled to the table. Abigail studied his rumpled appearance and said, "That shirt brings out your eyes, Jack," before adding in a scandalized tone, "but those jeans are so worn they're practically indecent!" Grinning unrepentantly, Jack took his seat and tucked into the stew.

The walls on this level of the house were painted a tranquil sage green. A tasteful chandelier with four tapered bell shades in etched white glass twinkled above Jack's head. A blue cloth was draped over the dining table, and matching cushions padded its four chairs. From his position, Jack could see the kitchen and salon. The built-in kitchen was austere but well-made, and over the years, the family had added its own unique bits of color and texture. Glazed terra-cotta backsplash tiles had been painstakingly installed, and the gap above the tall cabinets was decorated with a squat clay pot of faux flowers and two vintage wood crates used for hauling fruit, labeled with sunny, nostalgic images of apples and oranges. The furniture in the salon was crafted of reclaimed metal from oil drums, but the sofa and recliner had been stuffed with low-density foam and reupholstered in an indulgently plush, pewter-colored fabric. Pale-pink throw pillows further offset the bleak, industrial milieu. The seating was grouped around a foursquare coffee table and a huge video display embedded in the wall. In the corner, a towering ladder shelf brimmed with a menagerie of curios and weathered books and a glossy blue-and-white vase in the Chinese Ming style. At its foot, a fluffy gold pouf sat on a cream rug like an over easy egg. Olivia liked to sprawl on this rug to study or listen to music. Family photos were displayed on a gallery wall above a sideboard near the staircase that led up to the bedrooms. The area behind the bay windows was hidden from Jack's view, but a baby grand piano roosted there, easily the family's rarest and most valuable possession. Objectively, the Collins house was congested and sentimental, but to its inhabitants it was *home.*

A delicate bone china tea service had pride of place in the center of the dining table. Each creamy-white piece featured a motif of green vines with red flowers, a powder-blue border, and a lustrous gold rim. This was the family's most beloved heirloom, and instead of hoarding it away, they used the tea service every day. Abigail fussed with the pot. She poured two steaming cups and added milk. She passed the sugar bowl to Jack then took a seat beside him. The room was heavy with a somnolent quiet, dimly penetrated by Jack's zealous chewing and the tinkle of Abigail's spoon as she stirred her drink to cool it. She thumbed at a chip in the handle of her cup, debating the best way to broach what Jack had told Olivia.

Jack came up for air to tend his tea. "Dillon Tremblay was on the playground with a friend. He didn't pay me much mind because apparently, I'm cool." He flashed an ironic grin.

"Indeed," Abigail replied with an elegantly raised eyebrow. Then, wanting to continue the banter, she proffered some harmless gossip. "Actually, Margaret said that Dillon's been a handful lately—and not just with flouting his curfew." After relaying Dillon's antics, Abigail trailed off, and Jack watched her smile evaporate with the steam from the teacup that was poised at her lips. "I hope Olivia doesn't develop a rebellious streak," she fretted.

"Nah," Jack replied with affable confidence as he tore off a mushy hunk of his bread bowl. "She may be, um, *exuberant,* but she's far too sensible for any of that nonsense."

"She was very pleased to hear that you won't be hunting anymore," Abigail noted cautiously. "She looks up to you, Jack. Always has."

"God only knows why," he chortled self-consciously.

Abigail set her cup on the table and grasped Jack's hand. "I'm very pleased, too, darling."

"Mum, I didn't say that just to make Livi happy," Jack's voice quavered. He seemed hesitant to look at her, so she squeezed his hand encouragingly. "I-I don't know if I can explain. Something…uh, *shifted*…for me today, I guess. I intend to keep spending time topside, but I've given up hunting." His skittering green gaze settled on Abigail for reassurance. "I don't want to disappoint Dad," he whispered.

Abigail swallowed her son's tortured words. "Your father is proud of you, Jack," she soothed. "He would have wanted you to follow your heart. I am certain of that." Abigail watched as anguished tears shimmered in Jack's eyes and stuck to his lashes, reluctant to let go, just like her son. Time stretched taut as she chose her next words, sensing their import and refusing to hurry. "The Collins family may have been hunters, love, but they were also many other things." With that, the tension of the moment snapped like an overstretched rubber band. Jack inhaled shakily, squeezed his mother's hand, and nodded his head, jostling a few tears loose. He returned to his meal and mulled over their discussion. To give him space, Abigail returned to the kitchen and busied herself with household chores.

After a while, Jack was sipping a second cup of fragrant tea, and nary a crumb remained on his plate. He was slouched in his chair, an indolent straggle of limbs. Abigail kissed the top of his head. "Take your tea upstairs, Jack." He moved to gather his dishes, but she shooed him off. "Away with you now. I can do this. You need a shower." He headed for the staircase and sniffed his armpit when Abigail's back was turned, realizing sheepishly that he was awfully ripe from the hike and the rain.

The house was as still as a portrait by the time Jack emerged from the bathroom. Intending to check his email, he paced over to the computer nook that was tucked into a corner at the end of the hallway. The family used this space in lieu of a study. The desk was made of reclaimed pine that had a rustic, distressed finish. Knots and hairline cracks caused subtle variations in hue and texture. The desk's four deep drawers were augmented by a set of matching shelves that climbed the wall behind it. Despite the storage, the nook was filled to overflowing with books, woven baskets, photographs, and a golden tumbler in the shape of a pineapple. Hanging from a peg on the wall was a tatty black bowler hat that had belonged to a great-grandfather somewhere down the ancestral line. Jack sank into the swivel chair and spun around slowly until he felt dizzy. He accessed the computer and noticed that Olivia had visited some forums tonight, perhaps for a school project. A nature-lovers community caught his eye. Jack browsed the images, reminded of his meadow and the deer. He wondered if anyone here had had a similar experience. He found the most recent post and felt his stomach flip when he saw Violet's profile photo. He planted his feet on the floor to make sure the chair had stopped spinning.

"You're beautiful," Jack murmured, studying Violet's picture with yogic concentration. In it, she stood beside a chestnut horse on a sunshiny ribbon of trimmed grass. Brown hair fell below her shoulders in lush waves that framed her fair skin, sparkling blue eyes, and perfect Cupid's bow lips. She had a slightly upturned nose and high cheekbones. She was slim, almost petite, but well-muscled. With difficulty, Jack wrestled his gaze away from the photo to review Violet's profile, sighing softly as he finished. He was duly impressed and not a little intimidated. "I'm afraid you're way out of my league, m'lady."

Plagued by burning eyes and yawns that threatened to sprain his jaw, Jack decided that it was well past his bedtime. He would read Violet's post then retire. His posture stiffened. Her last two sentences were intriguing:

> I have a special connection to animals that seems to be on a different level. Does anyone know what I mean?

Certainly, his preternatural romp in the meadow qualified as "special" and "different." Should he reply to Violet? Would she think he was unhinged? Jack's thoughts swirled and his body sagged, until eventually, he was cradling his head in his arms and blearily staring up at the bowler hat. "Hats are cool," he slurred. He fell asleep and dreamed of behatted deer in rolling fields of purple flowers.

CHAPTER 8

THREADS

Before daybreak, Jack awoke with a tortured groan, his back stiff and keypad indentations on his face, while many miles away, Emily was earnestly apologizing to her supervisor at the museum.

"I'm so very sorry, sir. I do know what time it is. I needed to catch you early. I'm afraid I cannot deliver the lecture at the archives this morning. Due to an unexpected personal matter, I was unable to catch the last train to Apricus yesterday." Emily cringed, doubting that irresistible duck-feeding legitimately qualified as a personal matter.

She cringed again as Dr. Wong's sleepy voice turned angry, and loud. "What?! Dr. Steuben, this is completely unacceptable. Do I need to explain the Public Trust Doctrine to y—"

"Of course not, sir," Emily interrupted, before he could build up a full head of steam. "I am truly sorry about this. I propose that we swap topics with next week's lecture. I've already contacted Dr. Musa."

"You've already contacted—"

"Yes, sir," Emily barreled on. "She was, um, disgruntled to be awakened, but she agreed."

Dr. Wong sighed, but his anger was fizzling out like a spent match. "People are expecting *you*, Dr. Steuben. This doesn't look good for us."

"People will understand, sir. And Dr. Musa is very entertaining. They'll forget all about me."

"Hmph," Dr. Wong grunted. There was a pregnant pause, then he surrendered, saying, "Fine, fine. I'll handle the switch and give your regrets. When will you be in, Dr. Steuben?"

Smiling with relief, Emily answered, "I'll be there by noon, sir. Thank you for your understanding."

Dr. Wong grumbled his goodbye. Emily collapsed onto her bed, pleased albeit certain that she had not heard the last of this from her supervisor. Like most of the museum's staff, he did not approve of her living arrangements. Emily was regularly pressured to relocate to Apricus where she could (in her opinion) be at the museum's beck and call. However, precious few people trained to be preservationists, so her job was secure, and she simply ignored the bluster.

The room was chilly. Emily snuggled into the pillows and pulled the puffy duvet up to her chin. The fire in the hearth had burned out hours ago, and cold air was oozing down the open flue. The curtains were drawn, but one of the bedside lamps was switched on. The walls and ceiling were eggshell white with intersecting dark wood beams that cast hazy shadows in the semidarkness. An accent wall behind the headboard was papered in an intricate floral design of crimson, green, and gold that complemented the rose-pink of the linens. Across the bedroom, Emily spotted her flannel bathrobe on the boudoir stool of the vanity. She reluctantly abandoned her nest and padded over to fetch it. The furnace would automatically crank up at sunrise, but for now, she needed the extra layer over her nightgown.

Comfortably fortified, Emily opened the antique armoire that housed her wardrobe. The highly polished walnut befitted the sun and stars that were carved intaglio-style across the crown and door panels. The hardware was matted brass. A matching full-length floor mirror was angled near the thickset left foot. Emily swiveled in front of the mirror, holding up two dresses and assessing their relative merits. Not wanting to call attention to herself today, she selected a long-sleeved gray sheath with black trim.

An hour later, the cobblestone-click of Emily's bootheels punctured the still morning air. The horizon was veiled in thin stratus clouds streaked with the sherbety remnants of dawn. Shivering, Emily wrapped her arms around her torso and hurried across the courtyard. She needed to find a replacement for the wrinkled trench coat that she had left in a neglected heap on the floor after her adventure at the pond. The hinges squeaked as she opened the door to her parents' home. Emily and her cousin had been raised here. Now it was as cold and inert as a morgue at midnight. She triggered the hallway light and fumbled for the handle to the closet. Her eyes flicked to the staircase. Nearly a decade ago, her mother and father had succumbed to a sadistic illness in the bedroom upstairs. The family called for medical aid, but the team from Apricus did not reach Honey Hill in time. Both parents died within ten hours from what was later identified as a novel strain of dengue fever. After college, Emily's cousin resided in the house with his new wife, but they were killed in a storm last year when an uprooted tree crushed their truck. These days the building stood unoccupied, and Emily rarely visited. Unsettled, she pulled a black, double-breasted peacoat from a hanger. She was not sure to whom it had belonged, but it fit, so she buttoned it up and headed back through the court-yard to her grandparents' house, silently thanking her unnamed benefactor.

A savory-sweet blend of breakfast scents led Emily inexorably to the kitchen. "Ooooh, Grandma, something smells divine!" she exclaimed, crossing under the gothic archway from the mudroom.

Grandma Hannah pulled a tray of sesame bread rolls from the oven. "Thank you, dear," she beamed. "Sit down and get started before your grandfather eats it all." There were three steaming bowls of semolina pudding and a stack of floppy pancakes on the hardy farmhouse oak table. The air was redolent with vanilla and cinnamon.

Emily dipped back into the mudroom to hang her coat on a peg and took her place at the table. "Good morning, *solnyshko*. Heading to the train station?" Grandpa Dimitri's tone was matter-of-fact, but his crooked grin bespoke gentle teasing. Emily decided to play along.

"Yes, Grandpa. I should be able to catch the first train." She waited a beat before adding, "…now that the weather is clear."

"Ah yes, the weather." They exchanged knowing smiles, then Dimitri lifted his burly frame and walked over to the food generator for a serving of applesauce. His pale skin contrasted sharply with his dark-brown hair and eyes. The hair on his head had drastically receded, but a mutinous pelt still covered his arms below his rolled-up sleeves and peeked out the V of his work shirt.

Dimitri slathered applesauce on his pancakes and swallowed a king-size forkful. He sighed theatrically. After a second bite, he set down his fork, lamenting that the generated condiment did not even come close to the quality of Hannah's delicious cooking. He stared mournfully at his plate until a shower of powdered sugar rained down and he felt his wife's lips graze the back of his head. Emily listened with one ear as this habitual domestic drama unfolded. She was preoccupied with how to test the scope of her newfangled psychic ability. It would be weird if it applied only to ducks, she thought.

"Are the rolls for dinner?" Dimitri asked. The nostrils on his large, straight nose flared approvingly.

Hannah was washing her hands at the double-basin copper sink. Its hammered finish looked rosy in the gauzy morning light from the kitchen windows. "I'm going to freeze them," she declared. Dimitri harrumphed an unintelligible reply. In her periphery, Hannah could see him gawping at the rolls longingly. With a secret smile, she amended her answer. "Well, most of them anyway."

Emily ate with zeal, charged by the thrill of chasing an esoteric problem. The tenor of her internal dialog pinballed madly between cartoon speech bubbles and the erudite drone of a scholarly journal. In the end, she decided to stop spiraling and just focus on her grandparents. If she concentrated, could she read their thoughts and emotions?

Minutes passed. The kitchen grew quiet.

"This feels nothing like the pond," Emily mused. "They obviously love one another, but it doesn't take ESP to figure that out." A stroke of calloused fingers on her cheek startled her to awareness. Dimitri's broad forehead was creased with worry. Emily had closed her eyes, she realized, and she was blindly scraping her spoon into a pudding-less bowl. "Good Lord, they must think I'm having some kind of seizure."

"What's wrong?" Hannah implored. "Are you ill? Is Dr. Wong terribly angry?" Hannah had joined them at the table, but her body was twisted sideways on her chair, facing Emily. Heat and humidity from cooking had liberated a mess of silver strands from the coil on her head; the hair dangled in ringlets and wisps at her temples. Yet instead of a happily disheveled chef, Hannah now looked like a flustered matriarch. Regretful that her actions had wrought this change, Emily hastened to reassure her grandparents and restore a playful atmosphere to the rest of the meal.

Later, on the train, Emily stowed her coat and satchel and curled up on a seat with her DC. Using her work credentials, she searched the archives for references to paranormal phenomena. Inundated with results relating to ghosts, auras, ufology, and a host of other fascinating but irrelevant topics, Emily limited the search to telepathy and skimmed the output from dozens of cultural, pseudoscientific, and academic sources. Nothing seemed to align with the birdy bedlam of the previous evening. And aside from folklore, a cross-reference with common avian and animal phrases came up empty.

Undeterred, Emily left the archives and searched the online forums. She shelved the psychic angle and looked instead for fellow ornithophiles, which led her to a nature-lovers community. As she browsed the most recent posts, Violet's profile photo caught her eye. The woman in the image practically radiated love for the horse, and Emily felt an instant kinship.

> I have a special connection to animals that seems to be
> on a different level. Does anyone know what I mean?

Violet's word choice was compelling. Attention to detail was Emily's stock-in-trade as a preservationist, and she could not help thinking that the language was a deliberate lure. She nabbed a sesame roll from her satchel and chewed it pensively. By the time she was brushing breadcrumbs from her dress, Emily had made a decision. She uploaded her profile and drafted a short reply:

> Yes, I think I do. I have a particular affinity for birds.
> Lately, my connection to my flock seems to have taken
> on a new dimension. Perhaps we could chat about our
> experiences?

Enjoying a pleasant tingle of anticipation, Emily pledged to revisit the community after work. Then she put away her DC and mentally prepared for the dressing-down she was likely to receive from a bristly, fully awake Dr. Wong.

Jack spent the morning marooned in his cramped office reviewing the quarterly sales figures. It should have taken less than an hour, but he could not seem to concentrate. Whenever he tried to focus, his thoughts would scatter like the fluffy white seeds of a cottonwood tree in a breeze.

He thought about the frightened deer and the dovish joy of the sunlit meadow.

He thought about his mother's poignant wisdom.

Most of all, he thought about Violet. He wanted so badly to reply to her post, to dare a connection. But Violet was gorgeous and accomplished, and he was hopelessly unremarkable. She was a luminous rainbow arcing above his invariant gray sea.

By lunchtime, Jack had tired of his mental calisthenics and low self-confidence. He fetched a sandwich from the building's cafeteria and returned to his desk. Over a ham and cheese on brioche, he used his terminal to navigate to the nature-lovers community. "Now see here, Jack," his internal voice reproached. It sounded a lot like Olivia crossed with a drill sergeant. "Stop mooning over your crush and see if she can help you understand what the heck happened with that deer." He immediately noticed Emily's post and read it multiple times. Then he reread Violet's post. Then he read both posts again. His interest was piqued. It appeared that he might not be the only one wandering about the supernatural zoo.

Jack reviewed Emily's profile, wowed by her accomplishments. "Another attractive, brainy woman, eh?" he intoned between bites. "Well, ladies, I hate to buck the trend, but…" Permitting no further waffling, he uploaded his own profile and typed a short post:

> Hello. Recently, I had a unique encounter with a deer that left me scratching my head. Though perhaps it wasn't so unique. I'd love to join your chat to find out.

Elsewhere in Apricus, Mason was having a categorically bad day. En route to work, a dispatcher reassigned him from the train upgrades to coding at the Science Bureau. Several members of the Project Pioneer team were out sick, and the Infrastructure Bureau had been volunteered to provide provisional support. Mason debarked at the next station, flopped on a bench, and waited for a new train that would ferry him to Government Square. He called Trevor to grumble.

"Why are *you* complaining? I hear they're experimenting with next-gen AI and robotics. Maybe you'll get to work on that!" Trevor raved. "Me, I'll be working on the railroad all the livelong day. Uh, without the racist overtones, though."

Mason laughed at the reference to the old American folk song. They had played a variety of folk music during a project last month and endlessly analyzed the sociopolitical subtexts. He would miss his friend's company today. Nevertheless, Trevor's enthusiasm was infectious, and by the time the train arrived, Mason was in better spirits.

His good mood did not last long. His credentials were verified at the employee entrance to the Science Bureau, but no one came to collect him. After a long wait, he was redirected to the visitors' entrance where he was met by a blank-faced security officer and a soldier. In blunt contrast to the white lab coats of the scientists who stippled the entry hall, Mason's escorts were clad in black and gray, respectively. Hardly a word was spoken while his identity was reconfirmed. He kept himself entertained by indexing the shiny insignia on the soldier's uniform.

Mason gasped when he spotted the man's sidearm. Before Apricus was founded, at the pinnacle of human suffering, there had been countless more weapons in the world than people left to wield them. Warring factions fought for what little habitable land remained. Unconscionably, innocents who managed to survive megastorms, earthquakes, famine, and disease were routinely lost to man-made violence.

The Elbrus Armistice brought that shameful era to an end. All governments surrendered their arsenals then united to eradicate organized crime and pirating. The armistice fundamentally redefined the role of the military in society. It became the foremost institution for disaster relief, search and rescue, and humanitarian aid and for expertise in varied disciplines such as civil engineering, space operations, meteorology, and biotechnology. Militarized weapons were unequivocally banned. To this day, even personal gun ownership was rare and exactingly regulated.

Mason's gaze was glued to the holster. He was about to voice his shock when the security check ended and he felt his DC being shoved into his hand where it dangled nervelessly at his side. He inferred that the officer had been holding it out for him to take and got impatient.

"Come with me," the man barked. "Hold any questions. You'll be briefed shortly."

Hesitantly, Mason followed the officer into an aseptic gray corridor with flat lighting. The soldier fell in step last. There were no doors. The walls were bare. "We're inside the barrel of a gun," he thought. "A gun like the one that's not supposed to be on that soldier's hip. The soldier who is walking behind me. With a gun!" Disturbed, Mason asked if he could use a restroom.

"After the briefing," was the curt reply.

Near the end of the corridor, they passed a double-wide sliding glass door with a biometric scanner. It guarded a weakly lit room that glowed with the telltale aurora borealis of computers. Curious, Mason craned his neck, but he could see nothing before they turned the corner and boarded a rapidly moving sidewalk. He grabbed the handrail. According to the way-finding signage, the sidewalk connected the Science Bureau to the Security Bureau and military complex. Before long, it terminated at the mouth of a giant cavern that was buzzing with soldiers and equipment. The cavern had unnaturally smooth walls and was radiantly lit. Mason had to squint until his eyes could adjust. As they dissected the grotto to reach another hallway, he looked up at a bevy of light shafts that were considerably larger than any others he had seen in Apricus.

They stopped in front of a frosted glass door. The soldier entered a code on a wall-mounted keypad and inclined his head for a retinal scan. The trip from the lobby of the Science Bureau had taken no more than ten minutes, but the strangeness and tension made it feel like hours to Mason. He figured that only a maximum-security job would merit such an unusual reception. He wondered what it could be, shifting his weight nervously from foot to foot.

Mason was handed off to a military official once the door slid open. The copious ribbons and bars on her uniform shouted authority. With no preamble, she delivered Mason's so-called briefing at his assigned workstation. It was an unhelpful rehash of publicly available information about Project Pioneer, the canopy for all governmental space and terrestrial exploration initiatives. She explained that Mason would be editing code that crossed several areas. At her signal, a white-coated scientist stepped up to convey specific instructions, and Mason was quickly immersed in his tasks.

The room held nine other workstations. It was chilly and dim, making the glare from the omnipresent technology seem ultrabright and cutting. On the perimeter, a massive server room lurked behind a glass wall, emanating a spectral blue light. Mason was accustomed to working in cold, dark places; it was routine for the geeks at the Infrastructure Bureau. He was not, however, used to those qualities applying to the *people*, too. There was absolutely no chitchat in the room, and the atmosphere was intense and brittle, like a glacier ready to calve.

Mason's handler never left his side. He rebuffed nearly all questions, citing a lack of clearance. As soon as Mason completed a task, the scientist doled out new instructions. Although it was frustrating to operate without the big picture, the discrete tasks were challenging and Mason became too preoccupied to put up a fuss. It was obvious that the uptight team at Pioneer wanted him to *do*, not think. Inevitably, though, his right brain started to drift. Guns, floods, loneliness. Guns, floods, loneliness. Over and over in an uneasy refrain.

Mason was given no breaks. He was denied a visitor's pass, so he could not even use the restroom without an escort. He was indignant at first, but by lunchtime he merely acquiesced when a soldier deposited a tray of food at his workstation. He tried to brush it all off on military culture, but that answer was too simple. In the end, he resolved to report his treatment to his boss at the Infrastructure Bureau and let the higher-ups deal with it. He would mention the gun, too.

On the upside, the unrelenting pace meant that he was dismissed by late afternoon. While his handler was generous with praise, the man made no overture for Mason's return. He was escorted away with a rousing, unspoken chorus of "Don't let the door pinch your ass on the way out," which was perfectly fine with Mason. He rode home on the train before the evening rush and stopped at his favorite café for dinner. Au Naturel served mostly vegetarian dishes using fresh produce; only animal products like eggs were replicated. The friendly hostess seated him at his preferred spot outside, tarrying for a while to chat and casually flirt. The patio was festooned with brightly painted clay pots brimming with herbs, and each table had a colorful umbrella with twinkling fairy lights. Mason scarfed down an aromatic bowl of jambalaya and lingered over a square of lime cake. The convivial surroundings and a full stomach worked wonders on his disposition.

Pounce greeted Mason the minute he entered the apartment. She wove between his legs, forcing him to shuffle clumsily. "Hello, beautiful," he laughed. Mason crouched to scratch under the tabby's chin. He gazed into her slitted hazel eyes, but the potent bond he had felt with her yesterday was gone. "At least I can look at my cat again without feeling like I'm about to have a heart attack," he thought.

Mason went about his routine. When he was minty fresh and clad in sweats, he settled with a mug of cocoa at the small dining table that moonlighted as his computer desk. Longing for connection, he flicked through the online dating forums. After a half hour of fruitless searching, he got up to stretch and peered fondly at his cat. She was sprawled alongside the computer and had been lazily batting at his fingers as he typed. Her silver fur glistered in the bluish light of the monitor, and she was emitting a low, rhythmic purr. Inspired, Mason decided to look for someone who was interested in animals. He knew that most people feared nature and favored the safe, predictable haven of technology. He could not really blame them; after all, technology was central to his own lifestyle and identity. However, reading the posts he found online, he was surprised by how *adamant* they could be. Some people even regarded humanity as being "at war" with the earth.

Mildly disgusted, Mason exited the dating forums. He performed a broader search that unearthed a tiny nature-lovers community. He was instantly captivated. Starting with the oldest posts, Mason perused the comments and photos. He shared the most interesting tidbits with Pounce, who rolled over to watch the monitor and occasionally expressed her opinion with a throaty trill or a quick swat of her paw. When he reached Violet's post, Mason barely registered the words, so smitten was he with Firestorm. Something niggled at him, though, so he tore his gaze away from the horse and read the post more carefully, along with the two replies. He leaned back and reflected on the prior night's interactions with Pounce, stroking his trim beard like a seeing stone.

Decided, Mason uploaded his profile and prepared to type a response to Violet's post. Sensing the mood change, Pounce sat up. Her tail wagged loosely, and her ears were high and stiff. Mason's hand glided along her silky back as he studied the caginess of the other posts. "I prefer to be more direct," he said to Pounce, "but I'd better stop short of saying that you talked to me. It sure feels like that's what happened, though. Not with words, because cats can't talk, but somehow…" Mason trailed off, woolgathering, until Pounce roused him by walking across the keypad.

Have room for one more? I've always been close with my cat, but something odd happened yesterday that I'd like to be able to discuss with like-minded friends.

Message sent, Mason logged off and crawled into bed. He shifted the pillows and reclined against the headboard. Dwelling on the magnificent horse in Violet's photo, Mason called up *Black Beauty* on his DC. He had not read the book since he was a child. Pounce landed in his lap, but before she could relax, he reached over to snatch some tissues from the bedside table. "If I remember correctly," he cautioned her, "we're going to need these."

CHAPTER 9

TAPESTRY

I t was late. It was so late that the black ocean sky was streaked with undulant waves of stardust and the clotted smudge of the Milky Way oozed in purplish swells. Lying on her back in the freshly mown east pasture, Violet shooed the irksome mosquitoes and inhaled deeply. The air quality on Fulminara had been excellent recently. Steady winds were keeping the sooty pollutants offshore. Violet took another slow breath and rested under the starry canopy. It had been an arduous day. She had just finished loading the farm's pickup truck with grass clippings to be used as mulch in the outdoor garden beds and greenhouse containers. It would have been done hours ago, but a malfunctioning hydroponic system in the tower's rice bays tripped an alarm in the early afternoon. Since rice was a persnickety plant, she had to drop everything to handle the repair.

Dirty and hungry, Violet arose from the field and drove the stalwart old truck to the house. She gave the hood an appreciative pat before she trudged inside. Deciding to strip in the foyer, Violet left her grimy clothes in a pile by the door and shivered as her bare skin soaked up the chill. On the way to the bathroom, she very carefully lit a fire in the hearth, having learned from experience that naked enkindling was a dangerous business. One hot shower later, Violet swaddled her hair in a towel and made a beeline for the kitchen.

The refrigerator's oversize crisper was filled with chunky red, green, orange, and yellow vegetables as vibrant as a Matisse still life. Violet gathered the fixings for a salad. The hearth crackled merrily while she set to work at a thick maple cutting board. Although she was eager to check for replies to her post on the nature-lovers forum, she was ravenous from hours of hard labor. It would simply have to wait. She had peeked in the early morning. A couple of night owls had gushed about the horse in her profile picture, but nobody had responded to her message yet. As usual, her lovesome Firestorm had stolen the show.

After dinner, Violet moved to the study with a full stomach and a cup of chamomile tea. She launched the nature-lovers site while mentally replaying the perplexing experiences that had prompted her to find it. She saw that there were four replies, and her heart thumped with excitement as she arranged them side by side on her monitor. Violet studied the photos first, then she read each person's profile and message, in order.

Dr. Emily Steuben was a respected scholar, but Violet could tell that this was no frumpy, stolid academic. Emily wore a knee-length bodycon floral dress in her photo, and with her lustrous blond hair and generous curves, she resembled a starlet from Hollywood's golden age. Her impressive profile was suffused with self-deprecating humor. She was clearly a woman who refused to be stereotyped, and Violet liked her immediately.

Jack Collins worked in retail operations. His job sounded mundane, but every household relied on the products he managed, so his role was undeniably important. And Violet had the impression that there was more to this man than his short, dry profile conveyed. He was good-looking, with limpid clover-green eyes that seemed a bit sad. His dark hair looked soft and thick, and Violet got sidetracked for a minute imagining how it would feel to run her fingers through it. Taking a sip of her tea, she shook off the distraction and moved on. Jack's post referred to an experience with a deer. That was intriguing. Violet wondered how often he visited Fulminara, and why.

Companion animals were uncommon, so Violet was charmed to learn that Mason Agu had a cat. Mason was a passionate techie who served the Infrastructure Bureau with distinction. He had a brawny frame and compassionate brown eyes, and Violet wanted to hug him. She could not explain why; he just seemed inordinately huggable.

Violet stood up to stretch and wiggled her bare toes into the worn Celtic rug. She was entranced for a moment by the beauty and mysticism of the artwork. She remembered lying on the rug as a child, tracing the kaleidoscopic spirals and knots with her fingers while her father used the computer. It was a comforting memory that drew a dimpled smile to Violet's lips. She sat back down to compose a message to her new friends. She thanked them warmly for replying to her post and invited them to a video chat the next evening as a way to get to know one another and discuss their recent experiences. Logging off, she instructed her DC to alert her to any replies to the invitation.

Feeling calm and hopeful, Violet refreshed her tea and got ready for bed. She slipped under the covers and closed her eyes. In the blurry hypnagogic state between wakefulness and slumber, Violet heard three soft chimes. She counted them like sheep and fell soundly asleep.

The day passed in slow motion for Violet, Emily, and Jack. They checked the time obsessively as they went about their respective work routines. Fortunately for Mason, he rejoined Trevor on the train system updates, and the pair whiled the day away gossiping about his jaunt as a Pioneer grunt. At quitting time, however, even Mason felt a giddy nervousness akin to ascending the sheer slope of a roller coaster.

As the organizer, Violet joined the chat early. She wanted to greet the others as they arrived. She was seated at the desk in the study, raring to use her state-of-the-art monitor to engage with people rather than chromatograms and engineering schematics. She adjusted the chair until she was satisfied with how her image was framed by the intricate Tree of Life wood carving on the wall behind her. Emily's unapologetically feminine style had inspired Violet to choose clothing that connoted her own laid-back, outdoorsy personality. Aiming for rugged casual, she had discarded an embarrassing number of outfits that screamed "worn-out farmhand" instead. Ultimately, she opted for faded jeans and a finely woven chocolate-brown sweater.

Violet drummed her fingers on the desk. A chime tolled, and Jack's image filled the monitor. Violet startled then wondered how people could be surprised by exactly what they had been expecting. Jack was facing away from the camera. Violet admired his profile and listened to his exasperated voice say, "I've got it, Livi. Go away." She heard a scampish titter and receding footsteps, but Jack blocked her view of the room. Raking a hand through his hair, he turned and leaned back in his chair, only to discover that he was connected to the chat and Violet was smiling at him. Off-balance, Jack croaked out a tongue-tied salutation and tugged at his shirt collar, which suddenly felt tight.

"Hi, I'm Violet."

Jack willed her to continue speaking, but Violet just looked at him with a devilish glint in her eyes. Her smile was endearingly lopsided. Violet seemed to be enjoying his unease. It was almost like she was flirting. "Hold up," Jack scolded himself internally. "She's said all of three words. Let's not get carried away." Aloud, he explained, "I'm Jack, and er, you probably heard my little sister, Olivia. She was providing unsolicited technical help. It was, of course, an obvious ruse to spy on me." Jack's grin made it plain that he was amused, not mad. It also drew attention to his five o'clock shadow, which Violet decided suited him nicely.

Before Violet could reply, a chime heralded a new arrival. Emily's image appeared on-screen, and she greeted them with bubbly enthusiasm. "Hello, I'm Emily! Thanks, Violet, for arranging this chat." Emily was using her DC for the call, and the picture jiggled crazily until she got settled. She had had scarcely enough time to freshen up and grab a beer from the food generator before dialing in. She was perched on a stool at her kitchen island. There was a stained-glass window behind her. This was Emily's favorite spot for taking video calls. She quickly braced her DC and angled it perfectly. She was still clad in the sleeveless navy halter dress that she had worn to work that day, but she had removed her sweater. Backlit by the window, beer in hand, she was straight out of an old-world St. Pauli Girl poster.

Mason arrived on Emily's heels and joined the chorus of greetings. His lilac dress shirt was somewhat rumpled from the workday, and he could only hope it made him look devil-may-care, not sloppy. He was seated at the dining table with his laptop, a bowl of stew, and a tall glass of water. He had not eaten dinner yet and tried to gauge if the group was relaxed enough that he could do it during the call without seeming rude. He was encouraged when Emily took a deep swig of her beer.

When the thrill of first contact abated, Violet kicked off the call with a more formal introduction. "Since I'm the instigator here," she began with a grin, "it seems only fair that I tell you about myself. I live and work on a farm that I inherited from my parents when they died last year. Along with Firestorm, my horse, I am the last of the Murphy clan. I have degrees in biochemistry and applied physics, plus a lifetime of rigorous hands-on training in engineering and botany from my parents. I'm doing my best to carry on their legacy. It's my privilege to do it. I cannot imagine spending my life anywhere else. Running the farm is infinitely challenging, fascinating, and rewarding. And Firestorm brings me more joy than I can express." Violet looked down, cleared her throat, and blinked dampness from her cornflower-blue eyes. A beat later, she raised her gaze, and her smile was sober but warm. "I had never posted on a forum before, even as a student. A couple of strange experiences spurred me to reach out. But even if this ends up bringing me no clarity, I will be grateful for making new friends."

"Prost!" Emily crowed. "To making new friends!" She gestured with her beer stein and took another pull.

Mason whooped and held up a spoonful of lumpy stew to join the toast. Unfortunately for him, Pounce chose that precise moment to make an appearance. She leaped onto the table and jostled Mason's arm, causing him to spill the stew all over his face. The others heard an "oomph" on impact, but they could no longer see Mason. Pounce was perched in front of the camera, regal as a queen, soaking up the delighted, amused reactions of her audience.

"Oh my, aren't you a beauty," Violet burbled, eliciting a muted purr.

Mason scooped up his feline attention-seeker and held her in his arms. All traces of dinner were gone from his beard. "This is Pounce," he said. "She is *not* a clingy cat." Mason stroked her back. Her silver fur accentuated the flecks of pewter in his beard. "She's a bit of a loner really. But she does expect a little me-time when I get home from work. Being in a rush today, I was remiss." At this, he addressed Pounce directly. "I'm sorry, sweetheart." The cat gently thumped her head under Mason's chin and hopped to the floor.

Finding himself in the spotlight, Mason proceeded with his introduction. "I live in Apricus and work at the Infrastructure Bureau as a programmer and systems analyst. That's my official role anyway, but in practice, I'm a jack-of-all-trades when it comes to computers. I work a lot. Our way of life is inextricably linked to computer technology, but there aren't that many people who have the skills to keep it running. I'm not boasting. I'm trying to say that it can be tough. And lonely. The pressure is constant, and if I allowed it, the bureau would work me 24/7." Mason sighed gustily, then his lips curved in a weary smile. "Pounce is excellent company, but I'm glad to be growing my small circle of *human* friends. When I read your posts on the nature-lovers community, it just felt right to reply. Like we had something important in common."

The others nodded and smiled in agreement. There was a momentary pause, then Emily took a noisy sip from her stein and clunked it on the counter. "I'll go next!" she announced. "I work as a preservationist in the city, but I live topside with my grandparents on my family's estate. My job involves studying and protecting human history and culture, and while it is not a popular view, I firmly believe that the natural world is central to our human-ness. I cannot imagine leaving my ancestral home on Fulminara. Being there keeps me grounded. It also lifts my spirits in a way that nothing else can. It makes me feel whole. And I *know* it makes me a better scholar. How can we hope to preserve our past if we ignore our ties to nature and wildlife?" Emily took a breath and switched gears as smoothly as a classic Rolls-Royce. "I enjoy bird-watching, photography, good food, and strong ale. And it's lovely to meet you all."

Emily looked to Jack, signaling his turn. "Hello, everyone. I'm Jack, and I work at the Commerce Bureau in retail operations." Jack cringed inwardly. He sounded like a participant in a twelve-step meeting. "Er, I live in a row house in the city. It's the house where I grew up. I had my own apartment, but I moved back in with my mum and younger sister a couple of years ago when my dad died. I did it to offer my support to them, but frankly, his death hit me hard and I think I probably need to be there more than they need me. It's been a difficult time for me—depressing, confusing, and exhausting. When I was topside the other day, though, I had an epiphany. Or something. I don't understand exactly *what* happened, but it was profound. And at the end of that bizarre day, I stumbled onto the nature-lovers community. I wasn't looking for it. Then I read Violet's post, and I started to doubt that it was mere coincidence."

Jack's words settled over the group. The ensuing silence was loaded with all the things they were not sharing. Before the gap could become awkward, Emily said, "I enjoy feeding the ducks that visit the pond on our property. I've been doing it for as long as I can remember. Something new happened when I fed them the other day, and I was researching online to try to make sense of it. That's how I came across Violet's post. The phrasing piqued my interest. It seemed deliberate. *A special connection. A different level.* I think you were fishing, Violet, and I, *we,* took the bait. Are you going to reel us in?"

Violet chuckled. "You're right. I did choose my words carefully." Her eyes rolled up as if to seek divine assistance, then she forged ahead before she could lose her nerve. "Okay, here goes. I'm going to be blunt. I suspect that I can communicate with animals…psychically. That somehow, I recently acquired this ability. It appears to be limited, situational, and accompanied by a rather jarring physical reaction, including rapid heart rate and labored respiration. It may be triggered by strong emotions. The experience is best described as a telepathic conveyance of thought and emotion—just ideas and feelings, not actual sentences." Violet took a calming breath. "I have experienced this phenomenon twice. The second time involved Firestorm. I grew up with him, and nothing remotely close to this had happened before. It convinced me that my perceptions were valid and *real.* I was returning from an overnight stay in the city, and his emotions when I came home nearly bowled me over. I could *feel* his love and relief. I could *hear* him without language. It was incredible." Her last words were a breathy murmur.

Silence returned, and this time it was uncomfortable. The others looked pensive. Violet was unsure if they were comparing her experiences with their own or plotting to contact the nice men with the butterfly nets. At long last, Jack spoke. "Violet, what you described closely aligns with an unusual interaction I had with a deer. My reflections on that experience have been, uh, *muddled.* Your clear, scientific account is reassuring… and spot-on." Violet smiled at him. If her pre-call grin had been a flirty candlelight flicker, this smile was a blazing supernova. Jack felt a blush rise up his neck to paint his cheeks.

When Jack's engine stalled, Emily jumped in. "Let me tell you a little duck tale," she began with a smirk. The group was enthralled as she described the episode at the pond in loving detail. "I did some cursory research on the paranormal, but aside from folklore, it didn't turn up any links to animals."

"I did some research, too," Violet interjected. "I've been thinking about this as a form of empathic telepathy, but I couldn't find anything to connect telepathy and animals."

"Empathic telepathy," Mason repeated slowly. "I like that. It fits. You know, there are telempaths in the old comic books—individuals who can perceive thoughts and emotions. But even there, it's always a person-to-person thing. *Our* superpower is a bridge to animals…" he trailed off dreamily. There was a pause while everyone was deep in thought. Off-camera, somebody delivered a plate of cookies to Jack. Emily fetched another beer.

Pounce sprang onto Mason's table with a plaintive *reooowr* and sauntered across the keypad. "This must be the cue to tell *my* story," Mason said with a laugh. He proceeded to explain the incident involving Consuelo, ending with, "To be clear, my cat didn't talk like a Rudyard Kipling character. She didn't *talk* at all. I understood her without words. It was the damnedest thing. And to be honest, I wasn't really troubled by it. I wouldn't mind feeling that connection again."

"I don't know who Rudyard Kipling is, but I wouldn't mind having it happen again either," Jack replied. "I was distracted by the physical sensations. I felt like I was having an anxiety attack or something. That got in the way. In retrospect, though, I knew what I had experienced was special."

"You mentioned a deer, Jack. Will you tell us your story?" Emily asked.

"Actually, I'd prefer not to." Jack squirmed in his chair. There was a little crease above his nose.

"Why?" asked Violet. Her voice was a lure. He could not resist looking at her, but his green eyes darted away quickly like skittish frogs.

"If I tell you, you won't like me very much," Jack alleged with a bitter sigh. He was angled away from the camera, expression sad and lost. The cookies had left a streak of powdered sugar on his lower lip. No one on the call could imagine this man saying anything offensive.

Jack did not want his new friends to reassure him. He felt unworthy of their solace. Before they could try, he shared a photograph. In it, Jack stood beside his father in a wooded glen. A rifle hung over his shoulder, and the carcasses of a deer and two rabbits lay at his feet. "You're a hunter?" Mason whispered.

"No!" Jack answered fervently. "I used to hunt, but it's in the past. I didn't want to tell you, to alienate you. But I can't explain what happened without this context." He barreled forward, candidly revealing his struggles with loss and tradition and the pivotal encounter in the meadow. At the end of the confession, Jack lifted his soulful green eyes and awaited judgment.

Violet nodded her head once, slowly but decisively. "Okay," she said. She glanced at Emily and Mason, who indicated their agreement. She knew they would. The three had exchanged looks of sympathy and acceptance while Jack spoke, too pained and distracted to notice.

"O-okay? You, er, don't want me to leave?"

"No, man. Don't leave," answered Mason.

Jack smiled diffidently. No other words were needed. He had been accepted, warts and all.

Emily was eager to make the hunting photo disappear and to rekindle the previously upbeat tone of their discussion. "Jack, you said you took photos of the meadow. Can we see one?"

Jack displayed his favorite shots. "Wow, I think that's primrose!" Violet observed excitedly. "You don't find it very often on Fulminara. It's gorgeous…"

They chatted amiably for a few more hours. Their telepathic experiences were revisited and probed, and despite the limitations of those experiences and the lack of scientific evidence, the group was convinced on an instinctual level of their authenticity. At times, they got so animated that everyone talked at once until they caught themselves and dissolved into gales of laughter. Eventually, Mason yawned uncontrollably, and they reluctantly acknowledged that it was late.

"Let's meet in person!" Emily proposed. A final burst of conversation culminated in a sketchy plan to meet topside the following weekend and stay overnight at Violet's house. The group would firm up the details via email.

They said farewell and went about their bedtime rituals. The milky moon crept across the night sky. The cuckoo clock chimed. The city lights faded to black. The world was ostensibly the same.

CHAPTER 10

CLOSE AT HAND

Saturday bloomed sunny and warm. Violet was busy replacing the dusty linens in the guest bedroom and trying not to sneeze. Plumping a pillow, she stole a glance out the window. The hospitable weather was a good omen, she thought. Emily was used to the erratic conditions on Fulminara, but Violet did not want Jack and Mason to venture out of Apricus into a maelstrom. Violet was excited to open her home to them. This surprised her, as she was a private person, even a tad reclusive, and highly protective of the estate. But the group had bonded quickly, and they had traded many pleasant messages and calls over the past week that seemed to reaffirm the wisdom of her decision.

Violet carried an armful of linens downstairs. On the way, she passed her parents' room where Emily would be staying. Emily was reluctant to intrude, but Violet insisted. Wherever her mother and father were now, Violet was positive they would delight in having their beloved home reverberate with the sounds of revelry and companionship. Mason would stay in the guest room, despite his attempts to defer to Jack over email. When their amiable "No, I insist" debate had devolved into a record skip, Violet scheduled a call to finalize the sleeping arrangements and confirm the overall plans for their get-together.

She generated a random number on her DC that the men had to guess. Since Jack's guess was closer, his choice was honored. Violet had threatened to bunk them both with Firestorm, but Mason's eager smile told her that this was not the deterrent she intended. She snickered at the memory and piled extra pillows and blankets beside the sofa for Jack. His rangy frame might be cramped without a bed, but she could still pamper him with cozy bedding.

Before Violet set out for the barn to begin her morning chores, she detoured to the kitchen. Sunshine palpated the windows; it bathed the cabinetry, danced along the countertops, and lent the room an otherworldly glow. Violet proudly surveyed the food she had prepared the night before. She could not resist the allure of the fruit salad and shoveled out an enormous spoonful. Giggling and unrepentant, she grabbed blindly for a towel to catch the juice that dribbled messily down her chin. Breakfast was, after all, the most important meal of the day. Even though Emily would arrive early to help Violet with last-minute preparations for the picnic that would kick off their festivities, she had a lot to accomplish around the farm first and appreciated the pick-me-up.

Mason sat on the bench waiting for the train to arrive. A pair of bags were stacked neatly at his feet: a canvas duffel made from a recovered industrial tent and a straw tote. His legs bounced with nervous energy as he minded the countdown on the nearest video panel and registered every third word of the morning news broadcast. He had almost brought Pounce, but truth be told, he was too stressed to properly look after her. Mason had not left Apricus in years. The idea of lodging overnight on Fulminara was overwhelming. Therefore, he bade goodbye to his cat and promised she could come next time. He hoped he would calm down once Jack arrived. Some might call Jack boring (Jack being chief among them), but Mason saw his new friend as a steady little tugboat, reliable and true.

Looking more like an aircraft carrier, Jack's lanky body emerged from the arriving train. Mason had stood as the train glided to a stop and was waving excitedly. Wearing a chipper smile, Jack strode over and dropped one of his bags, leaving another bag slung carelessly over his shoulder. They shook hands vigorously, and Mason clasped Jack's empty shoulder with his other hand. "It's great to meet face-to-face!" Jack enthused. "I'm really glad you suggested riding together to Fulminara." Jack plonked down on the bench, facing the outbound track. Mason wrestled his luggage to the other side and joined him. The station was starting to bustle with activity. A klatch of legging-clad women with branded T-shirts were destined for a yoga class, and a couple of unshaven fathers who *already* looked tired were trying to herd their preschoolers. Jack offered his seat to an elderly man but was gruffly rebuffed. Shrugging it off, he watched the platform fill and chatted affably with Mason until their train arrived.

The men claimed a set of seats facing one another. The unit was not crowded, and by the time the train reached the last Apricus station, Mason and Jack were the only passengers. The final people to debark were a boy who kept running up and down the aisle yelling "eel" at the top of his lungs and his embarrassed mother.

Reveling in the blessed quiet, Mason realized that he was no longer anxious. Jack was good company, and now that the trip was underway, he felt exhilarated. "I was kind of tense about going topside," he confessed. "I haven't traveled outside the city since I was a teenager. As I was leaving the apartment this morning, the prospect seemed pretty daunting."

Jack nodded his head soberly. "And now?" he asked. He had noticed that Mason was speaking in the past tense and allowed a smile to tug at the corner of his mouth.

"Now, I'm thrilled," Mason replied. "I've been feeling caged up and overworked. This trip is exactly what I need." With a sly grin, he added, "I'm going to Fulminara on the eeeeeel!"

"No, no, make it stop," Jack groaned, and they both tipped over with laughter. Eventually, it petered out and Jack's stomach rumbled loudly to fill the void. "Pardon me," he apologized, a faint blush on his cheeks. "I missed breakfast. I was helping my sister get ready for an early soccer match. She couldn't find her shin guards." Jack pulled a beat-up gym bag onto his lap and rummaged inside. With a magician's flourish, he pulled out two sealed containers and handed one to Mason. "One for you. One for me."

Bemused, Mason took the offering. It was comfortingly warm to the touch. He watched Jack open the lid on his container. A heavenly aroma invaded the pristine, filtered air of the compartment.

"Go on, then," Jack urged. "My mum made a to-go breakfast for each of us. It looks like hard-boiled eggs and buttered crumpets with jam. I bet she baked the bread herself." Crumpet en route to his mouth, Jack froze when he saw the stricken look on his friend's face. "Mason? Uh, you don't need to eat anything. Mum didn't mean to be presumptuous. She'd understand if you aren't hungry or this food isn't to your taste or—"

"No," Mason cut in, distracted by muzzy family memories. Aside from Consuelo, no one had mothered him in a very long time. Mrs. Collins's gesture educed a bittersweet ache. But the pain was good, he decided, like the pins and needles you get when you awaken a disused limb. "This is wonderful, Jack. Thank you."

The two men munched and talked contentedly, and the time flew by with the scenery.

Irritating beads of sweat gathered along Emily's hairline and above her lip. Squinting up at the sky, she marveled at how quickly the temperature was rising. She hefted her travel bags into the back of the SUV where Hannah had already loaded several bulky containers of food. She heard the crunch of

CLOSE AT HAND 103

feet on gravel and turned to find her grandmother bearing another container. "Oh no, Grandma. You've already given me more than enough." Her tone was stern, but her smile betrayed her amusement. "There are only four of us!"

"Nonsense," Hannah replied, merrily dismissing Emily's halfhearted protest. "This is my potato salad." She held out the container with the studied reverence of a priest. "Be sure to tell Violet that I grew the potatoes myself in our garden. The rabbits don't touch them, though I can't say the same for my lettuce and broccoli. Of course, I don't have the heart to shoo them away, and it just made me sad to watch them sniffing around that protective netting your grandfather put up..." The women continued to chat while they secured the sacred salad, then they rounded the vehicle to join Dimitri where he was triple-checking the battery and the directions to Violet's place. Emily bestowed two grateful hugs and was on her way. The crushed-stone path was bone white in the morning sun and flanked by candescent grasses that undulated like the surf on a great gold ocean. The cool, dark forest lay in wait ahead.

Despite a few rough stretches of road, Emily drove without incident to her destination. She rarely had cause to travel to this part of Fulminara and devoured the unfamiliar scenery. The forest grew less dense as she approached the sheer cliff face of the coastline. The trees yielded to wind-whipped shrubs and giant sedges with copper straps. Resilient clusters of mountain sorrel and goldenrod were anchored in the rocky soil. Emily followed the sea cliffs for a while, watching for the unpaved path that would cut inland toward the Murphy estate. The turn was sharp, but Dimitri had warned her, and she was ready for it. The last segment of her journey led Emily back into the woods. Unlike the tracts of grassland, labyrinthian streams and ponds, and rolling hills that characterized the region around Honey Hill, the area around the Murphy estate was heavily wooded, with sporadic clearings.

At the outskirt of the latest clearing, Emily could just make out the stately front gate of Violet's home. Smiling broadly, she emerged from the shaded canopy onto a well-worn pathway of mortared stone. Opportunistic tufts of green clover and random wildflowers were growing in the cracks. Violet had opened the gate for her, so Emily passed under the arch and drove toward the house. However, she was promptly diverted by Firestorm in the adjacent paddock. He raised his head from a pile of new-mown hay and, seemingly pleased, cantered to the fence to check out his visitor. Emily's half-formed impression of aloof regality vanished in the breeze that ruffled Firestorm's mane. He puffed a noisy breath out his nostrils and observed her with guileless eyes. Bewitched, Emily had gradually slowed the SUV to a stop. She was still quite a distance from the house.

Violet stood on the front steps, hands on her hips, laughing. "Hey there!" she called. "Quit ogling my horse and come say hello!"

Emily finished the drive and hopped out of the vehicle. She wrapped Violet in a hug worthy of long-lost sisters. "It's so good to see you!" Emily said. She released Violet but held her at arm's length by the shoulders to prolong the moment. Firestorm neighed, feeling left out. He had followed Emily along the fence line and was waiting none too patiently to be introduced. The women approached, and Firestorm indulgently submitted to Emily's tentative petting. After a couple of minutes, he nuzzled her hand and trotted off to drink from a water trough near the barn.

"I think you've passed muster," Violet joked. "Come on, I'll take you to your room. You can get settled while I finish up in the kitchen."

"No, no, I want to help you. I just need to drop off my bags and make a pit stop in the bathroom. It was a long drive."

They walked back to Emily's purportedly white vehicle. It was covered in grime, and the women were careful not to rub against it. Emily started to unload while Violet connected the battery to a mobile charging port. "Holy goodness, something smells wonderful!" Violet exclaimed.

Grinning, Emily explained that Hannah had packed enough homemade food to last a siege. "There's a literal ton of potato salad. Grandma was adamant that I tell you she grew the taters herself." Violet beamed with wide-eyed delight. "Plus," Emily continued, "we have a variety of sandwiches on freshly baked bread and two dozen giant pretzels, half salt and half sesame seed. Oh, and Grandma made one of my absolute favorites, *apfelkuchen*. It's a scrumptious apple cake."

Priorities set by their appetites, they deposited the food in the kitchen first. Violet led the way through the house. Emily trailed behind her, soaking up minute details of the surroundings with her keen preservationist's eye. Her breath stuttered when she spied the graceful Celtic knot carved into the varnished hardwood of the front door. She was itching to hear about Violet's Irish heritage and the history of the estate. Humanity's diverse cultural roots were substantially diluted or lost; Emily felt privileged to be allowed to spend time in this hallowed place.

Given that Emily required the bathroom, the women did not linger in the airy kitchen. Violet guided her guest upstairs to the largest bedroom. Emily hesitated at the threshold. "C'mon, Emily," Violet coaxed. "My mother and father would be pleased for you to use this room."

Emily laid her bags on the floor at the foot of a sumptuous canopy bed and spun around slowly. "It's stunning," she breathed. The stone walls had been whitewashed, which emphasized the exposed wood beams on the ceiling. The linens and rugs were shades of blue with simple floral accents. An oversize beveled mirror in an ornate iron frame hung above the hearth, and a rocking chair rested fireside. Two antique nightstands and his-and-her armoires filled out the room, along with an incongruously modern chest of drawers with angled legs and cutout handles. Emily was drawn to the diamond-cut Waterford crystal bowl that adorned the chest. Awestruck, she ran a thumb over its curved rim and bent down to inspect it, afraid to actually pick it up. Violet waited good-naturedly while her friend made a dawdling circuit of the room, meeting her beside a towering window with thick drapes and an Irish lace sheer. On the inset windowsill, a vase of fuzzy purple flowers basked in the sun. Emily gasped when she realized that the flowers were real. "Oh, these are gorgeous…" She cocked her head and gave her hostess a puzzled look. "I don't recognize them, though. What kind are they?"

"They're violets, of course. My mother's favorite."

Emily spent long moments admiring the plant then reached out to squeeze her friend's hand. The melancholy warmth of Violet's answering smile glowed like a halo of sunshine around a dark cloud.

After using the en suite bathroom, Emily returned to the kitchen where Violet was playing *Tetris* with stacks of containers in the refrigerator, making room for Hannah's goodies. Even though the containers were insulated, the refrigerator was safer for perishables like potato salad, and she was confident that everything could fit. The pretzels were still on the counter. Emily opened the caddy. "Want to share a *Brezeln*?" she tempted. "I could use a snack."

Victorious, Violet closed the refrigerator door and eagerly accepted the doughy treat. "Is your family German?" she inquired between bites.

"Grandpa Dimitri is Russian, and we've incorporated his traditions. But Grandma Hannah was widowed *after* my mother was born, so technically, the Steubens are still 100 percent German stock. Grandma Hannah and Grandpa Otto arrived in Novosibirsk seeking medical care on the eve of the Sino-Russian Revolt. Otto died trying to get them to safety. Hannah found herself defenseless and bereft, with a newborn in tow. Dimitri discovered them hiding under the stairwell of his apartment building. He sheltered them for months and eventually snuck them on a transport to Fulminara to join Hannah's relatives on Honey Hill. Unable to say goodbye, Dimitri accompanied them and proposed a year later. Back in the day, there were several German families on the island. My mother and father met at an Oktoberfest celebration when she slipped on wet leaves and dropped a spit-roasted chicken on his lap."

Riveted by the tale, Violet startled when her DC pinged. "Looks like story time is over," she pouted. "We have to leave for the station." They grabbed a pretzel for the road and proceeded outside. As the SUV started rolling, Violet stuck her head out the window and hollered to Firestorm that they would be back soon. They paused to secure the gated archway. Emily inspected the stonework, admiring the artistry of the engravings that could only be discerned up close. Turning to Violet, she confessed her burning desire to learn about the Murphy clan. Violet gamely agreed, and the drive to the station passed swiftly.

Jack spotted Violet before the train had even coasted to a halt. She was waiting on the platform, luxuriating in the heat with her chin up, eyes closed, and sun-kissed hair tumbling down her back. Close by, Emily was examining some tall grasses that reminded her of Honey Hill. A smattering of wooly silver-pink plumes was stuck in her hair. The women heard the train and waved cheerily as the compartment doors slid open. Jack was blocking the exit but did not move. Rolling his eyes, Mason nudged Jack's shoulder when the warning bell rang. "Get moving, man. The doors are gonna close."

The women surged forward to greet Jack and Mason and assist with their luggage. For an awkward instant, Emily was unsure if they were "huggy" guys, but then she just launched herself at Mason who unhesitatingly wrapped his strong arms around her and laughed, and all was well. Violet followed suit with Jack. Floundering like a gawky teenager, he did not know what to do with his hands, so he basically stood there gripping his bags while she held him. His smile was liquid warmth, though, and she did not seem to mind. For Emily, he managed to free his left arm to embrace her shoulder.

They crowded into the SUV, which creaked under the unaccustomed weight, and chatted spiritedly the whole drive back. The temperature soared, and they teetered on the cusp of discomfort, but a breeze ruffled their hair through the windows and flowed over their skin like freedom, and no one turned on the air conditioning. As they reached the Murphy estate, its equine ambassador galloped into view. Violet got out to unlatch the gate, and Emily offered to take the bags to the house. Awed by Firestorm, the men made a clumsy clown car exit and stumbled toward the paddock. Mason failed to gain solid footing and tripped in front of the fence, slamming his knee into the ground. Worried, Firestorm ducked his head to peer between the slats, coming eye to eye with a hopelessly spellbound Mason. By tacit agreement, Violet and Jack hung back to allow their friend this moment. They listened to Mason murmur sweet nonsense while Firestorm exhaled deep, fluttering breaths through his nostrils. In due course, Firestorm lifted his head. Violet took this as her cue to make formal introductions, promising more time together later.

The group strolled up the uneven path as Violet explained the layout of the estate. The sun was feverish in a cloudless sky, amplifying colors and throwing edges into sharp relief. Firestorm kept pace on the other side of the fence. Meanwhile, Emily bellhopped the overnight bags to the guest bedroom and wrangled more containers into the fridge. She combed the stowaway grass out of her hair, then she made a ponytail and threaded a plume into the base as an adornment. When the others arrived, she joined Violet's tour of the house. The tour ended at the guest room, and the men broke off to unpack their belongings, even though Jack would sleep on the couch.

A short while later, everyone was laying out tableware and food on an expansive picnic bench that was draped in a festive tartan cloth and peppered with citronella candles to deter insects. The table and its two long, detached seats had been crafted from the remains of a veteran Douglas fir and worn smooth from generations of exposure and refinishing. The bench was located on a grassy knoll between the barn and the greenhouse. It was close enough to the paddock fence that Firestorm could join the festivities if he was bored with grazing and chasing squirrels. When the setup was finished, Violet proposed a show-and-tell. The friends idled around the table and admired the bounty for another minute or two, not wanting to rush. Jack, especially, was in no hurry. He snuck frequent glances at Violet, charmingly obvious in his effort to not be obvious. He was captivated by her freckles. "I want to create a star map of her skin," he thought, "like a Babylonian astronomer recording the constellations."

"I'm starving!" Emily chirped. "Let's eat!" Persuaded by the heat, she had eschewed her leggings and changed into a sleeveless, checkered sundress that fluttered in the breeze. She swiveled her hips to make the pleated skirt shift and flare, relishing the uninhibitedness of the motion. "As our hostess, Violet, you should be the one to start the show-and-tell."

Violet obligingly unveiled lemonade, roasted sweet corn, crudités with hummus, and minted fruit salad. All the ingredients were freshly sourced from the Murphy farm. Violet presented her offerings without fanfare, but her eyes were alight with pride, and her friends' enthusiastic responses raised a pink flush on her neck and cheeks.

After Emily explained the German origins of her dishes, Jack opened his containers to showcase the pork pies that Abigail had baked for them. "Mum uses our food generator for ingredients, but she makes the pies herself. She says that generated pies don't come out British enough," he chuckled, "whatever that means. Our family is English with a bit of Scottish and a scandalous touch of French. There's even a Collins coat of arms. And yes," Jack threw in cheekily, "we drink a lot of tea."

Playfully boasting that they had saved the best for last, Mason shared the creamy macaroni salad that he had prepared in his own kitchen, then he held up an oblong cardboard box. "Unlike you all, my background is a big mishmash. My family lived in the United States for a long time, and uh, they obviously embraced the whole melting pot metaphor. But if you go way back, my most distant ancestors were African, and my parents tried to connect me with that legacy in a bunch of small, subtle ways. That's what this is about." Mason lifted the lid on the box, revealing a dozen fragrant cookies. "These are called *Hertzoggies*. Food generators don't make them, and the recipe is too complicated for me, but a café near my apartment likes to serve African cuisine, and they'll whip up a batch if I ask." Mason's deep, expressive voice dropped a decibel. "*Hertzoggies* have always been my favorite. I used to love watching my mom bake them. She would let me lick the spoons and stuff, but really, I just liked to watch her and listen to her talk."

"I don't know about anyone else," Emily said, "but I'm starting with dessert." She plucked a cookie from the box using her thumb and forefinger. She inspected the confection from all sides like a gemologist then took a genteel sniff before biting into it. Eyes shut, Emily tipped her head skyward and moaned wantonly, causing Jack to clear his throat as the tips of his ears reddened. Violet's hand shot into the box to find out what all the fuss was about. Jack felt both relief and disappointment when her appreciative reaction was less vocal. Mason laughed, and the foursome settled in for a leisurely meal and conversation.

The white-bright sunshine turned to melted butter in the midafternoon, a lazy gold weight on their full stomachs. The group fell into a comfortable silence. Violet and Jack started to organize the empty food containers while Mason stretched out in the grass. Nibbling on *apfelkuchen*, Emily stared out across the paddock, absorbed in thought. Eventually, she said, "I have an important job. The city's museum and archives are crucial, now more than ever, when so much of the old world is gone. But they're not enough. Communities, families, individuals…*everyone* is responsible for preserving humankind's cultural and ethnic heritage." Emily grew animated as she warmed to her topic. "We are all shepherds. I've written and spoken on this subject many times, hopefully with some degree of eloquence. The fact remains, though, that while many citizens embrace this responsibility devotedly, like you all do, others…so many others…seem to crave homogeneity. It gives them comfort, a false sense of security. As if pretending everybody is the same, trying to *make* us the same, will prevent future wars and catastrophes." Emily slid off the picnic bench and paced. Violet, Jack, and Mason heard the strain in her voice and gave her their undivided attention. "Thousands of cultures have no living representatives, even fractionally. Yet instead of celebrating what's left, society passes measures like the Uniform Language Law and the Doctrine of Agnosticism. We suppress diversity in the name of peace. But me, I find no peace in it."

Emily dragged her focus back to her immediate surroundings. Her blue eyes sparkled with painful passion, and unexpectedly, Jack was the first to respond. He revealed his misgivings about having only one school system in Apricus and criticized the narrowness of Olivia's education, describing his sister as the idiomatic square peg that her teachers kept trying to cram into a round hole. The next hour was spent debating politics. Despite the potentially inflammatory and divisive topics, conversation flowed easily. The new friends were broadly aligned but did not always agree on details. Happily, such differences merely added energy and spice, and sometimes volume, to the debate.

Mason and Emily split off for an impassioned discussion of music. Unnoticed, Violet took Jack to visit Firestorm. He had ambled over in response to their raised voices and was grazing at the paddock's border. He eyed Jack, undoubtedly noting the stranger's close proximity to Violet. The couple's fingers brushed as they walked, but under Firestorm's appraising stare, Jack lost his resolve to hold Violet's hand, cursing himself six ways to Sunday when they attained the fence. Violet reached up to scratch Firestorm's ears, murmuring softly. When he was relaxed, she guided Jack to rub his neck. Jack marveled at the different textures of hair on the horse's body and mane. Violet pulled a sugar cube from the pocket of her shorts and showed Jack how to offer it. She was playing dirty, she knew. Firestorm was a sucker for sugar, and Violet really wanted him to like Jack.

"Oh man, can I feed him, too, Violet?" There was a little-boy whine in Mason's deep voice, and Violet caved immediately.

"Of course," she called. "Grab the carrot pieces that I left on the picnic table." Mason glanced at Emily sheepishly, realizing that he had abruptly ended their discussion. She chortled and waved him off, tickled by his childlike excitement.

While Firestorm was being pampered, Emily took candid photos on her DC. Ever the documentarian, she had been snapping pictures unobtrusively all day. As Mason giddily received hostler training, Jack shifted his attention to her. She was barefoot in the grass, meticulously framing a shot of the honeycombed greenhouse. She reminded Jack pleasantly of an unopened, shaken soda bottle—full of buzzy effervescence, barely leashed. When Emily gamboled closer to the greenhouse, Jack refocused on the others, awaiting his turn to interact with Firestorm like a visitor to an old-timey county fair. Mason looked damp and rumpled in his lightweight pants. Apricus was maintained at seventy-two degrees, and Mason had not packed workout clothes. He was overdressed for the heat, yet admirably, he was not letting it diminish his good mood.

After storing the leftovers, the rest of the afternoon was spent touring the farm, greenhouse, barn, and surroundings. Violet's knowledge was staggering, but she comported herself with gracious ease and unending patience, and her guests soaked it up with spongy enthusiasm, effusive in their gratitude to her for sharing her home in this way. Bracing her hip against a cool metal railing on level three of the farm, Violet spoke about a bygone world. "Agriculture used to be widespread. The earliest farming communities were established thousands of years ago, and agriculture has played a huge role in human history. It's gut-wrenching to see something that literally shaped civilization reduced to this," she said with an anemic sweep of her arm. "But the planet kept getting hotter, natural pollinators disappeared, and reservoirs dried up or got contaminated. Even today, the heat waves and storms make it hard to grow crops outside." She graced Mason with a fleeting smile. "Technology saved the day. Without food generators, we wouldn't be here. Replication and cultivation are different, though." Violet stroked her roughened palm over the tassel at the top of a cornstalk. "The substance remains, but the spirit is gone. A spark is missing…some undefinable essence we share with the bananas and the bees."

The quiet that followed was disturbed only by the numbing white-noise hum of machinery and the hiss and patter of irrigation sprinklers on the level below. Emily joined Violet by the corn. As she walked, she ran a finger along the row of yellow-green stalks like a harp. "In my job as a preservationist, I deal mostly with physical artifacts—objects of cultural or historical value judged worthy of study and retention." She made eye contact with Violet and continued earnestly. "You are a preservationist, too, Violet. Another sort, perhaps, but the underlying drive is the same. Your family has tried to preserve our natural world—the plants, the flowers, and the trees. That's a beautiful and amazing thing." The women shared a sad smile, then the sprinklers on their level spit to life and the tour moved on.

Late in the evening, the temperature nose-dived and the group settled by the fireplace, cradling warm mugs of cider. Though they were sleepy, they were not ready to say good night. Instead, they curled up on the cushy furniture in the salon and talked in soft, slurred voices until Hypnos was too pushy to ignore. Stretching and yawning, they wrapped up their conversation. "I visit the sensory chambers sometimes," Mason said. Fatigue pitched his voice even lower than normal. "I used to feel such a rush when I clipped a receiver behind my ear and walked into a room. I could go anywhere, you know? African savanna, ice shelf in Antarctica—*anywhere*. But lately, it makes me feel…empty." Embarrassed, Mason rushed to complete his thought. "I'm, uh, just really happy to be out of the city for real."

Emily gave Mason's shoulder a reassuring pat as she slipped past his chair to bring her empty mug to the kitchen. "I can't imagine living in a cave," she said. "It's hard enough to work there. Fortunately, I have flexible hours at the museum and the freedom to telecommute when my tasks are less physically hands-on, like when I'm doing research or writing. The earth-quake threat makes me nervous. Being under all that rock…"

"The caves are probably the safest place to be, actually," Mason replied. He slurped the last dregs of his cider and joined Emily at the sink with his mug. "The mountains on Potesta have survived the worst upheaval the planet has ever seen, and there hasn't been a cave collapse since they reinforced the armature decades ago."

Mason and Emily chatted in hushed tones apropos of the late hour while Violet helped Jack make up the couch, confiding that she often slept on it herself, either too weary or comfy to relocate. Jack studied her fluid movements and admired her little frown of concentration. In his distraction, he let the linens slip from his fingers every time she tried to tug them taut. After the third attempt, Violet chuffed out a fondly exasperated breath and gave Jack a pointed look. He got a grip, literally and figuratively, and assisted Violet with the couch. "I've always fancied the idea of a dome," Jack said, picking up the last thread of conversation he could remember. "It'd be the best of both worlds, really—outside but protected."

Violet rolled with the non sequitur. "Mmm, domes are interesting. Part of me, the problem-solver, wishes the government hadn't given up on the concept so easily, deciding that the terrain was too difficult and there wasn't enough space. But a much bigger part of me is relieved that Fulminara remains wild. Dome construction would have most likely destroyed the ecosystem."

Jack sank into the sheets. He felt chastised, though he was certain that Violet had only shared her perspective and did not intend it as a rebuke. She planted a kiss on the crown of his head, running her fingers through the hair at his temple. "Good night," she whispered, and it felt like forgiveness. Jack watched her lead the others upstairs, lit by the smoldering fire in the hearth. He stretched out as much as he could, burrowed under the blanket, and spent long, slow minutes marveling at his roller-coaster emotions before sleep finally silenced the noise.

The rest of the weekend passed in much the same way, filled with effortless camaraderie. They parted reluctantly and vowed to stay in touch.

As Violet caught up on chores, she reflected on how she had made similar assurances in the past, to schoolmates and suitors who drifted into her orbit and seemed important, only to witness the friendship float away like an untethered balloon. She was determined that this time would be different. This time she would hold on tight.

CHAPTER 11

CONSPIRACY THEORY

Three months passed, and the friends grew closer. They talked or texted nearly every day. Mason and Jack met for lunch on Fridays, a routine that Jack laughingly claimed made him feel like an old-school corporate executive. Emily treated the group to a daylong, private tour of the museum and archives. Violet taught Mason how to ride her scooter while Jack fretted on the sidelines. He scolded Violet for not wearing a helmet until she relented, outwardly grumpy but secretly touched by his concern. They visited the sensory chambers so that Mason could share his best-loved experiences, and in turn, they shared with him their favorite books. Jack introduced Violet to his family, and she occasionally joined them for Sunday brunch. It was unclear if they were dating. They had not labeled what they were doing; there was simply an unspoken acknowledgment that their relationship was qualitatively different from what they had with Mason and Emily.

In short, four people who were strangers became considerably *more*.

They rarely discussed the inexplicable telepathic experiences that had originally brought them together. They had exhausted all avenues of research, and it had not happened to anyone again. The subject was resurrected, however, one languid afternoon at Honey Hill when the group was grousing about the government's interminable census efforts. "It's insane. This has been going on for months," Jack growled. He sat cross-legged on the coppery cobblestones of the courtyard and raked his fingers through his hair in frustration, leaving messy tufts and spikes in their wake. "The reporting requirements are endless. Yesterday, my team finished a historical analysis of shampoo-purchasing behavior, cross-referenced with every conceivable demographic. It's just *shampoo*, dammit."

Violet laid a sympathetic hand on Jack's knee. "This year's census is unusual," she agreed. "The scope is intrusively broad." The cool dampness of the cobblestones bled through her trousers and up her spine. She shifted fitfully and leaned into Jack's shoulder, seeking his heat. "I haven't told you about the census team that came to the farm. Their visit started the chain of events that led to my post on the nature-lovers forum…to how we met." Violet sighed. "I'm sorry it's taken me so long to share this." Emily sensed that Violet was about to recount a disagreeable experience. She slid off the bench and parked next to Violet on the ground, tucking her skirt around her folded knees. Mason scooted closer, too, until the group formed a cozy circle. Distantly, they could hear the wind combing the tall grasses and the chatter of ducks on the pond. Violet began by describing the property inspection and the phlebotomist's assault on Firestorm. "The entire encounter was unsettling. It felt like…a violation."

"The census certainly is odd," Mason said slowly, the words slightly ahead of his thoughts. "It touches *everything*, from households to goods and services. Similar to Commerce, my bureau has fielded a ton of reporting requests, and speculation is rampant among us data geeks." A toothy grin accompanied the nickname. "The most popular guess is that the extra activity is associated with Project Pioneer, that the information is being used to prepare for our eventual relocation."

"That's a good theory," Jack said as he nodded, "but why not tell us that's what they're doing?"

Mason flashed back to his discomfiting day of coding for Pioneer. "I'm not sure. Maybe there's more to it than that. I have a hunch that there's a lot of stuff they don't tell us."

Before Mason could elaborate, Violet interjected with a question. "Did they take a blood sample from Pounce?"

"No, they didn't. I had a two-man team. One guy prowled around the apartment, making notes, nosing into my drawers and cabinets, and generally creeping me out. The other guy questioned me and took my blood. I have a license for Pounce that he called up on his DC. He had me confirm that she's a mixed-breed cat, but he didn't ask to see her. It's a good thing, too, because she was hiding under the bed and would have definitely, uh, resisted."

"That's interesting," Violet said dazedly, trying to reconcile their experiences. A second later, she refocused with a tenacious furrow of her brow. "I have more to share," she announced, and then she described her trip to the Science Bureau in vividly horrifying detail. Her affect was flat, a narrator safely removed from the story, but being unnatural, this only served to underscore her distress and confusion. "I just left them there," she finished in a quavering voice. "I could feel the pain, the desperation, all around me. They were suffering, and I fled. I was disoriented and selfish, and I fled…"

Everyone was reeling from the bizarre turn that Violet's tale had taken. It was quiet but for the jingle of Hannah's wind chimes in the breeze. Mason was the first to speak. "You were drugged," he asserted, leaning in and tipping his head to catch Violet's downturned eyes.

"W-what?"

"They drugged you. The coffee was spiked with something that loosened your tongue so they could pump you for info you wouldn't have otherwise disclosed. It probably made you more susceptible to the telepathy as well, though I doubt that was intentional."

"That sort of thing isn't done anymore," Jack protested, more confidently than he felt. "Are you sure you haven't been reading too much Agatha Christie, man?"

Violet pulled Jack's hand into her lap and ran her thumb over his knuckles soothingly. "It's a reasonable theory, Jack. It fits the facts, not to mention the, um, bad vibes I was getting. I've thought about that day a lot, but this possibility never crossed my mind because, as you implied, no one expects to be invited to the Science Bureau for a drug-induced interrogation."

Mason sucked in a breath. "Indisputably, there are many good people in our government," he stated, bouncing his fist against his knee. "But I've started to suspect that there's some darker stuff going on, too." By way of explanation, he described his stint as a temp for the black ops side of Project Pioneer and the shocking presence of weapons.

"God Almighty, haven't we learned *anything* from history?" Emily lamented. She leaned back on her hands and watched the billowy clouds fox-trot overhead. The air was laced with the earthy freshwater tang of the pond. She inhaled a calming lungful and sat up. "Why didn't you tell us, Violet? I can't believe you've been harboring this worry on your own." Turning to her left, she added, "You, too, Mason."

"I was shaken, yes, but it hasn't been weighing on me," Mason replied honestly. "Maybe it should have been. I'm starting to think it should have been."

"As for me," Violet said, "I was ashamed. I was also second-guessing the validity of my memories. But that's pointless because I *know* what happened. I've been wanting to tell you for a while." Violet surveyed her friends, locking gazes with each of them in turn. "I feel horrendously guilty for leaving those animals. And everything feels *off* somehow. When we were talking about the census, it just seemed like the right time to unload." She concluded her ramble with a self-effacing grimace.

Before the frown could fade from Violet's lips, the broody atmosphere in the courtyard was splintered by blaring, insistent quacking that rapidly escalated to a boisterous crescendo. The group erupted into cathartic laughter, eager to seize the sweet intermezzo unwittingly supplied by the ducks. Feeling a bit protective, Emily composed herself and playfully whined, "Hey, don't mock my flock!" The unintended rhyme coupled with her adorable pout led to a second fit of irrepressible giggles.

That evening, they lounged in Emily's salon, snacking on *Brezeln* and listening to music. Violet picked up the loose thread of their conversation and tugged. "I want to go back to the Science Bureau," she declared. "I need to rescue those animals."

Mason lowered the volume of the music and fixed Violet with a solemn, piercing look. "You can't simply waltz in, Violet. We need more information. Let me do some snooping, hack into their records. Akira Tanaka was your liaison, so I could start with her files. I'm very good, Vi—damn near undetectable."

"I trust your skills, Mason, but I'm partial to putting boots on the ground. I want to point to a closed door and ask questions." Violet's eyes were cobalt gems in the salon's muted lamplight. They were laser-locked on Mason, willing him to understand. "I don't expect to stroll in and start liberating captive animals. I can get the lay of the land, though, and maybe an answer or two. In any case, I need to try before I ask you to take unnecessary risks. The worst they can do is chuck me out the door. But you could lose your job and face criminal charges."

"I hear what you're saying," Mason replied cautiously. "But Violet, I'm not so sure that tossing you out on your butt is the worst they could do. They've already drugged you, girl."

Violet could feel the tension in Jack's muscles where she was nestled against him on the sofa. "Violet," he mumbled. She swiveled to face him, fingertips itching to soothe the creases at the corners of his pursed lips. "If something shifty is going on," he reasoned, "we need to be extra careful. The bureau would have had no motive to coerce you unless their questions were dubious or they wanted things they knew you were unwilling to share. I think—"

"And now I'll turn the tables," Violet interrupted. The timbre of her voice was antagonistic, driven by the single-mindedness of having already made her decision. Jack flinched. It was the barest movement, no more than a twitch, but Violet noticed. Instead of apologizing, however, she turned away, a coward and a zealot. "They obviously stole intel about the estate—unpublished work, my parents' private labors. They pillaged my house. So, I'm gonna pillage theirs...or at least I'm gonna try."

Emily stood to refill their drinks. "Okay, so Violet will try the direct approach first," she resolved. "And if that doesn't work, then Mason can show us his kung fu."

Violet rose from the sofa to assist Emily in the kitchen. She trailed her fingers over Jack's biceps in silent contrition. Mason and Jack were insular for the rest of the night. They were clearly unhappy but would respect Violet's wishes.

The president exhaled sharply and brushed his palm along the edge of his desk. An annoying hornet's-nest buzz seeped in from the adjacent conference room. He closed the report he was perusing and got to his feet. Acting on muscle memory, he straightened his tie and smoothed down the lapel of his tweed jacket. The dark colors and rough fabrics reflected his mood. He clutched his DC and strode next door to join his noisy vanguard. The room fell silent, and the president reveled in the peacefulness of it before taking his seat and nodding at the deputy on his left. Her features were pinched with strain as she addressed the group. "This meeting has been convened to deal with the public's mounting questions about the census..."

The president promptly tuned her out. The furniture in this room was constructed using salvage from a sunken minesweeper. For a couple of minutes, the president's gaze roamed fondly over the polished steel and exposed joints, but his meditation was repeatedly disrupted by the jittery movements of his staff. The senior deputies were crowded into chairs around a rectangular table. Key project leaders were stationed along the credenzas on the perimeter of the room. The space was at capacity and crackling with pent-up energy, as if they were a cast of nervous performers waiting in the green room before a show. The atmosphere was oppressive and did nothing to improve the president's mood. He refocused on the pale-faced deputy from the Communications Bureau just as she finished her summary of the problem at hand: "...but these measures have thus far been unsuccessful in quelling the rising discontent." Immediately, arms lifted and mouths opened to speak. All such gestures were aborted, however, when the president took over.

"Thank you, Jennifer." The president permitted himself a dramatic pause then continued, "It is time to mobilize Phase 2 protocols." Wide eyes and audible gasps greeted this news. The president reclined in his chair, crossed his legs, and folded his hands in his lap—the picture of insouciance. "Now, now, don't act so surprised," he remonstrated. "Phase 1 is finished. All critical objectives were met four months ago. I understand you'd like more time to complete noncritical items, but you knew this was coming. To the extent you can, build your open items into Phase 2."

It took no more than a lazy hand gesture and arched eyebrow for his well-trained deputies to spring into action. For the next three hours, goals, procedures, timelines, milestones, and risks were reviewed in exacting detail. The president worked on his DC, seemingly disengaged from the discussion, until he would suddenly lift his head and make a course correction that reminded everyone he was quite present. Eventually, he thanked his staff and adjourned the gathering with a parting thought that harkened back to the meeting's original purpose. The president loved symmetry. "Pushback about the census was expected. It is time to move on. Let's give the people something else to talk about."

He twisted lithely through a gauntlet of monochromatic uniforms on his way back to the sanctuary of his office. He had suppressed his bleak mood for expediency, but without the pressure of the meeting, he could feel the darkness resurging. When Akira Tanaka stepped into his path, he snapped his tongue loudly and thought maliciously that she was lucky he did not snap her neck instead. She recoiled slightly but continued to block his way.

"Mr. President, I was hoping to have a word with you in private," she implored, her voice a collusive near-whisper.

"Schedule an appointment, Dr. Tanaka."

He moved to sidestep her, but she blocked him again and pressed a pale restraining hand against his chest before she let it fall back to her side. "Please, sir," she insisted. It was a bold maneuver, he thought, but not bewildering. Akira had always been difficult to cow.

The president scowled, but it was mostly for show. His gaze raked Akira's body slowly, from head to toe. He admired the clean precision of her appearance, from her porcelain skin to the sharp-pressed lines of her lab coat. Her painted lips were crimson, and he imagined slapping her to see if they matched the color of her blood. He watched in fascination as her lower lip trembled and wondered idly if his expression had given him away.

Appeased by this crack in her stoicism, the president relented. "Fine," he barked. "You have five minutes." He removed his jacket and hung it carefully on the back of his chair. Gesturing for Akira to speak, he rounded the desk and leaned against it. His motions were predatorial. Akira moved closer and swallowed, returning the president's attention to her slender neck. He contemplated the many pleasant things he could do to her neck, in lieu of snapping it.

Akira cleared her throat. "Sir, Violet Murphy contacted me. She offered to return to the Science Bureau for, in her words, an information exchange. She is eager to learn about our projects, and in return, she is willing to share more of her knowledge, possibly even some of her parents' unpublished work." At this, Akira's brown eyes flashed. The president merely held her gaze and smiled. "Candidly, sir, this is highly suspicious. Ms. Murphy had a decidedly negative experience with us. It is unlikely that she would freely return. She claims that her visit stirred her scientific curiosity, but I believe that she is fishing for something."

"And what did you tell her, Dr. Tanaka?"

"I thanked her for her interest and said that I would bring her suggestion to my superiors."

"Very good," the president replied. He lifted himself away from the desk and stalked closer. "Deflect her, Doctor. Even if Ms. Murphy suspects that something untoward happened to her, she cannot prove it. And we have already procured what we need from her for now."

"Yes, Mr. President."

Akira turned to leave, but the president pushed into her space and she stopped. He drew his fingers up the straight line of her throat. "Schedule an appointment soon, Dr. Tanaka. A proper appointment. A long one. It's been a while, and we have unfinished business."

Akira tilted her head into his caress then fled like a panicked gazelle.

Two days later, monumental news was disseminated to every household.

Project Pioneer was an unmitigated success. Sadly, there was no salvageable territory on Earth, but no matter, because humanity had found a new home, and it was move-in ready. An advance team was already making preparations for relocation, aided by the census data.

A carefully orchestrated feel-good blitz went on for weeks. Video screens citywide blazed with digital fireworks and buoyant aphorisms. A lavish celebration was held in Government Square at which the president made an eloquent speech. Neighborhood parties were organized to commemorate humanity's fresh start.

Details about the imminent relocation were sparse. The Communications Bureau relied on nebulous phrases like *clean* and *safe* and close-up images of flourishing plants and commonplace objects. No hard data or verifiable facts were revealed about the new planet. In-depth briefing packets were promised in the coming months, and the masses were content to wait. Similarly, when they were told that Pioneer had found nothing on Earth that remotely approached the potential of their celestial destination, most citizens gave it no further thought. They *wanted* to leave.

A few strong-willed journalists tried to dig deeper, but they were quietly suppressed. The government's campaign proceeded unchallenged. Sentiment trumped substance, and the people did not push back. They were starved for optimism, even more than they had realized.

No one was complaining about the census anymore.

"This is ridiculous," Emily huffed. "We don't know *anything*. The president is not Moses, and I am not blindly following him to the so-called Promised Land. I want details, goddamn it." She flopped onto the pillows of her bed, pink-cheeked and irritable.

"I agree," Violet concurred emphatically. The unmistakable sounds of late-night dinner preparation attended her words. "We know nothing about the planet's size, atmosphere, climate, ecology, or geology. For goodness' sake, we don't even know where it's *located*." Violet sucked air through her teeth, and the background noise abruptly stopped.

Jack cringed in blind sympathy. "You okay, Violet?"

"Mmm, yes." She raised her voice so as to be heard over a gush of running water. "My knuckles are scraped up, and I got a smidge of salt on them. It's nothing."

Jack was certain that Violet would not want him to dote. He bit the fleshy inside of his cheek and envisioned pecking a kiss on her injured knuckles, then he resumed the conversation. "My coworkers call it 'a matter of trust.' *Pfft.*" Even without video, Jack's disdainful air quotes were loud and clear. "They trust the government. They have faith that we will receive the information we need when the time is right." Jack rapped on Olivia's bedroom door and wordlessly laid a stack of folded laundry on her dresser. She smiled and returned to her homework. "For now," Jack said as the door creaked shut, "they seem content to celebrate. There's a bloody happy hour almost every day. I'm lucky to keep my team at their desks past 4:00 p.m."

"They trust the government? What does that even *mean*?" Mason asked scathingly. "Three-quarters of the population is employed by a government bureau, and most of us are clueless about anything beyond our limited purview. We operate in silos, isolated, without transparency. It never seemed to matter much before, but now it looks like a big fucking problem. I bet only a handful of top officials are fully briefed on Project Pioneer—and as we've seen, they aren't inclined to talk about it." A drone of agreement drifted from where Mason's DC rested on the arm of the sofa. It was enough affirmation to keep him planted on his soapbox. "Remember what I told you about temping on Pioneer? Ultrahigh security and controls. Weapons. Secretive to the point of absurdity. In the context of the Big News, those memories are even more unsettling." Pounce reacted to Mason's anxiety by rubbing her cheek against his socked feet, which were bouncing restively on the floor. He reached down to pet her, and she licked his hand comfortingly. "Sure, it was only one day, but *nothing* that I witnessed was positive, optimistic, or even tenuously suggestive of us being on the cusp of humanity's salvation. The tone was way off. Add Violet's experience at the Science Bureau, and it's awfully hard to justify any level of trust in what's happening. Something is wrong."

After Mason wound down, the discussion meandered for a while. They did little more than paraphrase and reiterate, second verse same as the first. They wallowed in their collective disgruntlement until eventually, Violet rallied them to action. "I've contacted Dr. Tanaka twice, but she's not biting. Clearly, I am not welcome at the bureau. I hate knowing that animals are imprisoned there—animals in need of rescue that I abandoned because I couldn't get my shit together." Three voices piped up to dispute this characterization, but Violet barreled ahead. "*Plus*, I can't help but think that whatever is being done to those animals is connected to the Big News. Maybe they're being experimented on to see if they can survive where we're going. I'm not sure. All I know is that they were terrified."

The group shuttlecocked ideas, but Violet's drugged-up recollections were simply not enough to go on. When the grandfather clock downstairs chimed Westminster Quarters, Jack took it as a sign. "Mason," he said, "I think it's time for plan B." Oddly, he was reluctant to be more explicit. Feeling as off-key as the timeworn clock, Jack realized that he was genuinely concerned that their call might be monitored. It seemed utterly preposterous, and yet the others followed his example. It was understood that Mason would use his hacking prowess to snoop, but they shied away from discussing specifics.

Gradually, their prattle came to a natural end. Once they said goodbye, Emily rose from her bed and crossed over to a window. She slipped between the panels of thick, rose-colored drapery and peered into the night, her nose brushing the chilly glass. The sky was a bruised mass of black, navy, and plum sprayed with pinprick stars and gauzy clouds. The grassy hills were dipped in molten silver, and an enchanting fog clung to the far-off border of the forest. Emily inhaled the landscape like a dying breath. "You know the worst thing about this?" she whispered dolefully to the moon. "It's that leaving Earth isn't a reason to celebrate at all."

CHAPTER 12

HEADACHES

Mason pried open his eyes and stared at the nail pops that protruded from the bland drywall ceiling above his bed. "Cancel wake-up," he grumped, causing the gentle peal of Tibetan bells to die away. Pounce leaped onto the bed with a low-key meow, and the pair stretched languidly until the muscle in Mason's left shin involuntarily contracted. Mercilessly awake now, Mason massaged the spasming muscle and made an endorphin-fueled decision. Today was the day. He pawed under the quilt for his DC and called in sick to work.

Enjoying the rare freedom, Mason took his time with his morning ablutions and lingered over a decadent breakfast. Soon enough, however, he was buzzing with caffeine and eager to get started. He shimmied to the back wall of the packed walk-in closet beside the bed. Careful not to dislodge clothes from their hangers, he delved into two crates of custom computer gear that were concealed behind spare pillows and a stack of faded linens. After gathering the necessary equipment, he cleared the dining table and assembled his workstation.

Although Mason was keen to impress his friends, their safety was paramount. Therefore, no one knew that he was about to hack the Science

Bureau. They could not be implicated if things went sour. Only Pounce bore witness from her perch on the kitchen counter. Her tail swished lazily while she watched Mason launch a decoy program on his PC to simulate his usual online activity then boot up a Linux-like machine with complicated extensions. Settling behind an octopus of cables and hardware, Mason felt pumped about the challenge and excited to flex his covert skills. He created a spoofed IP address and took an array of other precautions. When he was satisfied, he chuffed a deep breath, ran a screaming-fast script, and began to stalk his prey.

In short order, Mason discovered that Dr. Akira Tanaka was affiliated with an ambiguously named Project Noah. Unlike Pioneer, Noah was not widely known to the public—at least, Mason had never heard of it. The two projects appeared to be closely related, though, based on the number of Pioneer references in Dr. Tanaka's files. Mason tried to probe deeper, but security was intense. He was begrudgingly impressed. He breached an interesting-looking file directory and caught some curious flashes of data, but mere minutes after his infiltration, he was being hotly pursued like ghosts on Pac-Man. Flop sweat prickled on his scalp and underarms. Pounce shifted and rumbled uneasily on the counter. Unable to shake his pursuers, Mason cracked into a folder called Testing Protocols and grabbed what he could before he retreated, worriedly covering his tracks.

Mason's finely honed instincts were blaring that he had been nailed. He hastened to transfer the downloaded file to a flash drive, then he disassembled his setup while distractedly recording his observations and adding them to the drive. "Come here, Pounce!" he hollered. Unsure if the cat was nearby and unwilling to spare the time to look, his voice was unusually strident. Pounce hopped onto Mason's vacated chair with a drawn-out yowl. "I'm sorry, I'm sorry," Mason cooed. "You need to hold this for me, okay?" He clipped the mini flash drive's carabiner to Pounce's collar.

Both man and beast winced at the sound of obnoxiously loud pounding on the apartment door. Pounce sprinted away with her charge, vanishing into the shadows beneath the bed. Mason eyed the gear on the table. He seized items wildly and tossed them into his kitchen drawers. "Hold on! I'm coming!" he shouted, but the hammering intensified, and Mason understood that he could delay no longer. He shoved the larger pieces of equipment under the sofa on his way to the door. The instant it was unlocked, two black-clad security officers pushed inside. He attempted to block the intruders, but a beefy hand landed on his shoulder and turned him around. Surprised by the physicality, Mason allowed his arms to be yanked behind his back where they were held in place with an iron grip.

Mason stewed in impotent fury as the other officer ransacked his home and piled his poorly hidden hardware on the dining table. To no avail, Mason insisted on receiving an explanation for the raid, and he wrenched his arms repeatedly, trying to intervene. Drawers crashed to the floor, furniture was displaced, and soft goods were scattered. The officer spent an inordinate amount of time in the walk-in closet, systematically dismantling it as if he were hoping to find Narnia and not just a recreational hacker's cache. When he finally emerged, he summoned a forensic team to collect the confiscated items and rejoined his colleague at Mason's side.

Up close, Mason recognized this officer from patrols in his neighborhood. The man had very dark skin that made the lightly pigmented birthmark above his eyebrow stand out like a flare in a salt mine. Although Mason had not gotten a good look, he guessed that the person restraining him was Birthmark's long-haired partner who sported a distinctive topknot. Mason had exchanged pleasantries with these men countless times, which made his current predicament even more surreal.

"Please, I know you guys must recognize me," Mason wheedled. He hissed in pain when he tried to roll his shoulders. "I'm not a threat." Topknot increased the tension on his arms and shuffled closer, choking Mason with halitosis and cheap cologne. "There's no need for this," he persisted, his voice high-pitched under duress. "You're hurting me and destroying my stuff. You haven't even charged me with a crime."

A cutting gasp echoed from the foyer. Mason was spun around to face the uninvited guest. His shoulders flirted dangerously with dislocation, and he had to blink hard to chase away tears. His vision cleared to reveal Consuelo in the doorway. She was wrapped in a tasseled burgundy shawl, hands on her hips, boiling like a teapot. It had taken a few minutes, but the cavalry had arrived, bidden by the kind of unholy noise that even a hearing-impaired supercentenarian would notice. Since the door had been left ajar, Mason presumed that sundry neighbors had poked inside and chose not to intervene. Consuelo, on the other hand, was 120 pounds of outrage. "What is happening here?" she bellowed. "Release him!"

The unfettered officer took an ominous step forward, and sirens blasted in Mason's head. Reeling from his own rough treatment, he did not trust these people with Consuelo. He instinctively jerked his arms again but stopped when the bones of his left wrist shifted unnaturally. "Consuelo, please. Go back to your apartment," he pleaded. "I'll be fine." The older woman peered at him for a suspended moment. "*Please.*" Something of his desperation must have bled out because Consuelo relented without comment, though her eyes were clouded with worry. As she muttered an impressive selection of fretful expletives, Pounce darted across the room and tailed her out the door.

Mason expelled a breath. He was relieved to know that his girls were out of harm's way. "We're taking you into custody," Topknot barked. He shoved Mason and relinquished his hold. Mason pivoted to face the officers. He flexed his arms gingerly and rotated his aching shoulders. He felt hot and sweaty, flushed from nerves and discomfort. His apartment seemed dreamlike and frayed at the edges. The officers were tense and watchful, but they gave Mason a minute to regroup while they conversed out of earshot. Mason measured his bad-tempered captors and tried to quash the burgeoning panic in his chest. The crime rate in Apricus was extraordinarily low. For the most part, the Security Bureau handled domestic disturbances and misdemeanors like public intoxication and petty theft. Officers were bound by well-established law enforcement standards and practices. Yet here Mason stood, toeing a dislocated sofa cushion on the floor of his ravaged home and cradling a swollen wrist. It looked like the fair treatment rule book had been forsaken, discreetly cremated by the government with bootleg copies of the Quran and *Fahrenheit 451*, and Mason wondered exactly how much trouble he was in.

"What are the charges?" Mason repeated. He lifted his chin and planted his feet in a wide stance, but his attempt at bravado was betrayed by the frightened wobble of his voice.

"You'll be questioned at the bureau," Topknot replied. "If charges are filed, you'll be informed." He gave Mason a once-over. "Will you accompany us willingly?" His fingers toyed with the shiny metal restraints that dangled threateningly from his belt.

"Yes," Mason gulped, swallowing the word, momentarily forgetting how to speak and breathe at the same time. "Fine. Yes. I will."

Jack propped his elbows on the desk and massaged his temples. The military had been stockpiling gargantuan stores of goods for relocation, and though this was understandable, it was becoming impossible for his team to fulfill day-to-day orders. His stomach growled, reminding him that it was late. He wondered if Mason would be interested in sharing a pizza. He would even spring for the caramelized onions that his friend liked so much. He texted Mason for the third time that day, with no better luck. When he called, he was routed to voicemail. His fingers tapped a twitchy rhythm on his thighs. Jack slumped in his chair and started to worry.

Apart from a crushing headache, the crosstown journey was easy and unexciting. The polished stone pathway to Mason's apartment complex shimmered with bluish lamplight, impossible puddles in the skyless drought of the cavern. Jack lifted his bloodshot eyes to the hulking gray structure that loomed ahead. He picked up his pace when Mason's unit came into view.

Poised at Mason's door, icy tendrils of apprehension skated up Jack's limbs. He touched the doorbell icon on the keypad then knocked with sufficient force to bruise his knuckles. On a whim, he jiggled the fail-safe door handle. The unlocked door drifted open, and Jack stepped cautiously inside. The lights were on, revealing an ugly scene. Mason's home was upturned, and its owner was nowhere in sight. Jack's headache hit a shrieking climax. He closed the door and made a quick circuit of the compact space. He checked the bathroom first, to confirm that the apartment was empty. Everywhere, there were ominous signs of a search, a struggle, or both. He righted furniture, picked up objects off the floor, replaced drawers, and straightened the lopsided wildlife photos on the walls. He called for Pounce as he worked, but she was as absent as her human. Jack's gut told him not to contact the Security Bureau about a possible break-in. He snatched an analgesic from the bathroom and left.

Back at the train station, the ambient lighting transitioned to a soothingly dim nighttime mode. Jack crumpled onto an unoccupied bench and thumbed a message to Violet and Emily with his eyes half-closed, willing the pain in his head to abate. He was being atypically terse, but in his present state, he could not bring himself to care. A gaggle of students in tacky university sweatshirts flocked the platform, and Jack's tension ratcheted up and up and up. To his relief, however, the group was rather subdued and bookish, not pub-crawlers. An image of a decked out, college-aged Olivia flitted by his mind's eye, making him inexplicably sad. He shrugged off the sensation and finished typing.

Violet replied almost instantly, with Emily hot on her heels. The women were expressly troubled and did not believe that Jack was overreacting. He could not decide if he was reassured or disappointed. Emily offered to meet up with him to talk about what to do. She was working late at the museum, supervising the packing of artifacts for relocation. Jack's stomach gurgled. He felt increasingly unfocused and emotional. His typing remained brusque. When Violet asked about his last meal, he admitted that he was feeling ill. It was enough of an answer.

A speedy train ride later, Jack dawdled outside the museum campus in a section of Apricus that was hectic during the day but eerily vacant and sparsely lit at night. In stark contrast to the utilitarian architecture of most public sites, the U-shaped campus was designed for beauty. The white-washed buildings were fashioned with sweeping curves and decorated with lively murals. A thick carpet of lichen clung to the adjacent cave walls, adding natural color to the scene. Emily snatched her overnight bag. She kept it in her office for when she lost track of time and had to sleep on the lumpy sofa. As she jogged down the front steps of the largest building, her footfalls cut the stillness like the heavy clip-clop of a Clydesdale. She spotted Jack easily, suspended in the pale glow of a VDU that was promoting upcoming events.

Jack raised a hand in greeting. Crossing the distance, Emily called, "Violet says you get headaches when you skip meals, big guy. Let's eat. There's a place near the train station that's open until midnight." When she reached Jack's side, they shared a fleeting, one-armed embrace, and Emily allowed him to remove the bag from her shoulder. "I'm going to miss the train, but I have my overnighter, so..." She motioned to the bag and gave Jack a sanguine smile.

"So, you can stay at my house, of course. I know how much you love my mum's cooking." Jack's grin was sincere but quickly melted. "Except I was thinking we might want to camp out at Mason's apartment."

Emily nodded and started to walk. She bit her lip, and worry lines marred the skin above her prominent nose. "Let's get to the restaurant so you can fuel up and tell me more about what's happened." They followed the footpath in companionable silence. The air smelled musty, despite the steady hum of the dehumidifiers, audible now that most businesses in the area were closed. Eventually, Emily sensed that they were not alone on the path. She peeked over her shoulder and relaxed when she saw the security patrol. At a fork in the path, Emily paused to check on Jack, and the patrol veered right. Jack's posture was stiff, and his hairline was darkened with sweat. "Hey, we're almost there. Are you gonna make it?" Emily asked half-jokingly, sculpted blond eyebrows arched in query. Ascribing his anxiety to the jackhammering in his head and the mystery of Mason's absence, Jack nodded and turned left.

There were hardly any customers at the restaurant, just a few inconspicuous people who had opted not to eat alone at home. The tables and chairs were crudely mismatched, and the walls were unadorned, but the establishment was clean and smelled wonderful. The soft lighting was borderline romantic, made moot by the muffled thump of rock music from the kitchen. Jack ate voraciously, and his headache subsided. Emily matched him in appetite and enthusiasm. When Jack suggested sharing a dessert, her retort was a saucy, "Get your own!" Between bites, Jack explained what had transpired and why he was apprehensive. He tried Mason's DC again, but it remained a dead end. Emily needed no further convincing. She folded her napkin decisively on the tabletop and agreed that they should return to their missing friend's apartment.

The front door was closed but unlocked, exactly as Jack had left it. He deposited Emily's bag in the foyer and headed for the bathroom. He noted sadly that the place was still in considerable disarray, in spite of his earlier efforts. Emily noticed, too, and felt compelled to tidy up. She scowled at the walk-in closet where Mason's belongings painted the floor like blood spatter at a crime scene. Tiredly, she leaned on the sofa to remove her boots. She heaved a whistling sigh, flexed her stockinged toes…and promptly stepped on a sharp object. Cursing roundly and imaginatively, in three languages, Emily bent down to identify her assailant. Alarmed, Jack tumbled out of the bathroom, hands clumsily fastening his pants. Before he could speak, Emily held up a wafer-like computer chip. "It's a safe bet that Mason was hacking today," she declared grimly, "and it didn't go well." She arose from her crouch and joggled her maligned foot.

"But he didn't say anything," Jack countered, wincing at the boyish whine in his voice. He looked over at the dining table where Mason's laptop was conspicuously AWOL. "Wouldn't he have told us if he was going to do it today?"

"Maybe he didn't want us to worry."

"Well, that worked out splendidly."

Emily collapsed gracelessly to the floor at the entry to the closet. Jack sat on the edge of the bed, facing her. His button-down shirt was wrinkled, and the collar was itchy and moist, chafing his neck. He rested his elbows on his knees and cradled his head in his hands. "We should update Violet," he said without looking up. "I know it's late, but…"

"Yeah," Emily exhaled. "She'll slay us if we don't tell her about this right away."

Jack joined Emily on the floor. They used his DC to initiate a video chat, smooshing together so that they would both be visible on-screen and elbowing each other like petulant children. They were surprised to find Violet in the barn. She was sweaty and winded. Her favorite chambray shirt was stained, and alfalfa was tangled in curls of hair that had escaped from her loose, lopsided bun. "I was restless," she explained, "and there's never a shortage of things to do around here, so…" The sentence trailed off, and her image jiggled madly. "Here. Say hello to Firestorm while I finish cleaning this trough." Violet braced her DC on a hayrack and ducked out of sight. They heard the slosh of running water, and then a wet muzzle filled the screen. Jack and Emily called out enthused greetings and were delighted to receive a cheerful neigh in return. Firestorm bobbed his head in reaction to their voices. They glimpsed his forehead and ears before his muzzle hijacked the screen again. He nosed the DC, which fell forward with a thud. The ensuing laughter temporarily staunched the dread that was intensifying with every hour of Mason's disappearance.

Violet returned swiftly, impatient for an update. She rescued her DC from the hayrack and sat cross-legged on a bench across from Firestorm's stall. Moonbeams dripped from a skylight above Violet's head. Her labors had sent jetties of detritus into the air, minute flecks of feed and bedding and dust that glinted in the light, sinking slowly, resembling snow flurries on a still night. The resultant tableau was earthy and ethereal in equal parts. Beguiled, Jack stared at Violet for a tick. But then he took the lead in briefing her, and the jovial mood leaked away as he spoke.

All of a sudden, Pounce slunk out from under the bed. She hesitated when the quilt was still draped comfortingly over half her body, but she continued at Emily's low, affectionate coaxing. Out in the open, Pounce was agitated. Her tail twitched sharply, and her ears were flattened. She did not withdraw, but she rebuffed all attempts to hold or pet her as she prowled across Jack's outstretched legs over and over. Feeling helpless, the trio conferred about the cat's troubling behavior until Emily broke the stalemate with a harsh inhale. She leaned forward to squint at Pounce's collar. On the cat's next pass, Emily gently grasped her collar at the bottom and twisted it up to reveal the carabiner that had been camouflaged by her silver-and-black coat. Pounce stopped pacing. She sat on her haunches and patiently tolerated Emily's manipulations.

"Look! It's a flash drive. Mason must have clipped it here for safekeeping." Emily's voice was spirited but strained. She was optimistic that the drive would have answers but troubled that Mason had felt the need to take this step in the first place. As she darted to her overnight bag to collect her DC, these feelings churned in a nauseating rhythm, interwoven, rising and falling like children playing double Dutch.

CHAPTER 13

DOMINO

In the molasses hours, when late night clung to early morning, sticky and slow, Emily burrowed her feet into the cushions of Mason's sofa and peered over to the neatened kitchen where Jack was rustling up a snack and feeding Pounce too many cat treats. Freshly showered, Violet squinted at the spreadsheet on her computer monitor and cradled a mug of hot cider. The flash drive's contents had been transferred to Emily's DC, and she was sharing her screen with Violet. They were disinclined to send the actual files, ever more circumspect as Mason's disappearance stretched.

Jack settled next to Emily on the sofa. He bore a glossy ceramic plate piled high with warm chocolate chip cookies that smelled enticingly of butter, vanilla, and brown sugar. "What do we know?" he asked. Pounce curled up beside him and fell instantly into slow-wave sleep.

Emily set her DC on the coffee table and activated the projector. Images bloomed in the air above the table, hovering, vivid and crisp. She nabbed a cookie, gesturing with it as she spoke, while Violet manipulated the screen remotely. "Mason's drive contained a folder called Testing Protocols. The properties identify the owner as Dr. Akira Tanaka, so there's no doubt he was snooping. The folder has only one file, but it's a big one." Emily took a bite of cookie, cupping her hand under her chin to catch any crumbs.

Being cookie-less, Violet picked up the narrative. "As you can see, the file name is Active Inventory, which is surprisingly vague. I would have expected Akira's records to be meticulously labeled, so my guess is that the genericness is intentional. The file holds reams of data."

"Considering the folder and file collectively," Emily piggybacked, "we can deduce that Akira's team is doing some kind of testing on the items in this inventory. At least, that's our working theory." Jack nodded; it was a logical conclusion. Emily's tired, itchy eyes darted here and there, looking for a way to dispose of her crumbs without getting up. Jack held out the plate. Emily smiled gratefully, brushed off her hands, and snatched another cookie. "For energy," she whispered conspiratorially as Violet started speaking again.

"I haven't had a lot of time to study the data, but much of it is recognizably biological. There are a bunch of codes, though, and no key. I would call that an oversight, except I don't see Akira being so sloppy. I have to assume that the key is purposely missing or housed in a separate file that we don't have."

Violet took an inelegant slurp of her cider in the unselfconscious manner of someone too keyed up to care. Emily filled the pause. "Even without a key, Violet was able to decipher enough of the inventory to determine that many of the items in it are plants and animals. We can't tell how or why they are being tested, though."

"That's right," Violet affirmed. "At least a hundred of the entries are plants." She spent the next few minutes deftly navigating the file to highlight her findings.

Jack tried to follow the tachycardial pulse of data, but despite the fact that he used spreadsheets daily at work, it was making him nauseous. Maybe it was the lack of control, or fatigue, or the infinitesimal flicker of the projector. Whatever the cause, it was time for him to interject. "They might be determining what to bring when we relocate," he offered. "Like,

which plants will survive in the new environment. Dr. Tanaka evidently has
a thing for plants. After all, she lured Violet to the Science Bureau and took,
uh, *extreme measures* to learn about the Murphy farm."

"I'm okay, Jack," Violet murmured. The grace of her smile did more to
quell the breakers of acid in his stomach than the fact that she had stopped
scrolling in order to focus on him. "But speaking of my misadventure at
the bureau," she redirected, "the inventory includes a substantial number of
animals. The file uses binomial scientific names, and animals are harder for
me to recognize, but I know enough to be dangerous. See item 147? Procyon
lotor. That's a raccoon."

"I think I prefer my field," Jack griped. "You know, the one where we
call soap, *soap*, not sodium hydroxide."

Emily nudged him teasingly with her elbow. "I'm impressed, Jack. I
wouldn't have guessed a suit like you would know that sodium hydroxide is
used as the saponification alkali for most soap."

"Saponi-what?" Jack sputtered. "You're just making up words…aren't
you?" Emily and Violet laughed, and Jack played right along, pleased to
make them giggle, even at his own expense. "And I'll have you know, I don't
even own a suit."

Too soon, the levity fractured and Violet pressed on, sobering as she
spoke. "Anyway, the animals are trickier for me to identify at a glance, but
the nomenclature is easy enough to look up. It appears that there may also
be some entries that are neither plant nor animal."

"You mean, like, minerals?" Jack asked.

"I'm not sur—"

Violet's reply collided with Emily's simultaneously uttered, "Shit!" as a
spray of airborne cookie crumbs disturbed the projector like a comet's tail
passing too close to the earth. "Shit, shit, shit!" Emily intoned, reaching for
her DC. "I just remembered!" To free her hands, she shoved half a cookie
into her mouth and continued talking, loath to spare the time to chew and

swallow. "There was an audio file on the flash drive that we haven't listened to. It's super short, less than a minute, but damn, we probably should have played it first. I can't believe I forgot about it!"

Emily stabbed at her DC, retrieving the wayward file with trembling fingers. Her blouse was peppered with crumbs, and a streak of chocolate painted her bottom lip. A splotchy flush stained her pale skin from cheeks to décolletage. Lost in a fluster of self-recrimination, she flinched when Jack's hand landed on her shoulder, hot and clammy but comforting. "It's okay, Em," he crooned. "We can listen to it now. No harm's been done." For an instant, Emily thought uncharitably that Violet had better drop her coyness and lay a conclusive claim on Jack or else Emily would make a move on him herself. But it was a transient thought, forgotten before she hit play.

Pounce roused immediately at the sound of Mason's resonant baritone. She sat at attention, ears and whiskers pointed ahead and pupils blown wide. Reflexively, Jack leaned forward in solidarity. Mason sounded harried. His breathing was fast and heavy as he pushed out his words:

Project Noah. N-o-a-h. Tanaka is the lead. Pioneer is referenced all over her files, but Noah is clearly its own thing. Highly technical data. Top secret security clearance. Had time to snag only one file, but it sees a ton of action, so it must be important.

"Damn… That didn't do anything to ease my mind," Jack fretted. "I've never heard Mason sound so, uh, frazzled. And that background noise was him manhandling his gear. Mason *never* does that. He treats his techie stuff like it's made of spun glass."

Emily sank into the sofa cushions and self-soothed with another cookie. Her eyes flitted around the apartment worriedly. "Yeah, he must have known they'd caught him," she said. Jack rose to fetch her a glass of water and a napkin. "Considering the state of this place, they weren't too gentle about taking him into custody. Should we try to find out if he's been charged with a crime?"

"Mason's smart," Violet asserted. "He would have erased his trail enough to avoid charges. Security is probably just questioning him, trying to scare him a little. If we meddle, it might do more harm than good." Violet hid her anxious expression behind her mug. She sipped her cider, wishing that she had had the foresight to fortify it with bourbon. "I say we wait a few more hours."

Emily agreed then watched Jack shuffle back from the kitchen. She hummed her thanks and guzzled the water, appreciative of his effortless kindness. Jack was a natural caretaker and nurturer. It was hard for his friends to fathom that he knew his way around a rifle.

"Meanwhile," Violet sighed, "we should talk about the content of Mason's message. Project Noah…" Violet pronounced the name slowly and pensively, as if she were casting a spell, compelling the letters to reveal their secrets.

"Noah could be a person's name," Emily posited, "but more likely, it's a biblical reference. If Project Pioneer is about getting the hell out of Dodge, then Pr—"

"Huh?" Jack's head was tilted like a perplexed puppy's.

Heavy-hearted, Emily puffed out a breath. "Ugh. Never mind." *Mason* would have understood the American idiom. She leaned her head against the sofa and closed her eyes.

"It's a reference to Dodge City, Kansas." Emily's head shot up in surprise. "What?" Violet smirked. "Cowboys are hot." Emily chirped a startled laugh.

For a moment, the women exchanged impish smiles while Jack stewed in confusion. "Okay," he drawled. "I think we're way off track here."

"It stands to reason," Emily resumed, "that Project Noah is about what to bring when we relocate. They must think they're being clever, a government that preaches agnosticism tipping its hat to an eminent religious text. Assholes. In the Old Testament story, Noah built an ark to save his family and pairs of all the world's animals from a great flood. Maybe the animals that Violet discovered at the Science Bureau were captured for an analogous reason: to be shipped out with the humans when we leave."

"I wish I could get back inside the bureau," Violet groused. "After Mason returns, I'm going to pester Akira one more time."

The subsequent hours were a slog. They studied clues and bandied hypotheses as their minds gradually decelerated like boots laden with heavy snow. When full morning broke, there was nothing bright or new about it. They were still gathered in the jetsam of their missing friend's apartment, drained and distressed. At length, Jack was lulled into a doze by the sonic choreography of familiar voices, and shortly thereafter, they decided to break for sleep. On the verge of disconnecting, Violet exhaled sharply. "Why is everything hush-hush?" she growled. "If we're in this together, as our president is so fond of saying, then why have top secret projects? Why withhold basic details about what's coming?" Then, avoiding eye contact, Violet unloaded a host of unexpressed feelings that were pressing on her. "I believe something is terribly wrong. But even if everything was copacetic, I would not want to relocate. Unfathomable effort has gone into this so-called emancipation of humanity. Imagine if we had put even half that effort into healing our damaged planet. Not to sound like a temperamental child, but I don't want to go. This is my *home*, my *soul*. It's Firestorm, my mother's flowers, and the labor of my father's hands. I cannot imagine…" Violet's lament was left dangling, a bottleneck of passion and weariness. And though the words lingered unsaid at the periphery, it was clear that Violet did not intend to leave, no matter what her briefing packet would promise or what she might lose.

Emily's heart beat in unity. Jack's heart ached.

Mason shifted his weight to alleviate the pressure on his hips and repeated the litany for the umpteenth time since Topknot and Birthmark had deposited him in the bowels of the Security Bureau. "I was curious. I work at the Infrastructure Bureau. I was investigating some interesting threads I came across on a project. I was just having fun. I didn't know it would cause so much trouble." For the first hours of his detainment, Mason's responses had been less syncopated. He had offered up plump sentences, ripe with irrelevant context to obfuscate the truth. But it no longer mattered. Mason would not be inveigling his way to emancipation. His captors had stopped listening.

The two-man interrogation team had started with simple intimidation. They strapped Mason to a slatted metal chair in a dank, caliginous room. They revealed their sidearms, making a clumsy show of it like a couple of novice strippers trying to act natural on the pole. They snapped rapid-fire questions at him and interrupted frequently to attempt to ruffle him. There was no good cop, bad cop; both officers were decidedly bad. However, the weapons and the inhospitable setting had lost a bit of their intended shock value due to Mason's prior exposure as a Project Pioneer temp—not much but enough to keep him calm. Thus far, they had been unable to shake him from his answers.

Mason heard shoe scuffs on the bare floor and muffled voices. Hopeful for release, he opened his eyes, which had been closed against the perpetual glare of the overhead light. The officers were huddled in a far corner of the room. Without the glinting metal accents on their black uniforms, they would have melted, ninja-like, into the shadows. "Those outfits are poorly designed," Mason thought idly. "Security personnel should be plainly visible to people in need." A bubble of hysterical laughter was rising in his throat when a voice jarred him from the bitter irony of his reflections.

"You're not giving us a choice, Mr. Agu." The man sounded almost regretful, and Mason's stomach lurched. Before he could reply, a third man entered the room.

The newcomer strode directly to Mason's chair. He gripped Mason's biceps and leaned in close enough for Mason to smell his stale, oniony breath. "Hello, Mr. Agu. It seems my men have achieved no results, so sadly," he said, not looking sad whatsoever, "it is time for more aggressive measures." He spoke with a pitchy, eldritch accent, unidentifiable and unpleasant to the ear. He squinted at Mason with beady eyes then pushed away roughly. "The bureau has been experimenting with inventive techniques to loosen a recalcitrant suspect's tongue, but alas, test subjects are scarce. How lucky we are that you have fallen into our lap."

Beady Eyes paused when the room's door slid open. He extended his right hand but remained in the light where Mason could size him up. He was tall and reedy with uneven stubble and a greasy mop of black hair. A decorated senior officer, his uniform was surprisingly wrinkled and some of the insignia were askew. Mason could tell, though, that it would be a mistake to interpret the man's lack of martial bearing as weakness. He was a rusty knife, more deadly in its state of disrepair. A stocky woman who was dressed in the telltale white coat of the Science Bureau dropped a small object into his outstretched hand and promptly exited the room. Beady Eyes closed his fingers around it and smiled sickly.

Clutching the object, Beady Eyes walked behind the chair and leaned in closer and closer until his breath raised goose bumps on Mason's neck. He curled his arm around Mason's shoulder and unfurled his fingers to reveal a recognizable device. "Doctors use these to draw blood or inject medicine. Ingenious, really," he purred. "But I'm afraid this one won't heal you. No, no. You'll feel better only after you've answered our questions satisfactorily." His volume climbed steadily on the last four words, and he punctuated the sentence by jamming the device into the crook of Mason's arm. The effect was instantaneous. It felt like all the nerves in Mason's body were firing at once. Every cell was doused in acid, burning, burning, burning him away, until nothing was left, not even sensation.

Mason regained agonizing consciousness. He immediately wished to return to oblivion, but the pain no longer crested the threshold to send him under. Beady Eyes was crouched in front of the chair, eyeing Mason hungrily and bombarding him with questions about what he'd seen, what he'd stolen, whom he'd told. Mason was a trembling, discombobulated mess, but he was angry, too, and the anger lent him a modicum of clarity. Pain be damned, he would not give up his friends or confess to the copied file. As he had been fielding the same questions for hours, he recycled his answers in a breathless mantra and diverted most of his energy to coping with the hurt.

Beady Eyes noticed that his quarry's replies were robotic, that Mason had sunk into a nearly meditative state. "Oh no, no, no. You cannot hide," the man admonished. He administered more of the drug, and fresh pain exploded like a solar flare. Shooting, stabbing, scorching, it reduced Mason to ash. An involuntary scream clawed its way out of his throat, ragged and hoarse. "Are you ready to share?" Beady Eyes laughed. He clapped Mason's shoulder, and Mason swallowed another scream. He wondered if he had passed out again. A sickening wetness told him that he had lost control of his bladder, but he could not spare the energy to be embarrassed. He was too busy gasping for breath and willing his erratic heartbeat to level out.

Beady Eyes seized Mason's chin and jerked his head up from where it was tucked against his chest. The same worn-out questions were shouted, and Mason muttered the same answers, lacking the mental wherewithal to come up with new ones even if he had wanted to. Time skipped as he roiled in and out of awareness. "They're torturing me," he processed woozily. "There's no other word for this."

"Denmark stinks to high heaven," he slurred, throat raw and eyes blurry with tears. Puzzled by the non sequitur, his inquisitor determined that Mason was too loopy to continue and granted him a blessed break.

This time, Mason returned to consciousness sluggishly. Though the overt physical violence against him had been limited, the insidious injections left his entire body in enduring pain. Realizing that he was alone and unshackled, he began to tentatively stretch his limbs. A new security officer entered the room. She was a statuesque blonde, distantly reminiscent of Emily. Mason's heart pulsed happily in memory of his friend until ungentle hands hoisted him out of the chair without warning. He stifled a whimper and collapsed to the floor when his shaky legs would not support him. To her credit, the officer looked remorseful when she realized the extent of his suffering. Her orders were to escort him to the bathroom, and hearing this, Mason forced his sweaty, shuddering frame to move. She waited in the hallway while he used the toilet, washed up, and gulped water from the faucet to relieve his wrecked throat.

Mason was returned to the interrogation room. During his break, wall sconces had been activated to supplement the overhead lamp. His towheaded escort guided him to the chair but did not strap him down. Left alone, bruised, and baffled, Mason pondered his situation. The Security Bureau handled graffiti and drunken bar fights. Why would it even *have* restraint chairs and torture drugs? His contemplation was cut short when Beady Eyes reentered with a spectacled twentysomething wearing a lab coat. They were having a heated argument at low volume. Mason could pick up only snippets, but he heard "drug interactions" repeatedly. Despite the obvious age difference, the scientist held his ground, and Mason thought ruefully that there might be at least one person there who did not want to kill him. Ultimately, however, Beady Eyes yanked a familiar medical device from the other man's hand and ended the conversation.

"You're softened up now," his tormentor said. "Tender and juicy. So, let's lower your inhibitions, shall we? Get you more comfortable." The creepy language and the calloused hand on Mason's cheek made him a far cry from comfortable, and he felt like a pincushion as the vulnerable flesh of his inner elbow was jabbed again. A colossal surge of dizziness threatened to topple him, but he battled to stay alert. His eyes clenched shut, and his fingers scrabbled frantically at his thighs. They had switched to a different drug, one that was designed to take down his guard. It became increasingly difficult to concentrate, and he wondered if Violet had been dosed with a similar concoction.

The vertigo receded, leaving Mason floaty and sedate in its wake. The blonde officer reappeared and lingered near the door with the scientist. Beady Eyes restarted the inquisition, but he quickly realized that he had made a grave miscalculation. Unremitting pain had depleted Mason physically, but it had also raised his hackles and shored up his psychological defenses. He did not deign to answer a single question. "Listen," Mason mumbled, "if you won't believe the truth, then I'll make something up." For two hours, he regaled his captors with stories drawn from every spy drama he had ever read, and he shunned all attempts to return to reality. The drug lent him dramatic flair, and he suspected that he was genuinely entertaining. At one point, Mason caught the scientist rolling his eyes and palming his mouth to hide a smile. "What? I'm just like Scheherazade, tellin' stories to stay alive," Mason proclaimed flirtatiously. "A big, Black, manly Scheherazade." He grinned dopily. Beady Eyes was at a loss.

It was dawn when a lackey announced that the bureau had found nothing incriminating on Mason's confiscated equipment. Though Mason could not make out the particulars of the discussion, he recognized it as good news. The pharmacological effects of the injections were waning, but his head was still cottony and his whole body hurt. "Even my hair is sore," he thought sullenly.

Chuffing with annoyance, Beady Eyes dismissed the lackey and confronted Mason. "Mr. Agu," he began stiffly, "the bureau is satisfied that you are a second-rate hacker and petty nuisance." Mason bristled at the insult but said nothing. "While your actions caused no identifiable harm, your clearance has been stripped as a precaution, and therefore, you will be assigned entry-level work at the Infrastructure Bureau for the indefinite future." Beady Eyes stalked forward. He pushed Mason's knees apart, stepped as near as possible, and leaned in, gripping the back of the chair. "It would be a dire mistake to publicize your experience here. Stay out of trouble, and we will not meet again. You have been very trying, Mr. Agu. I will be pleased to see you go." Beady Eyes's face was too close. The man was sweat-sheened and rank, and his bushy eyebrows were creased into a spiteful frown. Mason fought the urge to turn away, unwilling to jeopardize his release. Unfortunately, his submission made no difference. In a flash, Beady Eyes grabbed Mason's arm. Before Mason could react, a third injection of the torture drug ignited his bloodstream. Ravenous pain consumed him, reducing his world to a swirling miasma of blinding, seething agony. Mason's body buckled, and he cried.

The others stared spiritlessly as Beady Eyes bailed out of the room. The interrogation had yielded naught of value, and as the officer in charge, he would need to document this glaring deficit in the president's report. They did not envy him the task. He had taken risks with the suspect's treatment, and it had not paid off. If you gambled, the president expected a royal flush. They watched Mason inhale panting breaths, slumped in the chair. They were stuck there until he recovered enough to be transported home. The scientist turned to his fair-haired companion. "Science is not meant for this," he declared, gesturing at Mason. "When you join the Science Bureau, you take a vow to use your knowledge to help people, not hurt them. No one wants to see another Dhaka Plague." The woman grimaced but stayed quiet. "And you all," he said, "are not equipped to handle serious crime. You've never dealt with offenses like terrorism and treason. With all due respect, your supervisor totally botched this interrogation. He got angrier instead of smarter. He failed to analyze the suspect's reactions and expected the drugs to do all the work."

The security officer massaged her temples. "Stop," she replied wearily. "I agree. This was a complete clusterfuck. The powers that be believe that the instability inherent in relocation will bring about a rise in crime, so the bureau must adapt. But we'll need to do loads better than we did with this guy." She marched over to Mason and nudged his shoulder, hoping to get him on his feet. The mild touch pierced Mason as brutally as a dagger serrating flesh and bone. He shouted gutturally then folded over, wheezing and shaking. The officer squatted down and peered into his glassy eyes. "He's in no shape to move," she said over her shoulder. "It's gonna be a while." Averse to witnessing Mason's prolonged suffering, the observers left the room.

Midmorning, Mason was escorted home by a couple of resentful security officers who had to carry the weight of his barely mobile body. They dumped him inside the apartment without a word. Emily was asleep on the bed, and Jack was resting on the sofa. They both startled when the door opened and the foyer light switched on. Spying over the back of the sofa, Jack watched the retreat of two telltale black uniforms and waited for the apartment door to shut. Mason was braced against the wall, collapsing in slow motion, dripping down like wet paint.

Jack raced to his side. Too late to stop Mason's inevitable descent, Jack cradled his friend's head before it hit the ground. Emily tried to sort out his limbs where they had landed in an awkward jumble. Mason peered up at them with half-lidded eyes riddled with broken blood vessels. He tendered a shaky smile then lost consciousness, willingly this time, having finally recognized safety after the incessant stress of his incarceration.

Emily and Jack doctored Mason as best they could, constrained by their inexperience and their hesitance to remove too much of his clothing. Emily used her DC to monitor his vitals. Jack applied cold packs to the swollen bruises on his arm, wrists, and ankles. Pounce sat on Mason's torso, periodically kneading his chest like baker's dough. When it became clear that Mason would not rouse on his own, they were unwilling to leave him on the floor. Emily cajoled softly in his ear while Jack tapped persistently on his bristly, salt-tracked cheek. The strategy worked. Mason even eked out the vim to shower, zombielike, and nibble on toast before he collapsed into bed.

Mason gave a bare-bones account of his ordeal, not always cogent, and promised more later. Jack and Emily were shocked. The heavy-handed treatment that Mason described was unquestionably illegal, a castoff of humankind's ugly past. Emily reclined on the bed and grazed Mason's scalp with her manicured fingernails. He surrendered to her tender ministrations and drowsily watched Jack pace. Pounce was nestled warmly against his side. Drifting into a proper sleep, Mason mumbled, "Well, y'all, I'd say we're onto something." Jack let out a yelp of laughter at the understatement. Emily shook her head and smiled at Mason sadly, indulgently, as he started to snore.

The incident report was impressively thorough, but fastidious reporting could not hide the fact that the bureau's response to the security breach had been sloppy. Dissatisfied, the president summoned the lead investigator. Beady Eyes strode confidently into the president's office and spouted an overly rehearsed speech about enhanced firewall protections and encryption measures.

Interrupting, the president snapped, "Perhaps you should wait until I ask you a question." He adjusted the cuffs of his crisp white shirt and folded his hands on the desk. He jerked his chin to indicate the report that was displayed on a large monitor on the office wall. "As the author of this report, you deliberately downplayed the threat assessment and, knowing my penchant for detail, you tried to bury your investigative failures in a parade of irrelevant facts and distracting appendices."

"No, sir, that's not true," Beady Eyes denied.

Accepting the challenge, the president's left eyebrow climbed mockingly toward his hairline. He spent the next hour asking questions that simultaneously poked holes in the report and satisfied his curiosity about the incident. By the end of the meeting, Beady Eyes had deflated like a popped balloon. Having never been offered a seat, he was still standing in front of the desk, nervously shifting his weight. The president studied him dispassionately. The officer's handling of the breach had been messy, much like his accent, unwashed hair, and scuffed boots. "I encourage you to resign," the president concluded, leaning back casually in his chair.

"No!" Beady Eyes exclaimed. He shuffled closer. "I've given my life to the bureau. Please, sir." The president allowed the man to continue pleading for a minute, amused by his desperate sputtering.

"Oh, come now," he interjected smoothly, having grown bored. "Are such theatrics necessary? You would think I'd just given you a death sentence."

"Didn't you?" Beady Eyes choked.

The president did not reply. He merely pointed to the door, smiling like the Grinch. When the officer departed, the president called for his assistant. "Change him to red," he ordered, "and bring me an unsweetened iced tea with peppermint."

Armed with the findings from his tête-à-tête with Beady Eyes, the president reread the incident report and its copious appendices. An entry in the hacker's contacts list caught his eye: *V. Murphy.* The report speculated that Mason had befriended Violet and two others six months ago. All four background checks were clean. Suspicious, the president devoted his day to research, inclined to handle the job directly. He excavated personal histories in order to draft psychological profiles and risk analyses. He pored over travel logs and phone records. Swallowing bile, he scrutinized the online nature-lovers community. And then, when the jigsaw puzzle of Mason's associations took shape, the president made some disturbing inferences. Heedless of the hour, he phoned Akira. "Dr. Tanaka," he said without preamble, "when Violet Murphy contacts you again, I want you to accept her overture."

"Sir," a croaky voice replied, "I seriously doubt that Ms. Murphy will be contacting me at 2:00 a.m." Overworked and sleep-deprived, Akira felt reckless and punchy. She rolled onto her back and got tangled up in her nightgown, but she was unmotivated to do anything about it. She became mesmerized by the light from her DC that was dancing on the ceiling.

"This is important, Doctor. Wake up and drop the sass. Or perhaps you would prefer to come to my office in the morning so that I can be assured of your attentiveness."

Fatigue deafened Akira to the unsubtle warning. "It *is* morning," she grumbled. The president did not respond. He waited her out as moments ticked by, a handful of overripe fruits falling heavily to the ground. Akira recognized the danger in the ponderous silence. "You have my full attention, sir," she amended. "My apologies."

"We need to find out what Ms. Murphy knows."

"What she knows about what, exactly?"

"Project Noah."

"What?!" Akira bolted upright in the bed, impeded by her twisted nightwear. "How could she know anything about Project Noah?" With characteristic efficiency, the president briefed Akira on the security breach and Violet's connection to the hacker. "Why wasn't I informed of the breach?" she demanded. "As the project leader, I should have been told immediately."

"I'm telling you *now*, Dr. Tanaka." And though he would not stroke her bruised ego, he added, "The officer in charge of investigating the incident has been...dealt with."

Akira shivered.

"The hacker accessed classified Project Noah documents. It is reasonable to assume that he will apprise his accomplices and they will desire to know more. Ergo, when Ms. Murphy inevitably contacts you, I want you to invite her to the Science Bureau. We will lay a trap for her, and like Mr. Agu, she will reveal herself as a threat."

"What kind of trap?"

"You will step away to attend to an urgent matter," the president explained, "and let her off the leash for a while. Security will monitor her to see what she does with her false freedom. Don't be obvious, Dr. Tanaka. She cannot know that she's being set up."

"I'm not an actress, sir. This is out of my wheelhouse."

"Perhaps you misunderstand, Doctor. This is not a request."

"I know," Akira conceded. "I am bothered, though, by the flagrant incursions of the Security Bureau into Science Bureau affairs and how their mission appears to have strayed from public safety. Sir, you used to spearhead the advancement of humanity through scientific innovation and community values, but lately, your focus has been…well, darker."

"Darker," the president scoffed. "My duty is to guide and protect. Regrettably, a firm hand is required at times. That is not darkness, Dr. Tanaka. It's reality. I cannot be weak. Neither can our security substructure. We are too close to achieving our dreams."

"I understand, sir, but the Security Bureau espouses methods that harken back to undeniably *dark* times in our history. I-I cannot participate if Ms. Murphy will be drugged again." Even through the brume of exhaustion that emboldened Akira, she knew that she was pushing her luck. Taking a deep, fortifying breath, she finished with, "I am a scientist. I don't want to be your tool in this."

"You should, Dr. Tanaka. Tools are useful." The words were an infected wound, oozing menace. After a loaded minute, however, the president chose to back down. He needed Akira's cooperation, and he could grudgingly admit, if only to himself, that he valued her opinion of him. "No drugs," the president pledged. "No security personnel on-site. Remote surveillance only." Met by silence, he tried harder to placate her. "Akira, please listen to me." She thawed a little at the use of her given name. "Ms. Murphy knows the hacker. It is my responsibility to ascertain if Project Noah, *your life's work*, is at risk. All you need to do is host her at the Science Bureau and step away for a time. As a bonus, you'll have another shot at reaping all that Murphy knowledge. I'm certain there is more you want to ask about that damned farm."

Akira recognized that she was being manipulated, but she could find no faults in the president's argument and had always been a willow to his wind. In spite of her distaste for the brutes in the Security Bureau, she believed in the president's endgame. She believed in *him*. If only they could achieve their goals without losing their souls along the way. "Who am I kidding?" she thought resignedly. "I lost mine years ago." She assured the president of her support, and they ended the call. She snugged into her bed, pressed her heated cheek against a cool pillow, and secretly hoped that Violet had given up and would not contact her again.

The president deftly unbuttoned his carmine-red blazer and took his seat at the head of the conference table. He could not abide unsightly creases. Wasting no time on civilities, he signaled for the senior deputy from the Security Bureau to begin the meeting. The deputy had the chiseled body of an athlete, accented by his close-fitting black uniform. The president admired the view, then he dragged his gaze over the assorted others who were gathered in the room. His sweep did not falter when he spotted Akira. After all, as the leader of Project Noah, her attendance was mandatory. Even so, he registered her presence with satisfaction, and perhaps some relief.

As soon as the deputy completed his report on the hacking incident, the president announced that the timeline would be accelerated once more. The group's muzzle-flash reaction was predictable. All propriety gone, everyone spoke over one another, a hail of shrill voices competing for dominance. A high-decibel call to order by the military's top leader silenced the cacophony, and the president smiled his gratitude. Ignoring all questions and objections, he commanded that Phase 2 move faster. "I want the briefing packets distributed in weeks, not months," he said. "I see the mutinous expressions on your faces, but this is not up for debate."

"Respectfully, sir, this will put untenable pressure on our teams!" squawked the petite, rail-thin deputy from the Education Bureau. "Isn't this an overreaction to a minor security issue?" Numerous heads bobbed in agreement.

"This is not an overreaction," the president denied. "We cannot permit even the faintest spark of doubt to grow. The hacking infraction is indicative of a greater threat." He looked to the eye candy from the Security Bureau for corroboration. The deputy nodded obediently. "I have studied your status reports," the president said. His implacable hazel eyes made fleeting contact with every subordinate in the room. "Drastic acceleration of the timeline is feasible with reprioritization and meticulous allocation of resources." When several mouths opened to protest, the president raised his voice in a rare display of anger. "I said this is not up for debate!" he shouted. "*Make it happen!*" He slammed his palm on the tabletop and stormed out of the noiseless room.

Mason Agu had not acted alone. It was more than supposition; the truth of it resonated in the president's bones. And he recognized the implications, even if his staff did not.

This was no one-and-done anomaly.

It was a nascent rebellion.

CHAPTER 14

TICKTOCK

The briefing packets arrived without fanfare on an unremarkable Tuesday morning. A personalized packet was transmitted synchronously to every citizen's DC. Gloriously colorful and ebullient, the packets explained the logistics of relocation in painstaking detail but offered scant information about humanity's heralded destination. An effusive video from the advance team rehashed the same stale talking points that had been drilled into the citizenry for three solid months. Hardly any new photographs were included, all 2-D close-ups.

Stepwise instructions covered how to disengage from employers and schools, which would be gradually shut down in the coming weeks. A calendar marked the progressive curtailment of community services. But by far, the most exhaustive information concerned the departure shuttles. Multimember households would have private, full-service quarters on board. Single-member households were required to share. It was unclear how long they would remain on the shuttles and if they would be transferred to a long-range transport for a lengthier journey. Restrictions on what to bring were numerous, and cargo would be inspected before boarding. No food, no plants, no pets. Possessions were itemized, down to the number of undergarments allowed per person.

Most important, every citizen was assigned to a color-coded departure group that corresponded with a date on the shuttle schedule. The populace would be evacuated in waves, and the first group would leave in less than three short months. The aggressive timetable distracted otherwise intelligent, rational people from the shadiness of the operation. Preoccupied by who else was in their boarding group and the belongings they must shed, most citizens paid no heed to the packets' glaring omissions. There were *dates* now. Shuttles would be launching very, very soon. It was *real*.

And if a person here or there felt a pang of nostalgia for Mother Earth, they swallowed the feeling and buried it deep in their belly, beneath a heap of unasked questions.

On Tuesday night, the president's alleged rebellion gathered virtually using souped-up DCs. As soon as Mason had been clearheaded enough after his interrogation to recognize the danger, he had insisted on warding the group against electronic monitoring. He installed black market software to thwart hackers and sophisticated encryption programs. Though nothing could be done about physical surveillance, Mason's upgrades would seriously hamper any digital stalkers. Thereby empowered to speak freely, the friends vivisected the spectacularly uninformative briefing packets. Their heated conversation surfed on choppy waves of outrage and despair, roiling and sour, and all the while, they skirted their shuttle assignments, unready to accept that when the departures began, some goodbyes would be forever.

Violet paced the span of her moonlit kitchen, clutching a forgotten glass of juice. Fleet-footed clouds cast the pale cabinetry and glittery quartz countertops in passing shadow. "It astonishes me," she ranted for the fifth time, "that the government continues to divulge next to nothing about our mysterious new home, not even its celestial *location*. Lord knows where we're going, but hey, at least we're clear on when the shuttles leave," she joked sarcastically.

Niggled by a different concern, Mason seized the opening provided by Violet's jeer. "I'm in the red group!" he blurted. The disclosure was met with rattled silence. He blathered on anyway. "So is my neighbor, Consuelo, and Trevor, my best friend at the bureau. Our departure date is *to be determined*. Maybe I'm reading too much into it, but that seems, uh…inauspicious." After a beat, Mason inquired, "What group are you all in?"

Evading the question, Emily sought to reassure Mason. "The government must still be working out kinks in the schedule. You have ample reason to be mistrustful, Mason, but being assigned to the red group can't mean anything bad. My grandparents are in the red group, and they are about as law-abiding and unobtrusive as you can get."

"You think it's an administrative delay? Yeah, that makes sense. I mean, aside from their dubious taste in friends, Consuelo and Trevor are squeaky-clean, too." Mason's self-effacing humor fell flat. "What's your group, Em?" He shifted restlessly on the sofa, careful not to jostle Pounce where she was snuggled up on his abdomen. There was solace in the slight, steady movement of her sleeping body.

"To avoid confusion, they should have waited until everyone had a departure date," Emily said. "I can't imagine why they rushed the packets. It's just one more item on our long list of unknowns." Aside from Violet's hum of agreement, no one reacted, and the leaden weight of unspoken words slowly suffocated them like a funeral shroud. Emily picked the salt off a *Brezeln*. Finally, she rolled her shoulders and sighed. "I'm in the yellow group," she offered. "I thought families would be kept together, so maybe my grandparents will be moved from red to yellow. I don't know."

Jack answered next. He was lounging on the salon floor in an ungainly sprawl, all arms and legs, his head resting on the pouf so that he could watch

Abigail darning socks over on the sofa. "Mum, Olivia, and I are in the blue group." Jack faltered then, knowing that he was about to concede the group's imminent separation. He cocked his jaw and forged on. "We're leaving in ten weeks." There was an audible gasp, then nothing but the faint notes of the sea shanty that Abigail was singing under her breath. Retreating to the bigger picture, Jack added, "I have colleagues at work who are blue, yellow, green, and purple."

"I've been assigned to the orange group," Violet said.

Emily recited the colors through a mouthful of pretzel. "Red, orange, yellow, green, blue, purple..." She swallowed and took a sip of water. "It's a veritable rainbow."

"Mmm-hmm," Violet replied, "but what's at the end of it?"

For all their fellowship, there were significant topics that the group did not broach on Tuesday or in the charged days that followed. Topics like the "no pets" policy. Every night, Mason played with Pounce and plied her with treats. He cuddled her with fierce tenderness, mumbling over and over into her fur that he did not want to leave her. Pounce bemusedly accepted the extra attention. Mason was certain that Violet would not desert Firestorm, that the orange group would be one woman short, and he hoped that his friend would adopt Pounce. "Would you like to live on a farm, sweetheart?" he whispered. Pounce *mrowl*ed softly, and Mason felt his throat tighten with unshed tears.

On Saturday afternoon, they convened for a video call. Jack was staying with Violet for the weekend. He had left work early on Friday, a remarkably effortless feat now that retail operations were being dismantled ahead of relocation. Jack's department would be shut down in less than a week, though his briefing packet cryptically promised a future role commensurate with his experience. Emily and Mason were invited to the farm as well, but they opted out in order to give the slow-footed couple a chance to act on their romantic chemistry before it was too late.

While the government had served up an anesthetizing IV drip of propaganda all week, the four friends had been dogged by a mounting sense of urgency. Therefore, they had no appetite for chitchat and dove headlong into problem-solving. They were desperate to find answers to their most pressing questions before time ran out. But while the others brainstormed, Jack disengaged, helplessly drifting until the conversation was a muzzy whirr. He gazed at Violet, enchanted by the freckles on her nose and the firelight caught in the tips of her eyelashes. She was reclining against him on the floor. His back rested against the couch, and his long arms were slung loosely around her waist. Their legs were tangled under the porcelain-tiled coffee table on which Violet's DC was braced. Jack spared a glance or two to admire the table's fetching floral design and luminous stained-glass accents, but his attention inexorably returned to Violet. Jack longed to stay in that moment forever, ensconced in beauty and warmth. His heart was breaking and breaking and breaking, knowing that he could not have it, could not keep her. And cracking like an egg, words spilled out of him.

"I don't want to say goodbye," he said, choking on air. He forced his eyes to the camera. "You are the best friends I have ever had. Supportive. Kind. You make me laugh—to feel a kind of careless joy I thought I had lost. But I cannot leave my family. Mum and Olivia need me. I need them, too." Jack gulped a breath and pressed his cheek to Violet's head. Her silky hair caught on his stubble. She was wriggling, trying to angle her body to face him, and he stilled her with gentle but insistent hands. "I thought—I hoped, dreamed—that I might have a future with you, Violet. Pretty flowers and sun-warmed skin and the taste of wine on your lips. But I have to go, and even though you haven't said so, I *know* you are not boarding a shuttle. I want to hear you say it. I need to hear it. And Mason and Emily," he continued, refocusing on the camera, "I want to know your plans, too. I don't want to guess. We have to be more open about this. T-to talk about our f-feelings and fears and all that other rubbish that Dr. Devi goes on about." Jack let out a self-conscious groan but did not stop. "I mean, we don't know if we'll be able to stay in touch after the departures. We have no clue where we're even going." For a moment, his voice became darkly singsong, and his eyes were glassy. "Lemmings, lemmings, to the sea," he murmured, then he cleared his throat. "And maybe I'm paranoid, but I think I'm being watched. I have no proof. Still, it's been bothering me since shortly after Mason's detention, and I'm tired of not saying anything. We *have* to say things. It's important."

Jack petered out before his monologue could fully unravel into a Faulk-neresque stream of consciousness. However, the levee had been breached, and the others were unmoored. One by one they confessed their concerns, unburdening and comforting in equal measure.

"…*This farm is my home and my heritage. It's difficult to put into words how much it is a part of me, how integral. Losing you will be painful,*" Violet said, squeezing Jack's hand, "*but leaving here would be like cutting out my lungs and expecting to breathe.*" Jack kissed her temple, allowing his mouth to linger as she took a breath. "*And I'm worried, okay? I'm worried. Because the packets don't say anything about choosing to stay behind. Like it's not a possibility. Like they might try to force me…*"

"…*I'm reasonably sure that not all of the materials in the museum and archives are being preserved. I cannot fathom why. This is all we have left of our history.*" Emily was agitated. She chewed the corner of her bottom lip. "*The military made a pickup yesterday, but they left some of the items that had been packed for transport. That got me curious, so I examined the master docket. Certain collections aren't even listed on it!*" Emily leaned closer to the camera, still gnawing her lip. "*I know there's time. The docket may not be final. I know that. But I have a really bad feeling…*"

"...Pounce. My kitty." Mason lifted the cat in front of his DC, ostensibly for the others to see her but truly more as an excuse to hide his face. *"The rules say I can't bring her, and it's killing me..."*

Almost two hours later, the sharing circle ended. The friends were beset with cumulative grief yet also uplifted for having unloaded. After a break, they went back to debating ways to penetrate the government's infuriating opacity, the source of so many of their woes. Mason suggested another hacking foray, but he was promptly stifled. With no viable alternatives, Violet offered to angle one last time for an invitation to the Science Bureau. To up the ante, she would proffer unlimited access to the farm's current and historical records.

"No, Violet," Jack protested. "You can't barter your family's intellectual property for the flimsy chance that you'll learn something of value in return. Besides, it's too dangerous. You shouldn't go back, especially knowing what happened to Mason. Clearly, our government has little tolerance for snooping."

Violet turned to face Jack, her profile to the camera. They were nestled side by side in front of the couch with a fuzzy green blanket draped over their legs. A plate of blueberry scones rested on Jack's lap, mostly crumbs now. Violet had taken to sending Jack home with fresh fruits and vegetables, and Abigail delighted in using them in new recipes. Scones were a particular favorite—pumpkin, banana, lemon, even an adventurous fig with blue cheese. For a beat, Violet mourned the glimpse of earnest domesticity that was no longer within her reach. "I wouldn't offer up the records if we had any other option. I don't *want* to do it," she said, grasping Jack's hand where it was fisted on the blanket near her knee. The scientific community had always rejected, even mocked, her family's work. It was considered self-indulgent folly for the Murphys to live topside and nurture the land instead of moving to Apricus and using their talents in socially acceptable ways. In the early days, Violet's relatives were ostracized, but by her parents' generation, the Murphys were regarded more with puzzlement than ridicule. In the past decade, there had even been some tepid overtures from the Science Bureau for informal collaboration. Violet's parents had treated such requests with caution, aiming to help but closely guarding their research and expertise. Violet followed their example. She adamantly protected her inheritance, and the violation of her mind by Akira's psychotropic coffee was unforgivable. So yes, it was a big deal to release the farm's records. A very big deal indeed. "But I think my parents would understand. They would appreciate the stakes. For goodness' sake, humanity is about to vacate the planet. They would not see this as a betrayal."

Jack flinched. He had not meant to accuse Violet of disloyalty. He opened his fist and intertwined their fingers.

Violet's eyes were soft with forgiveness. "What's happening around us, *to us*, is monumental, Jack. This feels like a…a watershed moment. Like the Ring of Fire Catastrophe or the Elbrus Armistice. Plus," she concluded with a reassuring wink, "I know what to expect this time."

"Ahem," Emily coughed to get the attention of the star-crossed lovers. She waited until they faced the camera. "Jack's not the only one who feels like they're being watched. It's creepy. I don't want to take us off track with details, but I'm bringing it up because… I mean, we don't think that Mason gave us up. But, but what if he *did*—through absolutely no fault of his own—and just doesn't remember?" Emily's DC jiggled as she meandered around the house. She stopped near an open window where lens flare crowned her with a sunburst halo. "Violet, if you do manage to get invited back to the Science Bureau, they could already be suspicious of you."

Violet considered Emily's warning, curbing the reflexive denial that pooled on her tongue. "I think," she began deliberately, "that any uncertainty about what Mason divulged under torture has been nulled in the time that's passed since his interrogation." Mason looked aggrieved, but he did not interrupt. "There have been no consequences for any of us. And unlike you, I'm not worried about being monitored. I haven't noticed anything unusual. Unless they're flying surveillance drones over the west pasture, I think I'm good." When her joke flopped, Violet sat up straighter and adopted a more serious tone. "Look, I'm not saying we know for sure. But again, *we don't have any other ideas.* I'll be careful. It's worth the risk."

"*Nothing* is worth risking your life," Jack thought fervently, but he bit his cheek to keep from blurting it out in a fit of frustrated melodrama. He was tattering at the edges. He refused to forsake his family, but the prospect of losing Violet was some kind of disturbingly slow asphyxiation, choking out his hope for love. Their relationship had no future. He had waited too long to act. He could no longer do it, knowing their days together were numbered. He was stuck in an excruciating limbo, cruelly taunted by the fingertips dream of what he wanted but could never be.

From far away, Jack could make out voices, like muffled but familiar sounds behind a closed door. Then Violet spoke beside him, and it turned the tuner knob on Jack's old-fashioned brain. "The thing is," Jack heard her say, "it won't be enough for me to poke around aimlessly. I need to find those poor animals. I need to get Akira talking about Project Noah. Things have really accelerated. Jack's shuttle leaves soon, and we still don't know what's going on. If Akira accepts my proposition, we need to make it count. This may be our last shot."

"Then you'll need my help," Mason asserted. "And before anyone objects, I have an idea for how we can do this. How I can help Violet without being detected." No one objected. In fact, no one said anything at all, which somehow felt more damning. Mason scratched an eyebrow, cringing at the sting of their skepticism. "Look, I know I got caught. Security was insanely tight, and I wasn't expecting it. I'm still a better hacker than almost anyone in Apricus." Defensive, Mason explained how he used simulations to maintain his skills and participated in under-the-radar competitions with peers at the Infrastructure Bureau. He described a few of his most notable hacks, assuring his friends that the competitions had strict rules that prohibited theft and other harm.

After spelling out his qualifications, Mason said, "Frankly, I'm pissed. How they treated me was seriously fucked-up, and while I am certainly glad to not be imprisoned or, or worse…" Mason swallowed hard as his brain conjured unwelcome images of what "worse" might entail. "I'm stuck doing mind-numbing work that would bore an intern. My supervisors are unhappy, but they've had no success lobbying for my reinstatement to projects that match my abilities." Mason emptied his lungs in an explosive breath and slid his hands into his hair, tugging in exasperation. "So yeah, I'm upset. But I'm *not* reckless. I won't risk being taken into custody again. I have the skills, and this time I'll expect maximum resistance. I'm telling you, they're not as good as me."

Emily coaxed the last lingering beads of beer from a long-forgotten stein on her kitchen counter and wrinkled her nose at the stale taste. "Alright, cyberpunk, what exactly are you proposing?" Though her blue eyes were red-rimmed from strain, they sparkled encouragement where they peered at Mason over the empty mug.

For the next couple of weeks, the group spent hours and hours planning a two-pronged attack: Violet would be on-site while Mason infiltrated covertly. Mason's equipment had been confiscated, but he cobbled together the necessary hardware by swiping components from the Infrastructure Bureau and dismantling a disused computer in Emily's parents' house. They gathered face-to-face whenever possible, eager to socialize and antsy despite Mason's efforts to safeguard their tech.

Espionage may not have been on anyone's résumé, but the foursome was smart and determined, and they devised a solid strategy. When they were ready, Violet contacted Akira. Feigning excitement about relocation, she volunteered to release the farm's archives in exchange for a job at the Science Bureau. To turn up the heat, she noted that this would be her final outreach. It did not take long for Akira to acquiesce to Violet's last-ditch overture. Being Akira, she also included an itinerary for two days hence—meticulously planned, brutally efficient, and with quintessential disregard for Violet. Perversely comforted, Violet barked out a laugh.

The day of Operation Lemur dawned with gusty winds and distant thunder. Dishwater-gray light soaked the kitchen where they loitered over breakfast. Mason and Emily shared a heaping bowl of fruit salad. For a while, the only sound was the *tap-tap* of tines on stoneware. Eventually, Emily discarded her fork in favor of using her fingers to excavate her preferred berries. Mason called her uncivilized and chuckled as she pointedly sucked juice off her middle finger. Jack crowded Violet against the counter where she was eating a muffin, unable to stop touching her—hands, hair, neck, the graceful arch of a cheekbone. The mood in the house was grim but calm.

Picking a code name had supplied a cloudburst of levity when things had grown too tense overnight. "C'mon, the *government* names everything," Mason had cajoled. "But they use boring names like Noah, Pioneer, Rosetta, and Zeus. We can do better." The ensuing brainstorm was boisterous, goofy, and surprisingly R-rated. It was perfect for whiling away the starry hours.

After breakfast, Violet departed for the train station, sleep-deprived but relaxed. Her three similarly disposed houseguests hunkered down in the study to watch the clock and wait.

Akira's impeccably manicured hands gripped the edge of the reception desk, garnering a curious squint from the attendant. She ignored the lookie-loo and glowered at the bureau's monotonous gray walls. Her skin felt too tight, and her skull had been throbbing all morning, dissuaded by neither analgesics nor a torrent of caffeinated tea—and now, of course, she needed to use the restroom as well. Akira pursed her lips, anxious and supremely irritated about it. Mentally, she ran through a simple causal analysis:

Why has this appointment with Violet Murphy put me on edge?
Because the appointment is a trap.

Why does that matter?
Because I do not wish the woman harm.

Why do I care if she is harmed?
Because although I am dispassionate, perhaps even cold, subterfuge and intentional cruelty have never been my chosen methods.

Why do subterfuge and cruelty bother me?
Because they are anathema to my worldview. This is not why I answered the president's call to serve.

Before Akira's chain of inquiry could reach a potentially treasonous climax, Violet entered the building. She paused inside the door to pull the strap of her messenger bag over her head and scan the entry hall. Her thick hair was unbound and tousled, and though her clothes were clean and professional, she had the nonchalantly rumpled air of someone who was more accustomed to physical labor. Akira released the desk and stepped forward to greet her.

They detoured to the restroom then got down to business in a huddle room. Violet stiffly declined Akira's offer of a beverage, and the women shared an eloquent look. The room was located on a different corridor than the one where the animals had been hidden. Violet made no comment, but her body betrayed her disappointment; a pink tide swelled up her neck to her ears and made the freckles on her face stand out. She claimed the swivel chair facing the door, fiddled with the height and lumbar support to burn off some tension, and retrieved her DC and a portable hard drive from her bag. There would be no presentation this time, no other inquisitive white coats. In fact, the entire corridor appeared to be locked down or vacant.

"Society's dependency on food generators is disadvantageous and risky," Akira declared. This was an unpopular viewpoint, and Violet was instantly, grudgingly engaged. Her eyebrows shot to her hairline in surprise. Akira huffed dismissively. "It is a matter of practicality, Ms. Murphy, not philosophy." Akira folded her hands atop the table primly. Her sleeves pulled up to expose thin wrists and peculiar purple-green contusions. She slid her hands into her lap and continued, "Among our goals for relocation, the bureau has been preparing for large-scale farming and the construction of artificial biospheres. Your practical knowledge and experiential data are rare and valuable."

Violet accepted the halfhearted praise and sacrificed a couple of hours to stimulating conversation. She expounded and hypothesized with unfeigned enthusiasm, honestly fascinated by Akira's work. Akira, on the other hand, dodged her guest's every attempt to learn about humanity's destination, including even its weather and soil composition. She would say only that the bureau wanted to be prepared for all contingencies. Smooth as a politician, she paraphrased this deflection in an extraordinary number of ways, tap-dancing like Ginger Rogers to the president's Fred Astaire. Fed up, Violet confronted Akira point-blank. "Dr. Tanaka, I have a right to know where I'll end up when I board my shuttle!"

A pained expression guttered on Akira's face. "I am not at liberty to divulge more than you already know!" she shouted. "*Give it up*, Violet!" The uncharacteristic outburst startled them both into silence. They stared at one another for a protracted moment, then Akira picked up her tablet and pretended to be engrossed in her notes.

Violet took a few minutes to gather her nerve. Slowly, she pushed the portable hard drive across the table. "This drive contains the farm's archives.

If there is a free terminal, we can download the data, and I can explain the file structure."

Akira's eyes were fixed on the drive. "I'm sure I can figure it out," she said. Glancing back to her tablet, she asked a question about bacterial crop diseases. Violet contended that the information on the drive would address the question better than her extemporaneous thoughts.

Akira changed the subject to hybridization, but Violet cut her off. "Look, if I'm going to turn over my family's records, I want to at least have a proper handoff. This is a big deal for me. Let me show you the files, okay?"

Akira's umber eyes darted around the drab little room. She was certain that her squirrelly behavior was drawing unwanted attention and tried to marshal her typical clinical resolve. The drive was probably spyware, yet Akira continued to have mixed feelings about facilitating Violet's downfall. Akira was duty-bound to protect Project Noah. Nevertheless, she could not help but admire Violet as a fellow scientist, sharp-witted and useful. The president's goons would expect Akira to connect the drive, springing a trap on the hacker and implicating Violet. She frowned at the hard drive where it sat innocently on the table, black and glossy like the moral tarpit the situation had become.

Akira looked up to find Violet keenly observing her. An obnoxious buzzing in the pocket of Akira's lab coat delivered an ideally timed distraction. Relieved to escape, Akira retrieved her unusually noisy DC and excused herself to attend to an unspecified urgent matter. The sliding door had barely closed when Violet tried to reopen it using the adjacent control panel. It was locked. The panel displayed a menacing security override message in an incongruously delicate cursive script. The predictability of Violet's entrapment made it no less unsettling. She knocked on the door, purporting to need the restroom, but no one responded. Leaning her forehead against the cool metal, she relinquished her last hope of finding the captive animals. Even though it had been an unrealistic aspiration, not even part of Operation Lemur, she still felt regret.

Knowing that she must act fast, Violet shelved her remorse and strode over to the recessed computer terminal into which she had expected Akira to plug the hard drive. For the benefit of the concealed camera in the room, Violet connected the drive and typed gibberish into the keyboard. She tossed the drive back onto the table and returned to the control panel for the door. Praying that the red herring would confuse the watchers enough to buy Mason a few extra minutes, Violet knocked on the door with her right hand, reiterating her need for the facilities. Meanwhile, her left hand surreptitiously slipped a tiny flat node into the open port on the bottom casing of the panel, just like she had practiced on Mason's mock-up a hundred times.

The maneuver was executed beautifully, but the security team was on high alert and lost almost no time on Violet's misdirection. They detected Mason straightaway, and though they could not block him yet, they were in hot pursuit. Fortunately for Operation Lemur, Mason was highly motivated and much better prepared this time. He downloaded files and captured screen images at impressive speeds. He amassed a lot of information before he was cornered and forced to retreat. In the excruciatingly blind minutes that this played out, Violet could do nothing but pace the room and await Akira's return.

Down the hall, Akira listened to the president's briefing on her DC. Security had ousted the hacker, but they could not pinpoint the person's location. Regardless, the incident was framed as having provided strong circumstantial evidence linking Violet and Mason. The president acted decisively, comfortable in the knowledge that this mess would never be adjudicated in court. "You've confirmed that Agu, Collins, and Steuben are at the Murphy farm?" he asked. His tone was indifferent, but Akira could hear a subtle quiver of excitement underneath.

"Yes, sir. We've had them under constant surveillance, per your orders. We've had some trouble with their DCs, so it's taken considerable manpow—"

"Yes, yes. I've read your reports," the president interrupted testily. "Continue."

"Yes, sir. We don't know exactly how Murphy let Agu in. It wasn't the portable hard drive, but it had to have happened while she was in that meeting room, so—"

"Figure it out. Then guarantee me this sort of breach will never happen again."

"Yes, sir." The officer swallowed audibly. "Mr. President, Agu did infiltrate the servers that support Project Noah and Project Pioneer before we booted him. It's likely that he downloaded classified material."

"That's disappointing, but it doesn't matter," the president replied coolly.

"Mr. President?" Akira interjected before she could think better of it. The whole point of this charade was to protect her life's work.

"Ah, she speaks," the president replied. His voice was a chocolate-vanilla swirl of sarcasm and affection. "Mr. Agu may have pilfered some files, Dr. Tanaka, but we'll get to him before he has time to do any damage."

"Are you arresting Ms. Murphy, sir?"

"No, Dr. Tanaka. Finish your meeting. I want to see if she contacts anyone other than the three who are waiting for her topside. Go now, Akira. You've left your guest alone long enough." Once Akira dropped the connection, the president addressed the security officer. "You have your orders," he confirmed. "Act tonight."

Akira returned to the huddle room and hastily wrapped up the conference, spurred by a meager flare of conscience. She asked only two more questions before ushering Violet into the hallway. Violet noticed when Akira pocketed the hard drive on her way out, but she did not repeat her offer to explain the contents. Instead, she asked to tour the bureau's test gardens, but Akira curtly declined. As they walked down the corridor toward the exit, Violet tried to finagle her way inside the closed doors, abandoning all subtlety when she realized that she would not have another chance. Akira rebuffed her curiosity and rushed her through the entry hall, following her outside. At the edge of the flagstone square, almost to the train, Violet turned around. She could still see Akira in the distance, standing in front of the building, rooted to the stairs like a marble statue, unyielding and aloof.

CHAPTER 15

ASHES OF BABYLON

Outside the city's cocoon of stone, gale-force winds slammed sheets of rain against Violet's window, exacerbated by the ultrahigh speed of the train. Thunder rumbled, and a fulgent flash of lightning blinded her just before the train ducked under the waves. Violet blinked owlishly until her pupils adjusted, then she messaged Jack that she was on her way home. He replied with a red heart emoji. Violet smiled, relaxing into her seat. She stared out the window at the umbral remnants of a civilization past and wondered what Operation Lemur had revealed about their future.

At the Murphy estate, the study had been transformed into a full-on war room. Information was plastered over every inch of Violet's sprawling monitor and projected from three DCs. Dirty cups and plates, a pair of embroidered throw pillows, and a discarded cardigan littered the floor. Mason was glued behind the desk while Emily and Jack flitted about the room like humming-birds, browsing different files. In surprisingly short order, they confirmed Emily's theory that Project Noah focused on what to bring when humanity evacuated Earth. It took longer, however, to untangle its full scope and purpose. Evidently, the project team was harvesting, cataloging, and assessing the fitness of flora, fauna, and inorganic minerals. Only the best specimens were approved for relocation. Anything less than the best was disposed of. The friends called a brief timeout upon discovering the project's extensive kill sheet, sickened by the scientists' casual cruelty and God-complex arrogance.

And that wasn't even the real kicker.

Mason sorted the rest of the stolen files while Emily and Jack settled on the floor with the project charter. He heard them criticizing the scientists' bastardized Darwinian approach and grieving the captive animals that, as it turned out, had valid reasons to be frightened. Mason grew intensely fixated on the new materials, listening to the others with half an ear, then not at all. When they tried to engage him, he made a forceful swatting motion with his arm. It was raining heavily, so the pair decided to give Mason some space by checking on Firestorm who was sheltering in the barn. They dried Firestorm's coat and showered him with affection, an assuasive contrast to the noisy, pea-sized hail that pounded the roof. It had been storming intermittently all day, but this was the first appearance of hail. When the downpour eased up, Jack and Emily raced back to the house. They dallied by the fireplace for a while to dry off, shivering and smelling of wet horse.

Out of the blue, there was a vehement curse from the study. "Emily? Jack? Where are you?" Mason yelled. "Get in here now!" They arrived to find him pacing, hands clasped on top of his head, chanting "Shit, shit, shit" under his breath. The monitor was still covered in files, but these documents had Project Pioneer headers, not Project Noah.

"What's wrong?" Emily exclaimed in unison with Jack's, "What happened?"

"I can't fucking believe this," Mason huffed, "but it's right there, in a bunch of mundane, excruciatingly detailed Pioneer field reports." He gesticulated at the monitor then reclaimed his place behind the desk. "The Earth survey *did* identify other habitable landmasses. The sites are comparatively small, but they're stable and viable. According to these reports, they could support human settlements." Mason gaped up at two shocked faces. "They were all rejected and 'staked,' whatever that means."

"H-how is that possible?" Jack stuttered. "The government told us there was nothing salvageable."

"It was an outright lie," Emily snarled. "They lied. They *lied*, and now we can't trust anything we've been told. Holy shit, this is bad." She folded and unfolded her arms peevishly then drummed her fingers on the desk. "How were they able to keep this a secret?"

Mason took a moment to corral his frenetic thoughts. "I'm guessing that the work was fragmented and classified. Probably, no more than a few people were privy to the whole picture. These reports were 'for the president's eyes only.'"

The trio dove into the stolen records with outraged fervor. But the information was finite, so sooner or later, they had either thoroughly exhausted it or set it aside due to their lack of technical knowledge until Violet could participate. "Staking" stayed a mystery. Right when they were ready to call it quits, Emily made another gut-clenching discovery. It was buried in the unedited notes from a Project Noah team meeting. Despite what the pretentious charter implied, the systematic procurement of animals was not motivated by world-building or conservation. Rather, model specimens were being relocated "for entertainment and recreation."

Emily tipped over where she was seated on the floor and twisted into a fetal position. She pulled her blue pinafore dress over stockinged knees and picked at a spot of dried mud from her trek to the barn. Jack placed a comforting hand on her back. He had changed his rain-soaked pants, but with his arm outstretched, he noticed flecks of mud on the sleeve of his sweater.

"This is profoundly disturbing," Emily moaned. "There are so few animals left. I'm glad that the government is trying to preserve the remaining species, I truly am. But it should be done to safeguard and celebrate the diversity of life, not to fucking *entertain* us."

Mason listened to Emily's lament while he closed and organized files to make it easier for Violet to navigate. Poised to click, his glance snagged on the appendix of a recent Project Noah status report. In a short list of out-standing specimens to be appropriated, one line of text seemed to vibrate, tauntingly, keeping time with his galloping heart:

Equus caballus ("Firestorm") – Murphy Estate, Fulminara

Mason pushed away from the desk so hard that the chair hit the wall and chipped the bottom edge of Violet's Tree of Life. "No, no, no, no, no," he gasped. "That *can't* happen."

Violet inched her way home through the gathering dark, safely ensconced in Emily's borrowed SUV. The rain was sporadic, but there had been bouts of hail, and wind gusts swayed the vehicle, especially in the stretches of her commute that were outside the forest canopy. Although Violet was hankering to know the outcome of Operation Lemur, she could not risk calling Jack. She had to remain vigilant for fallen branches, flooding, and other hazards. Even during breaks in the rainfall, it still *seemed* to be raining; the insistent wind liberated fat raindrops from the trees and plunked them loudly on the roof. When Violet finally arrived at the path to her house, lightning continued to strobe the landscape, but the storm was weakening, leaving a sodden, moonless night at its heels.

Loose stones pinged the wheel wells as Violet drove through the archway. She put the truck in park and slid out to secure the open gate. Suddenly, every light across the estate blinked out. With the moon and stars obstructed by clouds, it was pitch-black beyond the reach of the headlights. The estate had redundant systems and fail-safes. Barring catastrophic damage or sabotage, a power outage of this magnitude was impossible. Violet scrambled back into the truck. The glass was foggy from having left the door ajar. She lowered the windows and swiped her sleeve over the windshield impatiently. Halfway to the house, Violet's heart lurched, and she

hit the brakes. Faint with distance, she had heard the clarion high note of
Firestorm's scream rise above the sounds of the moving truck. He almost
never made that disturbing vocalization. The fact that she could hear it from
a half mile away engendered instant panic.

Violet fell out of the truck and shouted to Firestorm, knowing that her
voice would not carry far enough but powerless to stop. The unlit house
loomed up ahead, discernable by its thicker hue of black, but Violet veered
away toward the barn. The wind surged, and the retreating storm spit icy
rain. Violet crooked her arm above her eyes to shield them as she walked.
Needing her DC's flashlight, she fumbled unsuccessfully in her pockets.
There was a disorienting lightning strike nearby. Violet debated returning
to the truck and simply driving it across the paddock. Before she could
decide, Firestorm screamed again. Her body moved on instinct, fueled by
adrenaline and a bone-deep certainty that something was dreadfully wrong.

After only a few steps, intense light ripped open the sky, but it did
not dissipate like lightning. Violet's dilated pupils contracted violently, and
she ducked her head. Firestorm's cries reached her ears, impossibly shrill,
and she ran toward the sound, heedless and desperate and blind. Blinking
furiously, she could see her horse being dragged out of the barn in some
type of harness. He was kicking viciously and making horrifying sounds of
protest. Then all of a sudden, Violet could *feel* his terror. She hit the ground
hard as her heart trip-hammered and her stomach revolted, but she swiftly
regained her feet and began shouting "Stop!" and "No!" at the top of her
strangled lungs. Firestorm was calling out for her, panicky and confused.
An aircraft hovered near the barn, spotlighting the crime, but she spared no
thought for it as Firestorm was lifted upward in the harness.

Firestorm's body wilted, and Violet's link to him was severed. Its abrupt
absence was a punch to the solar plexus that left her winded and rattled.
She screamed. Her voice was hoarse and strained, splintered like rotted
wood. She tried to run again, but she was flash blind, hyperventilating, and

disoriented. She slipped on the wet grass and nearly bashed her head on the paddock fence. Strong arms gripped her waist, pulling her back in time. It felt like she had arrived home an eternity ago, but in reality, it had been mere minutes. Temporarily nonplussed by the appearance of her friends, she watched Firestorm's lifeless form ascend into the aircraft.

Violet tensed to move, but Jack's arms squeezed around her. Firestorm's abductors began to rise by their own harnesses, and Violet fought Jack's hold with wildcat fury. When she blasted out an agonized, raspy scream, he almost faltered. But Mason and Emily were calling out what they could see through the zoom lenses on their DCs, and what they revealed made Jack hold on tighter. This was an armed military operation. The soldiers had weapons at the ready, practically daring Violet to make herself a target. Oblivious, she struggled on.

The aircraft extinguished its lights and withdrew soundlessly, thrusting the estate into blackness. The friends were marooned beside the lonely paddock fence that led to the swollen shadow of a soulless barn. Violet continued to call out for Firestorm long after he was gone. The others stood with her in mute sympathy.

Exhausted, Violet sank to the ground and began to cry. Viscid tears of loss and rage trickled down her red-hot cheeks. When she curled forward to wrap her arms around a fencepost, the piteous sight knocked Jack to his knees by her side. He rubbed her back and droned barren words of comfort. Leaning in close, he could hear her ragged voice repeating "Gone" over and over.

"Violet," he murmured, "you need to listen to me, okay? Firestorm was doped. He's not dead, darling. Are you listening, Violet? They don't want him dead." Violet loosened her stranglehold on the fence and lifted her face to Jack. "There's my girl," Jack breathed, pushing Violet's wet hair from her forehead. He shared what Mason had found in the Project Noah report and hypothesized that Firestorm had been drugged to prevent a heart attack or injury when he was lifted by the harness.

"H-he's still gone," Violet said in a small voice.

"Then we'll just need to get him back," Emily proclaimed with false confidence. It helped that she had to speak loudly to be heard over a howling gust of wind. With the rain intensifying, Emily crouched down and gently touched her friend's hand where it gripped the fence. "Let's go inside."

They hobbled to the house. As they moved closer, the cream-colored stones cut through the unlit night like a beacon. Once inside, everyone cleaned up and changed into dry clothes. They donned extra layers, for psychological comfort as much as to stave off the chill from exposure. Emily rekindled the fire in the hearth while Mason asked Violet to show him the control panel so that he could bring the estate back online. In the interim, Jack collected wax candles from a familiar shelf in the pantry, wistful for happier times.

One by one, they gravitated to the salon. The coffee table was well-laid with food and drink, of which they partook mostly in contemplative silence. Tending the fire, Emily reached up on her tiptoes to run shaky fingers over a horseshoe that was nailed into the stone above the hearth. Violet grabbed a handful of carrots to eat and meandered around the room with a candle. She gazed for a long time at one particular photograph. It showed her parents with Firestorm when he was a foal. They had acquired him after he was rejected by the mare who birthed him. In the photo, the little brown horse was resting in a patch of grass sprayed with silvery wildflowers. His coat was newborn dull, but even then, his brilliant white markings outshone the flowers. Violet's parents were reclining beside him. Her mother had a wildflower tucked behind her ear. Her father's head was thrown back in mirth. Violet touched the hardwood frame like a benediction then withdrew to the couch where she rested her head on Jack's shoulder. Mason was the last to join, over an hour later, after the power flickered on. They let the candles burn anyway.

Although they were all reeling from the day's revelations, Firestorm's traumatic abduction had knocked Violet's world clean off its axis. Being no strangers to loss, her friends wanted to give her time to regroup. Unfortunately, they did not have that luxury. Violet needed to know what Operation Lemur had exposed. They could only hope that it would distract her from her grief. Succinctly and urgently, Mason led a whirlwind brief. Jack and Emily interjected periodic comments. Violet was tucked into the corner of the overstuffed couch nearest the hearth, sipping honeyed tea for her shredded throat. Her body language was closed off, but her eyes were canny and attentive.

Unexpectedly, Violet's DC chimed with an incoming video call. She tugged the device from the back pocket of her faded flannel-lined jeans where she had stowed it after it had recharged. The caller's identity was blocked to her, and she had a fleeting impulse to disconnect out of spite. Instead, Violet flung the call to the video screen on the salon wall and shooed the others into the kitchen, out of sight. She stood in front of the screen and accepted the call, coming nose to nose with a grim-faced soldier. His uniform was bedazzled with several gaudy bars, though he looked much too young for a command. "Violet Murphy, you have been charged by the Security Bureau with multiple counts of criminal malfeasance and subversion. The specifics will be sent to your DC." Violet tried to interrupt, but the man was committed to his script. He talked right over her. "In light of the incontrovertible evidence, court proceedings have been waived. You have been found guilty on all counts." He recited the verdict blithely, as if it were not a gross miscarriage of justice. Surreptitiously, the color code on Violet's briefing packet switched to red.

Shaken but righteously indignant, Violet exclaimed, "This is insane! Why are details of our new home being withheld from the public? Why weren't we told that there are other livable places on Earth? Why is no one aware of Project Noah?" A look of uncertainty fluttered across the soldier's face. "I am not a criminal. I have caused *no harm*. I just want answers," Violet asserted. Her voice dropped deadly low. Through gritted teeth, she added, "And I want what was stolen from me tonight."

"You are in no position to make demands, Ms. Murphy." The connection was cut, and Violet stood numbly in her salon, stomach pitching like a noose twisting in the wind.

There was no time to rally. In the next instant, massive explosions shook the rock-solid foundation of the house. Violet staggered but kept her feet, frozen in horror as a yawning crack split the east wall. A shock wave blew out the kitchen windows. Jack, Emily, and Mason hit the floor hard and tried to shield their heads from shrapnel. Popcorn snaps drew Violet's eyes to the ceiling where the wooden beams were fracturing into deadly stalactites, ready to fall. On autopilot, she flew out the wobbly front door to find the barn, greenhouse, and a portion of the farm tower utterly destroyed. Violet's brain blue-screened.

The others untangled their boots and coats from the toppled rack in the foyer and joined Violet in the void. Couriered by the wind, drizzle-damp ash quickly settled on their skin and hair. It nested in their lungs, the cremated remains of a murdered life. Emily reached for Violet's hand. Mason coughed. But they were granted no reprieve. The false daylight of flames illuminated a sleek aircraft suspended above the wreckage, similar to the craft that had ripped away the last of Violet's family. Turrets on its belly swiveled toward the house. They had a split second to register the monstrous sight, then self-preservation prevailed and Violet bellowed, "Move!"

They fled as fast as their legs would take them. Jack made a dash for the gate, closing the distance with his long stride. When Emily fell too far behind, Mason backtracked, seized her arm, and hauled her bodily toward their goal. A mighty swell of heat and percussion slammed into their backs and propelled them forward. Emily tripped on the shock wave, and Mason dragged her along as she tried to regain her footing, unwilling to let go even as he regretted his brutality. At the gate, Violet looked back over her shoulder and seized up midbreath. She was cemented in place like Lot's wife, cursed to bear witness to the fiery hellscape that had been her home. Smoky craters pockmarked the ground. The trees nearest the barn were aflame. Live electrical wires sparked where they were exposed in the debris. Proud, comely structures of stone and wood and metal and brick that had endured for generations and weathered countless storms were reduced to rubble.

Leaning on the arch, Emily struggled for air and picked shards of bloody glass from her hands and hair. Mason and Jack fastened their coats and laced up their boots. Violet had dried everyone's outerwear once the power had been restored, but an icy drizzle was pelting them anew. When he had rushed from the house, Jack had had the presence of mind to grab Violet's coat and boots, not wanting her to get soaked again. He manhandled her into them. She did not protest and did not help. He brushed the stones from her socks before shoving her feet into the boots, too fast and rough. She gave no sign that she noticed, transfixed by the mangled paddock fence with wide black gaps like rotten teeth.

Violet was jolted from her stupor when the aircraft began to move. It methodically surveyed its handiwork using the same damnable spotlight that had accompanied Firestorm's assault. Realizing that they were too close, too exposed, Violet peered around frantically, away from the paddock and toward the untouched woods south of the gate. Aided by a lightning flash, her gaze caught on the skeleton of a building that had been destroyed by a tornado long before Violet was born, when the Murphy clan had been too numerous for one house. As the family dwindled, it was never repaired. Violet wished she could shelter her friends there, but she knew it was too risky to remain on the estate. She watched in alarm as the craft changed course sharply and inched over the perimeter of the paddock. There was no more time to think. She stilled Jack's hands on her lapel. "Into the woods!" she gasped, pointing to the welcoming embrace of the southern forest edge. "We need to get into the woods. *Go!*"

CHAPTER 16

YELLOW BRICK ROAD

They ran nonstop for as long as they could. Strictly speaking, they ran until they were shielded by thick old-growth spruce trees, then fell into a stumbling jog, then slowed to a hurried walk. The terrain grew wilder, and the adrenaline that had flooded their veins receded. Sooner than was prudent, they were forced to break. Emily was lagging far behind, and she was starting to hyperventilate. They collapsed in a copse of fir trees where the air was ripe with petrichor. Having suffered panic attacks into his early twenties, Mason was an authority on breathing exercises. He coached Emily until her inhalations were slow and deep. Unconsciously, Jack and Violet followed along while they inspected one another for minor injuries inflicted by spiky boughs and bramble thorns as they had barreled headlong through the woods.

Once their physical demands subsided and Mason could think clearly, he realized that they had to deactivate their DCs. He anticipated pushback. For most citizens, the mere idea of disconnection evoked a deep-seated, Pavlovian dread. "Listen," Mason implored. "They can use our DCs to find us. They can track our EMF. In the middle of a forest, the radiation waves emitted by our devices are a blazing neon We Are Here sign. We have to power down."

Moments later, an overconfident security captain blinked with disbelief as the four pulsing markers on his screen disappeared.

The fugitives moved on, slower now, but relentless. Violet tried to navigate using the partially obscured horns of the crescent moon, hoping to nudge them toward proximate estates. Their initial blind run had been disorienting, though, and she could find no familiar landmarks. The best she could do was pick a direction and stick with it. They hiked steadily south. The halcyon hum of the sleepy forest was drowned out by the lumbering din of four sets of boots ricocheting off the canopy.

In the ungracious 2:00 a.m. hour, they were crossing a slender clearing when they spotted a hovering, metallic-gray aircraft in the middle distance. Their pursuers were using the craft's unnaturally bright lights to penetrate the treetops. The group veered sharply and bolted into a cluster of white pines. Briefly, they watched and waited behind a wall of feathery teal needles. Then they raced away, in the opposite direction. They narrowly escaped again, about an hour later, by hiding under a rocky outcrop at the precipice of a ravine.

The pattern repeated twice more as the clouded stars gradually retreated to make way for dawn. Dense woodland continued to hamper the manhunt, and by this point, the friends were coated from head to toe in chilly mud and plant matter, which made it difficult to track their heat signatures using thermal imaging. In this one way, their discomfort was a godsend. Nevertheless, after nearly five hours of this tango, they were overcome by exhaustion, especially unathletic Emily who was unused to prolonged physical exertion and Mason who still lacked stamina after his interrogation. It was imperative to find somewhere safe to rest.

When the sun poked over the horizon, they understood straightaway that daylight would make the noiseless aircraft harder to detect. The flood-lights that lit up the nocturnal forest and low-lying clouds had betrayed the craft's position to them, even at a considerable distance. As Mother Nature slid the dimmer, they lost that advantage. Violet was in the lead, trudging a

path through a mess of cobwebby ferns that were flourishing under the conifers. She scrubbed angrily at the stress-induced tears on her cheeks. Mason
leaned heavily on Jack, who had not spoken in hours and bore a deep gash
on his neck that would not cease its listless bleeding. They paused at the edge
of a wide meadow that was sprinkled with hairy-stemmed, blue cornflowers.
Violet wrenched her eyes from the plants and studied the sky, straining to
hear the aircraft's imperceptible mechanical drone. Emily caught up with
the others and braced her aching body on the scaly trunk of an old cedar.
Hit with a surge of light-headedness and nausea, she scrunched her eyes and
tried one of Mason's breathing exercises, which she quickly aborted. "They're
south of us and approaching fast," she bit out urgently.

"How do you know?" Violet asked, squinting at the southern skyline.

Emily opened her glassy blue eyes and blinked stickily. "The birds told
me." Her countenance was sheepish but not uncertain.

Violet had been filtering out the sounds of the awakening forest. She
listened, and all at once, the trills and chirps and caws seemed inescapable.
"Good enough for me," she said. With a decisive nod, she scrambled northeast.

They hiked through rough terrain for almost an hour until their way
was blocked by a fast-flowing river, swollen from the storm. They slid down a
steep slope of flowering heather to the river's thin strip of shore. A short way
upstream, two smooth, flat boulders were wreathed in lichen near a fallen
spruce. The splintered tree trunk slowed the rush of water enough for them
to safely drink and wash. They crawled to the edge of the rocks and cupped
their hands in the river, drinking their fill and sluicing the grime from their
faces. Most of the water on Fulminara was no longer critically polluted, and
even if trace amounts of heavy metals or oil lingered in the river, the benefits
of drinking outweighed the risks to their dehydrated, overtaxed bodies.

The river was a blessing, but it was too exposed. After more than seven
hours without rest or food, aside from some underripe wild berries, they
were utterly drained. Locating shelter was imperative. Mason rolled onto

his back and turned his head toward Violet. "Do you have any idea where we are?" he croaked. The delicate skin around his eyes was puffy. Leaf scraps were embedded in his hair. Livid contusions on his face and neck were slightly obscured by his dark skin but unmistakable at close range. A gaping tear in the right knee of his pants revealed a seeping abrasion.

"I think we've hiked more than twenty miles," Violet speculated, "but we haven't been moving in a straight line. We've had to switch directions numerous times, even backtrack. I'm pretty sure this is the Draco River, though." Emily bobbed her head thoughtfully. Encouraged, Violet continued, "If we've gone far enough east, then the Johnson ranch could be nearby. They raise cattle and horses…" Violet trailed off, stifled by the body blow of her last memory of Firestorm. Mason gave her forearm a sympathetic squeeze.

Emily rolled onto her back with a groan and revived the flagging conversation. Her leggings were torn, virtually shredded in places, and a buckle was missing on her right boot. Despite the river water, her lips were stained indigo from the berries she had eaten. For hours, she had been compulsively separating her hair into a braid that kept unraveling without anything to secure it. The blond strands were dirt-streaked and wild. She could have easily passed for the frontwoman of a punk band. "The Garcia and Kumar estates might be close, too," she offered. "But I have no idea which way."

"We're personae non grata now," Mason said bitterly. "Even if we could find one of these families, who knows if we'd be welcome." Since no one could refute that disheartening nugget of insight, they concentrated for a while on the meditative rush of the river. Balmy beams of morning sunlight bled through the towering spruce and slender, white-barked aspens. It sparkled in the coarse grains of quartz and feldspar that speckled the rocks.

Off to the side, Jack was stooped over the river, splashing water on his wounded neck. From his vantage on the taller boulder, he caught the movement of a dark-brown lump on the shore of a lesser offshoot of the river's primary vein. Stocky with a flat, paddle-like tail, the beaver paced fretfully then swam to a rock that poked out of the stormy current in the main river, closer to Jack. It paused, slapped its broad tail on the rock twice, and swam back to shore. The sequence repeated several times, deviating only once when the beaver could not resist a leafy branch that was floating by. It stopped mid-swim to get a good grip on the branch and haul it to land. But it immediately abandoned its prize to return to the rock. Jack watched in fascination until finally, sluggishly, when the animal smacked its tail for the fifth time and flaunted a pair of uneven orange incisors, understanding dawned. Jack could hear the beaver in his head, but he could not decode the message. His pulse and respiration quickened. His ears began to ring. "No," Jack's inner voice chided. "None of your angsty bullshit. Just let it happen." He recentered his awareness on the beaver. The animal had not returned to shore this time. It sat on the rock on its haunches with its tail folded underneath like a scaly picnic blanket, blinking its black eyes in Jack's general direction.

"Shelter!" Jack blurted, louder than he intended. On the plus side, he had everyone's attention. "There's warm, dry shelter nearby. Someplace hidden." The beaver plopped into the water. Jack rose to his knees and pointed at the chocolate lump chugging toward the far shore. "He's going to lead us to it."

The group clambered downriver until they were directly across from the junction where the bloated waterway met a narrower, calmer vein. The area was littered with rounded granite boulders and fallen logs that were either too big or too tightly wedged to be moved by the current. The clusters of debris created swirling, frothy eddies. The friends took in the scene and mapped a safe path for crossing to the opposite shore where their furry escort was waiting patiently, munching on leaves from its salvaged aspen branch. Jack went first. He hopped from object to object like a life-size game of *Frogger*. He fell into the river when a log spun under his weight, but it was in the shallows close to shore. He emerged shivering but unharmed. He would never admit it, not ever, but the worst part was the embarrassment of being clumsy in front of the beaver. The others adjusted their path based on Jack's misfortune. Mason went next, but he waited one step ahead for Emily to follow. Violet tailed Emily. By unspoken agreement, they sandwiched Emily, helping her to make her jumps. The trio crossed the river in procession, without incident, apart from some superficial bruises and scrapes.

The beaver shuffled along the shoreline of the tributary. The water was jewel-blue and significantly less agitated. Colonies of hardy geraniums displayed blossoms of lilac and lapis. Up close, Jack observed the shaggy fur and rounded ears of their forty-pound benefactor. The animal smelled strangely of vanilla. Before too long, they came upon an expansive mound of interwoven branches, clumps of grass, and mud. A second beaver was fastidiously shifting a log atop the dam. It spared the visitors a perfunctory glance and resumed its engineering. The dam was impressive. Beyond it, the river pooled in a pond of deep, tranquil water. For an uncomfortable moment, Jack thought the beaver was inviting them into its home. But then it pivoted, climbed several paces up a grassy embankment, and twisted around to give Jack an expectant look. Jack returned the beaver's gaze dumbly. The ever-tolerant animal waddled higher up the slope then turned again. The embankment was steep. It was obviously not a preferred beaver byway. Jack perused his surroundings more intently until eventually, he noticed a structure tucked into a thicket of trees—and this one was decidedly man-made.

"Look!" he shouted, gesticulating at what appeared to be a stout, colorless building.

The others trotted to Jack's side. They had been following a fair way off, afraid to crowd the beaver. "It's a dome!" Violet replied excitedly. "This must be a scientific outpost."

The friends scrabbled up the embankment to get a better view. Where the land had been cleared, dapples of sunlight fell on a carpet of greenish-blue needles and woody pinecones. The dome was encrusted with dirt and draped with climbing ivy and flowering honeysuckle. It was acutely camouflaged; they would have definitely missed it without their web-footed companion. The door had a complicated metal latch, too tricky for curious animals and just barely workable for four exhausted humans. When the door opened, Violet, Mason, and Emily filed inside while Jack limped to the edge of the embankment to convey his gratitude to the beaver. He was pleased to see that the beast had loitered, gnawing idly on a slick branch. Jack's smile radiated affection and thankfulness. Feeling foolish, he gave a jaunty little wave. The beaver thumped its tail, grunted, and left.

The dome had two cots with lumpy, stained pillows and a stack of dusty blankets. There was a tiny bathroom with functional plumbing and a kitchenette stocked with ready-to-eat meal rations. The remaining space was dominated by two desks, storage bins, and a wall of equipment for tasks such as monitoring the weather and testing the water, soil, and air quality. Skylights peppered the rounded ceiling, but they were mostly obscured with twigs and muck. Fortunately, two fiberglass windows flanked the door and let in plenty of light. When Jack entered the dome, Mason was using the bathroom, and Violet and Emily were rifling through a rudimentary first aid kit. Now that a toilet was accessible, Jack's bowels decided that he could no longer wait. The instant that Mason withdrew, Jack brushed past him with an apologetic groan and shut the door.

The friends had fled Violet's house with no supplies, so the disused outpost was a bonanza. It enabled them to eat, bathe, and treat their injuries. It sheltered them while they rested. They chose not to start the generator for fear of discovery, but they could see well enough in the daytime, and the blankets were cozy. Jack had to strip down to his underwear due to his dunk in the river, but the others shed only their boots and hung their jackets on desk chairs and hooks to air out. Too drained to talk, they attended their most pressing needs and fell asleep. Violet and Jack entwined on one cot, oblivious to sharp elbows and stale breath. Emily occupied the other cot. She tucked her nose under her collar to inhale the comforting scent of her perfume where it clung faintly to the fabric. Mason stretched out on the floor beside her.

A solid seven hours later, Violet jolted awake as if she had been shocked with a defibrillator. Clammy-skinned and gasping, she shoved Jack off the flimsy cot, causing it to partially collapse. Jack's yelp and the ruckus of his fall woke the others. Violet's gaze bounced around the unfamiliar room. Rosy sunbeams streamed through the windows by the door. Clawing her way back from the nightmare, Violet focused in turn on Emily's concerned pout, Mason's palliative baritone, and Jack's tentative hand on her ankle. She had been plagued by bad dreams after her parents died and was sufficiently self-aware to realize that Firestorm's abduction had triggered a relapse. "I'm okay. I'm okay," she told her friends. "I'm sorry. I had a nightmare, but I'm fine. I'm okay. I'm sorry..."

Sleep had been restorative. Therefore, despite their sore muscles and injuries, they resolved to explore the outpost before dark. They took turns in the bathroom, but this time, they availed themselves of the bare-bones shower, which was separated from the toilet by a shabby, calf-length curtain. The shower was unheated, but a crowded shelf was stocked with basic toiletries and towels. In their current state, it was a veritable five-star spa. They still had to wear their torn and soiled clothes, but at least their bodies and teeth were clean. The women tightly braided each other's hair, and Mason tore up a kitchen rag to make canary-yellow ribbons to bind the braids. The first aid kit was put to good use, too. Most critically, Violet applied butterfly stitches to Jack's neck and Emily's hands and bound them in medicated bandages.

Ravenous, they raided the kitchenette. Mason chewed contemplatively on his peanut butter crackers, then he voiced what everybody was thinking. "So, Jack...that thing with the beaver...that was pretty cool."

Even in the diminishing light, the tips of Jack's ears shone pink. "Mmm," he hummed neutrally around a mouthful of room-temperature tortellini. After he had assuaged his initial panic, his "connection" with the level-headed rodent had actually been quite stabilizing. Jack could *feel* the animal's unflappable determination.

Sitting cross-legged on a cot, Emily gnawed on a chocolate protein bar and considered reminding her friends about the birds that had also helped guide them to safety. Instead, she opted for a theory. "Maybe we're elves," she suggested.

The others were amused, but their sniggers receded when Emily sat there with a straight face and they realized that she was serious. Jack snorted. "Come on, Em. Elves aren't real."

"You're right, Jack," Emily conceded. "The idea is implausible. You're right, of course." Emily waited a beat, licking chocolate from her lips, then she added sardonically, "I mean, we're *communicating with animals*. This certainly isn't the time to be thinking outside the box."

Duly chastised, Jack expelled a booming, highly contagious belly laugh. Though the merriment was short-lived, it was the first time that anyone relaxed in what felt like ages. Still grinning, Emily stood up and began to meander around the dome, preoccupied, while the others talked. They could not hide at the outpost much longer. They needed a plan. Emily reached out with unbandaged fingertips as she aimlessly roamed. They skimmed over a pH meter, an aluminum teakettle, and a trowel. They stilled in front of a map that was affixed to the wall near the door. It was disfigured by sallow blotches, ink smears, and curled edges, unreadable in spots, but Emily's mind cried "Eureka!" and she detached it with care. "Violet," she called, "come look at this!"

Emily pressed the document flat on a desk and beckoned her friend. Violet bent over to examine it. "Fulminara!" she exclaimed.

"Yes… It's a beautiful topographic map," Emily replied dreamily. "Look at the rich detail. It's a crime that they treated it so roughly. Printed documents are incredibly rare."

"I think the scientists were actually *using* it. Like, actively. See here?" Violet gently tapped on an area of concentric circles. "The font is different. It's penmanship. Someone added a handwritten notation about the valley between the Bisous Hills."

With nightfall imminent, Emily and Violet examined the map to determine their location and heading while Jack and Mason investigated the grounds outside the dome. Honey Hill appeared to be their surest hope. When the boys returned, mud-spattered and donning big, gummy smiles, Emily relayed the decision. "Honey Hill is our best bet," she declared, "but it's about fifty miles away. Violet and I have plotted the fastest practical route, but it'll probably take us two days to get there. I'll be the first to admit that I'm not in ideal physical condition for this kind of trek, but it's the safest option."

"I defer to your knowledge of the island," Jack said as he crossed to the bathroom to wash his hands. He left the door open and raised his voice. "But what if the bastards who attacked the farm are staking out Honey Hill?"

"That assumes they know about me," Emily countered. "Even if they believe I'm friendly with Violet and Mason, they can't link me to the hacking. At most, they might suspect that I'm tangentially involved. I doubt they would bother with Honey Hill." Emily recognized the flaws in her logic. She was trying to mask her fear with false bravado. Violet was not fooled. She linked arms with Emily where the two women were slumped side by side against the desk.

"The fact is," Violet said slowly, picking her words with care, "there may be no safe haven for us, but Honey Hill feels less risky than showing up at a random homestead and hoping the occupants haven't been poisoned against us by the government. I have been charged with crimes, big-league *crimes*, however bogus, and I dragged you all down with me." She flapped her free hand to curtail the predictable squawk of objections. "If Honey Hill's not being watched, we can regroup there. If it is..." Violet hesitated, giving her friend's arm a kindly squeeze, "then we need to check on Emily's grandparents. It seems to me that the only real complication is that we're tired, battered, and ill-equipped. A fifty-mile wilderness hike will be *hard*."

"We can help with that," Jack chirped. His smile returned, and he patted Mason's shoulder as the other man came back from his turn at the bathroom sink. Excitedly, they proceeded to tell Violet and Emily about the beat-up ATV in the storage shed behind the dome. It was a two-seater and only partially charged, but with some contortions and luck, they could drive it until the battery choked.

Mason snagged a waterproof duffel backpack from the floor near the door where it had been deposited unnoticed. "We found this, too," he said, tossing the bag to Jack who brandished it like an auctioneer, angling it this way and that while Mason chattered. "It had a bunch of instruments and sensors in it. We dumped those out, and now we can raid this place for as much food, medicine, and supplies as it can hold."

Energized, the group sorted and prioritized the dome's remaining stores. They loaded both the duffel and their coat pockets, empty from when Violet had dried the garments at her house. They had escaped with only their DCs, which they had toted protectively through the wilds even though the devices could not be used. In many ways, a DC was an extension of self. Citizens were nigh on glued to them from childhood, and apparently, being on the lam did not alter that.

By the time they finished packing, moonshine was seeping unevenly through the mucky skylights. They rotated through the bathroom and first aid kit, scarfed down unheated spaghetti and pound cake, and settled in for more sleep. Emily insisted on sharing her cot with Mason. She felt guilty about him sleeping on the floor but was unwilling to suffer it herself. They reclined head-to-foot, and after extensive shuffling and a near-miss broken nose, they were tolerably arranged. Violet and Jack spooned on the other cot. Violet burrowed into Jack's warmth and relished the soft, even puffs of air that bathed her neck. But when it occurred to her that almost twenty-four hours had passed since Firestorm's kidnapping, her fragile optimism was engulfed by a black hole of grief. She remained awake for a long while, tracking shadows on the walls.

Before the sun's disk broke the eastern horizon, they gathered by the ATV under a cloudless, periwinkle sky. Dragon's-breath fog swathed the river valley, and syrupy wisps of it billowed and rolled about their legs. As the most experienced driver, Emily slid behind the wheel and scrutinized the vehicle's controls. Being smaller than Jack, Mason claimed the passenger seat. Violet perched precariously on Mason's lap, clutching the handgrips. Jack was pretzeled on the cargo rack with the duffel.

"I hope the beaver isn't watching this," he groused under his breath, wiggling in vain to find a more dignified position.

As the ATV had no roof, roll cage, or seat belts, Emily watchfully bypassed the worst terrain. Even so, it was a bone-jarring ride. Lacking proper seats, Jack and Violet bore the brunt of it, and it was a minor miracle that neither was ever thrown from the vehicle. Violet's cheek was sliced by a thorny vine, but she made no fuss and declared it a bargain price to pay for the wheels. To maximize the regenerative capacity of the battery, they did not stop until it died. At that point, the ATV had carried them about twenty-five miles. They rolled to a stop at the bottom of a reedy hill adjacent to a swamp that Emily had been cautiously orbiting. She released her death grip on the steering wheel and alighted into a patch of fat cattails. This was a suboptimal locale for a break, but they were too stiff and achy to care. Beyond the cigar spikes of the cattails and throngs of fine, red-brown phragmites, the swamp was a glossy, clear-watered expanse dotted with hardwood trees and bald cypresses draped in fuzzy moss. While the women consulted the map, Mason and Jack set off to explore the area, brimming with callow wonder. Regrettably, they returned to the ATV in short order, their awe dampened by greedy insects and sharp-toothed plants. The group decided that even though it would be faster to cut across the swamp using its sporadic pockets of land as stepping stones, they could not chance getting their supplies wet. Instead, they climbed uphill where the swards were less dense, then they hugged the verge of the wetlands until they could turn east. Plentiful sunshine warmed their skin, curbed by a gentle breeze. From the higher elevation, it was evident that they had made the right choice. The sprawling swamp would have surely been too treacherous and disorienting without a Sméagol to guide them.

Hours later, they spotted a winding river in the distance. They paused to consult the pilfered map, then they hiked across the river's verdant flood-plain. The flat span was bejeweled with herbs and flowers. Fertile patches of sedge and wild rye mingled with a profusion of bluebells, mustard-yellow coneflowers, bloodred lobelia, and white buttercups. The view was such a sweetly painful reminder of her family that Violet's breath stuck in her throat. "You know," she rasped, "Firestorm likes to eat wildflowers when we go riding. He usually avoids the ones that are toxic, but he had a bad run-in with buttercups once. Now if one sprouts up in his pasture, he tramples it like it's Lucifer rising." Smiling, she brushed her hand over the blossoms in question. "He never nibbles on the flowers that grow in the pots and gardens around the farm, though. When Mom was alive, she used to show him the flowers she was cultivating. She'd lift a pot up to his nose and tell him he could 'look but not touch.' They had an understanding." Violet sniffled, and Jack and Emily reached for her hands. They bracketed her for a time while Mason walked ahead. He picked his way toward the water, guiltily cognizant of every flower he could not avoid crushing under his boots.

It was dusk when they hobbled to the river's edge and collapsed onto its sunbaked stones. The sky was royal blue with a thin tangerine ribbon at the horizon. Despite having taken a few breaks since they abandoned the ATV, their muscles were shrieking from overexertion. Emily unfolded the map and squinted at it in the dying light. "We skirted the Stillwater Wetlands," she said, giving the map a declarative poke. She traced a line with her finger and noticed that blood had soaked through the bandage on that hand. She ignored it. "Using the sun as a compass and watching for geographical mark-ers, I think we've done a good job pointing east." Mason handed her a protein bar. She shoved a hunk into her mouth and kept talking. "This should be the

Frost River. There's a stone bridge approximately eight miles south of Honey Hill where the road crosses the water. We need to find that bridge."

The temperature was dropping rapidly. The friends elected to nap before it became dangerously cold, then they would hike during the night to keep warm. However, their riverside position was too exposed and stony, not conducive to sleep. They shambled upstream in search of a better place to camp. As they walked, the ground grew muddier and more eroded, but there was also more vegetation. Stately alders and willows stabilized the bank with their industrious network of roots. Broad-leafed reeds cropped up in congested clusters and steadily pushed them farther from the water. As the stars sharpened overhead, the terrain grew steeper. They climbed higher and nested among two mossy boulders and the exposed roots of a downed tree. Tucked up in stolen blankets, they dozed fitfully for several hours. The disquieting sensation of insects crawling on his skin woke Mason repeatedly. Even after he was completely cocooned in blankets, he was too disturbed to truly rest.

Gusty winds blew in solid, featureless clouds while they slept. The clouds blotted out the moon, and without a celestial nightlight, it was very difficult to see. They tried to stay within earshot of the water, but hazards near the river forced them afield time and again. Mason scraped his other knee when jagged sedimentary rock gave way underfoot. His fall ripped another tear in his trousers for good measure. Emily slipped on a slimy tree root. She hit her head hard, but when her double vision cleared, she claimed to be uninjured. Monitoring her closely for signs of a concussion, they plodded onward. Eventually, though, they were surrounded by opaque forest with neither sight nor sound of the river. They had to call a halt.

Violet rested on a rutted granite boulder that jutted out from the peak of a steep rise. The rock was a lopsided ramp, and while Violet perched on the low end, Emily scooted higher to stretch out her legs and pluck burrs from her stockings. "At this rate," Violet sighed, "we're gonna miss the bridge."

Jack glanced up from where he was cleaning the new cuts on Mason's knee. Weak moonlight had started to escape through breaks in the fast-moving clouds. It filtered through the tree boughs to paint Violet in the shifting shadows of a film noir. With difficulty, Jack wrested his eyes away and resumed his task.

"The road is unpaved and overgrown. We could breeze right past it in the dark," Emily added morosely. "I don't even know if we're lined up to intersect it anymore."

They were quiet for a time, listening to the nocturnal birds and rustling leaves. But the longer they rested, the more Emily felt a swelling urgency to reach Honey Hill. She was running on fumes and worried about her grandparents. She crawled to the boulder's highest point and sat back on her heels to search for a landmark, something, *anything*, that might guide her home. A swarm of bioluminescent bugs buzzed in the nearby trees. A few buoys of golden light danced closer. A bold one landed on Emily's hand. She held it up to her face, considering. Her heart began to hammer, and she drew up on her knees. The firefly departed.

"Violet! Violet, come here!" she called. Exhausted tears clogged her throat. Emily reached down to haul Violet up the rock so that her friend could see the unbroken pixie-dust trail of bobbing, flickering light that was laid out before them.

"Look! They're showing us the way!"

CHAPTER 17

GROUNDED

Guided by the shimmering honey trail, aided by cracks of moonlight in the clouds, they trekked their way slowly to the bridge. Whenever a firefly floated close by, Emily whispered an emphatic "Thank you." She was careful to *think* it, too, unsure if they could understand her verbally. Mason vowed repeatedly that he would never swat an insect again. Unfortunately, their glowing escorts were oblivious to the ground conditions, and the rugged terrain tested the group's tenuous limits. When Violet slipped on a muddy incline, Jack grasped her arm and did not let go for nearly an hour, until he needed both hands to descend a rocky ledge. A short while later, the group finally regained sight of the river. Its black ribbon was illuminated by the falling moon like glitter on oil.

The fireflies were widely spaced once they reached the water, and the little bugs vanished entirely at the bronze break of dawn. This section of the river was broad. Steep gradients bred turbulent, white-foamed rapids. The shore was a silty accumulation of sand and pebbles, but it was risibly narrow, so the friends were forced to hike through the neighboring vegetation. The air smelled strongly of damp moss and the sharp, terpenoid scent of evergreens. While they walked, brighter light started to push through the canopy. Jack spotted a needle-covered deer path that they gratefully followed until they arrived at the bridge. Made of rough-hewn stone, the bridge had an ageless, three-arch edifice through which the river flowed. The water was tinged brown with runoff from the recent storm. A chiseled sign was partially hidden behind a welter of berry bushes. It read Welcome to Honey Hill. As they traversed the bridge, Emily took the lead. She trudged forth on autopilot, inexorably drawn toward *home, home, home*.

Parts of the road were overrun with clover and wooly thyme, but it was easy to follow. They listened to thready birdsong and did not speak. The grade grew steeper, murder on their overworked muscles. The thinning trees admitted warm, unfettered fingers of sunlight. Jack removed his coat and shoved it into the duffel. The group had eaten enough rations by now to make space. Jack regarded the duffel as his responsibility. His shirt was drenched in sweat, and his skin was chafed where the canvas laid against him. Mason had offered to relieve him, but Jack was too worried about his lately tortured friend to agree. Emily was not fit enough for the added burden, and the duffel was too big and unwieldy for Violet's five-foot-three-inch frame.

Midmorning, they passed a low stone wall with a weather-beaten placard that marked the official border of the Steuben estate. Beyond the wall, legions of prairie grass swayed in the breeze. Honey Hill was not, actually, one hill; it was a collection of hills and lesser hillocks. From the travelers' position on the old western road, the view of the main hill was obstructed. As they walked, plumes of black smoke began to drift overhead. They forced their bodies to climb faster. Minutes later, they heard the unmistakable snap of flames. The road crested, and the agony of Honey Hill was revealed.

Maddeningly hindered by fatigue, they closed the remaining distance to discover that all three of the estate's houses had suffered structural and fire damage. The adjacent prairieland was ash, but thanks to the elevated moisture level from the rain, fire was no longer spreading. A blast radius was clearly demarcated by far-flung debris, mostly masonry, shingles, and glass. Although the buildings were constructed of refractory brick that could withstand grassfires, the interiors were vulnerable once they were exposed. The top floor of Emily's parents' home was missing, and flames poured out of the gaping wound. The east wall of Emily's house had collapsed, and it, too, was bleeding fire. The third house was largely unscathed, but dramatic spalling and cracking was visible, and the chimney had buckled. The group circled the houses, impeded by the heat. They hesitated on the fringe of the courtyard, glass underfoot and cinder snowflakes above, shaken by the enormity of the crisis. The fire crackled and popped, *tick*, *tick*, *ticking* like a death knell.

Desperate to find her grandparents, Emily loped to their house as fast as her drained body would go. She glanced forlornly at the ruins of the other houses as she passed. Bent at the middle, she held her skirt over her nose and mouth to protect her from the billowing smoke, wishing that she could stop at the courtyard's water pump to dampen it. Terrified that her family was injured or worse, she opted to make do without. She tripped on a cracked flowerpot, then on a bicycle, and by the time she pushed aside the door that was hanging limply from one hinge, aggravated tears were making tracks down her dirty cheeks. She barreled through rooms and ignored the obvious dangers posed by a broken stairwell and a caved-in interior wall. She shouted for her grandparents between hacking coughs. Acrid smoke hovered thickly on the north side of the house, betraying an unseen fire and forcing Emily away.

Seeing Emily run straight for disaster jolted her friends into action. Jack shrugged the duffel off his shoulders and sprinted into the house after Emily. He made a pit stop in the mostly undamaged kitchen to dampen two dish towels. He forced one into Emily's hand when he found her coughing uncontrollably outside the primary bedroom. While they finished searching inside, Violet combed the grounds around the house, calling for Hannah and Dimitri in the loudest smoke-hoarse voice she could muster. Hope flared when she spotted the couple's garden shed and workshop. The building appeared to be unharmed, but the pungent haze that was pouring off the seething remains of the bordering tallgrass made it difficult to see. Violet did not notice Emily's grandparents huddled in the dirt, hiding among the charred vestiges of sweet corn and sugar beets, until she had nearly stumbled over them. They were blackened with soot, trembling, and disoriented, but they perked up instantly when they recognized Violet. Dimitri sported a swollen right eye and an amorphous red-purple bruise across the entire left side of his face, and they both suffered from minor burns and smoke inhalation, but on balance, they were remarkably uninjured. Violet supported the elderly pair, taking their weight as best she could, as they staggered to the courtyard to find Emily.

Meanwhile, Mason scoured the area for an engineering outbuilding. He hit pay dirt partway down the eastern gravel road where a sharp turnoff led to a small garage that was normally concealed by eight-foot bluestems. The door was unlocked. Mason started the backup power generator and hurriedly rebooted Honey Hill's disabled systems, prioritizing fire suppression and air quality. Flashing red symbols on the master display highlighted all the spots where the estate had been destroyed, but key safety features were still functional elsewhere. Concerningly, the recycling system was badly damaged. Mason rerouted the lines as a stopgap and tinkered with the estate's environmental controls, then he dislodged a first aid kit from its housing on the wall and walked up the hill to find out if his efforts had made a difference.

Mason picked his way past the beleaguered houses. He gave them a wide berth, pleased by the absence of flames yet wary of their structural soundness. The scent on the air was a nauseating potpourri of burnt plastic, scorched earth, and something akin to decaying fish. When he rounded the westernmost house, he saw his friends gathered on the periphery of the courtyard. He broke into a wobbly jog.

"Is this your doing, young man?" Dimitri boomed as Mason approached. Coughing, the elder gestured broadly to the dissipating smoke and the grimy water that was pooling in the grooves between the cobblestones. Dimitri's voice was raspy, and his smile was a lopsided mess on his severely swollen face, but his coffee eyes shone with gratitude and respect. "*Spasiba. Spasiba.* Thank you," he said, clasping Mason's shoulder.

Emily threw her arms around Mason and crushed him wordlessly. She plucked the well-stocked first aid kit from his hand and began to treat Dimitri's injuries. A family squabble ensued when Dimitri insisted on caring for Hannah first. As a compromise, Violet cleaned Hannah's burns and applied curative bandages while Emily tended to her grandfather. Dimitri held a chemical cold pack to his face, and Emily injected an anti-inflammatory using the kit's high-tech medical apparatus. Jack hobbled to the garden shed to retrieve another first aid kit and two sterile oxygen masks with a portable reservoir. He was surprised that the family owned such equipment, but on reflection, he realized that the residents of Fulminara had to be prepared for all manner of emergencies since there was no hospital on the island. In Apricus, medical help was only minutes away. Jack ferried the supplies back to the courtyard with a complicated knot of guilt in his belly.

The seniors benefitted immediately from the oxygen, and between the two first aid kits, ample medicine was stocked for everyone to receive a potent analgesic and a shot of restorative serum, which would significantly bolster and accelerate the body's natural healing abilities. Jack and Violet enthusiastically accepted their injections from Emily. When it was Mason's turn, however, he recoiled from Emily and batted at the hideously familiar gadget in her hand. He had to be talked down from a panic attack before he submitted over a half hour later.

Alerted by the bloodstained bandages on Jack's neck, Violet set to work replacing his mangled sutures while Hannah and Dimitri unmasked to tell the story of Honey Hill's demise. An armed security detail had arrived that morning with a military escort. Dimitri was walking to the east prairie to perform maintenance on the septic system. He heard the crunch of boots on gravel and called out a greeting. In a flash, two men were gripping his biceps. Another four proceeded to the houses and pounded on the doors. "I knew something was terribly wrong. All I wanted was to get to Hannah," Dimitri recalled. Hannah took her husband's hand and caressed his weathered palm reassuringly. "They were barking out questions. Hostile. They were looking for you, *solnyshko*." Emily made a piteous noise, ashamed of her culpability. Dimitri rested his other hand on his granddaughter's cheek. He swept away a teardrop with his thumb and gave her a good-humored wink with his unswollen eye. "I had no mind to tell them anything, so they tried some *physical persuasion. Pfft*, I survived the Moscow Riots. A rifle butt to the face will not faze me."

Hannah picked up the tale at that point, partly to cover Dimitri's mumbled stream of Russian profanities. She shifted restively, unable to find a comfortable position where they were seated on the stones, a safe distance from the wreckage. The afternoon was muggy, but the heat was tempered by a steady breeze that carried away the lingering smoke and fumes. "Dimitri found me as soon as he recovered," Hannah rasped, "but by then, these, these *interlopers*, had already torn each house apart, shouting for the four of you. They intended to arrest you. I wouldn't answer their questions, and when they got rough with me, Dimitri interceded. He took a few more punches for his trouble." Hannah gazed fondly at her husband, but her brow was creased with regret.

"Everything happened so fast," Dimitri added. His right eye had fused shut, and cinders were stuck to his balding head in mockery of the hair he had lost with age. "We did not notice the aircraft until it was directly above us. It blocked out the sun. The *soldaty* were lifted on harnesses, then the ship opened fire and set the Hill ablaze." Dimitri worked his throat. His prominent Adam's apple bobbed unhappily. "Hannah and I watched it burn. I thought such days were behind us…"

As the couple fleshed out their account, the ruined houses contributed irregular creaks and moans that spoke poignantly of irreparable damage and loss. The others offered what hollow comfort they could.

"I am so sorry, Grandpa," Emily choked. Her eyes were glazed with tears, but her body had grown too dehydrated to let them fall. "I'm sorry, Grandma. I'm so sorry..." Hannah stroked Emily's hair and shushed her, contending that it could not possibly be her fault. "But it is," Emily replied miserably.

When Emily failed to explicate, Hannah pressed her, "Tell us what is happening, dear. Why has your DC been offline? How did you get these injuries? What kind of trouble are you in?" There was no judgment in Hannah's tone, only concern.

Emily recounted a redacted version of events that she promised to augment later. "Right now, though," she stammered, "I need some time to myself, please." With life having mellowed to DEFCON 2, Emily felt irrepressibly dazed from prolonged physical and emotional strain. She limped off alone to witness the devastation of Honey Hill.

Jack empathized with Emily's need to grieve in solitude. To give her a modicum of privacy, he proposed inspecting the most undamaged house to surmise if it could be occupied safely. Hannah's kitchen and the rest of the ground floor had seemed fairly secure when he'd blown through it earlier. Everyone agreed with Jack's suggestion, so he and Mason fell to the task. Violet stayed behind to answer questions about what Emily had shared, though she obfuscated certain colorful details, such as those involving telepathy and torture. Violet activated a new cold pack for Dimitri and piled a stack of purloined blankets under Hannah to ease the woman's obvious discomfort. Together, they kept a weather eye on Emily as she orbited the rubble like a castaway adrift in a shipwreck. Stricken blue eyes peered into the charred maw that used to be the east side of her home. For endless minutes, she stared at the mutilated bones of her armoire, discernable among the piles of sooty, waterlogged debris by the sickly blue-green patina on its busted brass hardware.

At first, Emily's attention was riveted to the houses, but after a while, it shifted to the broader courtyard and pond. Seeing where his granddaughter was headed, Dimitri scooched closer to Hannah and folded his agitated hands atop his head. Hannah buried her face in Dimitri's chest and fisted handfuls of his grimy shirt. Emily was unaware of their distress. She shuffled blearily toward her beloved pond. Just beyond the hazy blast radius, she met a nightmarish scene. With a soundless scream, Emily doubled over, clutching her arms around her abdomen as if she had been punched. Dozens of dead ducks were strewn along the stony boundary of the pond or floating lifelessly in the water. Wings were bent at sickening angles. Listless puffs of smoke rose from smoldering pockets of vegetation. An obscene oil slick of blood and feathers coated the shoreline. Emily staggered closer to the carnage. Birds lay twisted on the cobblestones at her feet. The rusty scent of death filled her nose. She recoiled again, and her eyes slammed shut. She mumbled incoherently into her hands while painful, guttural sobs rattled her chest. A metallic taste settled on her tongue, which felt bloated in her mouth. Hannah and Violet rushed to Emily's side. "Why, Grandma?" she whimpered. "Why didn't they fly away?"

The ducks had been slaughtered before the estate was bombed. While prowling the grounds in search of Emily, a soldier accidentally knocked over a bucket of grain, and the ducks came running. They did not recognize the danger, having always been safe at Honey Hill. They toddled toward the bucket, *slap, slap, slapping* their little webbed feet on the cobblestones, quacking raucously, and flapping their wings in excitement. Irritated, the soldier began to shoot the guileless birds. He was quickly joined by others who made a game out of killing the ducks. Extra points for gunning down the ones that had instinctually fled to the sky.

"It was brutal and senseless," Hannah choked. "I am so very sorry, my dear, sweet girl." Hannah swept her hand in long strokes down Emily's back. Violet breathed exaggeratedly slow and deep from her belly, insisting that Emily mimic her.

Emily calmed down. Her dry sobbing subsided. Numb, she zombie-walked to the lip of the pond and knelt. She gazed despairingly at the cruel tableau, unwilling to focus on specific ducks, shying away from singed flesh and the atavistic horror of snapped wings. And everywhere, everywhere, feathers. A clean, brown covert sat near her left knee. She picked it up reverently and spun it between her thumb and index finger. A faint whistling bark reached her ears. Emily dropped the feather and followed the sound, crawling on her hands and knees. Tall shoreline rocks formed a small nook that was concealed on the water side by cattails. Inside, five teeny, shivering ducklings huddled close. Emily retrieved the ducklings one by one. She cradled them in her skirt and assured them that everything would be okay, uncertain how that could possibly be true, nearly gagging on the lie.

Hannah searched the courtyard for a pail. With Dimitri's help, she found one that was intact and cool to the touch. Emily started to transfer the yellow-brown birds to the pail. The traumatized hatchlings chattered softly, nonstop. The wounds on Emily's hands had reopened, and she became distracted by the blood seeping through her bandages. She lifted a hand and stared at it blindly. Hannah gently lowered Emily's hand, stroked her cheek, and said, "I will look after the ducklings, sweetheart." She lifted the last fluffy orphan from Emily's skirt and returned to Dimitri with her precious cargo.

Violet knelt beside Emily and drew her into a one-armed hug. Emily rested her temple on Violet's shoulder. "What are they saying?" Violet whispered tearfully.

Emily allowed herself to process the desperate, anguished call of the ducklings. Overwrought, she had been trying to block it out since the first sad chirp hit her ears. "It's just one word, one concept. Over and over," she replied. "Mother. They're calling for their mother."

CHAPTER 18

WHEAT AND CHAFF

His orders had been crystal clear: (1) Acquire the horse. (2) Raze the estate. (3) Kill the rebels.

Not necessarily in that order.

The mission was simple, backed by the full potency of society's cutting-edge military and security assets. Yet unbelievably, the so-called elite joint task force had failed on one count.

"All four human targets fled into the woods," the steely-eyed lieutenant had reported. "A go-team was rapidly dispatched, but the pursuit has been unsuccessful."

"Unsuccessful," the president echoed scathingly. A purple vein bulged on his forehead. His voice started out low and restrained, but it amplified with each word. "How could you lose them in the woods?! *Just burn the fucking woods down!*" he bellowed.

The lieutenant blinked, unsure if he had just received an order. He chose to ignore the president's outburst and stood his ground. "Storm conditions impeded our ability to track them—"

"You're telling me," the president interrupted, livid, "that with the most sophisticated technology in human history at your disposal, you cannot find four people, on foot, in a forest?"

"They deactivated their DCs, sir, and thermal imaging—"

"I don't want excuses! Find them. Find them, lieutenant, or you won't be boarding a shuttle."

Now, days later, the trail was cold. The task force argued that the targets could not survive, unprepared, in the wilderness, but the president never left matters to chance. With no prisoners or corpses to provide closure, he put the bureaus on high alert and convened his senior staff.

Unlike most staff meetings, the president entered a quiet room. The alert level had not been high since the early days of Apricus when the caverns were unstable and roving pirates cased the city like starving, rabid dogs. He trailed his fingers over the burnished alloy table and let his team stew a bit. "I will tolerate no bureaucratic bullshit today," he warned. They sat up straighter at his language. "There will be no droning report-outs, no number-crunching, no hand-wringing, and no debate. The best and brightest of our military and security forces have proved incapable of apprehending the four civilians who were implicated in the hacking of confidential files for Projects Noah and Pioneer. As a result, the bureaus were placed on high alert." Some of his people visibly relaxed, dropping their shoulders and releasing held breaths. It infuriated him. "The fugitives are a tangible threat," he insisted. "Since they have not been detained, we must fast-track our plans again. I am hereby ordering you to execute Phase 3, effective immediately." The collective gasp was as satisfying as it was predictable. He watched their bodies stiffen with tension. One or two deputies were obviously itching to speak but thought better of it. "I realize that it is not feasible to board the shuttles *today*," the president soothed. "You have twenty-four hours to modify your workplans and inform the populace of the new schedule. I want everyone evacuated within five days. Tell them that an imminent threat to the city has catalyzed us to adjust the timeline. Seismic activity, I'd say." He turned to the woman on his left. "What do you think, Jennifer?" The deputy nodded mutely. Her mouth hung slightly open.

The president had expected a blowup at this point, but the others all looked as unstrung as Jennifer. It was disconcerting. He leaned back and crossed his arms, wondering if it would be preferable for them to express what was on their minds. "I have confidence in you to make this happen," he encouraged. "What questions or concerns do you have?" The room exploded with shrill voices like an aerosol can left in the sun. "Nope," he decided to himself, "stunned silence was better."

"Quiet!" the president roared, unfolding his arms. The voices stopped short. "We have failed to catch the rebels, which puts everything we have labored for at risk." His shrewd eyes made a circuit of the room. The linear chandeliers tipped his eyelashes in gold. "I know you," he intoned. "You don't think you should have to scramble just because a few inconsequential citizens went rogue. Isn't that right, Kabir?" He stared challengingly at the wide-nosed senior deputy from the Housing Bureau.

"Sir, I have read the security briefs. Even if the criminals did escape, they have no access to Apricus and insufficient resources to cause trouble remotely. I am hesitant to rush after years of careful planning." Kabir's shaky hands raked through the clod of black hair atop his head. Razor stripes divided these longer locks from the shaven hair on the sides of his head. His fingers traced the stripes nervously.

"You have failed to grasp the situation, Kabir." The president waited, pointedly tracking the movement of Kabir's fingers until the man stopped fidgeting and tucked his hands under his thighs. "This rebellion must be squashed," he preached, "and for all our glorious technology, we cannot seem to manage that. Given time to breathe, it will become a hydra. Then, if we finally do manage to cut off its head, if we finally do capture the first four rebels, two more heads will simply grow in its place. Do you understand?"

"Sir, I-I-I know nothing about hydras, but I trust your judgment, of course. However, that does not change the fact that we are not ready to begin departures."

"*Get* ready," the president snapped. He rose abruptly, and the casters on his chair squeaked. The sound ricocheted as he strode to the door. "Meeting adjourned." From his office, he watched his staff spill out of the conference room. He knew that his orders seemed rash. In their minds, momentous undertakings should be as ponderous as a pahoehoe lava flow, inching forward with the gravity of importance. But the president was not reckless. He had already run the numbers. They could accelerate the timeline with minimal fuss. And it was too risky to wait.

Less than twenty-four hours later, an urgent message was pushed to every household conveying new departure dates for all briefing packet colors except red, which remained TBD. By way of explanation, they were told that experts monitoring the ocean floor had predicted potentially cataclysmic volcanic activity and consequent earthquakes and tsunamis that would pose a direct threat to Apricus. The government was unwilling to endanger lives when humanity was so close to deliverance. Therefore, they needed to move faster. It was vital, the message read, to shift one's mindset from *relocation* to *evacuation*.

VDUs across the city began to transmit departure bulletins on a never-ending loop, including frequent encouragements from the Communications Bureau to stay calm and optimistic. "The galaxy awaits," effused one of the bureau's favorite bokeh posters. "Our moment has come!" Concurrently, armed security personnel took up posts to supplement the usual neighborhood patrols. The sudden proliferation of alleged peacekeepers (with visible sidearms, no less) soured the public mood. Still, faced with a revised timetable and looming destruction, nobody had much bandwidth to lodge a complaint.

The afternoon sun was hot over Honey Hill when Jack and Mason emerged from the house. Combined with the heat of the burned-out buildings, it was almost too much. The men had stripped off their layers, retaining only their torn pants and stained white T-shirts with yellowing armpits. They cooled off at the old-fashioned water pump in the courtyard. The others were nowhere to be seen, so on a hunch, they tromped to the garden shed. Thanks to the breeze, residual smoke from the broiled grasslands wafted away from the garden. Violet and Emily were lounging on the ground with their backs against the shed's pockmarked brick wall. Hannah was on her knees, fussing over a handful of sorry-looking plants that might have survived. Dimitri was fussing over Hannah. "Good news!" Jack hailed. "The house needs major repairs, but to a layman's eye, most of the first floor is safe enough for shelter. Thanks to Mason, all critical systems are online." Jack fist-bumped his friend.

Mason smiled modestly. "The reboot snuffed out the fire," he expounded, "but electrical and plumbing repairs are needed. We'll have to put in some manual labor to fix things like the staircase, too."

"One of the interior walls crumbled," Jack reported, "but it wasn't load-bearing. We started to clean up the fragmen—" A paroxysm of coughing stole Jack's words. There had been a tickle in his lungs for the past hour. He and Mason had doubtlessly inhaled any number of harmful particles before the indoor air quality returned to an acceptable level. Dimitri affixed his used oxygen mask to Jack's face, explaining that the reservoir was not empty. It was not strictly hygienic, but Jack was in no state to object.

When Jack's hacking subsided, Mason quipped, "I guess the house has a new, more open floor plan."

Hannah found this exceedingly amusing, and Dimitri soaked up her laughter like a heliotropic flower chasing the sun. He helped Hannah to her feet and beckoned everyone closer to discuss next steps. They formed an imperfect circle, sweaty and squinty-eyed in the cloudless sunshine as the day's temperature hit its apex. Fulminara's weather was erratic at best, but luckily, it was not currently adding to their problems. They could hear the raw sounds of settling debris and the rustle of wind in the unscorched grasses, but there was a conspicuous absence of birdsong. It made sense that the local birds would steer clear of the dangerous conditions on Honey Hill, but Violet wondered if the uncommon hush might also be in deference to the fallen mallards. Not long ago, she would have dismissed the idea as whimsy. Now that she was privy to the complex inner life of animals, she was not so sure.

It was decided that Dimitri and Mason would start the most time-sensitive repairs while Jack helped Hannah to scavenge stable areas of the other buildings for household goods and supplies. Dimitri and Hannah refused to be sidelined, but they agreed to let the boys handle most of the legwork. Pushed well beyond her limit, Emily sat back down during the conference and fell asleep against the shed. Violet volunteered to stay with her and use the time to review the files that Mason had stolen during Operation Lemur. Since Mason could not activate his DC without alerting their enemies, he removed its memory chip via the pointy end of a planting hoe and transferred it to Dimitri's device.

Three hours later, Violet was deeply immersed. Emily snored at her elbow, drooling a tad on the hem of Violet's shirt. First, Violet had read the technical files that Mason had segregated, then she had tackled the rest. Presently, she was studying a compendium of unrelated documents from Projects Noah and Pioneer that she had intuitively curated. Vexed, she pinched the bridge of her nose, tired of trying to assemble a puzzle without all the pieces. It was also very hard to do this work on a handheld. Yet a prickle at the back of Violet's brain egged her on. She cycled through the subset of files again and again, until suddenly, she saw a link.

"Oh my lord," she whispered. "It can't be." Cross-referencing madly, she homed in on sporadic references to the briefing packets. Everything finally clicked, like a seat belt buckle before a roller coaster drop, a sickening fusion of relief and anxiety.

Violet roused Emily, but she did not disclose her discovery. She wanted to reconvene the whole group, ideally in Hannah's kitchen with clean hands and full bellies. The women stretched their cramped muscles, brushed dirt off their clothes, and walked to the house under a flat, vanilla sunset. On the far end of the courtyard, they could see the men solemnly disposing of the dead ducks. Violet headed over to assist while Emily went inside to find Hannah. When the disposal was complete, everyone crowded into the kitchen for fresh bread and a hearty stew. Dimitri and Hannah were seated at the table in the only intact chairs. Violet, Emily, Jack, and Mason sat on the floor, which their hostess had fastidiously swept of debris. They leaned against the cabinets and balanced their plates and mugs in their laps.

"I'm just gonna cut to the chase," Violet stated as she set her meal on the floor. She was still hungry, but she had procrastinated for long enough. "We already knew about Project Noah's policy to terminate animals regarded as unfit for relocation. Well, according to the files we obtained, there is a corresponding policy for people." Violet's jaw-dropper elicited a barrage of expletive-laced interrogatives. "Citizens assigned to the red group are ineligible for relocation," she continued. "They will be left behind due to age, infirmity, or even disposition in some cases—like, having an arrest record. The census appears to have played a big role in gauging a person's fitness using various physiological and psychological scales. Or maybe it was used for final verification. I'm not sure." Violet was briefly lost in mute speculation, but as soon as Jack touched her knee, she said, "Here, let me show you." She projected several marked-up files using Dimitri's DC and explained how she had reached such incredible conclusions.

Hannah was the first to comment after Violet's ad hoc presentation. Her voice croaked from inhaled smoke, but her tone was poised, anchored by hard-won wisdom. "The government's stance on this is appalling," she pronounced. "Immoral. To discard the old, the sick, the damaged. It has happened before, this quest for *purity*. We never seem to learn."

"You mean, like, the Race Wars that preceded the Elbrus Armistice," Mason said, scratching at the prickly scruff under his chin, "or the Dhirwa Jihad."

"Exactly," Hannah affirmed, "and there are nauseating echoes of Nazi Germany, too."

"World War II," Jack offered. "In the twentieth century." His handsome features were contorted in a grimace. Hannah nodded. Jack knocked back the dregs of his malty black tea.

"You are giving us a history lesson for a reason. Yes, Hannah?" Dimitri smiled knowingly at his wife and planted a kiss on her palm.

"Of course," Hannah replied, then she turned her shrewd gaze to the young audience at her feet. "As dispiriting as it is to see the dark past reemerge, it uplifts me to know that good people will fight it. They always have. You know, the Steubens were in the German resistance during World War II. Many of my ancestors were executed by the Gestapo. And though I want my grandchild to be safe, I am proud that she has followed such an honorable tradition."

Pleased, Emily tried to smother a crooked smile with her hand, but her dimpled cheek gave it away. Hannah beamed at her.

"I am proud of *all of you*," she went on, locking eyes with the others in succession, "for laboring to uncover the truth. Dimitri and I are with you. When the government abandons Apricus, it will be a death sentence for those left behind. Even on Fulminara, we will suffer greatly without the city's resources."

"*Da*, well," Dimitri huffed. He smacked his hands once on the tabletop. "We won't solve anything tonight. This day has been too long and troubling. I am a tired old man, and I'm still famished."

Emily dutifully rose to refill Dimitri's plate and ended up serving everyone. They ate in silent contemplation, exchanging looks and touches, too run-down for more conversation. Dimitri and Hannah distributed clean clothing and linens then retired to the guest bedroom. Their usual bedroom was upstairs, unreachable and possibly unsalvageable. Mason and Emily camped out on the furniture in the salon. Jack and Violet created a den on the kitchen floor. Periodically, the injured house would creak or groan, causing Violet to jerk awake. After a few hours of uneasy slumber, she wrapped a chunky crocheted blanket around her shoulders and sat at the table with Dimitri's DC. The clear night sky shot distorted moonbeams through the spiderweb cracks in the kitchen windows. Outside, patches of silver fog settled over the prairie where the surviving grasses swayed like ghosts.

The next morning was a flurry of activity. By 9:30, the inhabitants of Honey Hill were washed, well-fed, and dressed in different or newly laundered clothes, and repairs on the venerable brick house were underway. They bandied ideas about how to expose and disrupt the government's plots, but it was casual chitchat that yielded no real plans. One point was clear, though: there was little they could accomplish while they were cut off on Fulminara. They had to return to Apricus. But before they departed, the younger contingent was determined to make the estate as safe and operational as possible for Hannah and Dimitri. They would spare a couple of days to sweat and strategize.

At midday, Hannah was mashing boiled potatoes in a ceramic bowl when her DC vibrated inside her apron pocket. She set the device on the kitchen counter and read the notification while she wiped her hands on a towel. Alarmed, she pressed a hand to her chest and dropped into the closest chair. A flush raced up her neck to heat her cheeks. She activated the recessed video screen on the wall beside the kitchen table. The casing was cracked, but it worked. Hannah hollered for the others.

Mason and Dimitri were working at a control panel in the mudroom outside the kitchen. Mason wore a sturdy pair of Dimitri's utility pants that Hannah had tailored for him. His face was clean-shaven. On an impulse, he had also given the sides and back of his head a barely-there buzz cut, leaving only a tightly coiled mound of hair on top. The men followed their noses into the kitchen, unconcerned, just as Violet and Jack entered from a matching archway on the opposite side of the room. Hours of hauling debris left the pair perspiring and unkempt. Hannah pointed to the grave-faced news anchor and scrolling red text on the VDU, making it instantly clear that she had not summoned them for lunch. Mason opened the back door, shouting for Emily. Violet had insisted that someone else study the Operation Lemur files to verify her conclusions, so Emily had been sequestered all morning on a chipped stone bench in the courtyard. She was dressed in old overalls and boots that she had stored in her grandparents' guest bedroom, and as she hurried to Mason, he was struck by how strange it was, how *wrong*, to see her in pants, as if a vivid photograph had been tainted by a bundle of dead pixels.

Congregated around the rustic oak table, they learned about the fast-tracked evacuation orders. Dimitri muted the sound when the news restarted with a telltale "If you're just joining us…" The settling house creaked loudly. A territorial hawk screeched overhead.

"This doesn't feel right," Violet scoffed. "The Pioneer materials don't mention hazardous volcanic activity. Even if the oceanographers have their own server, there is obvious crossover with Pioneer, so it's suspicious that there's not even an oblique reference to their findings in our files. I mean, this cannot have snuck up on them."

Mason lowered himself to the floor and rested his head against a cabinet, eyes closed. "A significant issue like this should have been tagged in some way. I had to move fast, yeah, but I paid attention to highly trafficked files, flagged folders, stuff like that."

"I am skeptical, too," Dimitri rumbled. "This announcement reeks of more lies. But that is not our main concern. The first shuttles will depart tomorrow. You must get to Apricus. Expose the government before it is too late. Even if it changes nothing, people deserve the truth."

"I can't just leave you, Grandpa!" Emily moaned. Dimitri was seated at the table in the other chair, and Emily threw her arms around his broad shoulders from behind.

Hannah was the one to reply, "When we were put in the red group, the only group without a departure slot, it occurred to me that we might not be relocated. A couple of old topsiders? Humph, hardly worth the effort." Emily growled a wordless objection. "It's okay, dear. Truly, it is. Your grandfather and I love it here." Hannah reached across the tabletop to clasp Dimitri's hand. "We want to stay. We should have been given a choice. But we *want* to stay."

"What if the earthquake threat is real? The house is already damaged…"

"We will do our best, *solnyshko*." Dimitri placed his free hand over Emily's arm and thumped it gently. "There will be challenges either way. Even if there are no earthquakes, it will be difficult to survive on Fulminara long-term without the city's support."

"Is that supposed to make me feel *better*?" Emily sniffled.

Dimitri chortled warmly. "No, *solnyshko*. I suppose not. But I am Russian. We value our suffering."

A spray of wet chuckles filled the room, then the group was subdued for a time. In due course, Hannah stood up to finish preparing lunch. Her knees creaked as loudly as the floorboards when she moved. Violet assisted her while Jack and Mason left the room to continue restoring the house. Both men had been increasingly anxious to check on their loved ones, and now, they had graduated to a state of near-panic. Manual labor was a welcome opportunity to burn off some nervous energy. Dimitri and Emily huddled at the kitchen table, heads bowed, murmuring softly.

Over heaping servings of schnitzel and mashed potatoes, Emily and her friends agreed to work the rest of the day on the house and leave for the nearest train station in the morning. Jack and Mason focused on reconstructing the stairwell to the upper story while Violet addressed the most egregious damage to the roof, insisting that she was petite and light and therefore best-suited for the perilous job. Dimitri directed their efforts and hovered protectively. They were inexpert and rushed, but every completed task made the house safer and more comfortable.

Meanwhile, Hannah helped Emily to refill the duffel and cram two more hiking packs from the hall closet with food, clothing, and supplies. They picked carefully through the rubble of Emily's house to retrieve her time-released hormone pills from what used to be the half bath. Violet and Emily relied on these pills to prevent menstruation. The thought of having to deal with *that* while on the run made Emily cringe. Afterward, she hung back to salvage some personal effects from the debris: an onyx jewelry box, a hand-carved duck figurine, a framed photograph of her parents, and four books. She had meant to leave everything with her grandparents, but when her heart thudded a painful warning that she might never return to this place, she freed the photo from its spoiled frame and stashed it with the soapstone figurine in one of the packs.

They monitored the news for the rest of the day, but there were no further developments. In spite of their physical and emotional fatigue, sleep was elusive that night. No one felt good about forsaking Dimitri and Hannah to an uncertain fate. Nonetheless, Emily and her friends felt a visceral pull toward Potesta. They needed to reveal what they had discovered. And they needed to dig deeper. The shuttle hangar was in the city, and surely, answers could be found there.

"There's so much secrecy and misdirection," Jack slurred into Violet's hair amid languid, openmouthed kisses. They were tangled together under lightweight blankets, trading watercolor caresses on the cracked kitchen floor. The couple had been carrying on for hours, unguarded and hot and desperate. Whenever they came up for air, they confessed their innermost hopes and fears, which inevitably brought them back to the crisis at hand. This time, though, Violet's only reaction was a sleepy snuffle. Jack rolled over, flung his arm across his eyes, and tried to rest.

The cirrus-streaked dawn felt perversely ominous. Emily tarried near the pond where a luminous blush of champagne pink and gold stained the water. It was time to say farewell. Emily turned to find that Hannah was waiting nearby, hands resting on her hips. Her silver hair was stacked in a braided bun, and a fond smile curled her chapped lips. Emily tried to burn the image into her memory. "You know, dear," Hannah cautioned, "the public may go along with the government, no matter what you do. Even knowing next to nothing about their destination, people intend to board those shuttles today. Disclosing what you've learned may have little effect on them, especially if they believe that Apricus is in danger."

"That's true, Grandma," Emily granted, "but we need to try."

"Yes," Hannah agreed. She towed her granddaughter into a snug embrace. They remained that way for a long while, sunrise-glazed and sad, until Dimitri enfolded them both. Emily shifted to hug him properly and stared at the faded tattoos on his bare forearms.

In time, the others shuffled over to claim Emily and say goodbye, exchanging hugs and velvet words. Violet pressed her DC into Dimitri's meaty hand. "Hook it to some fishing buoys, turn it on, and chuck it in the river," she instructed shakily. "If we're still being hunted, the ruse might divert our pursuers. I don't need it."

It went unsaid that nobody would be contacting her—nobody good anyway. Her family was gone, and the only people she was certain she could trust were at her side. She declined Mason's offer to remove the memory chip and transfer the contents to Dimitri's DC. She would miss her files fiercely, especially the photos, but time was running short and she did not expect to return to Honey Hill. Fortunately, Mason did not push. Dimitri cupped her cheek and nodded. When Violet stepped away, she saw nothing but understanding and acceptance in two pairs of muddy brown eyes.

They set out on foot for the train station, hiking cross-country and avoiding the roads. The morning was sunny but cool. Tall switchgrass and wild rye rippled in the breeze. The land smelled rich and earthy, like buttered popcorn dusted with saffron. Under different circumstances, it would have been a pleasant walk, even with their burdensome gear. Jack carried the duffel. The new backpacks rotated among Violet, Mason, and Emily. The prairie gradually ceded to woodlands. Thickset, needly conifers became more and more populous. Fiery wintergreen cushioned the forest floor and attracted small, chirping thrushes. Before the hikers were completely engulfed by the trees, they stopped to catch a last glimpse of Honey Hill. Violet laid her hand on Emily's shoulder. The panorama was pristine. They were miles removed from the damage on the main hill, and Violet was glad that this remembrance would be unsullied for her friend. She lamented that her final moments at the farm had seen it ash-choked and aflame. That attack had been surgical and absolute, as if the powers that be had wanted to obliterate the estate and all traces of life and love it had ever harbored. In contrast, the violence at Honey Hill had been sloppy and unfinished. Preoccupied, Violet startled when Jack urged the group to keep moving.

Although they were less exposed in the woods, they remained quiet and contemplative, soothed by the warbling birds and rustling foliage. At lunchtime, they rested in a vast grove of red oaks and crab apple trees that was undoubtedly the secret to Fulminara's thriving squirrel population. They reclined against the ridged bark of a couple of closely spaced oak trunks and enjoyed a meal of fresh *Brezeln* and dried fruit. They were delighted when fluffy-tailed rabbits chose to graze in their vicinity and a skittish raccoon with a litter of kits made a short-lived appearance.

Time dragged in the afternoon, alongside their sore feet. They periodically drifted closer to the road to confirm that they were on course. Finally, they reached the unnaturally straight border of an expansive clearing. Not too far off, the island's busiest train station was an elongated, silver-gray structure with a subtle hint of blue on the roof. It looked like a hunk of freshly cut lead. The platform was indoors, but there were extra benches by the parking lot, adjacent to a dining kiosk and numerous VDUs. The friends sank into a bed of pine needles to observe and plan. They could see luggage-laden evacuees milling about the station's entrance. Teenagers were lounging in an open truck bed. A family with two rollicking toddlers was using the food generator.

A herd of white-tailed deer appeared at the eastern forest edge. They leaped through the scrub, glowing aureate in the dappled sunlight. Jack felt a stab of pain behind his rib cage, a pain that he had resolutely tried to suppress ever since Violet's farm was destroyed. "I need to get back to my mum and sister," he spilled in a rush. "They're all I have."

"You will, Jack. We're on our way," Violet reassured. "And you have us, too. We're in this together."

Jack twined his arm around Violet and kissed the top of her head. She wore a stretchy knit beanie, and he missed the texture and scent of her hair. Emily landed a hand on Jack's shoulder and shook him lightly in a gesture that was equal parts solace and pick-me-up. Jack considered his companions. He watched the last deer, an antlered stag, disappear into a copse of sugar pine seedlings. He thought about the beaver, fireflies, and ducks. And he realized that, whatever *this* was, they were indeed in it together—*all* of them.

Like a record scratch, Mason interrupted Jack's revelation. "Violet is right," he rumbled, "but to reach Apricus, we need to get into the maintenance tunnel, and that'll be thornier than I expected." Mason lifted to his knees and pointed at the coal-colored security squad that was patrolling the perimeter of the station. "Look."

Emily swore unintelligibly and stood up, tugging restlessly on her pant legs. "Do you think they're looking for us? Security might just be amped up for the evacuation, even all the way out here."

"Could be both," Mason guessed while getting to his feet. "The problem is that there are three models for these stations, and the entrance to the maintenance tunnel for this model is on the right side of the building." He pointed again. "Around that corner."

"Ugh, how are we going to get *there* without being seen?" Violet groaned. "It's bad enough we need to dodge security, but really, we shouldn't be noticed by *anyone*. Even though there was nothing about us on the news at Honey Hill, that could change at any time."

Jack leaned forward, arms wrapped around his knees, squinting. "The officers don't seem to have visible weapons."

"They probably don't want to freak out the general public," Emily said with a disdainful sniff.

The group fell into silence. The sounds of the forest were drowned out by a child's temper tantrum and the crunch of approaching tires on gravel. Mason leaned against a tree and dug his nails into its cinnamon-red furrows. "We need a diversion," he concluded.

They sat cross-legged in a circle to brainstorm ideas, knees bumping, jittery with worry about being at a standstill for too long. At length, Mason suggested that they split up. He would sacrifice himself as the diversion. "I can explain what you need to do in the tunnel. It should be straightforward. You don't need me to get to Apricus. I can be of more use by distracting the patrol."

His friends did not concur. It was written all over their lemon-pucker faces. "No way," Jack objected. He dipped his head to chase eye contact with Mason when the other man tried to look away. "We're sticking together. Even if we could manage the tunnel without you," Jack reasoned, adding "which I seriously doubt" under his breath, "you're the only one who can break into the government's servers once we get to the city."

"I don't feel like I belong with you!" Mason exclaimed. The others winced, taken aback by both the sentiment and volume. "You all have a common bond—the whole 'communing with nature' thing." He made dejected air quotes with his fingers then posited, "I must not have the same connection with the natural world."

Emily was poignantly reminded of the photos that decorated the walls of his apartment.

Mason dropped his voice. "I'm merely tech support. That other stuff doesn't come as easily to me as it obviously does to you. Not since my cat… and maybe that was all in my head. I miss my damn cat…"

Jack assured Mason that it did not come easily to him, either. "Are you kidding, Jack? Without your 'soul connection' with that beaver," Mason joshed joylessly, reprising the air quotes, "we would never have found the science outpost." Despite the sass, Mason's tone was desolate. His self-doubt had been festering for a while. "I guess I don't speak beaver."

"Listen," Violet implored, "we *all* have this gift. I have no doubt about that. We may not know how or why it's happening, but one thing is clear: this capacity is different for each of us. I couldn't hear the beaver or the birds or the bugs. But I could hear my Firestorm…" Violet said, choking on the beloved name, "and the animals at the bureau. Don't second-guess what happened with Poun—"

The unmistakable swoosh and crunch of movement through the under-brush presaged the arrival of a most unexpected visitor, punctuated by a series of resonant grunts. Everyone froze as a female bear lumbered through a veil of low-hanging pine branches laden with cones. The animal came to a stop about ten feet from their circle, snorting softly and idly poking its curved claws into a pile of dead leaves. Its muzzle was light brown, but the rest of its bushy coat was as black as a dreamless sleep. It observed the awestruck humans with round cocoa eyes. Mason's heartbeat was erratic. Though his lizard brain screamed that he should not look a bear in the eyes, that was precisely what he was doing. He broke out in a cold sweat, but it seemed that his body could spare no further energy for a panic attack. The bear looked away and continued walking, unperturbed.

Gulping air, Mason whispered, "I think I speak bear."

CHAPTER 19

RUN FROM THE WOLF

"It's beautiful," Emily cooed, stretching the adjective like warm caramel. "There are very few bears on Fulminara. They're almost never seen. Years ago, Grandpa spotted one near Shanshui Creek. It was foraging for insects inside decaying logs."

The bear paused again. It sniffed the air and clicked its tongue. "Uh, y'all? I-I think s-she wants to help," Mason posed uncertainly.

Emily quirked an eyebrow. "Help?" she repeated. "How?"

"I'm not sure, Em," Mason snapped. "She's not exactly using sentences!"

Emily and the others fell quiet while Mason focused on the bear. After a couple of minutes, he was able to elaborate. "I'm getting, like, really strong 'protect and defend' vibes from her. I think s-she wants to be our diversion."

Before Mason could even wipe the perspiration from his brow, the bear huffed loudly and broke into a run. It cleared the trees and headed straight for the station, surprisingly fast and agile. "Whoa…" Violet breathed, then all four humans jumped to their feet and scrambled for their gear. The time for reconnaissance and planning was over.

They raced across the belt of bulldozed land that buffered the station from the forest. Brambles thrived in the clearing, and there were many spalted stumps and exposed roots where trees had not been fully removed. When the friends reached the parking lot, the plucky bear charged toward the left end of the building, head down and rounded ears drawn back. Its behavior evoked abundant screaming and running, but no one was harmed. The furry freight train was intent on causing chaos, nothing more.

"Thank you!" Mason called to its retreating form. "Be careful…"

It took mere moments for the bear to distract the security patrol. "Please, please, please don't let them have concealed weapons," Jack prayed to any available deity, shamefully aware that at one time, he might have hunted this incredible animal himself. The commotion lured the patrol far away from the entrance to the maintenance tunnel. The officers began to herd overexcited people into the station while keeping a watchful eye on the cavorting bear. The four trespassers ran around the corner of the building at top speed and slipped inside.

Side by side, they stood plastered to the wall by the door, disheveled and ridiculous, like a police lineup in a Monty Python sketch. To the right, the tunnel was a uniform stretch of diffusely lit, unornamented oblivion. An overweight man in dull khaki coveralls eyeballed them from a circuit board where he was working. "This area is off-limits," he drawled.

Improvising, Emily babbled on about how they had made a break for the "staff only" door to escape the fearsome bear on the loose outside. The man was unmoved by her doe-eyed damsel in distress shtick and reached for his DC. Changing tack, Emily sashayed closer and kept talking but with less animation. She bit her full bottom lip while she searched for the name on the man's security badge. "You know, *James*," she purred when she found it, "you really should take a peek at the bear if you've never seen one. It really is quite something." Distracted by the tonal shift, James the Grade 4 Systems Technician allowed Emily to stroke his arm and gently tow him away from the exposed circuit board. Jack crept up behind them and crimped his arm around the technician's neck so that his windpipe was in the crook of Jack's elbow.

In a deft maneuver, Jack angled his arm and put the palm of his hand on the back of the man's head until he lost consciousness. Emily and Violet helped lower the body to the ground, all the while gaping at Jack. Misconstruing their reaction, Jack hastened to reassure them that the man was simply knocked out.

"What the hell?!" Emily blustered.

Defensive, Jack lashed out. "What? You don't like my methods, Em? Sorry, maybe I should have just wiggled my ass at him. Works for you, right?"

As soon as the technician had been immobilized, Mason had dashed down the tunnel to access a control panel and double-check his recollection of how the maintenance lines were organized. He could never have imagined being thankful for the boundless tedium of upgrading the train system's software, but the exposure was certainly coming in handy today. He whistled softly at Jack's half-truth/half-insult and tuned out of the rest of the quarrel.

"Hey, hey, hey," Violet interceded. "Let's all take a breath." But the combatants were not ready for the white flag. Emily was pink-cheeked and fuming. Jack was scowling at the cataleptic body. He clutched the technician under the armpits and hauled the man into a storage alcove that he had espied during Emily's ad-lib.

Emily followed Jack without helping him. "If I thought that a treatise on the historical importance of the common man's rebellion against oppressive government would have done the trick, I would have gladly stilled my hips," she seethed. "As it was, I used the best tools at my disposal."

"Your body is not a *tool*, Emily!" Jack barked.

"No, it's a weapon. Just like yours."

"Hold up, folks," Violet tried again. Her palms were raised in a placating gesture she typically reserved for aggressive badgers caught hunting squirrels in the farm's flower beds. "That's an awful lot to unpack, and we don't have time right now." She hurried to Mason who had just retracted the control panel and was striding farther into the tunnel. "C'mon!" she bade over her shoulder.

Mason led them to a streamlined, four-seater transport pod. Silver with steel-blue benches, the pod was a miniature version of a passenger train. It moved on a separate network of tracks but used the same subaquatic tube that linked the two islands. Mason shimmied behind the navigation display and shoved his backpack into the footwell. Jack sprang into the adjacent seat with his duffel, which left the back row to the women. Mason inputted their destination, and the pod glided forward, steadily gaining speed. They were heading for the first train station behind the force field that protected the city's main entrance. The energy shield was a technological marvel, though it was not impervious to tsunamis and could fall victim to power disruptions caused by earthquakes or flooding in the caverns. The shield was encoded to recognize and permit the passage of trains and approved foot traffic—salvagers, soldiers, scientists, and the rare hiker—but little else.

Luminous rectangular panels lit the way, spaced such that it was almost completely dark before the pod reached the next panel. Aside from a muted hum, the tunnel was silent. No one had spoken. At first, they were lost in private musings, then they were engrossed in scenery that differed from what they were used to seeing from the train. The pod's track ran beneath the train, so they were deeper undersea and exposed to new aspects of the crumbling buildings and murky waters beyond the translucent tube. Though comparatively few aquatic animals could survive the planet's inhospitable conditions, the oceans were not devoid of life. Microorganisms and several resilient species of invertebrates and fish had adapted. However, they tended to congregate in the more breathable, remote regions of water. It was unusual for anything but debris to drift among the bleak ruins. Hence, they all startled badly when an overlong, greenish-gray shape swam past the tube. Mason slowed the pod to a stop, hoping to see the fish again. It took a while for the curious sturgeon to catch up, but eventually, it hovered beside the tube to the delight of its human admirers. Thick whiskers dangled near its mouth. Its body was covered in rows of bony plates. Despite the armor, its flesh was scored like roughed-up concrete, and chunks were missing from its dorsal and caudal fins. As they watched it depart, Jack murmured, "He's very lonely," bringing an end to their excited chatter. Mason restarted the pod.

Before long, Jack twisted in his seat to look at Emily. "I apologize for what I said, Em. I was anxious," he said, practically swallowing his tongue on the word, "and I did a piss-poor job of expressing myself."

"There," Jack thought, "Dr. Devi would be so proud."

Emily held Jack's gaze. A pouty frown flickered over her features like the tuning of a staticky radio station. She debated being mulish, but Jack's sad little plaint about the sturgeon had already sealed his forgiveness. She wanted to move on. "It's alright, Jack. Apology accepted. I'm sorry that I screeched at you when you took that guy down."

"I gotta say, man, that was totally unexpected," Mason piped up. "How do you know how to do that?"

"When Olivia was going through a martial arts phase, she enrolled in classes at the recreation center. I took the classes, too, so we could spar. I enjoyed it, so I kept going even after Olivia gave it up in favor of soccer."

The four friends nattered amiably until the transport pod reached Potesta. The twilit sky was washed in a lavender afterglow, and the rocky mountainside was flecked with barely visible juniper and flowering lupines. At the cave entrance, the protective force field glimmered like the iridescent edge of a soap bubble. They collected their gear, anticipating the need for a hasty retreat from the maintenance tunnel, which would be much busier inside the city. When the pod cleared the energy shield, it veered onto an enclosed track that ran parallel to the train. From inside the windowless shaft, they could not see the city's portico or the grand colonnade that stretched out to the first train station. Mason monitored their approach in the navigation display.

Less than a mile from their destination, they hit a snag.

The senior deputies were wholly absorbed in Phase 3 implementation, so the president permitted them to proffer their reports remotely unless they were explicitly summoned to a briefing. After the conference room was disassembled, those briefings were moved to the president's office. He listened as the head of the Infrastructure Bureau answered his questions. The president loathed the man's ostentatious handlebar mustache, but his competence and dedication were unimpeachable. Averting his eyes from the hirsute monstrosity, the president perused the room. There were no sign-of-the-times moving crates or furniture pads. The office would be relocated, of course, but the president intended to delay for so long that his staff would be forced to leave the cumbersome desk behind. Presently, a handful of haggard deputies were seated in boxy, midback armchairs in front of said desk. A bevy of black-clad security officers skulked in the corner like a murder of crows.

At length, the president dismissed the deputies and called forward the security officers to discuss the unsuccessful manhunt for the four fugitives. "The task force has every conceivable tool at its disposal and the most highly trained security and military personnel. Explain to me how four *nobodies* with *nothing* have evaded you for days!"

When a skinny man with ebony hair and low cheekbones began to paraphrase the same tired excuses, the president cut him off. "I have heard all this before," he snarled. "Tell me something new." The spokesman flinched at the president's cross tone. His deep-set eyes darted to the notes on his DC.

"There have been no new developments, sir. Nothing unusual has happened in the past twenty-four hours. The only anomaly has been the unauthorized access of a maintenance transport on one of the train lines. But with all the evacuation activity, I'm sure it just wasn't logged properly."

"I see," the president said with a slow-motion nod. Though his cheeks were flushed, he appeared to accept the officer's report and changed the subject. "Is that the new weapon?" He pointed at a compact phaser gun atop the credenza.

"Yes," the officer replied excitedly. He retrieved the phaser and passed it to the president who was still seated behind his desk. "General Smith wanted to be here to show it to you, but he and his team are tied up with an issue at the shuttle bays."

"General Smith is a smart man," the president judged tacitly. He checked the settings on the phaser and shot the officer without a word. Other than a sharp intake of breath and slight shuffling of feet, the dead man's colleagues were motionless. The moment distended, straining like an overtightened fiddle string, ready to snap. Only then did the president stand. He inspected the sleek housing of the weapon. He hefted its weight in his hand as he strode around the desk. When he arrived at the body splayed out on the floor, he poked at it with the toe of his polished tan oxford. "Humph, it does seem effective," he remarked, with a moue of distaste.

A dark-skinned officer with wide-set topaz eyes stepped to the fore. "Yes, sir," she affirmed. Her speech was clipped but respectful. "The lethal setting causes instantaneous collapse. Total failure of all biological systems." She glanced at the body, blinking rapidly. "There is partial vaporization, which accounts for the, um, odd state of the corpse." She cleared her throat and trained her eyes on the president's left shoulder. "As you can see, though, the kill is completely clean. No blood spatter or other, uh, bodily substances."

Frowning, the president prodded the body again and shifted the man's lifeless arm. He gestured with the phaser. "There seems to be a powdery residue on the floor. Eliminate that before you start bragging about clean kills."

"Of course, sir. I will inform General Smith." Eager to not be the recipient of the president's laser focus, Topaz asked, "Would you care to see the video from the final trials?"

The president nodded his interest and returned to his chair. Topaz queued up the file on her DC and handed the device to him. He watched serenely as three people were executed in an unfurnished, grayscale room. Two were middle managers on Project Pioneer whose actions had marked them as security risks. The third was an autistic man from the red group. A soldier discharged the new weapon while a scientist observed. Timestamps corresponded with the three settings on the phaser. When one of the doomed managers died of heart failure on the second nonlethal setting, the president raised a neatly groomed eyebrow but did not comment.

The officer reclaimed her DC and awaited the president's dismissal. For a few minutes, he strung her along. He relished the silence of the room and thumbed at a groove on the edge of his desk. When he was good and ready, he addressed Topaz directly, ignoring the others. His voice was cold and steely. "The task force seems incapable of understanding the urgency of the situation with the fugitives. You must pursue *every* lead. Clearly, they left the godforsaken forest and are traveling to Apricus via the train's maintenance tunnels. Apprehend them, and put an end to this nonsense."

Topaz nodded curtly and turned to leave, but the president added, "Coordinate immediately with the Communications Bureau to announce that there are four criminals at large. Due to your ineptitude, they may have already breached the city. It is time to engage the public. Also, increase surveillance on their family and friends. Do not allow their circle to grow. *Find them.*"

The transport pod coasted to a stop. The controls froze, and a hazard symbol blinked in the display. The lighted panels in the tunnel switched to a dim, pulsing red, making it more difficult to see. A siren began to blare, rising and falling slowly in pitch. Its wail was painfully loud in such an enclosed space.

"We need to go the rest of the way on foot!" Mason shouted.

They clambered out of the pod onto a narrow walkway and hastily secured their packs. Mason blazed a trail to the train station, stooping forward and covering his ears with his hands. The others followed close behind.

Without warning, a pair of security officers emerged from a lateral corridor, mere feet ahead of Mason. Surprised to be head-on with the fugitives, they faltered long enough for Mason to punch the closer officer in the face. It was a weak hit, but its unexpectedness caused the man to lose his balance. His foot slipped into the groove in which the pods traveled, and he fell onto the sunken track, hitting his head on the way down. Mason and Jack darted forward, hoping that the second officer would go to her partner's aid. Instead, she ignored her unconscious companion and reached for her sidearm. She brandished her weapon but hesitated, unable to choose a target. Emily slid the backpack off her shoulders and swung it at the woman's face with all her strength. There was a revolting crunch, unheard thanks to the siren. The officer fell backward and knocked her head on the tunnel wall. Her weapon tumbled onto the track. Like her partner, she was out cold. While Mason and Jack reaped the officers' DCs and weapons, Emily positioned the woman so that she would not choke on the blood that was spewing from her nose. "You people need helmets," she mumbled, fretting that she may have caused more harm than she had intended.

"Should we take their uniforms?" Mason asked, straining his voice over the klaxon.

"No," Jack decided. He shook his head so that everyone would understand, then he spoke into Mason's ear to avoid shouting. "They don't match any of us physically. Besides, that uniform is covered in blood," he observed with a grimace.

"We need to move!" Violet barked. She was standing guard at the junction where the security team had entered the tunnel. Even though the group had been stationary for less than five minutes, she knew that the siren would attract more patrols.

Jack examined the confiscated weapons. They were trim and basically weightless, vastly different from traditional guns like his hunting rifle. He checked the technical controls and shuddered when he saw that they were set to kill. Gingerly, he adjusted each phaser to the least potent setting. He deliberated stunning the downed officers, but he was unsure what that would do to someone who was already unconscious. An experienced marksman, Jack pocketed one of the phasers. "Who wants the other weapon?" he hollered.

Violet volunteered right away. "She is such a badass," Jack thought fondly. Violet listened intently to the firearm lesson he spoke at light speed into her ear. As they resumed their flight down the tunnel, Jack's mind drifted to the archaic equestrian photos he had perused online when he'd first met Violet. He was intrigued by the tailored apparel and riding crops. Violet would never use a crop on Firestorm, but Jack had many a fantasy about her using one on him. Emily shoved Jack's back impatiently, ending his ill-timed daydream. He had not realized how slowly he was moving. Embarrassed, he sprinted forward. His rangy stride left Emily panting to keep up.

They took a sharp right into the next corridor that branched from the main tunnel. At the turnoff, an enormous numeral one was painted on the wall in fluorescent yellow. The emergency lighting made it look forebodingly orange. Mason guided them past some backlit workstations to a brushed metal door that was branded with another giant numeral one. Because the tunnel was on lockdown, the door did not open automatically. Mason crouched in front of the control panel. He felt around the casing then pressed his thumb at an angle until it popped off. The underbelly of the panel was a jumble of microchips and cables. It took less than a minute for Mason to hot-wire the door.

They eased through the exit. The cave was lit wanly for evening. Long shadows shielded them while they got their first look at the evacuating city. The railway platform was deserted. They sidled onward cautiously until the station's video panels came into view. A trio of seven-foot, double-sided flatscreens divided a lengthy row of benches from the track. The sound was off, but a spate of government alerts continued to roll by. The friends were skimming the alerts, trying to get their bearings, when their own names appeared on-screen alongside a tidy row of would-be mug shots. They were described as dangerous criminals and radical subversives who threatened public safety. Citizens were asked to be on the lookout and to assist the government in apprehending the fugitives before they could sabotage the evacuation. "Oooh, that's not good," Mason muttered as the screens transitioned to the next announcement. "That is so not good."

They scurried to the crossroads in front of the station, sticking to the shadows. They saw no one in any direction, not even a security patrol. "I don't like that they're calling us dangerous," Emily hissed while they gauged their surroundings. "We're only dangerous because of what we *know*. They're making us sound violent. People react unpredictably when they think they're in physical danger."

"I agree," Violet replied, "but I'm hardly surprised. What are they going to say? That we're nosy? I doubt that would enlist the public's help in catching us."

The walkways in this part of the city were laid with uneven brick pavers. People referred to them as the "pink paths." From afar, they did indeed look pink, especially in daylight. In reality, the individual bricks ranged in color from beet red to rose-tinted neutral. Most were made of iron-rich clay, but some were concrete that had been dyed to imitate brick. Small gaps separated the pavers for drainage in case of flooding. Jack turned right and led the group along that walkway. They were in a commercial area, but the businesses were vacant. Jack ducked into the entry alcove for what used to be a childcare center. Judging by the overturned moving crates and open door, the center must have shut down hurriedly when the departure timetable was accelerated. In the glow of the nearest lamppost, they could discern gaily colored stacking blocks scattered across the floor and the reflective eyes of an upside-down teddy bear. "That's not creepy at all," Jack remarked, too softly to be heard. He looked to the others and said, "It seems empty around here. I'd say we have a golden opportunity to put some distance between us and the train station before the officers in the tunnel are discovered." Huddled together in the alcove, they discussed their options. Jack's home was closer than Mason's apartment, so they decided to make their way there.

They used the pavers as a guide but avoided walking on them. They steered clear of the lampposts, too, and clung like limpets to the darkness. They hid in the shade of unoccupied buildings, and more often than not, the cave's knobby walls. Security cameras proved to be their biggest challenge. "I never realized there were so many," Emily griped after having been ungently hauled out of sight for the second time.

They were crowded behind the wide base of a finely detailed bronze sculpture of the Horae that marked the entrance to one of the city's environmental control centers. They had been traveling for a half hour without incident, but before they could plot their next move, sounds carried over from the pink path. Low to the ground, Violet peeked around the sculpture to confirm that it was a security patrol.

"This is ridiculous," a smoky-voiced woman complained. "It's nighttime. All these businesses are closed. Most of the residents in this sector are already gone. I should be at home with my husband and kids."

"Yeah, I hear you," her partner replied. "If those traitors weren't on the loose, I bet we'd be off duty." The man unleashed a gusty sigh. "It seems pointless anyway. I mean, what kind of trouble could they possibly stir up at this point? The city is shutting down, and security at the shuttle bays is tighter than General Smith's asshole."

Choked-off laughter could be heard, then the woman spoke again, but her voice grew fainter and fainter with distance. "It's absurd how many people can fit on those high-capacity shuttles. This place'll be a ghost town in no time…"

More than two hours later, they turned onto the footpath that served the humble row houses of Jack's neighborhood. The overhead lights were off for the night, and most of the portico lamps were dark. Before Jack's house was even in view, a familiar voice reached their ears, but it was distressed and abnormally high-pitched, cutting clean across the faint *thud-swish* of feet and clothing and the ever-present whirr of the city's life support systems. Jack surged ahead recklessly, but Violet grabbed his arm in time and pointed to the playground. He nodded curtly. The group rushed onto the cushiony tiles where they could be concealed by the equipment. Deprived of light from the adjacent houses, the playground was swathed in unusually dense shadows, almost solid enough to touch.

Abigail had one hand planted on the stairwell railing and the other on her rounded hip. A uniformed soldier loomed over her from a few feet away. With the front door ajar and no curtains on the bay windows, the home's interior lights illuminated the scene like a lighthouse breaching fog. Olivia was poised on the third step, fists pressed into her thighs. She was wearing her hair in lovely coronet braids that Jack knew from firsthand experience must have taken Abigail an age to style. Olivia never had the patience for it. "With all due respect, sir," Abigail said, heaving a deep breath and forcing a measured tone, "we are aware of the shuttle schedule. We are not leaving without my son. You are mistaken about him. I know my child, and he is no criminal. We will wait here until Jack returns, and then he will leave with us. Otherwise, we will not be leaving at all." Abigail tipped up her chin defiantly. Three steps above, Olivia mimicked the motion.

The soldier blew out a frustrated breath and took a rather menacing step toward Abigail. Olivia quickly descended the stairs. The man reconsidered. He pivoted to face the playground and clasped his hands behind his back. The fugitives were paralyzed in their hiding spots. The soldier's comportment and insignia revealed him to be a senior officer, possibly a presidential advisor.

"Nice to see my family rates top brass," Jack mused. His belly swirled with a confusing mélange of longing, fear, and pride.

After a moment, the officer turned back to address Jack's mother. "Mrs. Collins, I am not here to debate you," he stated resignedly. "I am here because you and your daughter missed your boarding today. You will leave peaceably or be charged with collusion. Security will return in the morning to either escort you to the shuttle hangar or take you into criminal custody—your choice." He started to walk away but stopped after a few paces to volley a parting shot over his shoulder. "There is nothing to be gained, ma'am, from clinging to people or places that are already doomed."

The altercation was over. Olivia wound her arms around her mother. Abigail kissed the girl's cheek and murmured soothing words as she led her up the stairs. Jack was shell-shocked. He wanted desperately to follow them into the house, but he was positive that it was being monitored. His appearance would put them in jeopardy. Jack flinched when Mason's hand alighted heavily on his shoulder.

"I have an idea," Mason whispered. "Get me to the commercial district that serves your neighborhood. I need to access a computer in one of the businesses."

Jack took a last lingering look at the house then led the way to another footpath. A few minutes later, the group was prowling among the shadows of a clutch of shuttered shops. Blackout shades cloaked the windows, and all signage had been removed. After some investigation, Jack slipped into a narrow service alley and said, "The building on our right is a spa—at least, it used to be. It'll have a computer. Plus, we can use the facilities to clean up."

Mason hustled to the entrance, dodging the red-eyed camera that was bolted to a lamppost down the block. He was prepared to override the locking mechanism, but the door was open.

Inside, a high-ceilinged room with velvet blond furniture and faux philodendrons was suffused with erratic light from an expansive monitor that was affixed to the wall behind a semicircular reception desk. The monitor had not been disabled when the spa closed. To the left of the desk, an unlit hallway led to the spa's treatment rooms. To the right, a half-empty moving crate was tipped over; its sundry contents painted the floor. The monitor was cycling through a cavalcade of public announcements. When it scrolled to their wanted poster, Emily scrunched her nose. "I hate that picture of me," she grumbled. It was the photograph from her ID badge for the museum. "I look frumpy." The others paid her no mind, so she curbed her trivial complaints and joined them at the desk, wondering gloomily what her work colleagues must now think of her.

Mason was bowed over the receptionist's computer terminal, nimble fingers flying. "You can't risk an in-person meeting with your family," he said to Jack, "but if I can hack a mainframe from here and work a little mojo, I should be able to scramble things enough for you to contact them without being detected, even if their devices have been tapped." Jack opened his mouth to thank his friend, but nothing came out. Mason heard the unspoken words. Smiling, he shooed everyone away so that he could work without distraction.

Jack guided the women down the hallway to explore the rest of the building. He navigated the dark space with sureness, grousing about how his mum often harassed him into accompanying her to appointments. Of course, his excited manner bared the fondness of his memories. With a flourish, Jack threw open an old-school hinged door and activated several rechargeable lanterns that imbued the room with merrily flickering light. As with many buildings in Apricus, the cave served as the back wall of the spa. A burbling waterfall tumbled through a slit in the ceiling and carved a wet path through a green mat of luminous moss. The water pooled in an enormous half-moon tub that merged with the wall. In sync, the women gasped a breath and eyed the tub yearningly. "Why don't you ladies relax in here while I take a couple of lanterns across the hall and use the showers?" Jack suggested. "The water in that tub is always warm and clean. It's siphoned from a geothermal pool or whatnot, and it flows through a series of filters. Even with the power off, it should be bonny."

Violet and Emily needed no convincing. Violet started to strip before Jack had even left the room. Emily shrugged off the backpack that she had wielded against the officer in the tunnel. She dampened a towel and tried to rinse the blood out of the fabric. Once she was reasonably satisfied, she joined Violet in the waterfall tub. "You know, Em, you don't look frumpy in that picture," Violet commented. "You've got that whole sexy librarian thing going." Emily rolled her eyes. "Besides, did you see *my* picture? They used my old university ID…" The women chatted and giggled unreservedly for a while, enjoying the unexpected respite they had been gifted while they waited for Mason.

Across the hall, Jack stared in the mirror, naked and dripping on the floor. There must have been some heated water in reserve because his shower had been tepid, not cold. Jack was shivering nonetheless. Unfamiliar fine lines puckered at the corners of his eyes. His rib cage was more pronounced. Inflamed insect bites reddened his calves, souvenirs from their most recent march through the woods. He would treat them later. He could not seem to move. If he moved, he would have to say goodbye to his mother and sister. Two knocks rang out in rapid succession, then Violet opened the door a crack and poked her head inside. She gave Jack an approving once-over before saying, "Hey there, handsome. Mason says he'll be ready soon. Get dressed, and come on out to the lobby. Emily and I are sweeping this place for supplies. We'll hoard as much as we can fit into the packs. Grab anything useful in here." Jack nodded numbly, realizing that he must have tarried in the shower room for a long time.

When Jack rejoined the group, he was squeaky-clean and beardless, and his duffel was full to bursting. "There you are," Mason called. He extended his arms above his head until his lower back popped. "Come here, Jack. I'm all set."

Jack ditched the duffel and stood behind Mason's chair. An inscrutable gush of source code was zipping across multiple overlapping windows on the computer. "It sort of reminds me of music or poetry," Jack noted, mostly to himself. Mason heard him, though. He looked up over his shoulder and gave Jack a delighted, toothy smile.

"Alright. I'm going to connect you to Olivia's DC. The camera is here—" Mason was pointing to the camera when Jack interrupted. "Wait, wait. I get to actually talk to them? N-not just write a message?"

"Yeah, man. You're gonna talk to your family," Mason answered with a kindhearted grin. "But you need to be quick," he continued sternly while pushing Jack into the chair and dropping to a crouch next to it. "Three minutes max. And I'll need to use the keyboard while you're talking." Jack bobbed his head, eyes glassy with unshed tears. "Okay, here we go. Three minutes."

After a beat or two, a small window in the upper right corner of the screen was swamped with a freckled nose and hooded brown eyes as Olivia fumbled with her DC. "Jack?! Jack, is that you?! My DC is being weird," she babbled. Her frown melted with joy when her brother's image broke through the interference. "Oh lord, it really is you!"

"Livi," Jack breathed. He inhaled and forced his voice to be firm. "Livi, get Mum. We don't have much time. I'm going to talk while you fetch her." Olivia's mouth dropped open to shout, but she snapped it shut and nodded. A stress flush colored her cheeks, and her lower lip wobbled. The DC began to jostle as she moved. "I know you've been hearing bad stuff about me and my friends. I promise that what they're saying is untrue. We found out that the government is hiding things, important things, from the p-public..." Jack stuttered to a halt when Abigail's beloved face smooshed in next to Olivia's. "Hi, Mum," he whispered. Before Abigail could speak, Mason tapped the desk brusquely and Jack barreled ahead. "They don't want us to expose them. But, uh, I don't have a lot of time, and that's not what I really want to say." Jack swallowed and looked directly into his mother's gorgeous, long-lashed eyes. "Mum, you need to take Livi and go. When they come for you tomorrow, board a shuttle and leave without me. Never doubt how much I love you both," he choked out, voice cracking, "and that if it is at all possible, I *will* find you."

Olivia started to protest. "No, Jack, we can't—"

Jack cut her off, unwilling to cede their dwindling moments to an argument. "Olivia," he said, raising his voice slightly. "I need you to do two things for me. I need you to take care of Mum. And when you get to wherever the shuttle takes you, I need you to locate a very special horse named Firestorm. Violet's horse. Do whatever you can to ensure his safety and care. Will you do that for me, Livi?"

Confused and frightened but trusting her brother, Olivia agreed. "Yes. Of course. I love you, Jack."

Mason smacked the desk again. Jack shifted his gaze to his mother. "Mum, I know you don't want to leave without me, but I need you and Livi to be safe. I couldn't bear to lose you, and right now, being safe means getting on a transport in the morning. Promise me, Mum." Abigail's cheeks were streaked with tears. She shook her head in short, jerky movements of mute denial.

"Jack," Mason said, softly but urgently.

"Mum?"

Abigail sucked in an audible breath. "Yes, darling. I promise. Please be careful. I love you."

"I have to go, Mum. I'm so sorry. I lo—"

Unable to wait any longer, Mason severed the connection. The window disappeared, and Jack folded over like a marionette with severed strings. "I-I wish I could have given you longer," Mason croaked. "It was becoming too difficult to evade detection and—"

"I understand, Mace," Jack broke in. He smiled feebly and relinquished his seat. "*Thank you* for making it possible for me to say g-goodbye." Jack gagged on the heartbreaking finality of the word. Violet took his hand and tugged him around the reception desk while Mason keyed away at the computer. She rose on her tiptoes to bestow a kiss on the downturned corner of Jack's mouth, a fleeting, unbearably sweet brushing of lips. She was deeply touched by Jack's remembrance of her pain in the midst of his own. She buried her fingers in his hair and dragged her blunt nails along his nape consolingly. Head bowed, Jack cradled Violet's cheek, and they said nothing.

CHAPTER 20

SPY GAMES

"Now what?" Emily asked no one in particular. She was curled into the corner of a plump love seat in the spa's reception area, nibbling on a *Brezeln* from Jack's duffel. They had powered down the computer and retrieved a couple of lanterns from the waterfall room. Emily had been trying to scrub residual blood off her backpack, but it was a lost cause. The bag was left to dry, braced against the alabaster wall like a scarlet letter.

Violet was lying on a different love seat that had matching upholstery, but its frame was constructed of natural wood, which was a rarity in the city. It was tragic that it had been left behind. Violet's auburn eyelashes fanned out over the thin purplish skin beneath her eyes. Her head rested on Jack's thigh, and her legs dangled off the seat's rolled arm. "I've been thinking," she replied, slowly opening her eyes. "They are way too afraid of us." She sat up and swiveled around to plant her feet on the floor. "They must believe we've uncovered more than we have. And whatever they're hiding must be truly reprehensible. I mean, yes, it's terrible how they perverted the census and used it to make decisions about relocation, *especially* if earthquakes are coming. But Hannah and Dimitri prove that perceptive people can infer the meaning of the red group all on their own, and nobody is rioting in the streets."

"That's true," Mason acknowledged. He leaned forward to rest his forearms on his legs. In this position, the sleeves of Dimitri's hand-me-down shirt rode up too high, and Mason pulled at them halfheartedly. "I see what you're saying. The government wouldn't expend all this energy on catching us or want to, uh, eliminate us unless they thought we knew something else, something that *would* cause a riot."

"Exactly," Violet said. "There's more to this."

For a while, only the faint hum of the monitor on the wall and the subtle *chew-smack* of eating could be heard. Mason polished off a packet of peanut butter crackers and brushed the crumbs from his shirt, heedless of the ones in his stubble. "I have an idea," he offered. As he rose from the love seat he was sharing with Emily, the cartilage in his knees crunched audibly. Emily grimaced. "We need to enlist some help," Mason said, starting to pace. "It's gotta be a person we can trust who hasn't been evacuated yet. I think we should contact my friend Trevor Zhou."

Jack stood up. Talking through a stretch, he asked, "That's your buddy from work, right? The one you were planning to invite to some of our Friday lunches." Mason nodded. "What makes you think he's still here?"

"The night the briefing packets were released, Mason told us that Trevor's in the red group," Violet recalled. "His neighbor Consuelo, too."

Jack bobbed his head and ran a hand across his mouth. "Right, right," he rebuked himself tiredly, feeling every inch the Ron to her Hermione.

"Trevor walks with a prominent limp. It probably disqualified him for relocation," Mason surmised bitterly. "He's a stand-up guy and a brilliant hacker. If we want to get back into the government's classified files, I'll need his help. Security will be unreal." Mason stopped pacing and peered beseechingly at his companions. "I think this is our best bet."

Jack crouched down to organize and zip his duffel. "I agree," he said. "It's a good idea, and we're running out of time. I don't think we should stay here, though."

Emily unfurled from the love seat and donned her high-cut hiking boots. "Initially, I assumed we would poke around Government Square or the shuttle bays. Break into an office or something. But with them broadcasting our faces on a continuous loop," Emily griped, pointing a well-timed index finger at the monitor above the desk, "that seems like a surefire way to get caught. We'd be too exposed. We should keep our distance."

"Let's go to my place," Mason suggested. "We need a base of operations, and my apartment is better than squatting in abandoned buildings. Besides, I want to check on my neighbor, and my cat."

With a groan, Violet swung the bloodstained pack onto her back. Mason hoisted the other one. "Your apartment is undoubtedly being watched," Violet said.

"Undoubtedly," Mason replied dourly.

Jack switched off one of the lanterns and wedged it into the duffel. "Let's head to Mason's area of the city while it's still nighttime," he advised. "We can figure out how to get inside the apartment later." When they were gathered at the door, Jack extinguished the other lantern. There was nowhere to store it, so he carried this one in his hand, reluctant to discard it. He made an aborted reach for the door's controls. As one, the group realized that they could not exit that way without risking detection. If anybody was nearby or the security camera was aimed in their direction, it would spell disaster. Jack reactivated the lantern. "I wager there's a service entrance," he said.

They spilled into the alley and crammed into a gap between the cave wall and a massive utility box. Being closest to the walkway, Emily scanned the vicinity while a transformer vibrated unpleasantly against her back. The coast was clear, so the friends began their crosstown trek, cleaving to the shadows like a school of snailfish in the hadal depths of the oceanic trenches. For hours, they sprinted and stooped and sidestepped. They encountered only one patrol, but many homes were abuzz with activity, and with the city's taverns closed, boozy people congregated in the communal spaces of several neighborhoods.

Shortly before dawn, they entered Mason's section of Apricus. The cavern's automated lighting was beginning its creeping ascent, and at the local train station, evacuees were already waiting to be transported to the shuttle bays. By the time the fugitives reached the path to Mason's apartment complex, there were so many people about that they were forced to take cover in a defunct fitness center. The main room contained an array of glum-looking exercise machines and a refreshment station featuring a rubbed metal bench and matching stools. The center also included an office and a gender-neutral locker room. The building's blackout shades were down, but enough of the cavern's artificial daylight seeped through the edges to make it possible to see inside.

Weary from prolonged psychological and physical stress, they decided to rest before planning their next steps. A rainbow of dyed rubber yoga mats was stacked in the corner. They unrolled the mats and unfolded the blankets from their packs. Jack declined a mat so that the others could each have two. He doubted that he would sleep much. Besides, the mats were matchbox sized for someone of his stature. Emily lay on her back with her legs straight and her arms at her sides, palms up. She tried to consciously relax her tense muscles. "This is called the corpse pose," she mumbled to Violet who was lolling nearby on her stomach. "I never realized how morbid that is." She fell asleep before she could change positions.

After hours of erratic sleep, Jack gave up on REM and shuffled to the locker room with a lantern. He used the facilities and squirreled away the toiletries that he found. He crept back to the main room and slid onto an unpadded stool at the refreshment station, his backside protesting its acquaintance with another hard surface. He was pleased to discover that the food generator was on. Generators in public buildings were free to all, and since this part of the city was still fairly populated, using this one might not trip any alarms. Following a brief mental debate, Jack concluded that the minimal risk was outweighed by the benefit of saving their portable and nonperishable food for times when there were no alternatives. He wanted to prepare a full-course meal, but the cabinets had been emptied of tableware and utensils, so he selected a variety of nourishing finger foods instead. With a nostalgic pang in his chest, Jack racked his memory for the appetizers that his mum tended to bring to school functions and serve when friends visited the house. He settled on sausage rolls, bacon-wrapped brussels sprouts, and spinach artichoke squares. In no time, the sleepers began to stir, awoken by tempting smells and the familiar whirr of a food generator. If anyone thought that Jack's menu selections were odd, they chose not to express it.

Periodically throughout the afternoon, one of them would peek around the rim of the hefty industrial shades to gauge the state of the evacuation and to scan the VDUs across the walkway outside. The endless procession of people and puffery was unnerving. The city was being drained at top speed. On the plus side, the mad exodus would reduce the likelihood of them being seen when they departed the fitness center. Having evaluated their options, they had resolved to leave as soon as the cavern lights transitioned to night mode. However, they would not go directly to Mason's apartment.

For hours, Mason had been tucked away in the office, using its sticky-keyed computer terminal to hack into the telecom grid. Contrary to popular belief, hacking was neither thrilling nor sexy. It involved an awful lot of waiting. Mason yawned like a reptile unhinging its jaw and crossed his ankles on top of the desk. Being unable to use his DC, he was thankful for the profusion of computers in Apricus. Same as the spa, though, he was saddled with an older machine that had not been upgraded in ages. This was probably why it had been abandoned. Lines of code flew across the low-resolution screen in a blur. Bored, bored, bored, Mason's jaw popped with another yawn. Suddenly, a new window opened. Mason sat up. His feet thumped loudly on the floor. Heart pounding, he started to type again.

The cave was lit for sunset by the time Mason mustered the others. As the office was overcrowded, Jack hovered in the doorway. "I've hacked Trevor's DC," Mason reported. He intended to send an encrypted message. It would manifest correctly for Trevor, but if the device was being monitored, it would look like he was listening to music. Mason's friends were impressed by the ingenious ruse. He preened for a contented moment then finished his explanation. "Trevor is working right now. I tracked his credentials to a terminal in Government Square. I tried to contact him on that terminal, but I couldn't breach the firewall. It was fortuitous, though, because using his DC will be even better."

Trevor rubbed his dry, stinging eyes until fireworks sparked behind his lids. He ran his hands up and down the sleeves of his cardigan in a futile effort to get warm. It was relentlessly cold and dusky in this building, and he was exhausted. Stifling a groan, Trevor rose from his workstation and hobbled unsteadily to the blue-lit server room to perform his assigned maintenance. Only three other stations were active today. The occupants looked burned-out and raw. No one made eye contact. He combed his stiff fingers through lank black hair that was badly in need of a wash and trim, then he got to work.

Trevor returned to his station an hour later. He was fixing a faulty line of code when he felt a vibration in his pocket. Intrigued, he glanced at the armed soldier who was stationed at the door. Despite the soul-crushing tedium of his post, the man was commendably alert at all times. Currently, however, his attention was elsewhere. Trevor seized the opportunity to retrieve his DC, then he immediately bent over as if to massage his legs. He was not proud to use his physical limitations as a ploy, but the soldier had seen his tottering gait, so Trevor hoped that the misdirection would allow him to check his DC under the desk, undetected. Suspicious and bored, the soldier's posture tensed. Trevor tapped into his inner thespian and moaned like a foghorn. He flexed his right leg and extended it to the side, just enough to be visible. The soldier regarded Trevor with thinly veiled disgust but gave him his privacy.

> Never was anything great achieved without danger.
> Machiavelli

Gawkily doubled over, Trevor squinted at his DC and smiled for the first time in days.

Across the city, Emily shot Mason a curious look. "Uh, Trevor and I have, like, a culture club," Mason clarified shyly. "We're mostly into classic literature and music. We, uh, debate and play games to pass the time when we collaborate on dull projects. Book quotes is our favorite game and the one we've been playing the longest. This way he'll know it's me." Emily was thoroughly charmed by this facet of Mason's personality. She enveloped him in an affectionate hug from behind his chair. She let go when Trevor's reply popped up on-screen.

> Everything is dangerous, my dear fellow. If it wasn't so, life wouldn't be worth living.
> Wilde

"Ha! We're in business!" Mason crowed.

Not a criminal.
Need your help.
Meet me at Au Naturel at 10:00 p.m.
Please, T.

Never doubted you, M.
Weird shit is happening.
See you soon.

They slunk out of the fitness center and made it to the café without difficulty. They studiously avoided the walking paths and met no security patrols. In fact, they spotted no pedestrians of any kind. Even the city's ubiquitous video panels were turned off. The cave felt hollow and deserted. The security cams were still winking, though, so they haunted the shadows across from their destination while they scoped out the safest approach.

Since the caves were climate-controlled and burglary was rare, the windows of many establishments like Au Naturel were not filled with glass or plastic. However, all nonresidential buildings in Apricus had been equipped with industrial-grade roller shades during construction. The evacuation protocols required that those shades be lowered when a location was permanently closed. Strangely, the café's shades were up. When the friends sprinted over to the half-closed door, the reason was obvious: Mason's best-loved restaurant had been vandalized. Upended chairs and shattered crockery covered the floor. The walls were defaced with savage, serrated chalk graffiti. With a resigned sigh, Mason crouched beneath a window to watch for Trevor. The vandals were probably aggravated teenagers whose world was being turned upside down by the evacuation. They were lashing out. Mason could empathize.

Trevor arrived alone, walking slowly but surely down the wide stone path. A threadbare crossbody laptop bag thumped against his hip with every step. He stopped within the dim circle of light shed by the lamppost outside the café. Even at a distance, Trevor looked haggard, and Mason noticed that his limp was dramatically more pronounced. The group observed the newcomer from the shelter of the building for a few moments, then Mason stood up and waved him over. Mason guided Trevor to a dark corner of what used to be the restaurant's patio and enveloped him in a tight, one-armed hug. Startled but pleased, Trevor returned the embrace and gave the much-larger man a genial pat on the back. When they separated, Trevor peered up at Mason's face and hissed, "You look terrible." Unlike their usual lighthearted banter, the words were spoken with genuine concern. Mason deflected that concern right back on his friend. Trevor muttered an ambiguous, "Yeah, it's been kinda rough," but he refused to elaborate until Mason explained how he ended up on the city's newly minted Most Wanted list.

Mason rattled off a CliffsNotes account of the events that had put him in the government's crosshairs and promised more details later. "I hacked into some restricted servers and swiped classified info about Project Noah, which is a counterpart to Pioneer. Noah used the census to pick who would qualify for relocation—and who would not." Mason fixed Trevor with a meaningful look. "Other files revealed that Pioneer did, in fact, locate more islands that are viable for settlement, but they lied to the public and 'staked' the land instead, whatever that means." Trevor was wide-eyed and rapt. Though he had a million questions, he did not dare to interrupt. "My friends and I were pursued topside by a strike team that razed two of my friends' homes. We returned to the city because time is short and there was little we could do from Fulminara." Mason heaved a breath. He signaled to Jack, who was keeping watch by the door. "We shouldn't dawdle here, so that's gotta be the end of story time for now. I guess, technically, we *are* criminals. But I swear, Trevor, we are not the bad guys." Jack, Violet, and Emily slipped onto the patio for hasty introductions, then Mason capped off his synopsis by saying, "We found some scandalous stuff. But the government, our government, tried to *kill* us. Someone must think we know more than we do."

Trevor crossed his skinny arms and swept his fingertips against the worn natural cotton of his cardigan. The dyed fabric was the clotted blue of interstellar space. His sister always said that it made his dark eyes look like obsidian chakra stones. He used to reserve the sweater for special occasions, but there was no point in that anymore. He had been wearing it every day. As Trevor considered Mason's tale, his eyebrow gradually ascended, Spock-esque. "I agree," he resolved. "They're overreacting. They must think you know more. *Which means* there is more to know."

They took a minute to recheck that they were alone. Their surroundings were static and soundless. The air smelled vaguely stale as if the environmental quality systems were defective. "Five days ago, I was yanked on to Project Pioneer," Trevor shared, talking fast. "They had me working eighteen-hour shifts. I tried to snoop, but they watched us constantly. I can tell you two things, though. One, there is *nothing* online about this impending volcanic disaster. It's like the government made it up as an excuse to rush relocation, though I cannot imagine why. Two, *everything* about the new world is überclassified. Every. Single. File." Trevor gulped air. He blinked up at Mason. "They grilled me about you, ya know. Twice. Real ableist dickbags, too. They were leery of me, but as the days rolled by, I think I was one of the only tech geeks left in Apricus, so they needed me."

Mason clenched his jaw and regarded Trevor regretfully. The corner of Trevor's thin mouth ticked up in reassurance. "Okay," Mason said to himself. "Okay," he repeated to the raggedy band bunched around him on the patio. "We're missing something crucial. We must be. Because, I mean, this is all dubious shit, but is any of it bad enough to burn Violet's farm to the ground? The punishment is disproportionate to the crime. Especially for a purportedly *nonviolent* society."

"About that," Trevor cut in. "I overheard some soldiers fanboying about a faction of scientists and engineers that's been developing military weapons for a Project Perses. Like, massive explosives. I thought, why would we make that kind of investment unless the new world is unsafe? I did a bit of poking, and I'm pretty sure I can hack the Perses files. The firewall has holes. I think we should start our investigation there."

"So, you'll help us?" Violet asked. She had been listening attentively and watching Trevor closely, not bothering to hide that she was sizing him up. Trevor turned his gaze to Violet and replied, "Of course" without hesitation. Violet grinned.

With a decisive jerk of her chin, Violet took charge. "Let's get moving," she ordered. "Next stop: Mason's apartment. We can strategize once we have eyes on it." Sensing that they had been in the open for too long, no one protested as Violet led them away from the café with their freshly acquired plus-one. Mason glanced back before the building faded out of sight. There was a palpable tug in his chest as he bid a silent farewell to clay pots, fairy lights, and buttery *Hertzoggies*.

The well-trodden path to Mason's home was wreathed in shadow. Deprived of light and kinesis, this part of Apricus felt considerably more like a cave than a city. They crept onward slowly, allowing Trevor to keep pace. Most of the lampposts were off, which helped to obscure them when they stopped short of the looming apartment block to observe. A weak but willful pulse of life was evident in the light-soaked fringe of draperies and the overloud clash of music and voices that drifted undeterred from a smattering of residences. A five-foot video panel sat at the T-junction in front of the long row of cookie-cutter, ground-level units. This one was still powered up and pontificating about the evacuation. They watched as a terse reminder about cargo restrictions melted into a red-lettered wanted poster. Accepting the mantle of their infamy, they hatched a plan.

CHAPTER 21

KNOCK KNOCK

Trevor hobbled past Mason's apartment. His astute eyes tallied the signs of a cavalier home invasion: safety panel dangling impotently from the wall, door slightly ajar, disturbing tread marks on the kitty flap. He came to a halt in front of Consuelo's unit feeling reassured that they had devised a good plan. A security team had obviously searched Mason's home, probably more than once. Trevor hoped that looters had not followed. He extended his hand to activate Consuelo's doorbell, irritated by the noticeable tremor. Before he could touch the panel, a familiar woman rounded the T-junction and shouted, "Stop!" Her shrill voice broke the night like a glass tumbler on concrete.

Trevor retracted his hand and pivoted to face her. "What are you doing here, Mr. Zhou?" Topaz barked. The skin around her eyes was puffy, her cheeks were shiny with perspiration, and the tousled springs of her hair were wild and frizzy. It looked like she had barely slept since she had hauled him into the bureau for questioning days prior. "It's very late for a social call," she drawled suspiciously.

"Consuelo Garcia is my friend," Trevor lied. "We had a chess date tonight, which I missed because I have had to spend every waking moment at Government Square." Given that Trevor had indeed been worked to the bone, this part of his story was easy to sell. Even his clothes were too big due to recent weight loss. They hung from his body like the wrinkles on a sharpei. "Do you need my DC for verification?" Trevor challenged. He extended the device to her, radiating frustration to cover his nerves. "I concede that the hour is late, but as far as I know, there is no curfew."

Topaz glared at him, too fatigued to rationally assess her options. Her silent stare stretched for so long that Trevor began to squirm. He repocketed his DC. "Look," he pleaded, "she's an elderly woman who may need assistance. The community services she relies on have been shutting down." It was the right tack. Topaz visibly wilted with guilt. She permitted Trevor to ring Consuelo's doorbell and even retreated a polite distance down the walkway.

After several agonizing minutes, Consuelo opened the door. She was dressed in a two-piece pajama set decorated with colorful birds and flowers, but she was not sleep-rumpled. It was as if the senior knew she was supposed to go to bed but had not actually been there. Trevor greeted her with forced cheer. "Hello!" he chirped. "I'm sorry to have missed our chess game." Consuelo quirked a patchy eyebrow. Feigning a hug, Trevor leaned in and spoke into her ear. "I'm Mason's friend, Trevor. Just play along, okay?" Consuelo quickly searched his face then nodded. There was a mischievous glint in her eyes.

Topaz was only half paying attention to them. It was almost time to patrol the complex again. Without a partner, she could not be stationary for long. The fugitives continued to evade capture, so Topaz had been denied permission to board a shuttle today with her husband and brother. The dreadful separation replayed endlessly in her head. She jumped when Trevor yelled, "Help! Please, we need help in here!" His plea was accented by a dramatic groan and the *crash-bang* of a capsized table. Topaz dashed to the open door of Consuelo's apartment. The moment her back was turned, Jack surged out of the walkway's inky margin and stunned her with the weapon he had acquired in the tunnel.

As it was not their desire to needlessly harm her, Trevor broke the officer's fall, nearly toppling to the floor himself in the process. Jack closed the door, disarmed the woman, and dragged her insensate body to the sofa. Meanwhile, Consuelo rummaged through a stout, handcrafted dresser that was situated on the raised platform beside her bed. The dresser was a hodgepodge of reclaimed wood and iron hardware. The copper detailing on its four drawers had a tarnished blue patina. Clutching a fistful of flamboyant fabric, Consuelo turned toward the sofa. She shut the plundered drawer with her hip and gestured for her unexpected visitors to take the scarves. "We need to secure her, yes?" Consuelo snapped. Taken aback by her quick-wittedness, the men nodded but did not immediately move. Consuelo huffed in exasperation. She descended the platform and approached the sofa with clear intent. Jack intercepted her and split the scarves with Trevor. They trussed up their captive like a lethal piñata, the fabric clashing brilliantly with her black uniform. Consuelo supervised them, arms crossed over her chest, looking more formidable than a petite, elderly woman in pajamas had any right to look.

Once Topaz was restrained, Consuelo blew out a wheezy breath. "You are Mason's friends?" she verified. Jack and Trevor affirmed, in unison. Consuelo studied their sober faces. Gazing up at Jack, she murmured, "Hmm, yes. You are Jack. I remember." She patted Jack's cheek with a wrinkled brown hand. He pressed into the gentle touch and smiled. "I do not believe we have met," Consuelo said to Trevor, "but I think...you work on the computers with Mason." Trevor nodded. "He has told many tales." She gave Trevor's shoulder an affectionate squeeze. Then, in a sharper, urgent tone, she addressed both men. "Where is *mi nieto*? Is he safe?"

The moment Jack had incapacitated Topaz, the others had snuck into Mason's apartment with the bags and closed the inoperative door as much as possible. It was a difficult feat to perform manually. When the door was more or less shut, Mason risked activating the lights. True to her name, Pounce collided with him instantly. She kneaded her body against his legs and meowed stridently. Mason lifted the agitated tabby to his face. She licked his cheek with her sandpaper tongue, a rarely seen behavior. Mason's heartbeat quickened, and his breathing stuttered. He staggered into the entryway table, overcome by a tremendous outpouring of relief and love, plus a biting hint of anger. "She missed me," he panted, "and I think she's miffed that I left her here alone for so long." Pounce squirmed in his grasp, vying to get closer. It struck him then, with all the delicacy of an F5 tornado, just how close he had come to losing her. "Thank the stars they didn't hurt you, sweetheart," he crooned into her downy fur. "You're okay. You're okay. You're okay…"

Violet and Emily stood by while a teary-eyed Mason lavished his cat with affection and reassurance. He spiraled for a few minutes before he began to relax. When he flopped onto the sofa with Pounce in his lap, neither party willing to separate, the women moved off to investigate the apartment. Even though it was obvious that the place had been tossed by unfriendly forces, it was mostly intact. After using the bathroom, Emily settled on the edge of Mason's bed and started the laborious process of unlacing her boots in order to apply healing ointment to her blistered feet. Violet found a durable leather satchel in the ransacked closet and set to stuffing it with essentials. She also included personal mementos that she thought Mason would appreciate having if he could not return. She wished that she had been afforded the same grace.

They had not gotten far with their respective tasks when Jack pried open the apartment door and slid inside with Trevor and Consuelo. Pounce leaped to the floor to give her human the freedom to confirm that their neighbor was unharmed. She orbited Mason's legs as he draped his arms around Consuelo's bony shoulders. When he pulled back from the embrace, his large, dark hands lingered, framing Consuelo's timeworn face like blackbird wings.

Certain that the feisty elder would refuse to return home, Jack wasted no time in hauling the door closed, leaving only a minuscule gap. Before he could turn around, Violet twined her arms around his midriff, relieved that he was uninjured and happy to be unhindered by the ever-present duffel. Jack rotated without dislodging her and brushed a featherlight kiss across her lips.

Jack introduced Violet to Consuelo, then together, they ushered the older woman to the sofa and tried to make her comfortable. Satisfied that Consuelo was in good hands, Mason hurried to the dining area where Trevor was setting up shop. Mangled computer parts had been scattered all over the table by the Security Bureau. Trevor's small nose wrinkled in disapproval. He shoved the detritus aside and fetched his crossbody from the kitchen where it had been deposited with the other bags. Mason helped Trevor to boot up his primary laptop and accessories. Unlike Mason's equipment, everything was undamaged and impervious to surveillance. Topaz's DC was added to the tech-laden tabletop, and with a theatrical *plunk*, Mason contributed the two DCs from the tunnel and the memory chip on which the Operation Lemur files were stored. The men acted quickly, worried that security goons would be dispatched when the napper next door failed to check in.

As soon as Trevor settled in front of the laptop, his hummingbird fingers took flight. Mason studied his friend in the brighter indoor lighting. He had uneven patches of black stubble on his typically smooth face and bulging purple eye bags. Sensing the scrutiny, Trevor glanced up. Mason felt a powerful rush of fondness. He said, "Thanks for having my back, man. I always knew you were smart and loyal. Had no idea you were so fucking brave, too."

Trevor's answering smile enlivened his tired eyes. "Dude, I practically pissed myself on the way to Consuelo's door. I was worried I was gonna be sacrificed like a goddamn redshirt!"

Mason laughed, but before he could come up with a witty retort, Consuelo beckoned him to the sofa where she was holding court. Violet draped a blanket across her lap. Jack handed her a mug of hibiscus tea. By turning on the lights, they would have already alerted anyone who was monitoring the apartment to their presence, so they reckoned there was no cause to avoid the food generator. As Mason approached, the couple drifted out of earshot. He realized that Consuelo must have requested what meager privacy the overfull apartment would allow.

She patted the sofa with her free hand, jostling the tea. "Sit with me, Mason," she commanded. He steadied her mug and sank into the cushions, pulling up a leg so that he could face her. "Tell me what is happening," Consuelo implored. "You are a good boy. You are not what they say, and I told them nothing." Mason winced at the notion of Consuelo being questioned, but her demeanor was defiant, and her amber gaze did not waver. "I tried to stop them from defiling your home, but this old body is too weak. I gave them a venomous earful, though," she amended with a wink. "And I grabbed Pounce before they could harm her. She was hissing and clawing at them. I feared they would lose their tempers." Hearing her name, Pounce vaulted onto the sofa and contributed a plaintive yowl to the story.

After a sip of tea, Consuelo continued, "These apartments have been vacated, top to bottom. Probably most of Apricus has. It seems I will not be leaving. They never sent departure details to the red group. Or at least not to me. Maybe I'm too feeble to make the trip." Mason opened his mouth to object, but Consuelo steamrolled him. "It's fine, Mason," she solaced. "It's fine for me. But not for you. You should be on a shuttle. You should be safe. I have lived a long life. Yours is only beginning." Consuelo's speech was slowing. She was depleted from a night of unusual excitement. Mason had yet to reply. His beloved neighbor was fading fast, and it seemed more important to allow her to finish saying her piece. He removed the mug from her hand. She rested her head on the seatback cushion and watched him from under droopy silver eyelashes. Drowsily, she slurred, "A flood is coming, Mason, but it won't be like the last time…"

Mason left Consuelo to doze on the sofa and beelined for the bathroom. On the way, his brain registered the whereabouts of his friends, but mostly, he felt floaty and detached. This was the second time that Consuelo had spoken of floods, and tonight, her words felt frighteningly more like prescient truth than the befuddled ramblings of an aged mind. Mason stripped down and adjusted the shower temperature to near-scalding. The water pounded his sore muscles. He washed and shaved, drawing comfort from the familiar surroundings and routine. Then, in the privacy of his bathroom, Mason allowed himself to grieve. He grieved for a hard-won life that had completely unraveled, and he grieved for the surrogate grandmother and cherished pet that could not go wherever he was headed next. Much later, Mason emerged from the bathroom in a cloud of steam, feeling lighter. He needed clean clothing. A white towel was wrapped around his waist. He nearly dropped it when faced with the scene that was rapidly unfolding in his living room.

A gun barrel protruded through the gap in the front door. Jack was plastered face-first to the adjacent wall. The intruder edged farther inside, suspicions piqued by the ill-timed swish of the bathroom door. Before the man could aim or speak, Jack made a brazen, one-handed grab for the gun. He jerked the man's arm up and yanked his black-clad body forward. Simultaneously, Jack used his other hand to stun the man with the weapon from the tunnel. The upward motion of the intruder's arm meant that the one shot he managed to fire hit the ceiling and posed no danger to anyone in the room. Jack's friends were flabbergasted, wondering again how these action hero instincts could exist within the shy businessman they had come to know. It seemed that Jack preferred his Clark Kent persona, but he could don the Superman cape when it was necessary. As the security officer sagged to the ground, Jack hurried to reclose the door. He toed the officer's weapon aside and lobbed the man's DC across the room. "Trevor, heads up!" Jack called. Trevor plucked the device out of the air, unfazed, as if stealing equipment from government agents was something he did every day, and he added it to the mushrooming collection on the table.

Mason rushed over to assist Jack in securing the officer. He was oblivious to his state of undress until Jack grumbled, "Put on some pants, man. I got this." For a desk jockey, Mason had a surprisingly athletic build. He was muscular but not bulky, built for stamina and agility like the big cats pictured on his apartment walls. Emily and Violet ogled him appreciatively. Jack, too, appeared mildly distracted while he dragged the officer into a corner. His eyes flicked to Mason repeatedly as his friend retreated to retrieve the requested pants. Violet snickered into her hand, then she moved to help Jack. "Should I be jealous?" she teased, tickled when it earned her a firetruck flush from the tips of Jack's ears all the way down his neck. Jack was unsure what flustered him more: Violet's flirtatious acknowledgment of their relationship or being caught checking out Mason, which was all but unavoidable when the man nearly fell on him wearing a towel the size of a postage stamp.

While Trevor toiled at the dining table and Consuelo napped, the others tore up Mason's spare bedsheets and used the percale strips to bind and gag the stunned officer. The humorous mood was unseated by a thrum of nervousness. They were considering a foray to check on Topaz, but they reprioritized when Trevor succeeded in disabling the biometric scanners on the stolen DCs. Jack, Emily, and Violet hunkered down to scrutinize the contents. Trevor turned his full attention to Project Perses. Mason booted up Trevor's ancillary laptop and sulkily poked his shoe at the flotsam of his own equipment on the floor.

A hush fell over the apartment, broken only by key taps and the subtle swish of clothing when achy bodies stretched. As the hours passed, Mason was never idle. If he was not backing Trevor on Perses, he was trying to worm his way into Pioneer. The two men ignored their growling stomachs and the numbness of their feet. At some point, most of the apartment lights had been turned off. It made the pendant above the dining table feel quasar-bright to their dry, gritty eyes. Pounce was curled up on Mason's lap, purring in her slumber. He took comfort in her closeness.

Morning limped in, unheralded. The cave outside the apartment did not light up at dawn. Consuelo was resting on her side, snoring into the sofa cushions. Violet and Jack were snoozing on the bed. Jack was curved protectively around Violet's slighter form. Emily had stayed awake with Mason and Trevor. She was slumped on the vinyl floor of the one-wall kitchen, cross-legged, rocking her body in a self-soothing rhythm. She held one of the DCs close to her face and squinted at it through half-mast lashes. The other DCs were fanned out in front of her. Suddenly, she jolted upright and fumbled each DC in turn. "Jack, Violet, wake up!" she exclaimed, shredding the lethargic atmosphere.

Jack and Violet roused in an instant. Consuelo did not stir. "An alert was just pushed to the stolen DCs," Emily reported. "The last shuttles are preparing to depart. All remaining security personnel have been recalled to the hangar." Emily choked on the shocking reality of her next words. "W-we're almost out of time. In forty-eight hours, they're going to d-disable all systems and cut the power to Apricus." Mason's gaze snapped to Consuelo, his heart in a vise. The government was not merely abandoning those who did not pass Project Noah—it had issued a death warrant.

Mason pushed out his chair with a grunt, deposited Pounce on Emily's lap, and excused himself to the bathroom. While Jack and Violet read the alert, Trevor opened a new window on his PC, typing furiously. A short time later, he leaned in close and cussed softly. On-screen, a preschooler clung to an elderly man's pant leg. Though the footage had no sound, the child's curly head was tipped back in an obvious wail. Her chubby fingers scrabbled for purchase as a careworn woman with matching hair pried her away and carried her up a boarding ramp.

"Everyone, come see this," Trevor implored. "I tapped into one of the cameras at the hangar." The group crowded around the laptop and bore witness to tragedy. A security officer ripped a young, freckle-faced man out of a woman's arms. The woman was escorted to the ramp, but she flailed and tripped multiple times, hysterical. The annoyed officer dragged her until she was out of frame. Meanwhile, a middle-aged man with a sizeable paunch and receding hairline appeared in the foreground. He zigzagged through the throng, running toward a sobbing woman and teenage boy who were clutching one another at the foot of the ramp closest to the camera. The observers watched in dismay as the man was thrown to the ground and kicked in the gut. He immediately struggled to his knees, shouting to his family, arms outstretched, unmindful of the weapon leveled at his head. "This is horrible," Trevor hissed.

"People are being forcibly severed from their loved ones," Emily lamented. "I can't watch this." Sniffling, she left to check on Mason.

"They don't even know about the shutdown," Jack added, clearing his throat. "The alert we read wasn't a public announcement." Frazzled, he snatched a garishly feathered cat wand from the kitchen counter and used the toy to burn off some stress with Pounce.

Violet bent in closer to the laptop and unconsciously shouldered Trevor aside. She was staring at a mob of white coats that had warily sidestepped the distraught man on the ground only to pause midway up their boarding ramp. One of the scientists seemed to be having heated words with the group's stiff-backed military escort. Her colleagues proceeded, but she stayed behind with a soldier. Facing the crowd, the woman made a sweeping gesture with her arm. She clasped a tablet computer to her chest like a life preserver. Its heaving movement revealed labored, irregular breathing. "Akira…" Violet whispered. "You're no innocent, Dr. Tanaka, but did you know about the cruelty, the shutdown? I'd like to believe this isn't quite what you intended…" Out of patience, the soldier tugged at Akira's elbow. She twitched out of his grasp and continued up the ramp on her own.

CHAPTER 22

BOMBSHELL

*D*ing. The scripts that were running had finally met with some success. *Ding.*

"The supply of medication in your bathroom is very low, Consuelo. Will I find more anywhere else in the apartment? Your dresser maybe?" *Ding.* Consuelo patted Mason's hand where it quaked on the sofa between them. She smiled sadly. Mason memorized the deep laugh lines beside her eyes. He was fit to implode from the weight of his own impotence and frustration. *Ding.* Mason glanced at the unmanned dining table. Trevor was in the bathroom. *Ding.*

"Go," Consuelo said. She squeezed his hand then shooed him away. *Ding.* "You have work to do."

Ding. Mason checked the laptops. Trevor was still rolling snake eyes on Project Perses, but it looked like Mason had weaseled his way back into the Pioneer mainframe. *Ding.* Galvanized, Mason cracked his knuckles ostentatiously (flouting the tuts of disapproval from across the room) and got busy.

For roughly two hours, Mason eluded detection and transferred a boatload of new files. Jack retrieved a gigantic portable monitor from Consuelo's apartment that would make reading easier. The ultralight device had been a gift from Mason to enable the aged woman to play games when she suffered from headaches or her eyes were particularly tired. While there, Jack confirmed that Topaz was unconscious and in no distress. In anticipation of the shutdown, Violet and Emily stayed occupied in Mason's kitchen, storing as much food, water, and cat chow as possible.

Mason withdrew before his incursion could raise a red flag and jeopardize Trevor's efforts on Perses. He grabbed a stolen DC and checked for news while he paced around the apartment to loosen his muscles. After a few steps, an alert popped up. "Hey!" he shouted. Worry made him sound unintentionally abrasive. "We just got another alert. It's the final boarding call for the shuttles. The trains will be disabled in an hour to stem the arrival of unauthorized people at the hangar."

Silence reigned for several minutes. Violet walked over to the bound officer slouched in a corner of the living room. Her lips were pursed, watermelon pink and puffy from nervous biting. She poked the man with the abraded toe of her boot. He did not wake. She planted her hands on her hips and poked him again, to no avail. "We should rouse our guests," she said over her shoulder, "and send them on their way. They'll need time to get to the shuttles, especially if the trains stop running." As the group was piloted more by compassion than spite, agreement was swift and unanimous.

Mason and Emily went to collect Topaz from Consuelo's sofa. Emily thwacked the officer's cheek where it bulged out around the gag. The strikes were rapid-fire and forceful, but Topaz merely rolled her head to the side without waking.

"Let me try," Mason said. He shook Topaz brusquely by the shoulders, which elicited a low moan. He shook her again and told Emily to pinch the woman's forearm. "Do it hard," he ordered. "I know you don't want to hurt her, but I'm willing to bet she'd prefer getting a bruise to missing the last shuttle."

A short while later, Topaz shuffled next door at gunpoint. Remnants of Consuelo's scarves trailed from her wrists and ankles like kite tails. The second officer was still out cold. Jack shook him vigorously but stopped when he heard the man's teeth clack. Emily stepped in to pinch the officer's limp arm. She burrowed under his sleeve to dig her nails directly into his skin. Mason rubbed the man's sternum with his knuckles. Jack gave him an inquiring look. "This used to work on my dad," Mason explained solemnly. "He sometimes drank too much after my mom died."

When both captives were alert and free of their makeshift restraints, Violet spoke to them, as unyielding and imperious as a thunderclap. "They have issued a final boarding call. We are releasing you so you don't miss it. The trains will stop soon, so you should hurry. All we ask in return is that you forget you saw us. Don't put this in a report. Stop pursuing us. Let us die in peace."

The officers nodded, squeezed out the door on shaky legs, and evaporated into the darkness.

Banking on their good deed, the group remained at the apartment. Trevor and Mason mainlined energy drinks while they hunted for faults in the Perses firewall. Mason also scoured his Pioneer haul, hoping for details about where the shuttles were headed. The dearth of information about Earth 2.0 nagged at everyone like a persistent itch that prickled just out of reach. Violet, Jack, and Emily reviewed the Pioneer documents on the portable monitor and took turns showering and eating, cuttingly aware that basic self-care might soon become a luxury. They tidied up the apartment and turned on all the lights, thankful for the ten-foot tray ceiling and open layout that kept them from feeling claustrophobic. They did not talk much. Baroque music played quietly in the background. When the others were occupied, Trevor reconnected to the security camera at the hangar. The crowd was smaller now but frantic. One of the shuttle bays was empty. Trevor closed the link and never looked again.

Mason's files corroborated their previous conclusions about Pioneer and Noah, but the rebels learned nothing new until, at last, Trevor circumvented a critical firewall protecting Project Perses. They basked in the high of Trevor's achievement for a while, finding that progress was a better mood enhancer than caffeine, and much kinder to their bladders. Unfortunately, a couple of hours after crowing "I'm in!" Trevor's hands were shuddering uncontrollably as he arranged select materials on his laptop screen and pleaded for someone to tell him he was wrong. When he withdrew to the bathroom, Violet took his seat. She studied his meticulously organized files for about twenty minutes while he regrouped. At the sound of the bathroom door, Violet locked gazes with Trevor and breathlessly declared, "You're not wrong."

Everyone gathered around the dining table to debrief. Trevor reclaimed his chair. Violet was glassy-eyed with shock, but she stood tall behind him, and her hand was a comforting weight on his gaunt shoulder. Though he was tentative at first, he became more assured with each word. "As we expected, Perses is the military's w-weapons program. But, uh, these are not c-combat weapons. I mean, there's some of that, too, which is disturbing…but, um, the majority of the development effort has centered on weapons with massive destructive capabilities. Like, obliterative destruction. Stuff we haven't seen on Earth for a really long time." Trevor craned his neck to peer up at Violet. She gave him a stoic nod. "Most importantly," he continued, "the weapons are not part of a defensive strategy. Once the shuttles are away, they'll be detonated. They are already installed. Probably have been for a while. At least some of them are planted in the old, disused light shafts around Apricus."

"Stop, stop, stop," Emily interrupted. "Some of *what*? I don't understand."

"Explosives," Violet clarified. "The government is going to detonate bombs to destroy the city. Their projections show complete structural dissolution and catastrophic flooding of the caves." Violet ignored the inharmonious medley of gasps and expletives that filled the room. "That's not all," she pressed on. "The government used Pioneer's exploratory mission to install explosives on every landmass they discovered that could foster life. We saw the term 'staking' in other documents but didn't know what it meant. Now we do."

"At least they aren't nuclear weapons," Trevor offered. "There will be no nuclear winter. It says here," he noted, jabbing at his PC, "that the president didn't want to risk the shuttles, in case they were still too close for any reason when the bombs were detonated."

"Nuclear or not, if these explosives detonate, they'll make the planet uninhabitable. They'll destroy what little is left," Violet countered despondently.

"So, even if someone who evacuated wanted to return to Earth," Jack murmured, "there would be nothing to come back to."

Emily asked, "Is Fulminara staked?" Her voice was thin and nasally.

Trevor replied indelicately, unaware of Honey Hill. "Yeah, definitely. Even without the bombs, though, people on Fulminara would be vulnerable without support from Apricus."

"To make matters worse," Violet said, unwilling to sugarcoat their findings, "if anyone does manage to survive on either island, the magnitude of the explosions will trigger tsunamis, volcanic eruptions, and earthquakes." Violet crossed her arms tightly and dropped her chin to her chest. "It's a manufactured apocalypse," she mourned. "The bastards are going to light Earth's pyre, then sit back and watch it burn."

The apartment grew quiet as the group tried to digest the enormity of the situation. Pounce rested on Mason's lap and purred as he stroked the fluff at the base of her ears. Emily sprawled on the bed like a starfish and stared at the drab ecru ceiling. Violet escaped to the solitude of the bathroom. Jack guzzled water in the kitchen, then he settled Consuelo on the sofa and doted on her until Violet returned. Emily sat up and scooted to the edge of the bed, displacing the patchwork quilt. Violet joined her.

"There isn't any kind of *natural* threat?" Emily queried. "The hullaballoo about 'imminent volcanic activity' is a lie?" Her fingers coiled into angry air quotes.

"That's what it looks like, yes," Trevor replied. He was slumped in his chair, squinting at his PC with bloodshot eyes. He had started to type during the lull in the conversation. The staccato *tap, tap, tap* of the keys carried on, undaunted, while he spoke. "I don't understand a sizable chunk of the information that I downloaded, but there are a few top secret briefing memos that were prepared in layman's terms for the president, and they make things pretty damn clear."

Violet bobbed her head. She had perused only two of the memos, but it was enough.

"We probably don't have much time, huh?" Mason's inflection made the sentence more affirmation than inquiry. He cuddled Pounce against his chest, not even noticing the sting of her untrimmed claws. She burrowed into his warmth, unusually clingy.

Trevor kept typing and squinting and scrolling. His movements were picking up speed. He sounded preoccupied. "My guess is that when they cut the power to Apricus, they'll also detonate the bombs. I haven't seen anything to confirm it, but it would make sense. The city will be defenseless without shields or structural assists."

Overwhelming despair compacted them like diamonds in their bleak mountain crypt. Emily wrapped her arms around her abdomen and rocked. She glowered at the frayed, purplish-red rug in front of Mason's sofa that, ludicrously, made her crave sangria. "What should we do?" she whispered loudly.

"You should leave," Consuelo replied with iron-clad conviction. She had been drowsy and withdrawn all day, but lucid. "Get away from the city. There is nothing for you here. Seek higher ground. Potesta is more than caves. *Climb*."

Loath to abandon ship, four heads shook in denial. They yearned to stop this madness, for Consuelo and everyone else the government had forsaken. There was no hope of doing that if they fled.

Fanning the prevailing maelstrom of emotions, Trevor announced, "There are fifteen explosives around the globe. I'm guessing they have remote detonators, or they're encoded to automatically discharge when Apricus is unplugged. Either way, it should be possible to disable them without physical contact. I'm going to try."

Pounce was unceremoniously plonked onto the floor as Mason gripped his secondhand laptop and skated his chair closer to Trevor. The two men huddled together, talking low and typing feverishly. It was relatively easy to slip back into the mainframe since Trevor had not raised any alarms during his initial raid on the Perses files. This time, the pair worked in tandem; Mason covered Trevor's cyber trail as he searched for the means to disarm the weapons.

Needing to be useful, Emily inventoried their gear and prioritized the items that would be essential up in the mountains. Her hands were shaking. It felt like razors were lodged in her throat, threatening to make her cry or retch, possibly both. Sensing Emily's turmoil, Consuelo shepherded her next door where they filled three carryalls with clothing, medicine, and personal care supplies while Consuelo recounted fascinating stories about her life. Freely and joyfully, she shared her belongings and her wisdom, instilling Emily with a calmness that unknotted her throat. They filled a fourth carryall with nonperishable food and a portable water purifier from the city's early days when the safety systems had been fickle. They stopped only when it was obvious that the hikers would be unable to carry any more.

Violet and Jack loitered in the shadows outside Mason's apartment. Jack leaned his back against the wall and gently pulled Violet against him. She pressed her fingers into his hips and rested her cheek on his chest, soothed by the steady thump of his heart. Eventually, her muffled voice popped their bubble of silent reflection. "My father once told me that as unimaginably horrific as the tectonic shifts had been, he liked to think that they had given us a do-over. Mother Earth had wiped the slate clean. Before the cataclysm, death and destruction were pervasive—war, pollution, plague, drought, overpopulation. But after, humanity chose a different path, and the planet began to heal." Violet nestled more deeply into Jack's embrace. "Now, we seem to have rejected our second chance, determined to inflict new damage on the world and each other."

With assistance from Emily when her hands would not cooperate, Consuelo had styled Violet's abundant hair into two inverted French braids. Jack pressed a kiss into the part at the top of her head, taking a moment to gather his thoughts. He inhaled deeply, smelling Mason's citrus shampoo and the clean, cucumber scent underneath that was uniquely Violet. It always made him think of air-drying laundry in a cool breeze. "Most people don't know what's happening," Jack reminded her. "Given a choice, I'm sure there are those who value what we have here and would choose to stay, like Hannah and Dimitri." Violet found consolation in Jack's words and in the tender kisses he rained down on her face. Temple, eyebrows, cheeks, nose, lips. They stayed outside for a long time.

When the twosome returned to the apartment, Trevor was excitedly saying, "Yes, I think I can! But I'll need to recode them one by one, and I don't know if there's enough time to get them all." It was swiftly decided that Trevor would work to disable the bombs while Mason rerouted the city's critical systems to bypass the shutdown. Mason wanted to assist with Perses, but it would take too long to bring him up to speed on Trevor's methods, and there was a risk of them getting in each other's way. Emily, Violet, and Jack combed the cache of downloaded files for *anything* that could help, and they alternated resting, eating, and caring for Consuelo and Pounce.

By morning, Trevor and Mason were beyond exhausted, but they refused to stop, fueled by desperation and adrenaline. Trevor had disabled three bombs at indeterminate locations, and with each success, he gained speed. He would have preferred to decipher the encrypted coordinates in order to give precedence to the explosives in Apricus, but the decryption was taking forever, and they could not spare the time. For his part, Mason had rejiggered the essential systems in his section of the city to continue to operate after the shutdown. Nobody at the Infrastructure Bureau seemed to notice. "Foolish," his internal voice chided. "Any geek worth his motherboard knows that you never, ever take your eyes off the grid." Mason began to tackle another section of the city, his fingers lulled to slowness by the soporific warmth and hypnotic babel of the apartment. At the sound of Emily's raised voice, Mason's stray thoughts scattered, and his chin jerked up. He realized that he had nearly dozed off. Emily was waving one of the stolen DCs. "A new message has arrived," she stated. "The last shuttle will depart shortly. Power to Apricus will be cut in twenty-four hours." Dread settled like a rusty anchor in Mason's stomach. He was no longer sleepy.

The public area of the shuttle was crowded. Olivia flinched every time a fellow passenger brushed against her. Abigail snaked an arm around her daughter's willowy form and pulled her close. The women were standing in front of a huge viewscreen that occupied the main wall. The vast, starkly lit space was dotted with monochromatic clusters of stingily padded seating that faced either the viewscreen or a wide, convex window. Currently, most people were gathered at the viewscreen to watch a live feed of the final shuttle departure. The shuttle was still boarding, so the watchers were being entertained with stock footage of the military's enormous hangar. The brassy orchestral score reached a crescendo as an aerial drone zoomed out of the hangar's reinforced metal doors to reveal a sheer drop off the side of the mountain. The hangar footage was followed by a dose of well-worn propaganda, carefully formulated by the government to keep its constituents fatted and docile. Flashy, overproduced ads praised their orderly evacuation, unwavering community spirit, and bravery for shedding the dangers and limitations of life on Earth.

The plethora of feel-good commercials misdirected the public and concealed the nasty truth that many citizens were being left behind. Evacuees wholly expected to reunite with loved ones who had different departure colors, including the doomed red group. People on later shuttles were suspicious, and some balked at being separated, but since DCs were confiscated prior to boarding, they could not contact anyone who had already departed. There had been an uproar when the confiscation policy was announced. People were *very* attached to their DCs. However, the angst subsided when the government promised that upgraded DCs would be issued in transit.

Buffeted by the ignorant crowd, Jack's family grew more anguished with each passing hour. They *knew* that Jack was not on another shuttle. The mesmeric white noise of the throng plucked at Abigail like an undertow, but she fought to stay alert for Olivia's sake. The teen had taken to staring sightlessly at the viewscreen while pressing her thumb to each fingertip over and over and over. Fed up with waiting for what amounted to the final takeoff from an aircraft carrier destined to sink, Olivia shook out her hands and turned to Abigail. "I don't want to watch this," she asserted. "I need to *do* something, Mum. Let's find out if this shuttle is transporting any animals. I want to find Firestorm. I promised Jack."

It was time to say goodbye. Everyone knew it. But no one seemed able to make the first move. The air in the apartment felt gooey and hot. Trevor's unending keystrokes sounded thunderously loud. Ultimately, the wisdom and fortitude of age prevailed. Consuelo rose from the sofa, shedding the quilt that had been transferred from Mason's bed. Tremors rocked her small body, but her voice did not falter as she ordered them to depart. Obediently, they gathered their bags. The others bid farewell while Mason stood paralyzed in the middle of the room. Though no one wanted to split up, the situation was most heartrending for Mason. When he saw Emily and Violet wrap Trevor in a compound hug and realized that the man was not coming with them, he moaned like a wounded animal. Logically, Mason had always known that Trevor could not accompany them. He knew. He did. He simply had not accepted it. Faced now with inescapable reality, he blue-screened.

Startled by Mason's cry, Trevor released the women and peered over the laptop at his misty-eyed friend across the room. "Hey man, it's okay," he consoled. "Until they find a cure for this disease," he said, smacking his hands on his thighs for emphasis, "I won't be climbing any mountains. I have enough meds in my bag to last a few more days, so I'm gonna stay right here and keep disabling these bombs." He flashed a sad, lopsided smile. Mason nodded rigidly. Trevor resumed his dire task.

Consuelo rubbed Mason's arm, shifting his attention to her. She assured him that she would look after his friend. He grasped her hand and stroked it lovingly. Her brown skin was mottled with darker spots, as beautiful as a bobcat to him. He fussed over her, tucking stray silver strands behind her delicate ear and reminding her to put on a sweater when she got cold. He hemorrhaged irrelevant, heartsick babble until Consuelo slipped a ring off her weathered finger and pressed it into his palm. There was a circular frame in the center of the gold band into which five gemstones of varying size, color, and shape were clustered. The edge of the frame boasted sparkling diamond accents and intricate beading. Mason recognized the ring as one of Consuelo's most prized family heirlooms. He could not speak past the cantaloupe-sized lump in his throat.

When Mason took leave of Consuelo, he shambled over to Trevor at the cluttered dining table. He racked his brain for an unforgettably sagacious quote, but all he could manage was to hug Trevor sloppily and thank him for being his friend. This was more than enough to unravel the other man. "This is just a 'see you later,' Mace," Trevor snuffled. "It's not goodbye." Trevor drew back with a close-fisted double thump on Mason's back. "I'll neutralize the rest of these goddamn bombs, and you'll be back home in no time. Enjoy your camping trip, alright?" Mason regarded Trevor's pallid face and felt an urgent tug in his gut to stay and help. However, they had all agreed that if the city fell, then Mason's skills would be needed in the aftermath. It felt profoundly wrong to walk away, but he could think of no compelling rebuttal.

Lastly, Mason sought out Pounce. The tabby was scrunched into a ball on the bed. "*Mrow?*" she trilled uncertainly. Her tail was tucked away, and her whiskers were pulled back. As Mason reached to soothe her, she gazed up with dilated pupils and keened "Don't leave me!" in his head, as sharp and severe as an ice pick. He stumbled backward and massaged his brow, gulping air as if he had run a marathon. Emily rushed to his side and steadied him by the elbow. Pounce dove off the bed and tried to climb his legs. Beleaguered and miserable, Mason tuned out the intensifying wail so that he could think. It was time to go. Fact. Pounce would be a burden. Fact. She was begging him not to desert her. Fact…

Mason broke from Emily to snatch a soft-sided kitty carrier from the closet that he could wear on his back. Pounce entered the carrier with unprecedented eagerness. Despite having no capacity for extra baggage, the others did not object. Each had been torn from family and would not begrudge their friend this choice.

Jack and Violet were in the kitchen wedging caddies of cat food into their bags when the torrent of file names spilling down Mason's laptop screen caught Violet's eye. With nothing to lose, Mason had infiltrated multiple servers and initiated a colossal document transfer a couple of hours ago. It had started slow, but the download speed had evidently skyrocketed. Violet bent closer to read the file names, and then she dropped heavily into the vacant chair and started to click. A short while later, she shot up ramrod straight and smashed into Jack's nose. She had not realized that he was reading over her hunched shoulders. "Wait, wait," she mumbled anxiously.

Jack prodded his stricken nose, covertly checking for blood. He squinted at the screen as Violet flipped between two files faster than he could process. "What is it?" he questioned.

"No, it can't be," she whispered.

More insistently, Jack repeated, "Violet, what did you find?"

Violet grappled blindly for Jack's collar and pulled him closer, pointing at the screen and murmuring to him heatedly.

Jack's eyes widened. His head bobbed in agreement. "You're right. It's spelled out here, clear as day. Bloody hell…"

By this point, the couple's pantomime had garnered the interest of the room. Violet inhaled deeply and got to her feet. "I know we need to leave," she prefaced, "but this is vital. The reason we've been unable to find specifics about the new planet, the reason the public has been kept in the da—"

Violet was shocked into silence when the apartment's powered-down VDU suddenly lit up. There, on the living room wall, the president appeared. Two-dimensional yet larger than life.

CHAPTER 23

THE LION SLEEPS TONIGHT

The president made a leisurely perusal of the room. His striking, thick-lashed eyes seemed to transmute from green to blue to brown as they moved, refusing to be pinned to a single hue. Trevor and Mason traded a loaded glance. It was unlawful to foist a bidirectional video call on someone without consent. Uncowed, Violet stepped in front of the screen. The president peered down his patrician nose at her. A moment later, his piercing gaze bypassed Violet and cut across the apartment again so hotly it should have left scorch marks. Emily dropped onto the sofa next to Consuelo. Too late, Jack and Mason shifted to block the president's view of Trevor and the laptops. Even if the president had not already itemized the room, the forced casualness of their movements practically shrieked "look here!"

"Hello," the president crooned. A self-satisfied smirk cracked his heretofore neutral expression. "I trust you know who I am. Be assured that I know who you are." From his perch on the wall, the president's penetrating stare swung from person to person like the Eye of Sauron. "My staff was having trouble tracking you, but you got sloppy. Tsk-tsk," he reproved with a condescending headshake. "Your relentless cyberstalking gave you away."

For a terrifying instant, they feared that Trevor's disablement of the explosives had been discovered.

The president moved on, though, with nothing more than a moue of haughty disapproval. "As did the fact that two officers failed to check in after having been on patrol in the vicinity of Mr. Agu's apartment. I would have contacted you sooner, but as you can imagine, this is an especially busy time for my administration."

In the supervening silence, time seemed droopy and distended. No one dared to rupture the Daliesque pause. Hysterically, Mason thought, "The president is taunting us. *The president.* Live on-screen in my living room. Nothing could be more bizarre." Pounce squirmed inside the carrier on Mason's back. "Yeah, okay. The telepathy thing is weird, too," he conceded.

Violet stepped closer to the president's smug face, jarring Mason from his frenetic reflections. Violet's shoulders were back, and her chin was high. "You are lying to the public, Mr. President," she accused. "You are laying waste to our planet. Your actions are unforgivable. You have betrayed this world in the deepest imaginable way."

"Ah, Ms. Murphy," the president said breezily, as if he were greeting an old friend. "You really are a spitfire. And so poetic to boot. I see why Dr. Tanaka has a soft spot for you." He pressed his perfectly moisturized lips into a thin, contemplative line. "I suppose there is no harm in addressing your allegations, melodramatic though they may be." A chime tolled in the background. The president's posture stiffened, and he turned away. His absence revealed a framed Impressionist oil painting of a glinting harbor peppered with sailboats and swans. It was a masterpiece, loveliness epitomized, and it was markedly out of place on the ascetic gray wall on which it hung. Slack-jawed, Emily bent closer to identify the painting, but the president reappeared. He rolled his shoulders and continued as if there had been no interruption. "This world deserves no allegiance, Ms. Murphy. It is irreparably broken. Dirty. Dangerous. I am giving people hope. A future untethered and limitless."

"Not all people," Violet corrected. "Only those you deem worthy of this supposed paradise. You used the census to study and sort the population, without their knowledge or permission."

"The census was firmly established as a necessity long before I took office. My team merely adapted it to determine eligibility for relocation. This is a pivotal juncture in human history, Ms. Murphy. We do not have the luxury of expending resources on the infirm or unstable." Realizing that the president was admitting to acts that were ethically dubious at best and epically criminal at worst, Trevor furtively opened a fresh window on his laptop and started to type, hidden from view.

"But those who didn't make the cut are not just being left behind," Violet volleyed, scrubbing her sweaty palms on her trousers. "They are going to perish. *We* are going to perish," she emphasized with a feral sweep of her arm. "You're making sure of that, Mr. President. Apricus is rigged with explosives." The president's eyes flashed like pulsing auroras, but his handsome face was unaffected, complete with plastic smile. "Fulminara, too. And several other livable islands that Project Pioneer discovered but you concealed from the public. These bombs will destroy the city. Destroy *everything*. Your scientists warn that the simultaneous detonations may even trigger another global cataclysm like the Ring of Fire." The president remained impassive as Violet's passionate indictment hit its peak. Her cheeks were ruddy. Her voice was husky, laced with anger. "And for what? There is no new planet, Mr. President! It's a *space station*. You're transferring everyone to a space station. And you're ruining Earth so they will have no choice but to live there." Distantly, Violet registered the appalled hiss of her friends. For all but Jack, this last revelation was new.

The president looked thoughtful but unconcerned. Another chime tolled, but he disregarded it. After a beat, he blurted, "Agricultural burning!" with a pert snap and finger-point combo. "Surely you are familiar with the term. Farmers used to use fire for vegetation management. After a harvest, they would burn fields and orchards to remove crop residue and weeds. It improved the health of the soil and promoted new growth." The president was pleased with his analogy—tickled, too, that something valuable had come from the droning lectures that Akira passed off as pillow talk. Nonplussed, Violet frowned at him. "We have created a utopia. A fertile new frontier where humankind can thrive. We can control and shape the environment to our liking," he raved. "Earth is nothing more than a harvested field."

"B-but you're making it so we can never plant on this field again." Violet clenched her jaw hard enough to risk cracking her molars. The president's reasoning was flawed, but she would not be sidetracked by pedantry. "We cannot simply relinquish our responsibility as stewards of this planet," she tried. "Project Noah collected specimens of animals and plants to transfer to the space station. Not for conservation, though. For *entertainment*. You're stripping life of something essential. It's not the same as being wild." Violet feared she was losing the tenuous threads of her argument, off-kilter in the face of the president's unwavering calm.

"That's true; it is not the same. It's controlled. It's better."

Violet perked up, finding her feet again. "If it's better as you claim, if you're doing the right thing, then why hide the truth?"

"Because humans can be foolishly sentimental." The president sighed theatrically. "Take your hippie parents. They clung to the belief that this dead planet is worth rehabilitating and resisted collaborating with my scientists." Violet opened her mouth to defend her family, but the president talked over her. "Fortunately, most such misguided citizens met…untimely deaths…in the years leading up to our triumph."

The murderous implication struck Violet like a punch. "*What*?!" she wheezed. "My parents… They… You—"

"Ah, ah, ah, Ms. Murphy," the president admonished with a finger wag. "There is no point in rehashing the past. Let's focus on the future, shall we?" He surveyed the apartment again, determinedly making eye contact with each occupant before circling back to Violet. "The shuttle passengers will witness Earth's destruction and embrace the station as their salvation. They will not know, of course, that we are the ones who destroyed it. They do not need to know. It's irrelevant. What matters is that they have hope for the first time in generations. I gave them that." The president's smile was reserved, borderline gentle, when Violet remained quiet.

"Well, Violet," he said with a conclusive handclap, "I have enjoyed our chat, but there is work to be done, and I don't want to have to jockey for a good seat to watch the world go up in flames. After all, I am the president, and that should come with a few perks. I have enjoyed this diversion, but all good things must end." The president was gloating, high on victory, a Goliath swatting at gnats. He was unaware that this conversation was being broadcast live on the shuttles.

The cat was out of the bag.

Except for Pounce. She was waiting patiently in her carrier for Mason et al to hightail it out of the city.

The president hesitated. A crinkle marred the unblemished skin above his nose. "You gave me no choice but to exile you, but I have no desire to see you suffer. The first aid stations in the city are stocked with painkillers and emergency syringes, enough for a speedy, peaceful end. Goodbye."

The VDU blinked out. Trevor pounded a few keys—*clack, click, tick*. Then he wilted in his chair, and the room fell silent save for the perpetual hum of the air filter. Fragrances wafted from the assiduously stacked food containers on the kitchen counter. The apartment smelled strongly of onion, garlic, oregano, cinnamon, and banana.

"Good God," Emily ground out. She squeezed Consuelo's hand and stood up. Her voice was strained. She fiddled with the polka-dotted fuchsia ribbon at the end of her braid. "He wants us to euthanize ourselves. He actually thinks he's being kind."

"I can't believe I voted for him," Jack groused. This elicited a desolate little chuckle from Violet, whom he immediately enveloped in his arms. She was content to hide there, face tucked behind the lapel of his jacket, while she recovered her equilibrium.

Wild-eyed, Mason strode over to Consuelo. Before he could sit, she rose to meet him, leaning on the furniture for balance. Mason was willing to procure a syringe for her, but he found that he could only gape mutely, incapable of articulating it. She stared back with unbearably compassionate eyes and shook her head. Gripping the sofa with one hand, Consuelo cupped Mason's scruffy cheek with the other and told him to go.

Somewhere, a doomsday clock was counting down, and they could delay no longer. With heavy hearts, four ill-fated rebels picked their way through the cavern to the nearest train station. Even though the primary lights were off, the spotty illumination from buildings and equipment proved sufficient. They intended to follow the train tracks to a service tunnel near one of the city's secondary entrances. The tunnel had been selected for its exterior hatch, which opened to a road that extended nearly twenty miles up the mountainside.

When the reluctant drag of footsteps died away, Consuelo lumbered to the food generator for chrysanthemum tea. "I relayed most of the president's call to every active channel," Trevor said. He noticed the pronounced tremor of the older woman's hands and moved to help her, wordlessly cursing his own trembling legs as he stood. "It wasn't even hard to do. I just overrode that Orwellian trash the Communications Bureau has been looping." He pulled two vibrant, hand-painted mugs from the cabinet, pausing to admire the dynamic pattern of chevrons and spirals. "Maybe the public will be angry," he mused aloud, plonking the mugs on the counter. "Maybe they'll demand justice. But if nothing else, we gave the bastard a goddamn PR crisis."

Consuelo filled the mugs with steaming tea. "You're a good boy," she clucked, tapping him gently on his wan, hollow cheek. Trevor leaned into the touch then returned to his laptop. Consuelo set both mugs on the table and flumped into Mason's vacated chair.

As they hiked across the deserted city, they kept an eye out for other castaways. Lights glowed inside numerous homes, and more than once, draperies twitched as the group passed by. However, they never actually met anyone. This was indubitably a blessing, for as much as they wanted to pied-piper the forsaken to safety, there was no time. Hoping to obtain supplies, they made a pit stop at every first aid station along their path, but the whole lot had been ransacked. They were sorely tempted to scavenge one of the city's many pubs for bottled liquor, but they could not justify the extra weight.

They reached the tunnel and ascended its narrow staircase. A stripe of bluish emergency lighting shone dimly above their heads. Though there was no safety railing, the metal stairs were textured to prevent slippage. The passage was barely wide enough for Mason's broad shoulders. Pounce yowled her disgruntlement as her carrier repeatedly bumped the walls. The endless climb was challenging for everyone, but Emily most of all. Red-faced and gasping, she refused to slow them down, so the others invented excuses for her to catch her breath. When Jack's boot became mysteriously unlaced for the third time, Emily realized what her friends were doing. She was too grateful to call them out on it.

A gust of alpine wind greeted them when they opened the hatch. The fresh, nippy air was a relief after the stifling tunnel. A hawk screeched overhead. They climbed outside and collapsed at the foot of a chubby pine tree. The stony soil was softened by a thick bed of yellowed needles and glossy green ivy whose tendrils wound up the pine's trunk. The hikers pulled in deep, wheezing breaths and drained a flask of water from the heaviest pack. Jack dug his knuckles into his temple. Violet pressed a protein bar into his hand. While Mason searched the medical supplies, he placed Pounce's carrier on the ground. The inquisitive tabby peered through the mesh window and swatted halfheartedly at the polyester walls of her prison. Mason announced that he was taking a stimulant injection. He was grievously sleep-deprived, and they had settled on this solution in advance.

After the barest rest, they began to trudge up the service road. Emily walked beside Mason to monitor him for any ill effects from the shot. The road carved its way through a splotchy montane forest. Hardy conifers with sloping branches were bunched in discontinuous patches, augmented by the occasional aspen and even an elegant willow or two. An assortment of low shrubs, including dense heather with bell-shaped, pendant flowers, sprouted beneath the trees and in rocky, unwooded meadows. The brash call-and-response of a family of jays accompanied the hikers for a while. In the far distance, they could see the jagged, snowcapped tips of the Olympus Range.

The course of the road alternated between flats and slopes, but the slopes grew exponentially steeper. Driven by the imperative to get as far from Apricus as possible before the bombs detonated, the four friends pushed ever onward, legs and lungs and hearts afire. And because this was not one of Mason's treasured novels in which the hero triumphs at the eleventh hour, every arduous footfall seemed to amplify the pathetic certainty that Trevor could not disable all the explosives in time; that no righteous revolution would rise up to protest the president's crimes; that they were simply too small, too powerless, and too late to stop the calamity that had been set in motion.

CHAPTER 24

THROUGH THE LOOKING GLASS

I n a far-flung corner of the congested public area, Abigail and Olivia were grilling a junior member of the shuttle crew about the vessel's cargo when the giant viewscreen flickered and flashed, snagging their attention. There was a grating blast of static, chased by the president's cultured voice. Curiously, his visage appeared in an off-center, inset box. His cropped brunet hair was parted neatly at the side, and he wore a royal-blue V-neck sweater over a white button-down shirt and black tie. However, most of the viewscreen showed the interior of an ordinary apartment. A swell of murmurs crested when the crowd recognized four of the inhabitants from the government's ubiquitous wanted posters.

Since the broadcast was unannounced and had started midsentence, it was fairly obvious that they were seeing a private call from the president's perspective. Unnerved, the crewman who had been speaking with the Collinses shouldered his way through the horde of riveted voyeurs to the closest hallway, presumably to report the issue. Olivia and Abigail were on the move, too. They strode doggedly toward the screen, wanting to be nearer to Jack in the only way possible.

The women listened, transfixed, as a familiar, freckle-faced farmer lobbed earth-shattering accusations, *literally*, at humanity's unflappable leader. When the call ended and Jack's image poofed away, they whined in protest and reached uselessly for the screen. Abigail was rendered speechless, unabashedly proud of Jack's morality but devastated to learn that she had abandoned him to certain death.

In contrast, Olivia was fury incarnate. While her mother grieved, Livi darted into the meat of the crowd. She searched the room fiercely, trying to find her disgust mirrored in the faces around her. Failing to see it, she shouted, "What is the matter with you people? There is *no planet*! We're being shuttled off to some space prison while Earth is blown to bits…" Gasping, her next words were wrenched out, "…with my *brother* still on it! We cannot just stand around and do nothing!"

In the wake of Olivia's outburst, a summery haze of hushed conversation hung thickly in the air. The viewscreen stayed dark, so the crowd gravitated toward the exterior window, either for a change of scenery or to flee the commotion. The public area was too large and populated for Livi to see everyone, but from what she could tell, nobody was overly flustered about the president's revelations. Most passengers avoided her, though some appeared thoughtful. Taking that as encouragement, Livi bolted through the crowd to stand near the screen again. People were still staring at it, eerily blank-faced, like junkies jonesing for a fix. Olivia flailed her arms and railed, "What is wrong with you?! Don't you care that we've been lied to?"

To Olivia's left, a middle-aged woman with a toddler on her hip called out, "It's too late to do anything about it." Farther away, someone shouted, "I trust the president. He'll clarify things soon enough."

Olivia stood on a bench to get a better view, ignoring the scandalized squawk of the hand-clasped couple that had been seated there. From her new vantage point, she could see tangled knots of passengers filing out of the public space to clog the hallways, mainly parents herding their children away from the drama. She was perversely satisfied to spot numerous people crying, no doubt having realized that one of their loved ones was facing a death sentence. Spurred on, Livi tried again. "We boarded this shuttle under false pretenses!" she bellowed. "We left innocent people behind to *die!*"

But the sparks from Olivia's tongue did not catch fire. The crowd remained placid, addicted to the hope the president had painstakingly cultivated. For a life outside the caves. For safety and stability. Livi jumped to the floor. She twisted her fingers into her untamed curls and pulled her hair in agitation. A man in his midtwenties with a tidy brush cut and extravagant sleeve tattoos placed a gentle hand on her elbow. "Look, kid," he said levelly, "we needed to get out of those caverns. Maybe our future looks a little different than we imagined, but it's still better than what we had."

Olivia jerked out of the stranger's grasp and screamed, "*It's not better for my brother!*"

The intensity of her child's wail jolted Abigail from her stupor. She pushed her way to Livi and babbled soothing nonsense in her ear while sweeping a hand over the girl's trembling back. In pockets around the room, murmurs intensified into full-volume discussions. Some sounded heated, and a few more people departed in teary huffs, but mostly, the voices were relaxed. Eventually, Livi untangled from Abigail and tried once more to rally the masses. Abigail participated this time, but it made no difference. Nobody was listening. When Olivia edged toward hysteria, security decided that it was time to flatten the Collinses' soapbox. The crowd parted like the Red Sea as a scowling officer advanced with his weapon raised, but before he could reach the troublemakers, Abigail pulled Olivia onto a bench and cradled her while she sobbed. Pressing a damp cheek into Livi's hair, Abigail glared at the officer until he relented. As soon as the man left, she closed her eyes and rocked her daughter in her arms. They wept, lost in a packed room, having no privacy yet totally alone.

For hours, the hikers followed the service road up into the mountains. Signs pointed to science stations along the way, but these outposts turned out to be scarcely more than blocks of equipment bolted into the rock face. There were no supplies to raid. After their third fruitless investigation, the friends disregarded the signs.

The weather had been overcast, but the clouds were starting to fragment, allowing radiant sunrays to pinch through the gaps. Though the terrain was getting rockier and more barren, the hikers continued to encounter wide wooded thickets. They often caught the movements of small birds eating seeds from pinecones, and they spotted several long-haired rabbits with tall, black-tipped ears. They even accidentally surprised a herd of grayish-brown deer from where the animals had been napping inside a network of grottos formed by sweeping low-hanging spruce branches.

The higher they climbed, the lower the tree canopy grew. Forested areas became more infrequent, too, usurped by sparsely wooded groves with negligible undergrowth. Late in the afternoon, the pavement underfoot transitioned to gravel. A string of gray-barked alders flourished in an old avalanche track parallel to the road. The group decided to rest in the shade.

A pair of surefooted mountain goats grazed on an outcrop nearby. While the friends were preoccupied drinking, snacking, and adjusting their packs, the nosy beasts wandered closer, undetected. It was not until they were nibbling lichen at the rim of the avalanche track that anyone noticed them. Jack heard vulgar chewing noises that he could not attribute to his well-mannered companions. He struggled to his feet and rounded the tree trunk against which he had been leaning. "Whoa!" Jack cried. The two goats were at eye level, less than a dozen feet away. The unexpected ungulates had bushy, bone-white coats accentuated by long beards with slightly scraggly ends and curved black horns with wickedly sharp points.

The goats were unbothered by Jack's outburst. They bleated when Violet, Emily, and Mason sprang up beside him, but they did not withdraw. Rather, the goats seemed content to forage languidly while the humans goggled them.

Too soon, Emily shattered the peaceful moment with a guilty realization. "Shit!" she exclaimed, earning herself a chorus of rusty-hinge bleats. "We need to warn the animals. We should have been doing it all day. They need to get to higher ground."

"How?" Mason asked. "How do we do that? How do we *initiate* contact?"

Emily looked to the others for suggestions, but Jack's textbook shrug and Violet's frowny head tilt plainly conveyed her friends' uncertainty. "I don't know," Emily moaned. "Maybe we just need to concentrate really hard?"

First, they spent a minute deciding what, exactly, to communicate. Then, all four humans focused raptly on the goats, hypothesizing that a collective effort would amplify the signal, as it were. With the utmost sincerity, they projected an urgent message of low-elevation danger and high-elevation safety. The goats bleated loudly and headed down the mountain.

"No, no, no," Emily called after them. "You're going the wrong way!" Defeated, she crumpled to the ground like a used napkin. Emily scrubbed her itchy eyes and half listened to the others shouting "Wait!" and "Stop!" She tugged at the sweaty bandanna on her head. She had wrapped it over her hair when she realized that her scalp was getting sunburned. The knot had loosened, and the fabric kept sliding out of place. Violet squatted next to Emily, brushed her fumbling fingers aside, and fixed the bandanna for her.

It would be unwise to dally, so the group collected their packs and tramped back to the gravel road. The gradient was uneven, and the crushed stones were loose. Going forward, they would need to pay more attention to their footing. "It's nonsensical," Emily bemoaned, wheezing her way up a steep rise. "Why do we have this ability? Why did it manifest *now* if we can't even harness it to save a few directionally challenged animals? I suppose it doesn't matter, though. I mean, what difference could we possibly make when the world is about to fall apart?"

Before anyone could answer, guttural bleating blazoned up the ridge, rising in volume. The group froze midstride to listen. The bleats ranged widely in pitch and power. A beat later, an enormous band of mountain goats bustled past, intent on climbing to a higher altitude with the humans. A number of goats came close enough to skim a timid hand over their wooly coats. The friends were awed. Beaming smiles made their unpracticed cheeks pleasantly sore. The band marched effortlessly over the dodgy road and the adjacent boulders and plants. Even the newborn kids were expeditious.

"Well, Em, we made a difference to those guys," Mason replied.

Heartened, they followed the goats.

Eventually, the tapering forest ceded to titanic expanses of shale and limestone as far as the eye could see adorned with constellations of treeless alpine vegetation. Near dusk, the travelers passed one last, lonely science outpost on the curb of the road. Its array of equipment was badly damaged. The gravel petered out at this point, and they were forced to hike an uncharted path through the wilderness. The terrain was severe, primarily cold sedimentary rock sequined with knots of moss-draped bushes, clingy lichen, and liverworts. Without the sun, the temperature plummeted even though they were many miles below the snow line. They were no mountaineers; it was slow going to find routes with solid footholds that could be hiked while laden with bulky, unbalanced gear. Nonetheless, their cloven-hooved chaperones did not desert them. In fact, when they floundered, the goats seemed to steer them toward safer trails. They lost sight of the band sometimes, but the furry fellows always reappeared.

The night sky was providentially cloudless and aglow with celestial light. The moon hung so clear and close that it seemed they could reach up and map its craters with their fingertips. Its luster made it easier to navigate, so they drove their bodies ruthlessly and stopped to rest as infrequently as possible. Despite their best intentions, however, breaks were inevitable. Scrapes and blisters needed tending. Mason required another stimulant. They added extra layers of clothing to fend off the chill.

Throughout the group's grueling ascent, they cautioned every animal they met: rabbits, deer, a skulk of red foxes, plenty of birds. They also tried to telegraph the danger generally, knowing that many animals would be out of view, especially after sundown. They went so far as to lie on their bellies to talk to the trout in a swift alpine stream, urging the fish to swim against the current. As silly as they felt at times, their efforts had an undeniable impact. Life was moving upward, rising like a helium balloon.

There was no way to gauge Trevor's progress, so they climbed and clambered and crawled until their bodies gave out. Less than two hours before the explosives were expected to ignite, Emily and Mason had exceeded the limits of their physical endurance. Shivering uncontrollably, they huddled in a patch of needly juniper shrubs while Violet and Jack investigated the surrounding area. The flora was denser and more diverse on this stretch of the mountain. Burgundy sedum and ivory yarrow splattered color across the pale, predawn landscape. The explorers came across a broad plateau where the ground was relatively level. There, by the side of a rushing stream, an obstinate pine tree grew, in defiance of the timberline. It seemed like a sign.

The group made camp. After only glimpsing the ocean all day, the plateau now offered an unobstructed view on one side, facing Fulminara. The smudgy glimmer of half-light on its surface was breathtaking. They ate heartily then replenished their water supply in the stream. Exhausted, they bundled up in blankets and shared a reusable chemical heat pack that Dimitri had stuffed into Emily's bag at Honey Hill. Conversation was patchy and hushed. They listened to the mountain breeze, the gurgling stream, the goats. Accepting that they were as far from Apricus as they could get, they rested.

At first light, they took individual positions around the camp.

Humming an age-old, melancholy show tune, Mason rested his back against a moss-cushioned boulder and stretched his aching legs. He extracted Pounce from the kitty carrier and settled her on his lap. She bumped her head against his bristly chin and made no effort to bolt.

Violet opted to sit cross-legged beneath the bristlecone pine. This put her too far from the edge of the plateau to see Fulminara. She figured that was probably for the best.

Jack paced lethargically. His gaze ping-ponged from the starry dawn sky to the seaborne horizon to the icicle summits. And always, always back to Violet. His breath condensed in the frosty air, reminiscent of winters of yore when regions of the world experienced distinct seasons. Violet, he decided, was winter starlight. She was not the powdered sugar twinkle of summer. No, his love was the breath-stealing, clarion sheen of midwinter. Wistful, Jack burrowed his hands deeper into his coat pockets and continued to pace.

Emily sat on a folded blanket near the rim of the plateau, mesmerized by the majestic ascent of the sun over the ocean. Though she had enjoyed myriad sunrises on Honey Hill, she had never seen daybreak painted on the infinite canvas afforded by such a high elevation. Emily reached blindly into the backpack at her hip. She traced the edge of her parents' photo with reverent fingers before closing them around the soapstone duck. She retracted her hand and cradled the duck against her chest like a talisman.

In the honeyed pink light of the golden hour, explosions rocked the mountainside.

Hannah lurched awake to an echoing boom of thunder. Dozy blue eyes registered the empty space in the bed beside her. Before she could call for her husband, the house convulsed violently, vomiting a deadly spray of glass, wood, and drywall into the room. Hannah regained awareness as

Dimitri was laying her on the rounded, weather-worn cobblestones outside. She was swaddled in the comforter from the bed. She expected to see dark cumulonimbi overhead, but the sky was stormless. The air smelled rusty. Something hot and sticky was matted in Hannah's hair. It pooled in the wrinkled grooves of her forehead and trickled into her eyes until she was forced to close them once more.

Dimitri moved Hannah to the garden with a meager supply of food and soft goods that he had been able to retrieve from the house. The couple nestled among the replanted dirt rows while, unbeknownst to them, Fulminara was reeling from massive explosions that obliterated measureless coastal portions of the island and sparked uncontrollable wildfires that raced inland. Situated atop Honey Hill next to a collapsed garden shed, Hannah and Dimitri were entirely defenseless.

The earth heaved with quakes and aftershocks. The heavens gagged on pungent smoke. The elderly pair, disoriented and afraid, eventually returned to the feeble shelter and false comfort of their fatally compromised home. It was unwise, surely, but it made no difference in the end. Over the torturous hours ahead, great gashes of Fulminara crumbled into the ocean and the rest was consumed by fire, until finally, merciful waves quenched the blaze and swept what little had survived to a watery grave.

Trevor hammered at his laptop until the very last second. His feet were numb, and burst blood vessels left scarlet smears on his eyes. The seizing pain in his shoulders and neck would have compelled him to stop under any other circumstances. Consuelo was a constant presence at his side, murmuring encouragement and caring for him as best she could.

Though the power sputtered ominously, it did not cut off thanks to Mason's wily hack. Even so, they gained no more than a spare moment of peace and a starburst of evanescent hope. Despite his herculean efforts, Trevor was unable to excise all the city's tumors, and the consequent explosions were catastrophic. The apartment complex was crushed under a limestone landslide as the structural integrity of the caverns failed. Consuelo died instantly from a critical blow to her head. Trevor, however, found himself trapped in a pitch-dark pocket beneath the rubble, suffocating, deafened, and slowly bleeding out from mortal injuries. Utterly, terrifyingly lost.

Unable to rest, Abigail and Olivia returned to the public area of the shuttle where flat, unemotional text filled the viewscreen on the main wall. Findings were pouring in from the scientific satellites orbiting Earth and assorted sensors on the planet's surface. Even though the reports on the viewscreen were simplified and redacted for public consumption, the scope of the devastation was clear.

Earthquakes, wildfires, and tsunamis have been verified in proximity to formerly populated areas.

Mammoth pyrocumulus cloud formations have developed.

A smoke plume laden with particles of soot and debris has already risen to the stratosphere where it is expected to persist indefinitely.

A volcanic eruption has been detected in the remote northern hemisphere.

All contact with Apricus has been lost.

Abigail curled an arm around Olivia and rotated her daughter's unresisting body away from the screen to face the floor-to-ceiling window instead. The women pressed up against the flawless glass expanse and peered outside. The shuttle was too distant to see what was happening on Earth. Their home was but one tiny dot among innumerable, indistinguishable other dots in the unfinished pointillism of space. They strained to find it nonetheless, hopelessly tethered, knowing that Jack was stranded there.

"I am a preservationist. I am a preservationist. I am a preservationist," Emily chanted miserably where she stood on the ridge of the plateau, bearing witness to unimaginable destruction, the very antithesis of her life's work. Dusk had just fallen, but copious smoke and ash polluted the sky, blotting out the moon and stars. Emily sniffed the air for brimstone, because clearly, this was Hell, or at least somewhere Hell-adjacent.

Even miles above Apricus, the stalwart mountains had spasmed with the force of multiple coincident bomb blasts inside the city, and the sonorous boom had been earsplitting. The four refugees hit the dirt as supersonic shock waves radiated through the Olympus Range. The stream beside Violet hiccupped and spit, and a hail of cones, spongy purple and hard-edged brown, pelted her as they fell from the pine. A thin, smoky vapor rose quickly, perversely beautiful in the palette of sunrise, followed by billowing, wraithlike clouds that hovered above the peaks like Dementors.

As the day wore on, the mountain airstream swept the most noxious pollution away from Potesta to shroud the open ocean. The dangling soot impeded the group's view of Fulminara, but not before they saw huge portions of the island fold into the churning sea, a brutal, man-made Krakatoa. At the horizon line, they could scarcely perceive other bleak plumes of smoke marking the ruin of a previously unknown island or perhaps an erupting volcano.

Even now, aftershocks rumbled through the mountains, and an avalanche in a distant part of the range choked up a fresh cloud of debris. Nightfall exposed the quivering ginger light of wildfire on Fulminara. Unseen tsunami waves jetted across far-off waters. The friends roamed their campsite, wrung out and filthy, damp cloths clinging to their noses and mouths. Despite everything, they chose to believe that Trevor's sacrifice meant that numerous bombs had been thwarted, that the annihilation was not total. They were, in fact, living proof of this, along with an admirably resilient, high-spirited band of goats. Potesta was still standing. They were still standing.

All day, they had oscillated between congregating and seeking solitude, unwilling to be apart for too long but unprepared to discuss what was occurring or what to do next. After dark, they gravitated closer and settled into a circle to share a meal by the light of Jack's rechargeable lanterns. They succumbed to exhaustion and slumbered fitfully under their blankets.

Frail sunshine tickled Emily's eyelashes. She was lying on her side. A warm weight covered her body, all the way up past her ears. Curious to know who had gifted her their covers, Emily peeked out from her cocoon. Mason was seated nearby, grubby but grinning, feeding water to Pounce. Violet and Jack were searching for something in a pack, sharing easy touches. Soft bleating drifted over from someplace behind Emily. She took in the scene, unnoticed, awash in a confused mash-up of grief and fondness.

Suddenly, a long-tailed jaybird landed on the ground by Emily's nose. The bird had dark-gray feathers with a lighter belly and a short black beak. As Emily watched it hop around, her heart began to thrash in her chest. She sat up slowly, careful not to spook her visitor. Untroubled, the jay sang a succession of low, melodious notes comingled with muted clicks. Through teary eyes, Emily watched it fly away. Then, she turned to her friends and said, "We're not alone."

The End